EARLY PRAISE FOR ACADEMY OF
UNHOLY BOYS

In ACADEMY OF UNHOLY BOYS, David Fitzpatrick writes with exquisite flair about the traps of young adulthood and what it's like to be in thrall to darkness, especially when it presents itself in the form of someone who's simultaneously brutal and charismatic, repugnant and seductive—a figure of cult-like power. At heart it's a novel about finding the tools to say no, which, in Fitzpatrick's hard-won vision, is a yes to staying alive on multiple levels. A timely, mesmerizing story.

— PAUL LISICKY, AUTHOR OF *LATER: MY LIFE AT THE EDGE OF THE WORLD*

Although ACADEMY OF UNHOLY BOYS is set in contemporary Connecticut, the story it tells is an old one—the struggle between the life force and the death wish. The main characters are adolescents who are old before their time and yet imbued with natural zest for life. The confusions they go through will touch you. David Fitzpatrick doesn't pull any punches as he shows that the path to clarity is bound to proceed through the travails of suffering. A beauty of this book is that, in the end, the value of taking responsibility is terrifically real.

— BARON WOR

In ACADEMY OF UNHOLY BOYS, David Fitzpatrick unpicks the deep, almost religious connection that can develop between traumatized young men. With his unique, elegant prose, Fitzpatrick probes the concept of the teenage secret society, skillfully peeling back layers of pain, need, and cruelty to examine how coming of age can damage or heal a soul. Fitzpatrick's Jay Souther and his friends are worthy successors to Holden Caulfield, Rue Bennett, Oscar Wao, and every other teen trying to survive the dangerous business of growing up.

— A.J. O'CONNELL, AUTHOR OF *A PERFECT FACEBOOK LIFE*

ACADEMY OF UNHOLY BOYS
A NOVEL

DAVID FITZPATRICK

Academy of Unholy Boys
Text copyright © 2025 Reserved by David Fitzpatrick
Edited by Ashley Crantas

All rights reserved.
Published in North America and Europe by Running Wild Press. Visit Running
Wild Press at www.runningwildpress.com, Educators, librarians, book clubs (as
well as the eternally curious), go to www.runningwildpress.com.

Paperback ISBN: 978-1-960018-52-6
eBook ISBN: 978-1-960018-54-0

Youth itself is a talent—a perishable talent.

— ERIC HOFFER

This novel is for Amy, Anna & Gracen...

SUMMER 2018

JAY SOUTHER

Before I met Foster Gold at St. Andrew's Prep varsity football camp, I smelled him; namely, the blended aromas of vanilla aftershave, pine, and cut grass. It was about six months ago, in the early summer of 2018, and I was a sixteen-year-old third-string sophomore punter on the Cardinals' squad, trying to make varsity. We'd just run brutal wind sprints, so I was catching my breath. Coach gave us ten minutes to hydrate.

"Gotta want it so damn bad. *Who* wants to play ball here?" Coach hollered.

"*We* do, Coach," we yelled. "*We* want it so damn bad."

"*Bullshit!*" he said. "Show me how bad you want to play. Prove it, or you're finished. We'll forfeit the goddamned year—I don't give a shit."

"*No way,*" we said. "We need it bad, Coach, *we need* to play ball for you."

In the sticky June humidity, we wore helmets, shorts, shoulder pads, socks, cleats, and light practice jerseys. I noticed Foster right away. He was eighteen, and the starting senior defensive back, but we had never spoken.

DAVID FITZPATRICK

His perpetual sidekick was eighteen-year-old senior Bear Santos, a *Parade* magazine All-American tight end two years running, and Foster's best friend since the beginning of time. There was a certain mystery about the pair, known as the Dynamic Duo, roaming halls of the local parochial schools since fifth grade. They were both popular but didn't hang around in a mass posse like other kids—they were usually off to themselves, playing video games, listening to audiobooks, watching movies, or drinking.

Foster had a clean, well-scrubbed look despite all the sweat, and though he didn't appear capable of a beard, that faint scent of aftershave lingered in his wake. He swaggered by, carrying his helmet, not terribly out of breath. When I glanced up, he smiled.

"Stand up, man," he said, and so I stood, fidgeting.

"Uh, hey."

"You punt the football like a ballerina," Foster said, playfully hooking his left arm around me. "Hang with me and Bear —we'll bring you safely out into the world of good men. And, for now, Bear has some edibles for you, okay? Our gift to you."

"I dunno," I said, but then Bear Santos, all six-foot-five, 235 pounds of him, came over and dropped a yellow cannabis chew into my palm. I caught Foster's fresh scent again, that aftershave, woodsy-vanilla stuff.

"I don't do drugs," I managed to say, right as Bear swallowed his share.

"Our lives will be wonderfully famous, Jay," Bear said. "Plus, these gummies are good for our souls."

"Who says that?"

"In the book of Jeremiah, I believe. God says weed is holy and tremendously redemptive."

"Horseshit," I said as Foster swallowed his edibles, too. I paused as they both stared at me. I looked down at my palm

ACADEMY OF UNHOLY BOYS

and the harmless-looking candy. It was just a little weed. All it would do is make me chilled out and hungry, right? I gamely downed mine with gulps of water and laughed self-consciously. "You both aren't too worried about the piss tests around here, huh?"

"No worries at all," Foster said. "Every base is covered for you."

"How so?"

Foster offered a disarming 100-watt smile. "You're the chosen sophomore," he said.

"Why me?" I asked, thinking *that friggin' edible isn't chilling me out at all.* I thought these were supposed to take time to kick in. But my brain was scattered, jumpy. Pulse racing, heart still hammering from the wind sprints. I felt silly, peculiar, and giggly as hell. Whirling colors zipped through my capillaries, and I felt ready to burst. I wanted to explore every constellation in this blessed firmament.

"Absorb this," Foster said. "From this moment on, no one in the school or town can touch you, Jay—you're like a revered relic, a golden Buddha. Hell, by Thanksgiving, you'll be the goddamned star of Bethlehem!"

Foster slammed my shoulder pads repetitively with both fists, grunting increasingly louder with each pop, and I felt bizarrely aroused. Hair stood up on my arms, as well as on the back of my neck. Throughout the next hour of conditioning, my fears and inhibitions melted, propelling me into making numerous unprompted shrieks for school spirit.

"He with you, Foster?" Coach asked, looking my way.

"Young man really wants to punt the ball for you, Coach," Foster said, offering him a thumbs up. Coach deferred to the senior defensive back when it came to strong personalities and quirky underclassmen. "Sophomore Jay Souther wants to play varsity so damn bad."

"I like that in a player," Coach said. "Any of you who want to play varsity might start howling like Mr. Souther here today, or don't even bother trying out."

So, everyone howled for a long while, the desperate, harried notes vibrating in my chest, ricocheting inside my whole frame. I was breathing in green grass and salty sweat, exhaling humility on a practice field.

Even while I was following the directions of Coach's shouts, I stepped into another dimension, unhinged in time and space. Distantly, in some stranded recreational corner of my mind, I started to question if those gummies were really weed. Helmets became the bright, pastel lights of a beach arcade. The grass became the choppy, flashing waves of the Atlantic on the Jersey Shore fifty years ago from an old postcard mom keeps up on our refrigerator, and I had morphed into a popular pinball machine under a wide orange canopy tent on the boardwalk.

Ragged-breath teens juked and thrust their bodies against my rectangular frame of metal, springs, wires and so many damn lights and silver spheres. I enjoyed watching the balls bounce off the bumpers in the clanging and glittery parts of me. I enjoyed it when the talented kids pushed me harder than anyone ever had before.

My fugue seemed to go on forever, but it had probably lasted only five minutes, and then I was back on the gridiron at St. Andrew's varsity football camp, doing more wind sprints and jumping jacks. The whole pinball machine reverie felt like a wet dream, and I was embarrassed, shaking my head, confused by every sensation, desire, and the addictive, unholy brilliance that had lurked inside the edible.

I now knew this gummy was stronger than I had first thought, and could be trouble, so I promised myself to not get in over my head. After practice, Foster caught up with me.

ACADEMY OF UNHOLY BOYS

"Your life will be a breeze from here on in," he said. "*Guaranteed.*"

"And what exactly am I giving you in return?" I asked.

He tousled my black curls. "We'll figure something out."

"What did Bear slip me?"

"Peace of mind," Foster said. "Freedom, a break from your petty, obtuse fears."

"Petty, obtuse fears?" I repeated.

"Webster's Dictionary says *obtuse* means 'dense or slow to understand'," Foster said. "Means if you were smarter, you wouldn't be so damn afraid of everything."

"Either way, that gummy felt dangerous," I said. "It screwed with my circuits."

"No worries, Jay," he said. "We practice the utmost caution with our chosen sophomores. Haven't lost one yet."

"I'm not the only one?" I asked, but Foster was digging in his bag for a Sharpie.

"See you tonight. In my basement," he said, stopping us both. He held my forearm steady with his tanned left hand and wrote his address on my wrist. "I got something else for you—I saw it on Instagram. I kept reading this quote nonstop. A new favorite of mine."

"What'd it say?"

"'*No one will ever know the violence it took to become this gentle*,'" Foster recited. "Nitya Prakash, an Indian scribe, wrote that."

"I like it," I said.

"It applies to my life in numerous ways," he said.

I read my wrist again. "Huh," I said. "It'll make a cool tattoo."

"When you come by my house tonight, don't knock, just come right in, okay?"

"Hey, are there other chosen sophomores or not?" I asked.

7

DAVID FITZPATRICK

"Just let yourself in, my dear boy," Foster said.

BEAR SANTOS

The sophomore waddled into our lives like some awkward tourist with a fanny pack interrupting an expensive movie shoot. He was decent enough, friendly and all, but so remarkably naïve. You could smell his virginity from a mile away. Foster would never have admitted this about his relationship with Jay Souther, but he fell in love. Or at least, he adored the power he had over that kid. Jay was an infant, man. He had never smoked a joint or gotten laid. That type of person made Foster Gold's mouth water. The kid was good-looking, but so green, as if he had not grown into his body yet or was not a complete human being.

Granted, all the team laughed and found themselves endeared the day Jay flipped out at practice and started screaming and doing wild jumping jacks and twirling wind sprints. My yellow edible had fired our boy way up. The other underclassmen trying out screeched in solidarity and carried on like hyenas. Too funny. Coach rolled with the punches and wisely figured,

"I'll just let Foster deal with it—besides, he's only a third-string punter, what's the worst that could go down?"

As far as human interactions go, I was interested in Jay in the same way a scientist is fascinated with an especially combustible experiment. Our newly formed trio would either go smoothly or it would implode, but I knew Foster and I were betting on devastating eruptions. Plus, each afternoon at practice, I now get to hand out the daily edibles. It felt cool, like I had a new power over him, as well.

As the sun blazed just before setting and sweat stung my eyes, I felt the rush and buzz of the cherry-flavored gummy.

BASIL SOUS

Permanence does not apply much to my life. Same goes with Aunt Peg; she is my current guardian and tries hard to assist me the best she can, to offer me a version of normalcy. She had never signed up to be my boss, but my parents bailed on me on my fifth birthday, disappearing into the jungles of Costa Rica, and have not been in contact since. They let it be known that Peg is in charge, so my aunt stepped into some big shoes, although if my parents wore anything at all on their feet, it was cheap and damaged flip-flops.

Anyway, I was hustling out of the mudroom the other day to grab my skateboard, but I tripped on our cardboard boxes. Peg and I keep these cheap moving boxes close by. Currently, we are living at a periwinkle blue Saltbox just off Route 146, overlooking the marsh. This is our second year in Gently. It feels weird to have been in the same place this long, honestly. It's like I get an itch after a few months and start automatically tossing everything back in our ripped-up cartons.

Sometimes we refer to our boxes as "Samsonites," as if we're traveling leisurely, and when we are feeling real pissed off, we call 'em "Louis Vuittons" or "Coaches." At the very top of my smallest box, wedged in a book, I keep my Polaroid of the three of us. But he is long gone now—Avery, I mean. A frat house binge-drinking disaster snuffed him out years ago.

"I keep tripping over this Louis Vuitton shit," I say. "So, I'm off to get my head shrunk by Dr. Athens."

"Wear your helmet, please," she says. "I'm getting tired of bandaging your skateboard war wounds every day, okay?"

"Sure," I say.

"Love ya," Peg says.

"You too," I say, and headed into town. I have always felt in a general manner that my life is a crapshoot, sometimes boring or sublime, but always sour and tragic. There does not seem to be much rhyme or reason, at least one I have figured out yet. Peg and I never hold a definite spot for long. These days, she does some accounting for a Honda auto dealership, trying to save enough for a permanent abode.

A social service agency in Gently set us up on the marsh. The owners are traveling across Europe, so we house-sit, feed their cats, change the litter three times a week, and look after their Great Danes, Reg and Clegg, who are massive, spotted, and slob and drool all over us, but I love them, anyway. I think of Peg and I as modern-day housekeepers, helping with the housework, the cooking. I got a job at Wave Café not too long ago, so I can purchase my own clothes and start saving for college.

The idea that pouring enough lattes for soccer moms will get me closer to college tuition is somewhat ridiculous, I know, with it being so damn expensive to go anywhere for college. Plus, after Avery died, I'm not so sure going to any university anywhere would be a smart move. That said, even the mediocre schools feel beyond my reach.

Peg would tell you I get out all my rage and frustrations by

ACADEMY OF UNHOLY BOYS

skateboarding everywhere, all over town. Yesterday, as I was putting my new Fucking Awesome sticker on my board, Peg kissed my forehead and said, "I'm so glad you've found an athletic way to escape the terror of the grown-up world." So, I get flying sometimes up Water Street on my board and if the distance was ever measured, I think we're only talking three-quarters of a mile before we hit the Gently Green, and a little farther on to Dr. Athens, so I just hop on the sidewalk and soar.

On Fridays I see my psychiatrist—he is a bearable person who surprised the hell out of me. I thought I would loathe him, because my last social worker was so severe and cold, but I like this guy. He is handsome in a nerdy way with tight black curls and olive skin —his name is Dr. John Athens. "Sounds like a Greek joke, I know, especially with this particular nose of mine," he said on our first day. "But it is on my birth certificate like that, and no, I have never visited the country. Not yet anyway."

"Yeah, me neither. Would be cool if social services found us a place on the Aegan," I say.

Dr. Athens lets me unload and say anything I wish, whether that is cursing about Peg's cleaning liabilities, mourning Avery, or bitching about the lack of maturity of other students at Gently Public High. It might not sound like much, but I feel lighter, less stressed when I leave my psychiatrist's office. I spring from Dr. Athens' lovely leather chair after thirty-nine minutes or so, and I am free, and that is a good thing.

There is an awkward and tall skinny guy who sees Dr. Athens on Friday, just before me. I've seen him at the Wave café— he mumbles into his left hand, or scribbles down his order on paper. A waiter at Wave calls him "Lurch," which is cruel, so I refuse to do that. The following day she tells me the young man just turned nineteen and his real name is Tuck and is in the special needs program at St. Andrew's. "Just don't ever call him 'Smiley.'"

Apparently, Dr. Athens accepts a sliding scale fee from Peg and me, which is cool of him. But that's a secret only the three of us share. I keep a diary, too, something the good doctor suggested on my first day. Granted, it's a bit silly, and I know I'm not suffering like Anne Frank in Amsterdam or anything, but I do like the idea of wrapping up each day with a summation. A balance statement. I do not even think other kids ponder stuff like that, but as Avery used to say, "You know, B, there are times when you're nothing but wrong."

When you live like Peg and I do, you discover how kind some people are, how they come through in the clutch, while others turn away, not always antagonistically, but because they don't know much about being alone in the world.

For my sixteenth birthday, Aunt Peg gifted me an Ashley's ice cream cake, and some gift cards to local shops, like Evergreen, and a face-to-face chat: "I know the last thing you need is a lecture on drugs, but I thought my friend Benny might help you see things with a bit more clarity."

Which sounds ridiculously awkward and silly, but what Peg did not know was that I had already taught her friend Benny how to ride a skateboard. Well, not really ride, but she came right over to me as I crossed the Green and said, "Damn. You don't know me, but you look so cool on that board." So, Benny and I got to talking and I bummed some Hubba-Bubba watermelon gum from her and soon we bonded, and now we're friends.

Peg faithfully goes to Alcoholics Anonymous and swears it has saved her, kept her sober for a decade plus. Benny was born in Hong Kong and half her head is shaved and the other part has tumbling red hair, but she tucked it away tonight beneath a dusty yellowish reggae cap. It looks odd, at first, as if some-

ACADEMY OF UNHOLY BOYS

thing's oozing out of Benny's right ear, like brains or crimson foam. Aunt Peg knows that Benny and I are pals, and the third time Peg mentioned her niece or so, the penny finally dropped. At first, Benny said Peg was a little baffled at the pure coincidence, but after a moment, she laughed and said it was fate. I kind of have to agree there.

"So, it's your sixteenth birthday, right?" she asks me. "And you're feeling pretty good?"

"Yes," I say. "Things aren't too shabby now, I guess I'd put it like that."

"Are you ready to hear my tales of woe and hardship?" she asks.

"Tell me all about it, Benny," I say.

So, she removes her jean jacket, and has sunken bluish-green eyes that look fatigued, with deep shadows between her nose and eye sockets—her whole frame looked thoroughly exhausted and *lived in*. Benny also had intricate blue veined markings, like underwater vegetation, sea grass of sorts, leaping off her left arm and hand.

"I've seen my fair share, Basil," Benny began. "There's a shitty little apartment down by the Gently docks, and years ago —and I'm not talking *that* many years—I stayed in a shitty little bedroom and barely came out. Only for food breaks and to use the bathroom, and that was it."

"Okay," I say.

"I'm telling you this, Basil, I was very low."

Benny wore a navy, short-sleeved T-shirt, and a long aqua skirt with black boots.

"I put black cloths over every mirror," she says. "I was so disgusted with who I was, I couldn't look at myself, couldn't bear it."

Benny's face tensed.

"The black cloth," she continues, "wasn't a religious thing

15

or a spiritual code of arms. I simply thought of myself as wasted flesh."

Benny tapped her fingers on her thighs.

"I couldn't stand my own face. That's depression, drug addiction, and dangerously low self-esteem wrapped up in one." Then she dabbed at her eyes with a Kleenex Peg had handed her, and she went on. "I felt I was poison, like I was lower than a dog, okay? So, I found harsh men who treated me worse than they would a mongrel stray."

"Tell it straight, Benny," Peg says.

"Since I believed I was an asshole," Benny says, "nothing but measly crack addict, there was no hope whatsoever for me."

"How'd you fall into using?" I asked.

"We came to Bridgeport when I first arrived from Hong Kong as a toddler, and our family had some real hard times," she says. "There was drinking, divorce, and some nasty domestic violence, and—eventually—everyone I knew was doing it. My aunt, my two cousins, and even my older sister, so I picked up, too."

You could imagine Benny's tattoos rustling in the currents of a rip tide around her, caught helplessly deep inside her body. In the ripples of color on her left forearm, one could see something akin to a human oil spill that had occurred. It clogged, overwhelmed, and reached every inch of her nooks and crannies, stinging her, yet maintaining her energy.

Benny's right arm was like a shallow creek with luminous goldfish darting left and right, some even jumping clear of the water. They flowed back and forth in a rainbow pattern along her forearm and under her right bicep and into the shoulder, and underarm. Her right arm features a kaleidoscope of veins and ropey cords, and waves in indigo, yellow, sapphire, and cherry-red. Seeing all the colors mixing and meshing was like attending the greatest masquerade ball in history. I could've studied those colors for days. The designs were riveting and sad and spectacular, just like Benny herself.

"So, how'd you come out on the other side?" I ask.

"Only matters how it ended," she says.

"How'd you get to a lot better spot?" I ask.

"It was several years ago," she says. "I can't believe I got out, but good people came through for me, like your Aunt Peg. Emotional support, housing, a job, a strong, resilient community, and working the twelve steps. And that's what we're trying to help you see right now, Basil. Take care of your body, mind, and soul. Nourish it. Get involved in the town with the right young women or men, whatever lights your fire."

"I like guys," I say.

Benny squeezed my hand. "Peg helped me," she says, "so now I help you, understand? You pass it on, you pay it forward —the world works best when we help each other."

"I hear you," I say. "Thanks a lot, Benny."

"The world is not that evil of a place," she assures me. "But when your self-esteem is shot, and drugs are hovering, and others are using them freely, forget it. Never give up on yourself, though, young lady, because it can be hard to find people who will be there constantly."

"Right," I say, before she embraced me tight, kissed Peg on the cheek, grabbed her jean jacket, put it on, and slipped out the front door and back into the night.

JAY SOUTHER

One maddening fact about Foster Gold is that he has so many gifts beyond his physical beauty. Like his photography: stark black and white shots of the Virgin Mary and Joseph, or decaying saints and archangels in many cemeteries, or of Jesus Christo himself stuck in some slushy snow on a raw Wednesday morning in November. So many graves are decorated with flora and mementos: crosses, candles, rosary beads, prayer cards, and stuffed animals. Foster also shoots funky grottos inside backyards in West Haven or takes pics of the Long Island Sound, and on occasion, he'll drive his cherry-red Audi through sketchy neighborhoods of New Haven, and when his eye finds decay, he takes shots of run-down, rusted out Chevy pickup trucks with wildflowers sprouting from the steering wheel. It's nothing fancy—he just searches out entropy, crumbling bricks here, or collapsing stone walls over there, or at least that's what he explained to me.

Foster puts them all on Instagram, like "a steady, gentle river." He calls the habit his favorite and healthiest addiction that consistently buoys him. His rare color photography is

ACADEMY OF UNHOLY BOYS

immaculate, as well. I end up staring at close-ups of his unforgettable eyes—one green, one blue. I started seeing the maestro in action, just how he works and breathes and loves both the outer world and the one within.

A week after meeting the Dynamic Duo, I came home from practice and found a tote bag of books on my bed. They were from R.J. Julia Booksellers in Madison, a wonderful independent bookstore. In the pile, I saw *The Great Gatsby* by Fitzgerald, *Franny and Zooey* by Salinger, *Great Expectations,* Donna Tartt's *The Secret History,* a sci-fi novel called *Logan's Run;* further digging revealed Wendell Berry's book of poems entitled, "The Peace of Wild Things," a short story collection called "Emperor of the Air" by Ethan Canin, and a nonfiction book on the Jonestown nightmare back in 1978.

"What's with all these books here, Ma?"

"A friend of Foster's, named Al Basque, said Foster wanted you to have them. He wants you to read them, or at least, listen to them as audiobooks."

"He hand-delivered them here?" I asked, incredulous.

"Yes," Ma said. "He's the handsome partner of Mrs. Gold. Watch your step with these older boys, though." Mom was sipping an early martini in front of the TV, gearing up to watch a full night of Home Shopping Network or QVC or maybe both; I had stopped trying to figure out mom's consumer tastes years earlier.

"Why say that?" I asked.

"Folks don't give you free books for no reason, Jay," she said. "Donald Ayo at church said that Foster is spoiled, fickle, and has totaled his 2016 Audi twice. Strings are forever attached. Promise me you'll remember that?"

"Sure," I said, "but I believe you're overreacting. Books are good brain food, right?"

19

"I hear what I hear, Jay," she said. "But why would this angel of a young man buy you a book on Jonestown?"

"Did I ever describe him as 'an angel of a young man'?"

"Sort of," she said. "Your voice goes up an octave talking about Foster, I've seen him, he's a handsome young man....so it concerns me."

"Because I have a new attractive male friend who bought me some great books as a kind gesture?"

"Look, you're constantly in search of a strong male role model to replace your invisible, disintegrating father," she said. "Just be aware of that fact going forward, okay?"

"I'm not sure what you're getting at, Ma," I said, feeling oddly defensive. "And I know you don't go to church any longer, would you just admit to that, finally?"

"Don't start being a smart ass, Jay," she said. "I'm aware I haven't attended church in five months, but that doesn't mean what Donald said last year was false."

"Okay, okay. Good point, Ma," I mumbled placatingly while rolling my eyes.

Later, I went to Foster's that evening and just about every night for a few weeks running. We had a blast, laughing our asses off, singing and crooning like slick and cheesy Atlantic City lounge acts, shadow boxing, arm wrestling, watching movies, playing video games, and eating take-out. Those muggy, blissful evenings that summer were potent and precise, the memories a cheerful golden blur of the three of us driving around aimlessly, listening to the audiobook of *Great Expectations* and all those other poems and stories Foster loved so much. We posted social media madness, stopping by the vegetarian diner whenever Foster, Bear, and myself switched from bulking up with several orders of chocolate chip pancakes each to cutting calories with salads and diet soda. Without even realizing it, I gradually came to

ACADEMY OF UNHOLY BOYS

enjoy the cannabis edibles instead of feeling psyched out by them.

After ten nights in a row, I got up the nerve to question Foster about the books, but he shook it off. "It's what friends do," he said. "Part of our blood brother bond. Bear, me, and now you, Jay—we take care of one another, stand guard."

"I'm broke, though," I said. "I can't afford to even buy you a paperback."

"Have you ever read *The Great Gatsby*?" he asked.

"Skimmed through its freshman year," I said.

"Go back to it with intent, okay?" Foster said. "Extend yourself, especially the beginning and the ending of the story. Or if you don't have any steady concentration skills left within your psyche, listen to it with us at night. Jake Gyllenhaal's narration is marvelous; a part of me wants to cry as I listen. Fitzgerald was at the top of his game, I'd say."

"You prefer listening to books than reading them?" I asked.

"Listening to an audiobook for the first time blew me away. It was *The Secret History* by Donna Tartt. That tiny woman-scribe-hero from Mississippi bursts with confidence, and her novel kicks a tremendous amount of ass."

"What time is it, folks?" Bear asked, awaking from napping on the couch.

"Time for a change of pace," Foster said, and so we headed upstairs to refill our munchies bowl, mostly Doritos and pretzels, and then Foster roused Bear again from the couch and found Al Basque taking pics of the dinner he was cooking for Foster's mom. Al was St. Andrew's sports equipment manager, and Mrs. G's boyfriend extraordinaire; born and raised in Madrid, he was in his mid-forties with salt and pepper hair and obligingly took constant photos of Foster's life.

If Foster wasn't filming, he insisted on being filmed. He wanted everything captured. From his ultrasounds in Mrs. G's womb to everything that happened since; and he means everything, I'd come to learn, from his Bris to his first-grade graduation to his bar-mitzvah to his first kiss and more. Sometimes just photos, other times recordings of every glance, every giggle in a waking day. Foster rarely admitted he was influenced by pop stars, but he told Bear and I that he got the idea of recording every second of his existence from iconic singer and performer Madonna. "She's got serious chutzpah."

Al and Mrs. G and Foster were an odd, but very contented family, and after they added their chocolate cocker spaniel Swiss Miss, they seemed like they were ready for a *People Magazine* spread. It certainly was not my mom and I or Bear and Reverend Santos who had the tightest, closest filial bunch in the Nutmeg state.

Al did everything from fixing household appliances to gardening to making sure Foster, Bear, and I never got in trouble with our urine screens at St. Andrew's. Al was very much a Renaissance Man; he had his hand in everything.

"Let me steal your camera right now, Al," Foster said, and then turned back to me and snapped multiple shots of Bear and myself, smiling all the while. Then he led our trio like a pied piper to three yellow lounge chairs set out on the back lawn of his mom's sprawling home. There was a small gray-stone fire pit in the middle. As Foster came back around for a close-up, I popped up from the chair and stepped away, not ready to be posing for anyone.

"What do you like to read besides your trashy pulp or porn fiction, Jay?"

"Not sure," I said, and he smiled again.

Too charming and handsome for words, I thought. *And why is he always staring?*

"If you're stuck on an island and can only bring five novels?"

ACADEMY OF UNHOLY BOYS

"I like the ones you bought me," I said.

"Disappointing and lame answer, Jay. Which novels? Give me at least two."

"There's a middle-grade book called *I Am the Cheese* that I still read. Necessary fiction for me."

"Robert Cormier penned it," Bear said from his lounge chair, fooling around on his phone. "A New England native, it says here."

"Offer me one more title," Foster said. "And then sit your ass down right there; time to relax. We got delicious chips, pretzels, and dip here from Mom and Al."

"I know it sounds archaic, but I still love *Catcher*, okay? Holden doesn't give a flying freak, so I worship him. He's like my forever friend, always ready with another snappy comment or detached zinger. Plus, I love Franny Glass with all my heart, I want to find and marry her as soon as possible."

"Interesting," Bear said. "*Delusional*, but interesting. But my mind is currently doing flips because you two morons are like biplanes showing off at Big E State Fair."

"I'm too drunk to show off," Foster laughed. "Do you adore me, Jay?"

"The fuck?" Bear spat, pulling a face.

"Get over yourself, Bear," Foster said, before coming in close to me with the camera, an inch away from my chin. "I was just joking, Mr. All-American tightest- tight-end in town."

"Yeah, right," Bear said.

Foster was pushing buttons on the camera's settings. "Will you show me yours if I show you mine, Jay?"

"You're very odd," I said, still not sitting down. More like fidgeting and moving around a lot. "Closer to certifiable, in fact."

"I want you, you want me, what do you say?" Foster asked,

dancing around with the camera still focused on me. "Are you attracted to me, Jay?"

"Honestly, I can't ever follow you and Bear's conversations," I said. "It's like a morbid morse code, all the goofy, singsong seventh-grade sexual innuendo crap."

"I'm drunk and high and a tad numb," Foster said. "But I feel your eyes on me in the shower after practice, know what I mean, Jay?"

"That's patently untrue," I said, even as I can feel my face heat. "You can't just make crap up like that, Foster. It's slanderous."

"Whatever," Foster said with a smile. "After I get everyone's picture here, we'll go sit in my Cove and listen to amazing novels, poems, and perhaps speak of darkness."

"You and Bear are always flirting with melancholia and doom."

"Just having fun, I guess," Foster said.

"Death and fun don't go together," I commented. "Like oil and water."

"Tell Edgar Allan Poe that," he said. "Or Gillian Flynn, Stephen King, Truman Capote, or true crime podcasts. People can't get enough of dark stuff...it's addictive."

I had no reply to that. "Point taken," I said.

"My boy, you need to look at these things with the right aperture," Foster said. "All this stuff fascinates me, plus all these books are just to show you what I'm absolutely not."

"Is that true?" I ask.

"For some of us, death can be a comfort, a place to seek shelter... I get going myself with bad suicidal ideation, periodically, okay?"

"I'm sorry to hear that," I said. "What helps you fight against it?"

ACADEMY OF UNHOLY BOYS

"Flirting with Bear and you," he said with a grin. "I'm a people-person."

"So, why'd you throw in that book about Jonestown?"

"You're asking me why I filled your mind not only with stellar poets and writers, but also with the story of the victims who drank grape Kool-Aid and cyanide at The People's Temple in Guyana on November eighteenth, 1978." It was a statement, not a question. Like he was gauging me, taking my temperature.

"Why bring up that much suffering to me?" I asked, walking back and forth between the yellow lawn chairs, but not yet sitting down beside Bear. "A thousand victims, that's so messed up."

"To be exact, nine hundred and nine," he said.

"It's freaky that you know that number by heart," I said.

"I share all this with you because I care a lot for you. I wish for you to see the massive difference between a sociopath-idiot-like Jim Jones, David Koresh, and us, Foster Gold and the amazing Latino athlete, Felipe Bear Santos."

"You're saying you're not obsessed with death and dying?"

"Not at all, it's just wild speculation, a hobby. We ruminate about life's mysteries in the Cove, and learn from everyone on Planet Earth," Foster said. "Numerous lessons."

"Like what?" I say, finally sitting down in a yellow lounge chair as if hypnotized by Foster's smooth, caramel voice.

"We need to be sponges absorbing the world with passion and verve. Perhaps we'll learn romance languages and study Latin, French, and Italian, or practice breathing lessons with a talented Yogi, or even hit the gym."

"And?" I asked.

"We'll study more about civil rights," he said. "Or disabled, gay, trans rights, or even learn about wild bobcats, and the honeybees buzzing about."

"Why wild bobcats and honeybees?"

"Because I don't know jack shit about honeybees, and that's a shame," he said. "They keep the world fed, pollinating all around us left and right, and a lot of them are dying unnecessarily."

"You offer variety in a maddening fashion, Foster," I said. "You go low and morbid with your obsessions, and you end with buzzing bees and a skewed sense of optimism."

"Life and death are mysteries that no one will ever figure out, Jay," he said. "I like exploring all the options available to a young, happening dude like me, okay?"

"I guess," I said and watched him preach.

"Let me dance around you and croon a tune, my boy," he said. "How'd you like the free beer and the cannabis edibles offered again today?"

"I underestimated their strength—I don't enjoy feeling out of control, but thanks for offering them to me."

"Well, I like to be sky-high, as does Bear."

"I'll tell you this much, Jay," Bear said. "Foster loves photos and books, bits and scraps of media that will outlive us long after we die. I think you should listen to him, think about what he's saying; don't dismiss Foster as being on the fringe. He's just so far ahead we can barely see him."

"By the way, you made varsity football," Foster says. "Coach told me to tell you of that wonderful, tantalizing, and spectacular fact."

"Seriously?" I said, as I jumped up and made a fist.

"Absolutely," Bear said. "We're both proud of you."

"Thanks, I never made anything in my life," I said. "Wow, that's pretty cool."

Foster put his camera on the ground and started mumbling words and phrases as he spins with his hands out flat, whirling. He moved around in circles, spinning past Bear and me on the lawn chairs, saying, "It's my privilege to invite you to a snazzy,

ACADEMY OF UNHOLY BOYS

amazingly fantabulous, all-souls, heaven-can-wait, devil-may-care fundraiser with three varsity jocks dancing and twisting off the goal post at St. Andrew's on a huge day of gratitude, prayer, and random acts of carved turkey, kindness, cranberry sauce, and violence."

"Thanksgiving, huh? Sounds ambitious and dubious."

"Football is violent, life is brutal, too," he said. "Did you ever see Quentin Tarantino's *Inglorious Basterds?*"

"No, but that's a great description of your duo," I said, standing up once more and walking away this time, shaking my head. "You act like hope and peace are curse words."

"No need to walk away tonight, Jay," Foster practically shouted, staggering to a stop. "I do love our trio; we've got a lot of things to do together. Look, man, I also enjoy all the love and light in the world."

"Did you really total your Audi, twice?" I shouted back to him. "Yes or no?"

"What are you, a cop?" he said, running after me, grabbing and turning me around to face him. There were beads of sweat on his brow, his multi-colored eyes, one green, another blue, stunning as ever, and I thought, *I wonder if he'll ever try to kiss me?*

I didn't want that ridiculous and discomforting thought rampaging around in my head, so I grit my teeth and thought, *not cool, not cool at all!*

"I am just a guy seeking the truth, hoping to hear it now, okay?" I said.

"Yes, I smashed everything up when I first learned to drive, that's two times in a row," Foster said. "I'm very human. Why don't you chill out and return to us?"

"I'm going home tonight, but thanks for the honesty," I said. "Promise me the cult deaths in Guyana aren't like some wild inspiration for you?"

"That's a bizarre thing to say," he remarked as I started walking away again.

"My mom had the same thought," I said. "She's not a huge fan of your book gifts. She said there's always strings attached to every present, including going all the way back to the Ten Commandments."

"I love both your mom and you, Jay," he said. "Isn't there a place for simple kindness in the world?"

"Will Jay Souther be a trusted leader for tomorrow?" Bear asked ominously.

"We'll discover all that and more in these next three and a half months," Foster went on as I continued walking away. "We love you, Jay."

"Tell me I just didn't join a cryptic high school cult," I called over my shoulder.

"We're definitely not a cult!" he shouted. "That's my solemn promise!"

"Superb. I'll hold you to it," I muttered. "And I did make varsity."

"Congrats on making punter," Foster said, reading my mind. "Huge deal."

I turned and offered a thumbs up and Bear shouted, "You must know that the chosen sophomore would never be passed over."

Foster picked me up in his cherry-red 2016 Audi with the somewhat-dented hood two days later and took me out for Sunday brunch at a retro diner in Old Saybrook. We discussed listening to fiction and how my maestro's imagination had grown exponentially since he started audio books. He wore his

ACADEMY OF UNHOLY BOYS

light khakis, a black flannel shirt, and moccasins. He was acting lighter, friendlier.

Foster didn't speak about himself for nine minutes straight, only listened and laughed, asking me about my life, any funny stories I might have heard. I mentioned a heavyset teacher I had in second grade, and that when she'd lose control of the class, she'd sometimes resort to sitting on rebellious students.

"No shit?" Foster said.

"She was so fed up with one kid, she sat on him and broke his wrist in two places," I said, "After that, we never saw her again. Mom told me she ran off to Key West with a plumber, and played guitar well, singing tunes four nights a week. She developed a following there, and put out an album, too. To this day, she's still playing and singing at a local bar and grill."

"Cool," he said. "Well, that's a great little story."

"You're being so kind to me today...is there something wrong?"

"I feel bad about how rude I was the other day," he said. "I don't like that part of myself."

"I'm a big boy."

"Of course, you are," he said. "I just feel like a shit and am sorry for coming on too strong around the holiday bash."

I looked at him. "Thanksgiving, right? Did you mean it'll happen in the end zone or on the goal post itself?"

"It'll include everything and everyone," he replied. "We are taking baby steps in the beginning, though, understand? We won't miss a thing – that's my promise to you."

"Sounds cool, and thanks for apologizing," I said.

"I told Bear on the first day," Foster said. "This sophomore kid Jay is so damn unique at St. Andrew's."

"How so?"

"You're real and true," he said. "My mom noticed it, as well, and said, 'That kid is a sweetheart, make sure you're good to him.'"

I smiled. Foster's attention felt like sunshine beaming down on my face, healing and empowering. "It's rare, especially for guys our age," he said. "We're always so competitive, macho, ready to fight over anything."

"That's you," I said.

"Absolutely," he said. "All I can say is you've also got twelve different kinds of laughter, Jay," he said. "It's one of my favorite things about you."

"Really?"

"You got every kind," Foster went on. "Carefree, slapstick... vulnerable, screwball, anecdotal, ironic, deadpan, morbid, even lyrical and burlesque."

"I'll write them down so you can keep track."

"No need, my friend," Foster said, tapping his temple with his finger. "I got them all saved up right here."

And I guess that's part of the reason I spent the rest of that Sunday, and most of the autumn beside Foster, listening, soaking up his quasi-sermons. It's why I followed him into battle so blindly, like a damn fool. Don't get me wrong, Foster can still be a dick and get ugly, but who else recognizes your twelve versions of laughter? Who ever listens that close? It was the rare days like that Sunday that made my time with Foster seem worthwhile, even blessed.

Until I'd fallen in with Foster Gold and Bear Santos, I'd managed to avoid drugs, weed, even booze. I'd never been interested much; does that sound too naïve? It was the truth for years—until I made varsity football that June. By July I was consuming on the regular. I had decided I'd only drink and

ACADEMY OF UNHOLY BOYS

have some edibles, all the rest of the stuff—blunts, coke, pills—I'd skip. Foster and Bear directed me where to go for urine screens.

Through the months that followed, and despite my fear of Foster and his morbid and bizarre ways, I felt a disorienting pull—a desire to make physical contact. Periodically, I even fantasized about brushing against him. Some nights, I tossed and turned, obsessing about his tight belly and thighs.

"Stop this, Jay," I'd scold myself. "He's your friend."

But the fact remained I could not heed my own words. I studied him frequently, though I hated to admit that. Foster had morphed from boyhood into manhood exceptionally well, with nary a pimple in sight. He had blond hair and a taut, toned body, though he was not that much taller than me at five-nine. He had a touch of arrogance—he knew he looked great.

"Knock it off," I told myself. *Why is he in your head so much?* I thought. *Move on, let it go, for Christ's sake.*

On Instagram each night, I examined collections of anonymous pictures of scars and blisters around a male's belly button —I think it was male, anyway; tight abs with slight blond hair. I wondered if it was Foster. Would he post pictures of his marred skin like that? No comment, no hashtags? In the afternoons at St. Andrew's showers, I tried my best *not* to ogle him, but I think I might have seen puckered scars around his belly. I wondered if they were self-inflicted or from his abusive father all those years ago.

I felt sick as I admitted to myself that I wanted to trace and touch those damn scars. Wasn't that peculiar? I would shake my head and slap my face for wanting to kiss the wounds and all that abundant flesh. *Was I hopeless for thinking like that? For my mind to be going in that direction?* I asked my conscience.

"Yes, you absolutely are," I scolded myself.

The next day, I attempted to shower at St. Andrew's gym without getting a hard-on. I heard students bragging in the locker room about a new girl in town with her full, buoyant breasts, heart-shaped ass, and ruby lips.

So, I tried to think of morbid thoughts, tried to use words and images that would deflate me. *Would you grow the hell up, Jay Souther?* I chastised myself, thinking, *reduction, subtraction, deflation, retiring, subduing.*

His exposed flesh wrecked me. Outside, I ogled Foster on the football field, but in the showers, I soaped, shampooed, rinsed, and got the hell out as quickly as possible. I couldn't bear him knowing I fantasized about him like some perv. But I couldn't control my thoughts. What struck me most during the long days at football camp were Foster and his damn shorts. The fit, tight over his muscular hips, so snug. Soccer legs, strong thighs, and rounded, knotty calves. His shorts had three stripes: peach, rust, and sandalwood…at least I think so, but I can't be a hundred percent certain of any of it, as I was usually getting smoked by our conditioning, distracted, a mile high from the edibles he fed me, and woozy in the summer heat.

I guess I do brag about Foster. There are implications of mystery and darkness all about the gentleman, or is he instead a classic bullshitter? On Instagram, he posts numerous pics of dark wells and mysterious railroad tunnels, or videos with kittens, alpacas, llamas, souped-up Audis, and baby pigs. Foster Gold's work could be like a balm for many who've seen enough in their lives and cannot stand it one second longer. He is a multi-talented human being who never stops searching for the next huge thing, and if he happens to sense it living deep inside of your chest wall, well, by God, run hard, for he'll hunt you down and spirit you away.

BEAR SANTOS

Even I'm not sure what kind of arrangement Foster had with Al Basque, the stealthy equipment manager at St. Andrew's Prep. Maybe Foster paid him with drugs, or stacks of cash. At any rate, Al worked with a select few on the team—our trio and some other seniors who liked to indulge.

Al Basque made sure none of us got tripped up with petty infractions. In between wind sprints and dry heaves, there was a lot of laughter about the questionable hiring standards of St. Andrew's. Not that any soul complained. Al was a peculiar figure—and we all benefitted from his peculiarities.

Al and Mrs. G were quite affectionate with each other, and it was obvious to everyone who visited the Gold house that they were in love. Al Basque's hot cocoa-inspired cocker spaniel seemed perfectly content there. Swiss Miss climbed all over them and ruled the roost; from what I could see, it was a tight-knit family. At Foster's place, there was laughter and affection and love. And so many cameras, of course. Post practice, we gathered at Foster's expansive backyard, and there would be Al Basque, present on the periphery, helping Mrs. G prepare

ACADEMY OF UNHOLY BOYS

dinner or recording Foster in action. My leader claimed it and I certainly believed in a single fact; A camera had been kept on constantly for one purpose: visual authentication.

"We're always live here, men," Foster said. "Al Basque helps make some of that possible for me, for you, for all of us."

"My son is so convinced he's going to be the biggest star ever in the history of constellations," Mrs. G said.

"You nailed it, Mom," Foster answered. "Only for a short blip of time, however, I won't be around that long, I'm afraid."

"You have a massive ego," Mrs. G said. "I fear that will come back to haunt you down the road."

"*Whatever*, Mom," Foster said, turning his attention to Al Basque. "Are you getting my good side here, Al?"

"I'm doing my best," Al said. "Being captured in living color twenty-four-seven can be quite an expensive undertaking."

"As it should be," Foster said. "But we've got the cash, and I've got the scars and bruises to prove it, thanks to my dear old Pop."

"What can I say?" Al said to me while filming the senior. "Your best friend here pays me extremely well. And he's a riot to be around—doesn't seem to fear a damn thing in the whole world."

"Yes," I said. "I noticed that, too."

"I was just the opposite in high school, Bear," Al said to me. "I had no clue which end was up."

"What was it like growing up in Madrid?" I asked.

"We were poor but had fun and played a lot of soccer; *everyone* played a lot of soccer," Al Basque said with a laugh. "I was a wallflower throughout school, you get me?"

"I get you," I said.

"I did play baseball my last year, though," he told me. "I was a semi-decent second baseman, and then my sister was

35

suddenly attending school in New York and the world sort of opened up like a rare lily for me, for us."

"Where'd she go?" I asked.

"New York University," he said. "She loved the Greenwich Village campus. She used to take me around Washington Square Park all the time, show me the ropes, introduce me to her lovely, whacked-out, eccentric, and bizarro friends."

"What does she do now?" I asked.

"She got her doctorate and teaches kids in Barcelona all about theatre; Shakespeare, Miguel De Cervantes, Sarah Ruhl, Lin-Manuel Miranda, Annie Baker, Neil Simon, and more. I visited her once in New York, and I never went home again. Lovely women everywhere in NYC—hard for me to leave, understand?"

"I can imagine," I said. When Al wasn't recording Foster, he often helped spruce up Gold's home, painting the shutters or planting veggies in the garden. He observed us kids without a hint of judgment. It's hard to say exactly when Al became part of the scenery, no more substantial or important than the musty cardboard boxes of old CDs in their basement, or Swiss Miss dashing around with his tongue hanging out of the side of his mouth like a massive slab of bologna.

JAY SOUTHER

Before school, in the weeks after I'd first met Bear and Foster, I was offered a sense of belonging I'd never felt before. During that hot, seemingly endless, bizarre, and scary summer, Foster spirited us around in his 2016 Audi, and drew up intricate truth-or-dare games, and dished out booze, edibles, and bizarre challenges. When we weren't out playing football, listening to amazing short stories, poetry, and novels, or hanging out in The Cove, we were champions in Foster's creations, "Tests of Spiritual and Physical Glory."

One test was wild, freewheel surfing on top of his Audi. He'd put me or Bear in full-dress football uniforms on the hood of his car and drive ten, fifteen, then twenty miles an hour in the old Walmart parking lot, seeing how much speed we could take. Then he'd hit the brakes. Because of Bear's size, he took some particularly bad spills.

"Do you want it to hurt, my dearest gal?" Foster shouted at him through the open window.

"Give me everything you got, and make it sting, chicken-shit."

The Surfing Challenge frightened me. Bear and Foster both seemed unbothered like it was no more daring than a stroll around the Green. Surprisingly, Foster didn't mind if Bear and I dented his prized Audi's hood with our cleats.

"No worries," he said. "I won't need the vehicle too much longer."

Another glory test was OUCH, a sport that had Bear and me wearing next to nothing in Foster's backyard, only a baseball catcher's mask with a neck protector over swimming goggles, athletic cups, and steel-toed boots. Foster would tee off and drive golf balls right at us from only feet away. He thoughtfully put up a thin mesh net behind us that recovered the balls, preventing them from striking any of the neighbors' property.

The test was dangerous, insipid, and painful. It hurt like a son of a bitch, leaving welts, and it even fractured my left index finger, which ended our summer season of OUCH. I told my mom that it had all happened at football practice but when the swelling didn't recede, she yanked me down to an Urgent Care. As I sat on the papered table, and the doctor pummeled me with questions, I managed to keep the truth to myself.

Through most of it, Bear and I had laughed uproariously, calling for more. "Who wants to eat this golf ball?" Foster howled. "Who needs it in their gut today?"

"*I do,*" Bear roared. "Nothing will break my abs, sir—*I'm a rock.*"

"What about you, Jay?" Foster asked with a grin, knowing he had this maddening control. The winner of OUCH was the player who somehow stayed silent during the impact, who absorbed every blast of the golf balls and swallowed the pain. Foster never let me or Bear drive golf balls at him, nor did he put himself on the Audi hood for freewheeling surfing days. *That* wasn't allowed. Foster was forever in charge, always the Wizard, I guess, delivering his orders.

ACADEMY OF UNHOLY BOYS

Mrs. G came out on her porch once, observing us play on the back lawn as Al Basque recorded the games without any protest. "Come on, boys, fight back, disagree with him," Mrs. G said. "Don't put up with my kid's bullshit."

"You wouldn't understand, Ma," Foster said, waving her off the porch. "It's about football, brotherhood, and civic pride."

"My son is completely nuts, Al," Mrs. G said to the camera. "A dangerous boy, a future autocratic tyrant of the world, I believe. He's certifiable and whacked out of his head—mark my words."

"Just exit stage left," Foster said to his mom. "We're girding our loins here, preparing for an epic, monstrous battle."

We rarely questioned Foster's games. I imbibed his alcohol while Bear hoovered his drugs. We would run through brick walls and spit fire for the guy.

"Guide," Bear called out to his best friend, *"lead us."*

I shook my head as Bear said that. Bear's faith, his reverence, was unshakeable. Bear would sit enraptured at Foster's feet, eyes wide and unblinking, mouth slack, when the maestro would go on his rambling speeches in the basement, nicknamed "The Cove." I, on the other hand, would be thinking, *how did Foster get so far beyond the rest of the free world? Can we walk it back somehow? Can we get Foster to tone down his vibe?*

Then Bear would take a hit from Monster, a massive, five-foot teal bong which Foster described as his, "oldest, most loyal friend who never lets you get discouraged." Bear would sink into the damp, tattered, and mildewed sofa, which was covered with repeating designs of orange tulips in an indigo vase. Foster would often be scantily clad in that basement, bouncing around in his colorful athletic supporters, cut-off T-shirts, and bright knee-high socks.

The two were like manic seventh graders with their petty jousts and rapid-fire insults. And they had this weirdly frank, homoerotic thing going on, whether it was Bear slapping Foster, or the pair catcalling "Do me," and "Bend over, sweet tits." Almost everything between them was couched in sexual sarcasm. Their voices ricocheted off the basement walls.

"Blow me, Bear."

"I want a meal, not a snack, cowboy."

"You could never take me, bitch."

But as I listened and observed them daily, I found myself struggling to put the pieces of our friendship together. What did our bond consist of? What kept us from walking out on each other? Was it fear of loneliness, fat gobs of despair, or ugly, repressed rage? Did we ever stop to discuss the larger picture? Beyond even the classic and contemporary novels and the insightful poems we heard weekly, daily, even? Or examine our own aching loneliness, and realize that we felt as alienated and shattered as every other suburban Catholic high school student in America?

Hell no, we insisted we were stellar and unique and sucked in our breath and charged on with our macho games. Our toxic rage and the culture's bombardment of violence left gaping wounds all over our trio, although no teacher would dare take us on, or challenge us. We should have been knocked down a few notches, but no one seemed up to the task. That meant we were powerful and unchecked, a dangerous combination.

The three of us had formed a lopsided gang, to say the least, and we often found ourselves in Foster's Cove that summer getting drunk, listening to novels, or playing videogames, watching movies, texting, and posting our stupid antics on social media. Foster had quite the following. Several females from St. Mary's, our sister high school in North Madison, texted him. A few times he would text pictures of his hard-on to them from a burner cell. That said, when girls texted back their

ACADEMY OF UNHOLY BOYS

bare bodies, or "their brilliance" as Foster put it, he appeared uninterested. Bored, even.

I hated to think it was just *ennui*—a word Foster liked to fall back on when he couldn't think of another term to use. For he was a charismatic yet negative force, and when his mood grew dark, he made the Grim Reaper appear like a jolly and neighborly guy.

* * *

In late August, I started receiving the first of many anonymous notes. I got them at my house twice a week, usually Tuesdays and Thursdays. They were typed in bold font on copy paper and folded inside a manila envelope. The first one read:

"Jaye Sudder—don't throogh your life awaye 'cuz two depressed senor dolts r messin with yor guuey brainz. Listen to yor gutz. Avoid shrooms or ascid, cut wey bak on boozee. Don does not take life fur granted any long er. Be strong, and stae positive—here if you need mee. Do nut ever give in, man. Never die yung, ether."

T"

Initially, I panicked. *Somebody out there already knows everything about The Greatest Show,* I thought. *How do I respond? Should I tell Foster and Bear?* After I debated for a day, I kept quiet and hid the notes in the bottom drawer of my dresser.

I spent more and more time in Foster's basement. Mrs. G was cool about all of us drinking, and she even looked the other way when Bear and Foster smoked. Foster's dad was rarely mentioned; he was a fired, felonious insurance exec from Hartford, and was long divorced from Mrs. G. He lived off Route 80 deep in the woods in North Gently, although he used a red barn in Mrs. G's backyard as a storage facility for his miniature antique models and collectibles. The three of us avoided it—off limits.

A St. Andrew's rumor had it that Al's great-great-grandfather was a champion bullfighter and was said to have gotten so shit-faced with Papa Hemingway that he woke up blind, naked, and writhing in the dirt of a Palermo bullring.

Al was full of crazy stories similar to that, and he had a great joy retelling them to the three of us. Life at Foster's was more loving as time went on. There was much kissing and snuggling between Al and his mom, and this seemed to mellow Foster out, and his personality became less harsh, more supportive. I was grateful for it, and although it was hard to read him, I think Bear was, too.

BEAR SANTOS

Since the fifth grade, Foster Gold and I had thrown insults back and forth at each other, the nastier the better. In the end, we had no choice but to become pals, because most everyone else in the town feared us. I was always bigger and more muscular than the others in school, at the playground, or on athletic fields. Plus, Foster gravitated towards me because he envied the respect I got from the other kids. Eventually, they'd respected him too, even more than me, but back in middle school, he just couldn't help himself with his sarcastic retorts; he always had the funniest comments flying out of him.

"Jesus, that little Jewish kid has balls," I muttered to myself, watching him flail about in the snow. It was winter, and a snowball fight had broken out as we all waited for the bus. Foster got hit with an ice ball, and he just lost it, cursing at two sixth graders out something fierce. I was impressed with Foster—he never gave up.

"You're nothing but a cheap-ass Jew," one of the boys shouted.

Foster burned with a rage so hot I was surprised the snow

didn't melt around him. I thought, *they will regret this forever,* and joined teams with Foster; thus, the Dynamic Duo was formed. After we scared off the little shits, I reflected on a time when a couple assholes called me a "beaner" and "greasy spic" years before and how that hurt had overwhelmed me. "You think you're some hot shit because you can catch a football?" the older kid had spat.

The incident had truly stung me something fierce—there was anguish and something akin to shame that sat low in my gut and throbbed for hours on end. My father told me, "Son, look to Psalms: *The Lord loves justice. He will never leave his faithful all alone. They are guarded forever, but the children of the wicked are eliminated.*" So, the next day I found the older sixth graders and they left with bloody noses and split lips, and no one ever pushed me around again.

I think, at first, some kids stayed away from Foster and me out of fear, but eventually they offered us a grudging form of admiration after we got into football. We ended up being inseparable, and as time passed Foster stood clear of most trouble: he stayed out of detention and even earned good grades. He relied on his creative and persuasive mind, and before long he realized the value of being a classroom charmer.

Two years later, during eighth grade, Foster disappeared for over half a year. Vanished into thin air. So, I thought I'd lost my best friend. But on Valentine's Day I received a surprise call. It was Foster inviting me over. This was way before the basement days, so that afternoon we sat on opposite beds in his room, not having a clue what to say.

"I have a weird gift for you, man," Foster finally said, rising. "Even though you're still nothing but a lousy ball and chain."

"You're a no-good meddling wench," I said, smiling. "Mrs. Drama, day in, day out. A constant and massive pain in my ass."

ACADEMY OF UNHOLY BOYS

He handed me a homemade Valentine's card that had been crafted out of orange and yellow construction paper and even had a ribbon. I half expected a crude joke or a belligerent drawing, but this had been crafted with surprising care.

"How kind," I replied, not sure whether I was expected to be sarcastic or genuine.

"Did you miss Sharon while he was gone?" he asked.

I fell mute and placed the card on a side desk. I didn't know what to say. Foster had told me several times that Sharon was his actual first name. He said a rabbi had sat him down long ago and told him the moniker was handed down from God himself. It seemed fine to me, but I knew he loathed it. "Sharon's a good name," I commented. "It's cool. Most kids don't give a crap about that kind of thing—we're nearly in high school, man."

"You get tired of hearing Bear, though, right?" he said. "Doesn't it piss you off? Felipe."

"A bit," I said, wanting to change the subject. "Where the hell have you been, though?"

"Around, I guess," he said, his handsome face flushing.

"We missed you," I said. "Or, at least, *I* did."

"Thanks," Foster said. "I was far away, though, long gone." I watched him pick intently at his thumbnail. "The place I went to was like the isle of misfit toys."

I nodded at him like I understood, but I didn't.

"A zoo," Foster said. "A bughouse in Missouri, outside of Columbia."

"Bughouse?"

"A frightening spot," he said. "Sick, burnt, bleeding, messed-up, and depressed bugs, some getting zapped, beating themselves up, or starving to death."

"Like a mental hospital?" I asked, and Foster's eyes spilled, and he nodded.

"Promise me you won't ever tell a soul."

"Never," I said. "We're friends, we're tight."

"I feel that, too," he said.

"Was it hard to make friends at the bughouse?"

"We were all broken, our minds, *my mind,* wasn't working," he said.

"So, like, what was it all about, Foster?"

"Pop."

I sucked in air through my teeth. "Your father?"

"He beat the living shit out of me," Foster said. "Still can't hear out of my left ear. He busted my jaw, nose, and broke so many bones, fingers, and both of my ankles."

"Holy shit." I couldn't bring myself to use the phrase "I'm sorry"—it seemed like such small words for his huge wounds; so I fidgeted around and scowled and finally added, "God, that's terrible news."

"He used to be an insurance exec," Foster said. "Fired after almost killing me. A bigot, too. If he sees you with me around town, he's likely to call you nasty names..."

I suddenly realized that his dad never mentioned that he'd cornered me after the ice skate accident. "Like *'beaner'*?"

"Worse."

"I've heard worse," I said. "Plus, I'm bigger than him now."

"Yes," Foster said. "You've really shot up."

We were both quiet for a few minutes.

"Why isn't he sitting in jail, though?"

"An insipid clerical error by a paralegal who worked for the prosecuting attorney helped Pop go free. So, he got off easy if he attended mandatory AA meetings five times a week," Foster said. "My dad must stay a mile away from me and my mom. And he had to pay us a shitload of cash – almost four million."

"But no jail time?"

"No. *Car for a scar.* Good deal, right?"

ACADEMY OF UNHOLY BOYS

"Not really," I said. "Want me to come back tomorrow? You know, to read the special card?"

Foster barely smiled.

"Would it be okay if I came back?"

"Sure, man," he said. "I just hope you won't tell anyone about all this shit. I don't want everyone harassing me about it."

"Foster," I said, "no chance, never."

I left the Valentine's card with him, unopened. It's not that I felt threatened by Foster, only that I wasn't up for anything too odd and uncomfortable that day. And with my old friend, Foster, that was always a possibility.

I learned fast that no family is perfect in the world. It certainly wasn't my father, the ghostly Reverend, and I, nor Jay Souther and his frequently imbibing, out-of-touch mom. Funnily enough, the closest thing to a friendly, loving, and supportive household was by far, Mrs. Gold and Al Basque.

JAY SOUTHER

Bear Santos had ruled our high school football field—he was amazing at baseball and basketball, too, but football was his passion. Colleges had been drooling over him since ninth grade. Six-five, lean, mean, and fast, the Latino star had chalked up receptions and touchdowns throughout his sophomore and junior years.

I saw Bear work his magic in several games, catching three or four touchdowns at every gridiron battle. Announcers will say thing like, "It's like an adult playing ball with kids out there today," and while cheesy, that was exactly how it seemed on St. Andrew's field. Bear moved fluidly, with an almost preternatural grace, twisting and juking and maneuvering the ball so efficiently, like some ballet dancer out there, avoiding his pursuers with ease and spins, a beautiful thing to watch.

Bear was a triple varsity athlete, but I didn't catch many of his baseball or basketball games. From what I saw and heard about in school, Bear's swing was explosive, and he was a force to be reckoned with on the basketball court, as well, aggressive and so dominant. Bear was like perfection out there and no one

ACADEMY OF UNHOLY BOYS

else could keep up with him. But his glory seemed to demand a dramatic fall, and during his junior year, he was the victim of the cheapest, most sickening tackle heard 'round the world. At least, that's what a kid in my homeroom dubbed it.

Let me be clear—I wasn't on the field for that, or even on the team yet, but the loudmouth kid described it so dramatically. How long after the whistle the hit took place, the sound of Bear's helmet *thunk*ing against the ground, the sympathetic groan from one of the assistant coaches; it was beyond unfair. "Foster Gold is a total slimeball," the kid said. "The cruelest motherfucker that ever stepped on a field. I don't care who hears me saying that, either."

This was how Bear got his third concussion. In a frigging scrimmage game. Instead of driving the Dynamic Duo apart, though, it strangely appeared to solidify their bond. Later, I'd piece together that this is when Bear got in deep with the drugs, and Foster sunk the hook in. Off the field, Bear liked to mess around with weed and other illicit treats, "indulge his senses," as he called it, but after concussion number three, he seemed high around the clock.

Shortly after their senior year summer camp began, Bear tripped and awkwardly fell onto a piece of concrete, smacking the back of his head. It was such a simple and clumsy thing that no one could believe it. He got concussion number four, and the university scouts who had been courting him slowly evaporated from our sidelines. Bear was pretty broken up about it, or at least that's what I absorbed. It was such a heartbreaking loss, his whole future, his escape from his father, and a free ride to college...gone, just like that.

Foster became kinder to Bear after that, but with that compassion and good humor came a stronger grip on his constant companion. I think, looking back, this is when Foster's coercion of the world became more alluring, the frenzy subdued to bouts of mania; curbed by Bear's deepened dependency. If you looked at Foster from a certain angle, you could see he was like an evangelical provocateur on steroids. Except, he was Jewish. But he penetrated people's psyches in ways you wouldn't believe. Although he was chivalrous and sweet toward my mom, but she never bought it. "He's like a baby-faced serial killer from the eighties," she'd seethe.

I thought that was unfair, for Foster was genuinely defensive of Bear and me. Plus, it wasn't his fault he possessed golden-boy looks, set off by two different-colored eyes: one baby blue, one light green. "Heterochromia iridium," Bear told me. "It's a rare and wondrous thing." It was like he was a pollster selling his favorite candidate to a swing voter. "A genetic mutation at work inside this singularly gifted man."

I wondered if Bear was reading a script. Foster loved that kind of thing though, and I had no talent for poetry, myself. We went for late-night Audi rides, just our trio in his shiny cherry-red sedan with windows down and moon roof open, head hanging out, recording everything. Foster would write these lovely lines down each night. One post was: "I enjoy slipping through darkness with the cold wind in my ears. The steep, sweet hills by school, jittery lights of our village photographed from way up high."

Bear was the first person to like it. Occasionally, I wondered, *Is Bear serious? Or is he just so devoted to Foster and the cause that he'll say anything at all?*

Another of Foster's gifts was how he could take Bear and me to the edge. It's curious—I never paid Bear much attention. We rarely interacted without Foster, and even when we were interacting *with* Foster, it was not really inclusive of one another. Our Intro to Psychology text would call us parallel players, both of us beside each other, but always focused on Foster. Was I cognizant of all this occurring in real-time, or was

ACADEMY OF UNHOLY BOYS

it happening too quickly for me to stop and ponder it? Even now, I cannot tell. But I remember one day, sitting at lunch, I had a sudden image of going to class reunions five, ten, fifteen years down the line, getting nostalgic but then I thought, if you continue in this dire and reckless direction, and leave the world with Foster and Bear, you won't even matriculate to junior year. DOA.

Like I said, I'm not perfect at keeping all the drugs away all the time. But I did my level best. Certainly, I never want my own kids to behave in the manner we did in the Audi or in the Cove. I'd teach my kids right from wrong, to respect their elders, and be kind to the world, and not mock every other person in the universe. I would have never allowed that sort of self-destructive behavior to occur under my own roof. Because life demands structure and rules, and discipline is elemental.

My mom's not exactly the leading authority on that discipline stuff, but she does a decent job of it. I tried extremely hard not to follow the seniors down too many of their hellish, doomed trails, mostly so as not to stress my mother out. She is forever on my side and had my back through that bizarre summer and autumn that neither she nor I ever want to repeat.

BASIL SOUS

It's a peculiar thing observing Foster, Bear, and Jay out and about at Wave Café. They're quite loud, cocky, and irritating—it's clear they think they're the top dogs in our small town of Gently. Their antics draw fleeting attention from most customers—moms cover their kids' ears, middle-aged business-people chuckle at first, but after a while, they start clearing their throats and rolling their eyes. And tall, gangly Tuck sits way in the back, sipping his cocoa and studying the trio the way a mouse watches a cat.

I possess this oddly accurate radar about bullies and those who produce significant amounts of horseshit, and Foster oozes that stuff. Then there's Bear Santos tromping around behind him like a giant mannequin full of suppressed rage, and poor Jay Souther doing his best to keep up, making sure he looks sly enough for the younger fillies of the world.

It's fun to watch Gently and its famous Green come to life each Saturday, and I am learning to love the art of people-watching from behind the barista counter. One part of the job that bites is that I must wear a hairnet and take out my nose

ACADEMY OF UNHOLY BOYS

ring. The owner is a hard ass on the jewelry rules but really is a sweet lady who calls me "the eyes and ears and moral center of Wave."

We have some truly wonderful regulars. There is the local hardware store lady named Athena who helps Aunt Peg and me when our fridge goes on the fritz; she always orders two Granny Smith apples, a granola bar, two peanut butter cookies, and a latte each day for lunch. My fellow skateboarders look to me to sneak them free blueberry scones, or a few shots of espresso.

Some customers swear all they desire for Halloween or Christmas or New Year's is a single cider donut. I shake my head and say, "I'm really sorry, but that's not going to happen now or in the foreseeable future if I wish to keep this job."

My favorite shift on Saturday is the opener, helping everything get organized and set in its precise and proper way. It is satisfying. Plus, I work with a lot of developmentally disabled employees who help bake the bread and cookies, brew the coffee, ring up the orders, and tidy up our gender-neutral bathrooms.

There is an old man with a shock of white hair that used to be red, but everyone still calls him Reddo, and he loves his coffee black. He habitually enjoys a toasted bran muffin with raspberry jelly, two cinnamon-flavored toothpicks, and today's *Boston Globe,* which we rarely have, but which I always look for because when I do find a spare *Globe,* Reddo takes off his Fedora and belts out, *"Start spreading the news..."*

JAY SOUTHER

As a boy, I sprouted a burst of white hair on my left temple, a Souther family male trait. The rest is curly and black. Some kids called me "Skunker" in middle school, but that subsided in high school, resurfacing occasionally, but only in the locker room.

Despite the light teasing, and my father's troubles, I loved most of my life in those first sixteen years. People in the world had an odd way of charming me. I found I was not as cynical or depressed as my two senior colleagues. It was taxing to hear them ramble about life's redundancies. It grated against my nerves like Styrofoam squeaking away. My mom would go as far as to say I could be nauseatingly buoyant for a sixteen-year-old male.

"You could use a touch of gloom in your personality, you know," she once said. "Some girls find that mysterious."

One thing Mom does find mysterious and alluring is my synesthesia. She tells people all about it. My senses overlap so colors become flavors and physical sensations become images: a pretty girl's sweater brought the scent of strawberries, a glossy

ACADEMY OF UNHOLY BOYS

licorice-dark car could make my fingers buzz like they'd be on ice, the lemon sun tasting tart like the best Italian ice. Mom tells me the trait comes straight from dad.

Basil Sous' blush is closest to cinnamon. Despite the danger and lethality in Bear and Foster's Cove, I'll always see lucky number seven there. And the smell of hail tastes like a Martini to me, which is what Aunt Carol and Ma guzzled when my dad had his nervous breakdown. My dad's leather chair is perpetually scented with Old Spice.

"He was grievously faulted, believe me," my mom once said, her hand reaching for the chair but never touching its soft surface. "But he was also quirky and endearing. Like my one and only Jay."

My aunt tells me I'm the spitting image of young Geoff Henry Souther, but my dad remains a bona fide mystery. The sort of mystery that my mom didn't want to talk about.

As the 2018 school year approached, a weather event struck Gently with a ferocity that made me sob. It was a massive August gale, two parts hurricane and one part out-of-season Nor'easter. The sky that day had turned midnight black an hour before sunset. I knew the thunder and hail usually made me jumpy and nervous, so I cranked the music up in my headphones until the rain and wind faded into the backbeat. But on that night, I found no solace in music—Spotify failed me in a massive and ugly way.

I never had asked Foster what was in the various edibles he doled out, already trading implicit trust for—what? Gratification? Validation? Love and affection? That day, he must have given me speed, I mean, why else would I twitch at every thunderclap? As the lightning crept closer, I feared a white-hot bolt would slice my body into fifths. I tried doing pushups or sit-ups and then running in place, anything to loosen up the wildness, the excess energy inside my bones. I gazed into the bathroom mirror and for a second, I saw nothing but my dilated pupils, the blackness dominating my face. My reflection seemed haunted, even stricken.

At first, it was nothing but soft little tickly sounds, like cat claws on a screen door. But then a cacophonous roar brought thousands of golf balls and avocado pits made of furious, enraged ice cascading to earth. A blinding flash and crash sounded and *SNAP!* a tree fell to the earth directly across the street.

Why did I rush out into that nightmare so fast? All I know is when the tree cracked and tumbled, I slipped on my helmet, bit into my mouthguard, and dashed out into the scrum. I could not stay in the house a moment longer. It was as if Coach himself had ordered me to take on Mother Nature and slay that bitch.

I bolted down the street, and ran like a terrified animal, dodging debris. Initially, I didn't feel the frozen rain or hard unforgiving rocks of ice banging into me. It would only be later that the damage would be seen in terms of bruises and welts on my scraped-up body. The storm raged and I sprinted on, passing cars and some more downed trees, and even a crushed motor scooter. Some minutes later, on Dunbar Road, something struck me, a thick branch fell and hit the top of my helmet and scraped up my forearm. I was never as thrilled to be on the varsity football team as I was at that moment; without that helmet, I'd be dead, or maybe faced with a TBI.

I was down for a moment, but popped up and sprinted away, screaming and carrying on like a rabid ocelot on coke. I ran without a direction, even as the hail pummeled my protective gear. I felt sheltered somehow in my little cage of foam and plastic. I glanced back and saw a neighbor's screen door being torn off the hinges.

"Holy Jesus, keep running," I told myself. It wasn't exactly

ACADEMY OF UNHOLY BOYS

a twister, but it was damn close, and the winds were fierce. There was a storm all around me and a storm within me, equally vicious, and I was so full of terror and fire it felt like my bones would erupt and immolate. There were more lightning strikes, more wild crashes of branches and trees.

My pulse pounding so loud in my ears, for a time it drowned out the outside storm, as I pumped my knees, dashing through puddles and hail. I was blind with rage and fear and, surprisingly, grief over what exactly I was not sure. Maybe something about messing with substances that could obliterate me.

I am not sure how long I ran; it must have been over three miles because I finally looked up and saw my reflection in the glass of Foster's front door, my appearance not dissimilar to a frazzled feral cat. I had been so deep into my sprint, I hadn't realized I had kept my mouthguard in the whole time, and the tang of lemonade bubble gum temporarily soothed me. I shook my head, looked back, and saw that the worst of the storm was clearing, leaving Gently and headed toward Branford Point and beyond.

When I turned away from the fleeing weather, Foster was there in the doorway. I was soaked to the bone, exhausted, with tears streaming down my face.

"Take it easy, Jay," Foster said, shaking his head, helping me into the house. He helped me remove my helmet and held me in a gentle, careful embrace as I wept.

"Don't know why I ran here, I split, don't know...stupid, really, no good reason for any part, sprinted like a bastard, a fool, and you brought up my dad a few days ago..."

"It's going to be okay, man," Foster said. "I got you, you're safe. No one is going to get at you now."

Foster continued patting my back, telling me to relax, to take deep and easy breaths. It sounds ridiculous, I know, but it felt miraculous to be inside a warm home. A part of me had thought I was going to die out there in the storm. Time shimmered and shifted in Foster's arms as I breathed in that aftershave that I had first noticed at football camp some months earlier. Pine trees, freshly cut grass, and vanilla.

That moment stopped, twisted around, and before I knew it, I was sitting waist-deep in a tub of soapy water. I grabbed a bar of soap and washed my bruises and contusions and winced when I got to the nasty scrape on my left arm. Foster came into the bathroom with hot cocoa.

"For you," he said, and I nodded my thanks. Even after he left, it was like I could still feel his eyes on me. Later, my clothes were in the dryer, so I sat in shorts and a sweatshirt that Foster had loaned me. I phoned my mom and she sounded concerned but relieved to hear I was okay. Then it was almost eight, I was stoned, and Mrs. G brought chicken salad sandwiches and soda down to us. After she went back upstairs, I said, "I feel a lot better, Foster, thanks."

Foster smiled. "That's what is so fantastic about having a Monster around the house. He is a healing entity."

"Doesn't it piss your mom off?"

"Mom says as long as I keep it here, within The Cove," he said, "it's cool, just do not 'abuse the privilege, and stay in control' she says. 'Do not overdo it' is all she asks."

"But overindulging is absolutely what you and Bear are always about," I said.

"Yeah, I guess," Foster said with a fatalistic laugh. "Honestly, I try not to rock the boat anymore."

"And Monster somehow helps you achieve this?" I asked.

"He absolves us," he said. "Forgives us for our life failures,

ACADEMY OF UNHOLY BOYS

and the neurosis which we face in school, and out in the world."

"How does he do that?"

"He just does," Foster said. Then he tilted his head. "You have a melancholy air, Jay, did you know that?"

"What?"

"You mentioned your dad, Geoff Souther, earlier in the week," Foster said. "Did your dad let you down in any significant way?"

"I don't know," I said.

"Sure, you do," Foster said. "I know my father was a deranged man—beat me up something silly. He must stay far away forever from Mom and me, that's why I got so much cash on hand right now. Why we can have all this fun—smoke, drink, order pizza, weed, buy books, do whatever we need or want, because the law kicked his guilty fat ass all over the courtroom and he had to pay up with four million."

"I always wondered about that," I said. "But as far as my own dad..."

"Spill the beans," he said.

"It was a minor event, I guess."

"Reveal thyself, anyway," he said.

"Six years ago," I said. "My dad was carried out of my house by two Aryan-looking female EMTs during a bad hailstorm."

"No shit?" Foster said.

I shrugged, looking away.

All the kindness and gentleness of Foster really threw me. Each night we'd dabble in some form of alcohol or weed and listen to chapters of different stellar fiction or some poems. It was wonderful and mind-expanding, but now I felt tight, like there was pressure, something subtly growing, increasing, pushing against me. Eventually, after we'd worked out way through a pack of edibles, I asked him to take me home.

The night was muggy after the storm. As the Audi's headlights carved their way through the dark, he said, "It's so great to do these things together. This is how it should be forever..."

I knew he wanted me to say the same. I couldn't quite bring myself to commit to the eternal bond Foster wanted, so I just said, "I just like to hear stories, all different kinds. And you make a good one."

"That's why Bear and I love you so much—you're like a dream, you deliver great product. I feel appreciated when I'm in your company."

"Well, thanks, man, I feel the same way," I said.

Despite our time together, I was still unsure what to make of him. He was handsome and charismatic, peculiar, and so damn nervy, and on so many drugs, as well. He'd fed me so many, I feared I'd float away. Nothing holding me down in the car but the seatbelt now. As we drove by the Gently Green, Foster asked me how I was feeling deep inside myself.

"Aside from the fact that I'm so high I can hardly sit upright?"

"Yes," Foster said, smiling. "Aside from that minor point."

"I don't know how you drive with all that weed," I said.

"I've got a pretty good tolerance built up."

After a moment, I asked, "Can you offer me some clarity? About our group?"

"Our trio is meant for wonderful events to rock our society —transformational things, I'm speaking of. How does that hit you?"

I shrugged.

Foster pulled his 2016 red Audi up to my home. "I'm rarely a nonsensical type, Jay," he said. "I'm a rational man, a straight shooter across the board."

ACADEMY OF UNHOLY BOYS

"Yes, of course," I said as my mind drifted up and away.

"Bottom line, Jay," Foster said. "We're going to be by your side forever."

Foster opened the driver's side window and spat. I felt the warm rush of air on my face before he closed it. The car's dashboard glowed orangey red, spooky, as if it were radioactive. I imagined it emitted earthy, mystical powers to anyone in the vehicle. I felt myself slip out through the moon roof and twirl eighteen times in the night sky before gazing down.

There was a surge of clarity within. Foster tapped my left thigh twice. I felt like I was melting—my eyes, my chest cavity, my brain, my hair, and flesh—everything was dripping, thawing, pooling onto the floor beneath me.

"You listening to me, man?" Foster asked and I blinked my wet eyes, nodding twice.

"Yeah," I said. "I mean, I think so."

"My father was an evil goon," Foster said, so soft I almost didn't think he expected me to hear him. "I still strike myself periodically. Strong, sharp punches to the head, sometimes. Carrying on his violent traditions, I suppose."

The night was quiet, but as we idled by the curb, I could see half-melted pellets of hail glinting in the street. "Did the EMTs take your father away to a psychiatric hospital, Jay?"

"Must have, huh?"

"Quite possibly," Foster said. "A trigger for you now, I imagine, yeah? The hailstorm and everything? Must be terrifying, man."

"Yeah," I said. "It was, and now, I guess it still is."

"Yes," Foster said. "I'm so sorry about that."

"Me, too."

61

BEAR SANTOS

2-18-14

So, I did return to see Foster after that Valentine's Day visit. He opened the door with a smile, and greeted me with a, "Hello, Dolly."

"Good to see you, peaches." I held up the apple pie I'd bought at a local store. "Is your mom around?"

"No, she's out," Foster said, taking the pie and placing it on the kitchen counter. "She'll love it." He led me back to his room. "We got the place to ourselves."

He handed me the valentine again.

"Hope I didn't ask too many questions yesterday," I said. "Thanks for trusting me."

"Brothers forever," he said. "We're despairing, ragged fools —horny, lost souls drifting through time and space."

We sat down next to each other on his bed.

I opened the card and saw a photo collage of me and Foster from our school pictures and sports teams, but our faces had been glued on top of porn models from dirty magazines. Some had been taken from out-of-print magazines like *Hustler* and *Screw*, others from more raw stuff, like an imposing transgender

ACADEMY OF UNHOLY BOYS

soul with huge breasts and an angry erection in a classroom. I found it so disorienting, confusing, and compelling that I gagged for a moment.

"Hilarious, right?" Foster said. "The best of humor on display here today."

"Yeah," I said, thinking, *my dad would grab his pistol from his top drawer and shoot me dead if he saw this.*

"I'd like to show you something," Foster said. "Learned it in Missouri, actually."

He took out some weed and rolled a blunt; I instantly got jumpy, anxious. I had tried weed once with my cousin and had felt so paranoid afterward—like twisted ghouls had ransacked my bone marrow and were devouring it in gulps. I was all set to say no to Foster, but then he leaned over and gave me a hit, and then rolled up his shirt and burned eight blisters around his belly. The smell of singed hair and burnt skin rushed up my nostrils and nearly got me sick. I wanted to say something, but what was there to say? Foster's expression hardly changed through the process, just a tightening around the eyes and his flesh sizzled faintly.

"We called it belly button blisters," Foster said. "No one will ever see them."

"...Okay."

"Battle scars," Foster said. "Something you earn through emotional wars."

"Doesn't it hurt?" I asked, and he shrugged.

"Pass me that stuff," Foster said, so I grabbed a tube of Bacitracin on the edge of the desk and handed it over, and he rubbed the ointment in his wounds. "It doesn't hurt *that* much. Gives you a bit of a high if you do it right...we'd dare each other to see who's the toughest in the bughouse."

He gestured with great animation, like a fake television preacher. "Always one guy going too wild, but that's probably

DAVID FITZPATRICK

why he's there in the first place, you know?" He rambled on; his pupils were so very tiny.

"Are you using other stuff right now, Foster?"

"I'm *always* on something, Bear," he said, laughing. "Everything is simpler on weed, pills, or dope, or whatever. It protects me."

"From what?"

"Offers a buffer from my harsh life," Foster said. "Like some life-preserver... rescues me from getting all shook up. I mean, doesn't the world scare you?"

"Terrifies me," I said. "The only place I don't panic is in my sleep or on a field."

"There's no way one person can take it all. Hunger, terrorism, threats of nuclear war..."

"Our generation's fucked," I said. "School shootings, systemic racism, climate change, kids so afraid of going online that they put bullets in their heads to avoid it."

"I know."

"Is that why you always talk about going out with a dramatic bang, Foster?" I asked.

"Let's say it's my... creative solution. And hopefully, you'll embrace it, too."

"I don't know, man," I said.

"Life is so much easier with a plan, Bear," he said.

"Yes," I said. "But this isn't a plan. It's just an escape."

Foster nodded. "Even better. Why play a game you're guaranteed to lose?"

"How about another hospital or a talented shrink?" I asked. "There are excellent people out there that could put you on the right path. Turn your life around, don't you think?"

"There's only my path," he said. "Others whine or bitch— my plan delivers."

ACADEMY OF UNHOLY BOYS

After I burned myself, Foster reached out and embraced me and said, "I love you, man."

"You too," I said.

There wasn't that much desire or want in his gesture—only a rare moment of innocence. A friendship. Two of us doing this belly blister thing as if it was something we'd been doing for decades, like building a fire in the woods or hunting for food.

"Nothing more all-American in the world, right, pal?"

"You bet, buddy," I said, and everything was settled.

Foster reached around me and shut off a small recorder behind us and removed a tiny chip.

"You recorded all that?" I asked. "And the drugs? You can't do that, ass-wipe."

"It'll never see the light of day, Bear," he said. "It keeps us honest."

"Can't go through life blackmailing people, Foster," I said.

"Our friendship is now built on a solid foundation of trust."

"Not if you threaten me with exposure," I said. "You can't record every person in life into owing you—that's not human interactions."

"Not a problem for me, bro," Foster said.

"Bullshit, it's not your problem." I stood up and he blushed, signaling me to sit, to stay calm.

"I won't do that to you again, okay?" he said. "Never again, I swear. A mistake."

"What're you gonna do with the chip, though?" I asked.

"It goes into my safe," he said, "packed away forever."

We vowed at that point never to make physical contact again after burning ourselves. We were insistent. A hug would only bring complications. Best to stand clear and avoid the mess, as much as I longed for it. We could watch the other guy burn himself. But we would never touch it afterward.

Distance, Bear, I told myself. *Always keep your distance, no need for anything else.* No more embracing, especially with Foster's recording devices a constant in each room of his house, or wherever he ventured out in the world. His mantra of "let's record absolutely everything" could get tiresome, but I put up with it because I cared for him. I believed in his spirit, and desired him, too.

SEPTEMBER 2018

JAY SOUTHER

My dad had been a notable architect and possessed an understated decency. As a boy, I loved it when he swooped down and picked me up, flew me so high in his big, strong arms, and made me feel like I was a supersonic rocket piercing the upper atmosphere. But dad cracked one night when I was ten, and he hasn't been seen since—I'm not sure if gravity tugged too severely on him and sucked him into the ground, or just gave up on him and released him into the stars, but Mom doesn't discuss it, so he remains a shadowy figure in my life.

God knows, I have enough photos of my father to look at since I raided the boxes in our basement; I even pasted them to my bedroom walls with double-sided tape, despite my mom's warning of what they do to the paint beneath it. But the images don't remain in my mind—I stare at them and they're sweet, but then I look away and Dad's features turn to ash like weed in Monster.

Mom's an inconsistent personality and a huge Carole King fan—she's seen her Broadway musical, *Beautiful*, eight times with her sister. After the breakdown of Dad, Mom compensated by drinking lots of Martinis and listening to King's 1971 album, "Tapestry." Mom drank Martinis so she didn't feel the need to fret about what her child was doing out late with upperclassmen Foster and Bear.

Sometimes it was like I had two moms. A real Jackie and Hilda. By day, she made me cucumber sandwiches and asked about my life and schoolwork. But after sundown, once the potion began to flow, she became a base creature from whom indifference was the best I could hope for.

She was somehow already fiercely against Foster and picked up on my schoolboy crush. The alcohol only provoked her. She began teasing me, calling him my, "sweet, tender, and dearest friend." *Is it that obvious?* I thought to myself. *Is that me?*

During the summer months, when I would come home after midnight, she would typically greet me half-zonked on the living room couch, her sarcasm defused by her slurring. She would rise in her wrinkled, blue satin bathrobe, the same one once worn by her own mother, with "number one grandma" stitched on the back, and offer me a half-finished Martini.

The Home Shopping Network or QVC would be blaring on the mammoth flat-screen tv, and her credit cards would be spread out on a coffee table, like a twisted, high-stakes game of solitaire—which, in a way, it was. "You want a sip, hon?" she would say, the gin slopping up to the edge of the glass.

"You should watch all the drinks you guzzle every night, Ma," I said. "They'll catch up with you and destroy your liver."

"You have no moral high ground to stand on whatsoever," she said. "You're like a walking stinking, blunt that has no business lecturing anyone. *Period.*"

"Give me a break," I said.

"All you're doing is spending too much time with Foster, the resident liar-in-chief."

ACADEMY OF UNHOLY BOYS

"Grow up, Ma," I said.

"He's an idiot, a sly con artist."

"You can be a witch, Ma," I said. "So mean and cold, do you know that?"

"Foster Gold is not some magical Peter Pan, son," Mom said. "I mean, all he did was give you some novels and poems in a fancy tote bag."

"He's a senior that's trying to help me improve my life skills and expand my mind through poetry and literature," I said. "We listen to classic books or poetry on audio as we drive around Gently—"

"Getting high as a kite," she said.

"Not always, we're harmless teens trapped in an excruciatingly mellow town. I mean, don't you want me to socialize and further my education?"

"I do, of course," she said. "But will you make a promise with me now?"

"Which one?"

"If you agree *never* to fall in love with Foster Gold, I'll go back to church."

"Of course, I won't fall for him, Ma," I said. "No chance. But you'll go and find Jesus and some good friends."

When I was feeling lonesome and fatigued by Foster and Bear's nihilism, I'd remind myself of a gutsy high school sophomore girl that flew around town on her skateboard, her sinewy, muscular legs and graceful arms so at ease in mid-air. Last summer she added varying stripes of pink and green as her hair grew back. She and her pals hung out near the library and town hall, sometimes jumping the handrails with their longboards. She's a waiter at the Wave café on the Green, and I was infatuated.

The first day I spotted her there I thought, *where does someone so young find the guts to transform so completely like that?* A friend caught me staring and told me her name. Basil Rutherford Sous wore thin yellow, orange, and raspberry ribbons wrapped around both of her biceps, and when she moved, she seemed to be soaring and colors whirled behind her like better versions of shadows.

"She's like a skywriter leaving messages to a lover on the ground," I told Aunt Carol. I was sold on her fast.

Sixteen and diminutive, Basil blazed brilliantly and when her hair wasn't parrot green or pink, she shaved everything off. Her graceful neck was regal and poised. Her eyes were light blue, and her lips were thin and added a bit of restraint to her whole groove. I had never kissed a young lady before, which was embarrassing, of course, if not pathetic. Sixteen and not even a peck. One day, I tried to wave her down, but she flew past me several times. Finally, she slowed down, wheels thudding over the cracks in the pavement as they lazily rotated.

"Do you always stare at strangers?"

"Only when they're as stunning as you."

She rolled her eyes but there was also a touch of pink on her cheek.

"What do you want?"

"Just to know you. Talk to you."

"Oh, really? What would you say?"

"I go to St. Andrew's Prep. I'm a sophomore..."

"Try something unique, ace."

"What?"

"This is where you say, 'I'm Jay and I go to St. Andrew's Prep.'"

I paused, admiring her smirk. "I admire the way you carry yourself."

"And what about you? Your *countenance?*" she asked, emphasizing the word vocab quiz style.

"I didn't even know I carried myself. I'm just here."

ACADEMY OF UNHOLY BOYS

She nodded at that before skateboarding off.

* * *

I wrote an essay for a composition class I was in; the assignment was to turn a mirror on myself, musically. A reflection of how tunes affect me, and to jot down some of my favorite singers and bands, figure out what did and what did not move me. I wrote that I enjoyed the journey of Kendrick Lamar's, "To Pimp a Butterfly," Billie Eilish's dark, fearless tunes, sprinkled with some jazz brilliance from the likes of Branford and Wynton Marsalis.

The blues specialists the Alabama Shakes echo when I'm in the pits, often accompanied by the slow, spiritual reflection of Sufjan Stevens. Sometimes classical instrumentals stream from my Spotify account, maybe Yo-Yo Ma playing Bach Cello Suites to help escape the world. Timeless, genius sounds slipping and soaring through the decades. And if you don't mind going way, way back, I love that singer, Sade. She was the coolest customer in town back in the eighties—in my humble opinion. Maggie Rogers is certainly gifted, too.

I adore shutting the lights off in my room and twirling around, imagining myself in an artful music video, highlighted by lens flares and judged only by the open gaze of my favorite artists and their understanding admirers. They show me a flamboyant and joyous type of transcendence. What that means, exactly, with the lights on, I am never sure, but in the dark, with all that freedom and the music playing, it feels obvious and unstoppable.

In my head, while my favorite artists perform their tunes, I rush over to Basil with her colorful hair and the tie-dyed short shorts and curves, and I kiss her belly, spin her around, moving in the moonlight in some primal dance, breathing in her sweat and roasted coffee and everything else.

Foster and Bear listened to bands like Iron Maiden, Seether, and Five Finger Death Punch to start and end their day and nights, which makes our world seem darker, oozing with portent. At least, for me, that is. For a while, the two seniors even droned on about Ayn Rand and all her mystery and innate power in each of her sentences. All my buddies had done was read the Spark Notes for *The Fountainhead*. Once I informed Bear and Foster that Ayn Rand is a big lure for right-wing fanatics, they kind of stepped back and chilled out with their hero worship. Turned it down a whole bunch.

"Oh, she's alright, I suppose," Foster said after some additional research. "It's not like we were ever *that* into her, we're certainly not rabid fans. I would never go out on a limb and say something like that."

TUCK REIS

"Smiley face, Smiley boy, yo, little Smiley man." That was all I heard ever since I was three and a half because I couldn't talk. *Smiley.* It was either a sob or grin, and who wants to cry into their milk twenty-four-seven? I was a tiny kid, and I accidentally drank some lye water, and it seared my vocal cords. My cousin Maxwell was babysitting me, and he'd been making soap the old-fashioned way for his home-economic assignment with lye, lard, and oil, and somehow when Max wasn't looking, I drank some lye water off to the side and nearly died.

From then on—friend and foe alike—dubbed me Smiley. It definitely wasn't Max's fault, but some bullies started calling him Mad Max, and spreading cruel rumors that he had somehow poisoned me, his tiny cousin. He was in seventh grade when it occurred, so he started freaking out with panic attacks, and tugging out his hair, something called Trichotillomania, and he also developed these horrid ulcers. At fourteen, he was a nervous wreck, really stressed out. In one way, we were both haunted forever by my childhood mistake. Max is gone now, cremated after his death a few years back. I remember Aunt Jill whispering under

75

DAVID FITZPATRICK

her breath as I left the kitchen once, "You watch, my Max will beat himself up something fierce for that accident with Smiley."

I wrote to him early on when I still couldn't speak: *It's not your fault, Max. It was an accident, that's the truth. Come home now and we'll sort it all out. I know you never wanted to hurt me. I love you, cousin, everything will be just fine.*

But he never forgave himself, and so he never came home.

* * *

"My son's proper name is Tuck Reis," my father told Dr. A on the phone. "He speaks only to rare souls, and he's chosen you to be the latest one."

"Why am I a rare soul?" Dr. A asked.

"He spotted you on YouTube some months ago," my dad said.

"I don't think I was ever there, though, Mr. Reis," Dr. A said.

"*Inside Edition,*" he said. "Something about you saving autistic kids once."

"Christ," he said. "That was nine years ago, and I didn't save anyone, just offered kids some decent counseling. I was still in med school."

"Tuck grows obsessed with fame and what the ramifications of it are," Dad said. "And how an object—a painting, song, photograph, book, sculpture, or even a human—becomes palpable art."

"Are we on speaker with him right now, Ben?"

"Yes, Tuck's listening in on his own line..."

"Hello, Tuck," Dr. A asked. "Are you interested in—"

I slammed the phone down. A day later, I found myself inside Dr. A's office, which was admittedly very cool. Deco-

ACADEMY OF UNHOLY BOYS

rated with funky, textured yellow wallpaper with some Salvador Dali prints on one wall, and a large, gurgling aquarium with several expensive, gently gliding fish on the other. It was a custom-made one-hundred-fifty-gallon fish tank. Dr. A had to get a special permit to house the fish and hold all that water gurgling away like some alien being up on the third floor.

He also had twenty glass hummingbirds around his space; they're tiny and colorful, and he shifts them around different spots each day, or at least in between the three days I see him for therapy. Sometimes the pastel birds rest on his desk—other days on a windowsill or scattered about his many bookcases. It's so cool, like a moving, shifting rainbow inside there—lime, yellow, lavender, pink, cobalt, cherry-red, forest green, and indigo.

Dr. A shook my hand on our first day, a firm, dry grip, and said, "Your dad told me you rarely speak with him."

"He can be a real turd, Doc," I said. "For people I respect, I'm quite vocal."

"Give your dad the benefit of the doubt," Dr. A said. "Will you try to do that for me from here on in, Tuck? A special effort to be a lot kinder to your father?"

"Yes," I said. "I'll try."

"Your dad said you have a favorite actress."

"Emma Stone," I said. "The redhead from *La La Land*. Once Emma won the Oscar in 2017, I followed her career quite closely."

"How closely?" he asked.

"I listen and watch Emma's films on my iPhone," I said. "When I need a lift, she sings to me in her charming, self-deprecating way."

"A big fan, huh?"

"When she got engaged in real life, I wept legit tears, Doc," I said.

"And why cup your left hand around your lips when you speak?"

"I was a breech baby, Doc," I said. "Nearly strangled to death by the umbilical cord."

"And so?"

"It comforts me to keep my left hand up," I said. "Like a guardian angel or even a teddy bear might."

"It keeps people too far away from you, though, Tuck," Dr. A said. "A huge wall."

"Maybe," I said. "But it offers a sweet catchphrase."

"Let's hear it."

"Welcome to the Great Wall of Tuck," I said, "climb me if you dare."

Dr. A smiled. "What illness do you think you have, son?"

"A strain of selective mutism, a serious anxiety disorder," I said. "Jane Leete, my teacher who reeks of Pantene shampoo and caramel chews, she said I got serious PTSD thrown into the mixture."

"Yes, I'd agree," Dr. A said. "Many SM students use iPads, but your dad said you refuse to do so, why's that?"

"Too much tech is destructive for my stressed out, developing brain."

"What about the iPhone you use to study Emma Stone's career and life day and night?" he asked.

"I admit there are some gaping holes in my argument," I said.

"Who were the last folks that mattered to you, like I do now?"

"Footballers Bear Santos and Foster Gold," I said. "I was taken with Foster's habit of recording every second of his own life. I wanted to be part of it, I guess, wanted to be

ACADEMY OF UNHOLY BOYS

captured in that same manner, but he gave me a Swirly when I wouldn't try out for the damn football team sophomore year."

"Swirly?"

"A dated term—means he tried to flush my head down the toilet," I said.

"Lousy bastard," Dr. A said.

"We're not friends now, of course," I said. "He's obsessed with death."

"Does he still harass you, Tuck?" Dr. A asked.

"Foster Gold moved on, for the most part," I replied. "He prefers to work on a huge canvas now."

"What does that mean, exactly?" he asked.

"He's into protracted melodramas and enjoys hurting other human beings," I said.

"Sometimes, Tuck, you speak like you're an old man."

"I agree," I said. "Trauma leaves some real scars, like emotional crow's feet all over me."

"How would you describe your speaking voice today?" Dr. A asked.

"It hurt me to talk for a while," I said. "Couldn't do it for a few years, even. But I got a lot of help, and now it sounds close to decent... I'd guess I'm now probably a tenor."

"Emma Stone's voice is throaty," Dr. A said. "Would you agree?"

"Yes."

"Do you find that ironic?" he asked. "You've spent years working on improving your own voice, only to find your favorite gal has the most imperfect one?"

"I love her voice," I said. "Every part of it."

"I see."

"You're my professional friend now, Doc, huh?" I said. "An expensive peer, true?"

He smiled again. "Indeed. You and I are professional friends."

"Dr. Ed Benzo said this nutty stuff once," I said. "He said everything was dad's fault because my dad was an only child."

"What a crock of shit," he said. "Dr. Benzo sounds like a fool."

"Yes," I said. "Dad felt that way, too."

"I'm glad you're done with this Benzo character," Dr. A said. "He doesn't sound healthy in the head. What was the last thing Dr. Benzo said?"

"He said without his guidance, I'd probably die. Basically, *rot from within*."

"Dr. Benz sounds like a dangerous, unharmonious man."

I frowned. "Is it inharmonious or unharmonious?"

"I always thought unharmonious," Dr. A said. "Let me check on that and get back to you, Tuck."

"Mortality is never a joke, Dr. A," I said. "But it can be quite humorous."

"How so, Tuck?"

"There's a romantic spin of dying young, etcetera," I said. "I mean, 'To be or not to be?'"

"Your father told me you don't believe in Shakespeare, though," he said.

"I don't," I said. "But it's impossible to avoid the brilliant words, even as it melts and oozes into my famished brain stem."

"I see," Dr. A said.

"No way one soul wrote every one of his plays, though, Doc," I said. "Impossible feat."

"Then who on earth did?"

"Three women and two men pooled talents, and split the gold, and had wild Elizabethan orgies in between shows," I said. "Those were amazing days."

"Sounds like a shifty conspiracy theory, Tuck," he said.

ACADEMY OF UNHOLY BOYS

"It's all crammed down our throats daily," I said. "But I'm only showing off to the most promising shrink in New England."

"Most promising shrink, huh?" Dr. A said. "What other conspiracies do you feel are being crammed down your throat?"

"Beer ads, sex, violence, racism, paranoia, xenophobia, football, democracy, God, and guns," I said. "Media bends it, serving it to us horny kids, morphing the truth."

"You speak extremely well," Dr. A said.

"Your kind but possibly delusional, Doctor," I said. "I only talk to you—I prefer it."

"To make progress with Tuck, though, we must step into the hurt and rage, okay?" he asked. "We need to confront what scares us."

"Shit," Tuck said.

"What is it?" Dr. A asked.

"You want me to talk of the Dynamic Duo, right?"

Dr. A nodded. "You have a lot of... feelings inside about those two."

"They're dicks," I said. "The less said about them, the better."

"I disagree," he said. "I want you to write about them, and about you. Writing is essential as we look within. I'll give you many prompts and you write everything that comes into your mind at home, and read it to me for the following session, okay? Write anything down that comes to you and present it to me."

"Got it," I said. "I love to write, sir."

"Well, you'll be doing a lot more of it in the future," he said.

BASIL SOUS

I saw a flickering film of myself in suburban Calhoun, New Jersey in 2012—was it a fugue, or some waking dream? Perhaps the flickering aspect was caused by my low blood sugar? Or was it too much caffeine? I was ten, crouched behind a buddy's Sears-brand fencing, looking out through failed daffodils, wilted pansies, dried-out mums, and dead tulips. I snuck glances onto an open lot—the local boys called it a Hazmat field.

So of course, I believed it truly was a hazardous waste site—bizarre, twisted things crawling from the soil night and day. The land was four hundred yards long, and half again as wide. The clumps of grass, dirt, rocks, fire ants, scrub pines, moles, mice, broken beer and liquor bottles, and more than a few rat snakes were proof of its toxic potential. The property was several years away from having affordable housing constructed on it, although eventually drab Soviet-looking throwback of beige buildings would rise from the rubble and be called, "Hidden Valley Oaks."

Months after its ribbon cutting, an intoxicated neo-Nazi

ACADEMY OF UNHOLY BOYS

nicknamed T-Rex would hurl a Molotov cocktail through a bedroom window, and the subsequent fire would kill a young immigrant Guatemalan girl, along with her disabled grandma. The sweet bedroom community of Calhoun that was never all that sweet to begin with would soon become known from then on as "the venomous village not far from the sea," thanks to several leading newspapers from the Garden State.

As my Aunt Peg had reminded me daily—*anything* can happen in America. "Never underestimate this country," she said. "Especially if you don't have enough funds to get you through the next week's dinner."

Our pear-shaped neighbor, a CPA and Libertarian named Robbie, was ever the contrarian. "But the world is much improved, Peg," he insisted. "Look around—before cell phones took over the world, we kids raced around un-chaperoned, doing anything we wished."

"You're a nostalgic-over-the-hill fool," Peg said. "With too much cash in your bank account to give a damn about hurting those around you."

"Perhaps," Robbie said. "But we egged houses in the seventies, set our flatulence on fire, shot robins with BB guns, played kill-the-guy-with-the-ball, sniffed glue and turpentine. There was always one kid with a buzz-cut and a soiled shirt who choked a feral cat in the woods, and would eat mud for a nickel, insisting: 'I enjoy the taste, the graininess—what's it to you?'"

But before all that, back on Hazmat field, the early afternoon was becoming overcast, and thunder was growling. I watched some of my fourth-grader buddies dart from their best hiding spots, a group of ninth-graders chasing them across the field toward me. They had toted out wheelbarrows to cart away the seized kids; one large hoodlum and hide accomplice tied a tomboy's hands and feet to a beam and they disappeared into a maroon barn. I had to make a run for Peg's apartment, or I'd be found.

The barn seemed to be their headquarters for whatever was being done to the captured kids—surely trauma, pain, and various perversions—which was not going to happen to me. I made a mad dash for it but was captured by a pockmarked goon with curly red hair and a purple scar on his forehead. I tried to dive away, but he was huge compared to me, and he grabbed my left arm and dragged me to the barn like it was nothing, my other elbow getting all scraped up.

"You're in trouble now, bitch," Lenny growled. But as I was pulled, yelling and shouting and biting, down the drive, I saw a green Chevy careen across the road towards us. Avery stepped out onto the passenger side with his trusty Louisville Slugger. His friend, Jack Welsh, parked his green Chevy pickup there, and they both ran at the bullies. Jack was the star southpaw pitcher on the high school team, and Avery was the starting shortstop. They were returning from practice, and they looked angry.

"Let her go, you piece of shit," Avery shouted at my attacker, and swung the bat at full speed into the bully's left ass cheek. The redhead stumbled and I ripped my arm from his dirty nails.

"Jesus Christ," Lenny cried, "How could you hit me like that, Sous?"

"She's my baby sister, asshole," Avery said, swinging again. *That's how.*"

Lenny was on the ground then, holding onto his left buttock, sobbing, his beet-red face covered in tears and snot. Avery embraced me and said, "Don't come near my sister again, Lenny. And you dipshits better let everyone out of the barn — Jack and I are calling the police."

"Already done," Jack said. "Cops are on their way."

ACADEMY OF UNHOLY BOYS

"We were just having some fun," Lenny said.

"You should be ashamed of yourselves, picking on fourth graders," Avery said. "You make me sick."

And so, my older brother swept in and rescued me like Clark Kent himself. We had moved from Missouri a few years earlier and, though we didn't know it at the time, we would head on to Connecticut in a few more years. Avery was off to Cornell the next semester, getting a free ride because of his smarts.

As we cleaned up my scraped arm that afternoon, Avery carefully applied some Neosporin and a Band-Aid. Then we scrubbed the bathroom clean as a favor for Aunt Peg, who tended to drop the ball with most domestic chores.

"You okay, B?" Avery asked. "Were you seriously hurt?"

"No, no, I'm good, thanks for saving me," I said. "I'd be lost without you, Avery."

"You're growing up so damn fast you'll soon be kicking Lenny's ass all on your own," he said. "You could destroy that fool with a well-targeted insult or two."

"I'll be missing you a lot when you leave for college, Avery," I said.

"Me too, B," he said. "I'll feel lost without my little partner around."

* * *

Gladys, my hair stylist, spun me around in the chair and suddenly it was me going forward six years to the present at Capture Hair Salon on Crown Street in New Haven, Connecticut. And I'm no longer watching a flickering film of me as a kid, but life has slowed to a crawl, and is a Hollywood still: Basil Sous is sixteen in the stylist's chair getting her hair dyed.

Gladys, a proud Italian American woman with gorgeous nut-brown flowing hair and dry wit, was running a brush dipped in parrot green on my tips. We all should be like Gladys, like how she wore her pastel six-inch long, quarter-inch wide ribbons on her upper arms that fluttered behind her as she moved through the salon. I admired them so much that after my first hair appointment, when I'd initially moved to Gently, I decided to copy her style when I went out skateboarding.

Gladys asked if there was a young man on my horizon. I quickly said no, but then I started pondering the situation. There was that awkward sophomore from St. Andrew's Prep on the other end of our village. I'd seen him more than once near the library while I skated by, stopping to lurk in the shadows and watch me with his skittish eyes.

When we eventually made eye contact, we smiled at each other as if we were sharing a long-held secret. It was like the Little Prince and the Fox, him as the creature to be tamed. I mentioned some of this to Gladys. "What's he like?" she asked.

"Sexy with those famished eyes," I said. "Black hair with a small patch of white on his left temple. One fetching character."

"Like a smooth and cagey predator, huh?"

"He's quite shy, though," I said. "He blushes a lot."

"So, what happened next between you two?" Gladys asked.

"After we acknowledged each other, his gaze ran all over me—I mean, he doesn't even pretend to be sneaky about it anymore."

Eventually, he reached out, but he could barely get a conversation going. And so, my taming of the fox began. Sometimes you don't really know a frigging thing until you start speaking about it. And as I sat with Gladys and had her work magic with my hair, it dawned on me that maybe I liked that boy.

JAY SOUTHER

School had begun almost two weeks earlier, in mid-August, and once again I found myself inside the Cove with my two senior cohorts. It was nearly midnight, a Tuesday in early September, and Foster's teal bong sat stuffed with the finest hashish Foster could find in our conservative shoreline town. We were also eating heaps of Chunky Monkey and chasing that with bourbon.

Bear was hunched over Monster playing his role of, "young man who just saw his last chance at a free ride to university disappear a day previous" perfectly. Foster stood in the middle, wearing only a giant gray-and-white fuzzy donkey head with eyeholes, a white jockstrap, and knee-high yellow athletic socks. He was doing an endless number of curls with an eight-pound barbell. Strewn around him were various game consoles, a half-broken rocking chair we called Rocky, and a black beanbag chair that had seen better days.

I lay partly sprawled on one end of the couch, picking dry skin off my left palm with intensity, a sign of either manic distress or just being drunk. Ever since Foster had described how the Greatest Show might involve our trio hanging *from, near, or around* the goal posts om Thanksgiving, I remained anxious and obsessed.

I knew the themes of mortality always played a major role in the maestro's life. And the way he spoke of *Logan's Run*, a 1967 sci-fi novel by William F. Nolan and George Clayton Johnson, a futuristic world where people never live longer than twenty-one, confirmed Foster's hyper-fixation. The book also has a young, charismatic male leader and a sect of zealots who end their lives at eighteen. Foster rarely mentioned the movie version of *Logan's Run*, which debuted in January of 1976 and was *absolutely not* his favorite. "In that story, the population lives to thirty," he said. "Isn't that so bizarre? Why would they ever go and change that fundamental detail and ruin the whole film?"

My own question for the seniors was what exactly is set to occur on Thanksgiving just before dawn at St. Andrew's football stadium? To cope with this gloom, torment, and death business, I drank too much and ate so many edibles. I knew it was stupid, counterproductive, and dangerous, but my mind said, "Give me anything to keep the horror away, please let me not think of the heinous act straight on."

I wished to forget everything; my mom, dad, and aunt, and instead just swallow edibles and drink booze and not obsess about Foster's holiday festival. The past three days, though it had been only dazed thoughts and my uncomfortably numb mind that kept returning to the fact that I had implied I would take part in their dark and morbid games. Even though, I know I clearly said "not interested."

My cruel mind taunted me, saying, *oh, yes you did, oh, yes you did, you frazzled freak, you signed up for the nightmare, you are an idiotic fool and you're headed for rigor mortis in the end zone.* I couldn't deal with it. I didn't bother to ask Foster

ACADEMY OF UNHOLY BOYS

more about it, for fear he would convince me his intentions were serious. Below me on the floor, near the musty boxes of CDs, I spied two old calendars, one featuring black-and-white photos of otters and their pups in Yellowstone Park and the other glossy color shots of busty waitresses washing muscle cars in wet T-shirts and soapy bubbles in Hollywood, California.

"Colleges never wanted the *real* me," Bear said, exhaling a thick cloud of smoke. I jumped a little. I had forgotten they were there. "They never knew what I had down deep."

"Never appreciated your nuances, right?" The donkey head retorted.

"Bastards missed it all," Bear said.

"They didn't pay attention," Foster's muffled voice said. "In three months, the nation will drop to their knees and say, 'How did we miss the signals from those hurting, damaged teenagers?'"

"They'll twiddle their thumbs," Bear said, "asking, 'What more could we have done for these perpetually lost boys?'"

"Bingo," Foster said. "Revolution will be delivered straight up the school's ass. They'll never escape the residual damage of our deed. Academy of Unholy Boys forever."

"Always essential to have a catchy name," Bear said. "Good branding's a must."

"You guys are too much," I said.

Foster laughed, pointing at me.

"Hold on, my dear boy, we're going for a fright-filled ride and you're coming along whether you like it or not."

"No can do," I said. "I never agreed to any of your morbid games."

"Ha," Foster said, and placed the barbells down on the floor and began braying and spinning around, pausing just long enough to adjust the angle of his Life Cam.

"Give it to us now, leader," Bear said, and I straightened myself up on the couch.

"Barnum and Bailey Circus is old news, a veritable antique for a decade," Foster said, gesturing like a seasoned politician. "We shall step in and borrow their trusted mantle, becoming for one day 'The Greatest Show on Earth.'"

"How?" Bear asked.

"No more caged animals," Foster said, "or vicious, red-nosed clowns riding a mini-trike on a tightrope or acrobats soaring so high above."

"Okay," I said, and Foster took a deep breath.

"Instead, three varsity high school jocks share a sad truth: Life is a lie—so too da loo, *au revoir, adíos,* and piss off, our time together is nearly up."

That's twisted shit, I thought, studying the dynamic duo. I know I didn't ever agree with them, I know I wouldn't have openly signed on for any of that forever death muck. But doubts stick me like pinpricks, taunting me like a churning and punching internal 24/7 bully.

"Why twist me all about with the Greatest Show, Foster?" I asked. "You mislead me completely and willingly. That's not something a supposed friend does to another friend."

"Frankly, Jay, the Greatest Show can be a tough sell for me on some days," Foster said. "And I was already feeling suicidal myself, unusually *blah,* and your lovely face was all googly-eyed and gung-ho and you wanted to believe in me with everything you had."

"You're too cynical for prime time," I said, and thought of my anonymous letter-writer. "You scare lots of good people away."

"Don't quit on me, Jay, okay?" Foster said. "Can you give me the benefit of a doubt tonight?"

ACADEMY OF UNHOLY BOYS

"What's the point?" I asked. "It'll be even more untrue tomorrow."

"Can you reward me for the weekend? Just a few days, can I get an amen here, please?"

"Amen," Bear shouted on cue. "*Alleluia.*"

"Fine," I said. "You have the weekend."

"That's why you're so wondrous, Jay," Foster said. "Your curiosity is alive and well. You want to chase Bear and me down a thousand and one rabbit holes, hoping, striving, pining for our cosmic secrets and bountiful, semi-divine wisdom."

"I looked up the football game, Foster," I said. "Our gridiron battle is on Thanksgiving morn, 10:15 with St. Andrew's Cardinals versus Madison Tigers. No mention of a fundraiser featuring violence, wild dancing, thumping music, or random acts of kindness, turkey, Irish Bread, cranberries, and Mom's sweet potato pie."

"Our event will be live-streamed and archived," Foster said. "Everything elemental occurs before the football game starts. Before dawn. Don't panic. It'll be copasetic for all involved, and that's a vow I intend to keep."

"God, help you, then," I said. "And God help me, too, I guess."

"Quiz time," Foster said. "Which side of the plate do you like to swing from?"

"I haven't played in ages," I said, and when Foster smirked, the true meaning clicked. Cotton-mouthed and drunkenly honest, I stumbled, "I don't know, I guess I believe sexuality is liquid."

"I want concrete, tangible answers, though."

"Everything's liquid, okay? Nothing but blurry lines at sixteen-years-old."

"Are you asking me that?" Foster asked, squinting his eyes. "Or telling me?"

"I'm in the middle somewhere, I guess," I said.

"No need for any shame or guilt," Foster said. "Life is for all of us—everyone gets in the pool. Life spans each spectrum and continuum, whether going left or right, some on top, others on bottom. Some choose women, others, men, some on the side, some are solo all the way. We also have available binary and non-binary. Essentially speaking, you, Jay, seem to prefer both."

"Yes, both, I guess."

I watched Bear crumple a can of Sprite. The crackling, popping sound sent showers of orange through my head.

"Is that a final answer?"

"Both."

"Give me a straight answer," Foster said. "That's all I seek tonight... all I want is truth."

"Both," I said. "Probably, or so I'd guess right now."

"*Fine,*" Foster said. "We'll postpone the quiz on *your needs* to a later date."

BEAR SANTOS

Now if there was a promise that none of Foster's recording devices were present, I told myself, maybe more emotion could be shared between us—not just a silly infatuation, but a love, a hungry heat rising to the surface that is undeniable, at least on my end. I wanted a stable relationship, and at times I thought Foster did too. Or at least, that he'd pursue it if things were different. What elements and qualifiers needed to change, I wasn't sure. Sometimes I thought it was me, sometimes him, sometimes just where we lived or our age. But he could be sweet when he wanted to. But rarely in public unless he was purposely trying to charm some third party. But one day, he kissed me full on the mouth in front of strangers.

We had left a package store after getting carded during our junior year, and two townies called us "fags" as we returned to Foster's car. My friend pushed me back against his cherry-red Audi, and whispered, "Just go with it," and kissed me for a long minute; a beautiful, tender kiss. I tasted weed and bazooka gum and wasn't surprised to feel my erection straining against my fly.

Foster spun around to face the hecklers and said, "If any of you pathetic, slimy homophobic dirtbags want to step up, my unstoppable name and address are online." The townies whispered, giggled, and trudged into the liquor store. While I was excited by Foster's open display of affection, it confounded me because that behavior became increasingly infrequent through the summer and into the autumn. The young man ran so hot and cold. I had all sorts of activities worked out in my mind, romantic getaway trips that Foster and I could take if only he would fully commit to a relationship with someone besides himself.

If he did that, well, then maybe I could tell Foster about the difficult pressures I face, reveal myself fully, like the swirling, bubbling and harsh reality of being a revered stellar Latino athlete in a white town like Gently with only a blank space at home as a dad, a ghost of a man.

We ate dinner together at times, but I didn't exist in his life, save for being a drain on his system, a deduction on his taxes each April. "Just don't ever get in my way," he told me repeatedly. "Do your sports if you wish, be dancing, prancing, twirling monkey for the masses, or don't do any of it. Partake in life, be a belly dancer if you desire it. That's really the gist of my feeling, is that clear to you now, Felipe? Let's stay out of one another's way from now on, got it?"

"Yes, loud and clear."

I confronted him once a few years back about his lack of affection, and he waved his hands at me like I'd spat on him.

"Seriously, Dad, what is your problem?"

"Do not ever refer to me as 'father,' Felipe," he said. "Your response should only be 'yes, sir' or 'no, sir.'"

I took a deep breath and said, "Okay, got it, sir."

"If you're going to be a man, you can't depend on anyone else. I'll be around doing the whole life act, but that's it. Are

ACADEMY OF UNHOLY BOYS

you a shepherd's son, or a sheep? I'm the minister, so don't embarrass the church. *My* church."

"How can you say that?" I asked.

"Listen closely," he said. "Here it comes now... we'll stay out of each other's way. It's what's best. Whatever you choose to do, I don't care so long as you keep it to yourself."

"Yes."

"Yes, who?" he barked.

"Yes, sir," I spat. "I'll never need, no sir. Never. I'll absorb your wise counsel and carry on fruitfully without an ounce of need."

"That's it precisely," the Reverend said. "Stay far away, and I'll do the same."

* * *

I get these weird, awful headaches a lot. Migraines. First, everything gets this weird fuzzy halo of light —so then even the smallest sound is elevated to rock concert decibels. I squint a lot, and it feels as if a giant claw is squeezing my head, trying to make it burst, its tips are like talons, and they are cutting through everything, my skin, my bones, and my gooey brains. And there's that fuzzy outline around my vision, an "aura" it's called, I believe. It's why I spend so much time loving up on Monster in The Cove with Foster and Jay.

The weed and booze are the only things that relieve the pressure and make the migraine auras seem miraculous. But when those headaches grip me while I'm at home, there's nothing I can do but lay in the dark and let the pain take me. Without Monster, I'm basically lost in space.

Sad, but true.

After each subsequent concussion I suffered, it became more difficult for me to process information. I don't want to overstate it, though. I mean, I wasn't an idiot—I knew my schedule, attended classes, practiced daily, and spoke with my teachers in a coherent, lucid manner.

But when I'd focus intensely, I'd feel these shooting pains up my neck and into my skull, the kind Advil never eased. Foster took over for me late junior year, said he'd take the wheel. He helped me with homework and finished a good deal of my papers, but I don't know if he bought the reports and essays online or penned them himself.

I still struggle with my rage toward Foster for my third concussion. He was kind and sweet afterward, doing all sorts of extra work with no complaints. But he'd made it happen in the first place. I mean, the play was long over. It was an intra-squad game, a soggy early May Day, and I had caught a pass and was tackled. The ref blew the whistle, everyone stood, set to jog back to the huddle. But Foster came screaming out of nowhere right then, and nailed his helmet against my left temple, knocking the living crap out of me, nearly twisting my face-guard around.

"Coach, what the hell do you call that?" I cried, my head throbbing. "What kind of shit hit is that?"

"Pay attention to the whistle, Foster," Coach said. "Bear is an All-American, you just can't make that hit on him *ever*."

"Goddamned cleats, Coach," Foster said as he helped carry me to the trainer's room with a couple other players. I was fuzzy, woozy, and sore, even though I'd endured way worse tackles. "My cleats wouldn't stop when I pulled up, I swear to God."

"Bullshit hit, and you know it," I shot back.

"Sorry, bud," Foster kept on saying to me, as he let the trainer and coaches look me over. "Coach, he's my best friend. I'd never hurt the man."

"You're jealous that no big schools are looking at you, slimy

ACADEMY OF UNHOLY BOYS

bastard," I yelled. The coaches were grabbing my shoulders to keep me from thrashing at him. "So, you're trying to fuck my chances over. Just screwing me, you selfish piece of manipulative shit."

"Okay, gents," Coach said. "It was a mistake, a huge mistake, Bear, an awful error on Foster's part."

"I appreciate that, Coach," Foster said. "He's my best friend in the world.'"

From that point on, Foster said he'd think for both of us, so I could chill out and not feel so much pain. And he was wise, Foster, I mean. He even broke down one time at The Cove, I couldn't believe it. "I'll never let you down again," he told me. "I am so sorry, man." Plus, he started feeding me endless amounts of weed. Whenever I needed it, Foster made sure it was there. Drags off the pen before school, edibles between breaks, joints after practice, and our beloved Monster for all the rest. He had loads of it to soothe my worries, where it came from, I never knew, although he was frequently chatting about all the cash his mother and Foster won in the abuse and divorce trial.

I'm swimming in cash, man, he'd say. Or if I asked too many questions about that hard tackle, Foster started jerking me off in The Cove, something to leave me smiling and sated. It started happening so often that Foster once joked he could probably never step foot in my father's church.

"Not that I ever could," Foster said.

"Face it," I said. "You're headed straight to hell, man."

"At least, I'll go with your love, Felipe," Foster said. "God bless you and keep you."

"Sharon, you're too much," I said, to cover the funny feeling in my gut. Foster never hesitated when he put his hands on me, but we barely ever kissed, and in public, we joshed around so much that I'm sure anyone who didn't know about the Dynamic Duo thought we hated each other a little.

After those experiences became frequent, I never brought up the topic of that third concussion again, but I pondered it, tried to recall it with more clarity. It had grown so warped and distant in my head. So much so it hurts to think about it, even now. I don't think Foster really wanted to ruin my scholarship plans. He wouldn't have done something that cruel to his best friend in the world, right?

TUCK REIS

"Are you ready for me now, Dr. A?" I asked, standing beside the bubbling aquarium in his office. I placed my writing for the day on top down on a four-foot wooden podium he said he'd carted in from home and leaned my forearms against it.

"Deliver your words to me as if we're gathered at your first book reading, Tuck," he said, sitting across the room in his leather chair. "Standing room only tonight at the cozy Breakwater Books in Gently, Connecticut. People have come from all around to hear you today."

"Just start reading?" I asked.

"Good posture, elocution, and clarity are wonderful traits in a reader," he said. "Have at it."

"Once upon a time, I thought I was destined for greatness," I said. "Like my painted-over black and white photos would hang in the Wadsworth Atheneum, or The Met, MOMA, or the Fricke, or even the Louvre, although in the end I almost decided *I* should hang, egged on by cruel, nihilistic peers during my sophomore year. And then my rampant, epic desire for young women and anything that pulses and breathes. I mean, why is it so hard for me to walk down the streets without wanting to bang everyone in it?"

"Go on."

"And what about the ones who ruthlessly mocked me?" I asked. "Like the bastards who called me Smiley when I couldn't speak? Even the pompous prick who dunked my face in a toilet. Why do I still need him by my side?"

"Big finish now, Tuck," Dr. A said. "Project that voice for everyone."

"It's the buzzing within me," I said, "a ringing in my gut. The energy I feel when I'm aroused is the same energy when I'm creating which is the same energy when I'm humiliated. One never-ending live wire stuck straight up my ass into my vertebrae and into my cranium and *KABOOM*, nothing left but blinding, whirling, and frenetic lights."

"I love that ending of yours, Tuck," Dr. Athens said. "We're going to take your credo apart very carefully. We'll toss it high in the air, examine it like it's the best gourmet pizza in town. See what it has to offer, and what it can become in the future. Sound doable to you, son?"

"Absolutely, Doc."

"I'll give you more writing queries that keep your creative juices flowing," he said. "Like, what does your nineteen-year-old brain obsess about right now?"

"School shooters popping up on every horizon," I said. "It's a dangerous time to be alive."

"I thought the rate of school shootings was going down nationally," he said.

"Perhaps so," I said. "But when catastrophe is broadcast over the loudspeaker in the form of lockdown drills at St. Andrew's Prep several times a year, Dr. A, there'll always be emotional casualties. I mean, how do we test the seams without fraying the fabric?"

ACADEMY OF UNHOLY BOYS

"Astute point," he said. "What else is on your mind?"

"Breasts and buttocks that bounce, shake, and jiggle," I said.

"Sounds healthy," he said. "Any more tidbits?"

"I'm not impressing you any longer, am I, Dr. A?" I asked.

"You don't have to impress me, Tuck," he said. "See me three times a week, speak often, take many vocal and life risks, and work hard at school."

After a few moments, when Dr. Athens asked why I bother with my own darkroom at home and the old-fashioned cameras and gadgets, I admitted, "I love ancient things— decay and ruin fascinate me. Even the aging process is a cool perk."

"Wait until you're thirty-three," he said. "You might change your mind on that one."

"Jesus Christ was crucified at thirty-three," I said. "Do you believe in him?"

"Generally, historically... Jesus sounds like an amazing human being," Dr. A said.

"I didn't think respectable shrinks were allowed to believe in him," I said.

"You mean we're not allowed?" Dr. A. said. "Why on earth can't good shrinks believe in God's son if they want to, Tuck?"

"I'm not sure about that one."

"Everyone's got surprises up their sleeve," he said. "Surprise me now, Tuck."

"I paint neon-yellow smiley faces, or lime green, orange, and purple handlebar mustaches, or oblong alien-looking violet dudes on top of my black and white photos. And I scribble non-sequitur "s" words in tiny English upside down on my pictures: Snooker, salacious, sartorial, sinister, subterfuge, sanguine, sluice, and slacker."

"Fantastic, Tuck," he said. "These are wonderful, stupendous images."

"Are they really that cool?" I asked. "Even if there are others who create parallel work?"

"Always respect what has come before you," Dr. A said. "But keep pushing at your own boundaries—don't ever stop that stuff. Not for one second."

"Right," I said. "Thanks, Doc."

"Tell me now, Tuck," Dr. A said. "What does it feel like to have words flow so freely from your lips?"

"Feels wonderful," I said. "Like I'm finally in charge of my life."

"Is this a safe place, here on the third floor with me?"

"Very much so—I feel at ease and proud of my voice up here," I said. "It's like the bubbling aquarium and all your cool fish settle me down."

"Where don't you feel as safe?"

"Wave Café," I said. "Well, really, it's a mixed bag there—when I sit and have a chat with a new friend and waitress named Basil, she gives me a feeling of security."

"But other times?"

"The Dynamic Duo scare me," I said. "Bear Santos, Foster Gold—those two are hostile, they intimidate everyone, except maybe Basil. She doesn't fear Foster."

"Why not?" he asked.

"She said Foster is nothing but a windbag."

"Right," Dr. A said.

"She said Foster's nothing but a low-class bullshitter."

"Why are you so afraid of him, though?" Dr. A asked.

"He shoved my head in the toilet bowl sophomore year, Doc," I said. "Threatened me, said he'd slice off my left baby toe if I ever told anyone about it."

"Sounds scary," Dr. A said. "An ugly bully on the loose."

"Absolutely," I said. "A real creep, Doc. As a matter of fact,

ACADEMY OF UNHOLY BOYS

he seems to exist in a bubble, floating high above us, up beyond everything and everyone."

"Right," Dr. A said. "Tell me more about this particular asshole."

"He can attract people to his mission without much effort," Tuck said. "Not unlike a cult leader, or, say, that Tyler Durden dude."

"Yes," Dr. A said. "Could you use my help, maybe?"

"It may sound silly to say this," Tuck said. "But I think, I've got it under control. Does that sound stupid?"

"Nothing you say sounds stupid to me, Tuck," Dr. A said. "Ever."

"Thanks."

"And I'll respect your wishes to stay out of it for now, but if you need me, I'm here. Any time of day. Got it?"

"Got it," I said. "Thanks, Dr. A."

BEAR SANTOS

During those eighth-grade days, with Foster Gold inexplicably gone from my world until mid-February, I'd get so anxious and uptight that at times I'd nearly piss my pants. His return, and my first time seeing him again, brought immense relief, better than a migraine vanishing, even if it was a little strange and charged. That's just how Foster was. When he was ready to announce his return to the public, he phoned me and said, "Let's meet at the skating rink. We'll play it like it's our first time seeing each other. Does that sound cool?"

"Sure," I said, although I was not what you called a natural at the ice-skating rink—I rented the skates but figured I'd just hang around and never get on the ice.

I spotted Foster—he was dressed in jeans and a sweatshirt, skating around, twisting left and right with the other eighth graders. It was winter and Foster had not yet officially returned to school, so he surprised everyone else. All the girls were skating up to Foster with numerous flirty questions.

Foster appeared to be having a grand time, encircled by three twittering girls. One was recording him doing spins,

ACADEMY OF UNHOLY BOYS

while the other two glided and weaved around him. Wherever he was, he attracted many young ladies, who invariably recorded his every move. That said, he didn't appear to give the time of day to any of them.

Foster spotted me standing by the desk and shouted, "Hey, Mademoiselle Bear Santos."

"How can this mysterious fellow be of help, my lady?"

"No mystery with you, Bear. One look and I know every secret. I read you like yesterday's news."

"Maybe you're no surprise to me, either, Ms. Foster," I said.

Foster shook his index finger as he glided up to the boards. "I'm a riddle you can't figure out, little bird," he said. "Plus, I'm all about the soul—let's see you top that."

"Smile, you two," a young girl in a neon-orange T-shirt and black jeans teased, balancing her phone in one hand.

"Ever been soul-kissed by a real lady, Bear?" Foster asked.

"Once, playing Truth or Dare," I said, before I realized he was only joking.

"What good are you, then?" he asked, laughing and skating away, joining the throngs of teens moving around the oval, while a begrudging twenty-year-old DJ played 2015's big hits off his Mac Book. Foster glided around for what felt like hours, disappearing into the morass of faces, his sly grin beckoning me. He returned ten minutes later to find me wearing a pair of skates and clinging to the boards.

"Can't skate, Bear?" he said. "Come on, I got you."

"I don't want to embarrass—"

"You already did that a long time ago, man," Foster said, grabbing my hands and pulling me forward. We moved, awkwardly, around the edges of the rink, many people watching, laughing *with* us, not at us.

"So, you're back, huh?" I asked, and he shook his head, pointing to his bad ear.

"Oh, right," I said, now louder. "HOW ARE YOU, MAN?"

"I'm adjusting," he said. "I went from one zoo to the next. Fostered at different places, you could say." He smiled at his pun, then tilted his head, quiet for a moment. "What the hell does *'Bear'* signify to you?"

"I eat people," I said out loud, but thought, *if I had any balls, I'd admit Bear was never my choice.* Only a label passed onto me by regulars at every sports game I'd played since I was five, my size and talent somehow giving them permission to write over my existence, as opposed to securing my autonomy. Felipe was my given name, though just like Sharon Foster Gold, I wasn't comfortable using my real one either. People already had their picture of me. Why confuse them?

"Tell me, lonesome dove," Foster said. "Are you good? You're trembling. Do you want to take a sedative? As you know, I've always got something on me."

"No thanks. You using 'em to cope?"

"Life's never easy," he said. "I'm okay, though. And I missed you, sweet tits."

"You too, man," I said, smiling.

"How would you like to run away together to California, maybe meet up in a palatial mansion in Malibu?" Foster said before my left skate slipped, and my growing frame collapsed on top of him, fracturing his right elbow. He hollered in pain, and soon an ambulance took him off to the nearest Urgent Care. As I left the rink twenty minutes later, Foster Gold's dad, a former insurance exec with a hobby of listening to ham radios, threw me against his black Ford F-250 pickup, as kids watched outside.

"If you go near my son again, greasy lazy beaner," he said, his vodka breath warm on my face. "I'll snip 'em right off."

"Was an accident, sir."

ACADEMY OF UNHOLY BOYS

"Promise me you're done with Foster," he said, hollering. *"Promise me!"*

"I promise," I said, but he only shook his head and cackled.

"Gotcha, Bear Santos," the man said. "Scared you to death tonight, right?"

I tried to smile.

"Scared me good, sir."

"No worries," Mr. Gold said. "I hear you can catch a football well. Don't get too cocky when you make it to high school, though, okay? Remember the little people."

"Will do, sir," I said, swallowing my rage, and disappearing into the night, feeling pleased for one thing: that it was dark and so no one saw me piss my pants in front of Foster's dad.

OCTOBER 2018

JAY SOUTHER

10.10.18

Foster seemed to have taken what Bear had said about good branding to heart. He began a three-word success campaign: "Visualize. Organize. Execute." The three terms were everywhere. Foster made bumper stickers with the words, embroidered ugly T-shirts with them, emblazoned on his bedroom wall with them, painted the words in huge black letters on his basement floor. Even paid $117 so the vanity plate on his tricked-out cherry-red 2016 Audi would read *VOE-11-22*.

Foster Gold was like a cult leader. Inundated by his language, I even had a repeating nightmare of his favorite verbs developing blob-like shadows with wiry, hairy legs that hunted me down on a Komodo dragon-infested island.

I was trying to understand how an intelligent and charismatic soul had become so hell-bent on suicide as his main topic of conversation. I don't remember how we arrived on the topic, but Bear went upstairs for more Jack Daniels, and I'd tried to steer the conversation away from death, asking what I thought was an innocent query.

"Did your father ever take you fishing?" I asked, and Foster burst into tears, before savagely punching his head with both fists twice, directly on each temple. *Punch. Punch.* After the second hit, he only wept, shaking his head.

"Are you okay?" I asked. He grimaced and pointed up the stairs.

"Don't ever tell Bear," he said.

"Maybe he can relate, you know?" I asked. "His dad doesn't sound so—"

"Enough," Foster yelled, pointing up the stairs. "Just leave."

"You told me, though, Foster," I said. "The night we got high after the hailstorm, you spoke about the Greatest Show, and said your dad was a terrible man."

"Right," Foster said, sounding exhausted. "Sorry, so I did. He was not the most compassionate gent in the world."

I certainly didn't celebrate the fact that Foster was ailing, but he did become more human to me. It wasn't exactly schadenfreude that I felt seeing him strike himself, but it was the first major crack I'd seen in Foster. I saw his weakness, and this was my first inkling of doubt that he might not be the answer to my wishes. Might not actually have *all* his shit together.

"You pay attention to me now, Jay?" Foster asked. "Listen closely and absorb. Got it?"

I nodded.

"'All is never as it seems,' is a favorite quote a female shrink told me when I was a fractured, frightened eleven-year-old boy at a children's hospital near Columbia, Missouri, one my mom had read about in *Time* magazine a year earlier. The doctor's words were a simple enough statement, but I found it to be the wisest one I had ever heard. I had a broken nose, jaw, and I had to adjust to a left ear that didn't hear sound any longer. Some ribs, both ankles, and two of my fingers, too. All fractured by

ACADEMY OF UNHOLY BOYS

my father, Evan Linus Gold. Nineteen bones in all. 'Your dad is… a drunken, evil man, Foster,'" I was told multiple times.

"Yes," I said.

"My dad's attack had made the network and cable TV news, and front pages everywhere. He was fired as CFO at his large insurance company in Hartford, paid four million in damages to my mom and I, but he didn't serve jail time. A procedural error in the litigation process saved him from a cell-block, so he got to keep two Rottweilers, a trailer, and a collection of ham radios. I was only a minor, so I was never mentioned publicly, but people who lived in town put two and two together."

"Right," I said.

"My shrink was a striking, compassionate lady—her skin ebony, eyes and often clothes very green. She typically wore a bright melon dress, or these tight Kelly-green pants. I loved that color from then on, and she had the longest legs I'd ever seen—they appeared to go on forever. I was late to puberty, but God, how I loved Dr. Check."

I watched Foster's eyes turn almost wistful.

"She embraced me as I left after seven months of intensive therapy to return to Connecticut," he said. "I wrote to her for a while, but freshman year at St. Andrew's Prep I stopped cold. It was too juvenile, I felt. I saved her phone number and business card."

"What did she possess that was so outstanding?"

"Dr. Check had a way of easing those lonesome and ugly hurts within me. She was an exceptional listener and was precise with her phrases—they worked like a salve on the tender spots of my psyche. I told her she was probably a poet in a past life. I called her a few weeks ago—we hadn't talked in three, maybe four years. It was just ten here, which is around 8 p.m. in Missouri, I think. 'You taught me how to breathe again, Dr. Check,'" I told her. 'You saved my life.'

"She said she'd always hoped I'd phone her, and that she was touched I reached out. I wanted to say more, to dig deep and tell her everything, how no other therapist ever approached her in skills," he said. "Just Mom and Hazel Check, MD—those two women were all I needed. I didn't tell her I was making huge mistakes as of late, taking too many drugs, and letting the power go straight to my head."

As Foster spoke to me, he paced the basement, visibly agitated, gesticulating like some dictator. I thought of throwing myself down in front of the maestro to stop another episode of two punches to his temples, which I sensed might occur again soon. Was that form of self-harm a comment on the arc of Foster Gold's brief life? An unceasing rage pulsing just below the surface, which could erupt and seal his fate come holiday time?

Our leader gathered himself, describing the one soul he had allowed himself access to in his life. "Dr. Check's mantra: 'All is never as it seems,' caught up with me. No one else, not Bear, Mom, teachers, or coaches ever understood where exactly Foster Gold was coming from and that was my error, I believe. I do know what Pop would say about all this fire, gunk, and war I've got percolating in my gut ever since: 'It is what it is, Sharon Foster Gold,'" he'd say with a smirk, slapping my head three times. "'Get used to it.'"

Foster embraced me then, awkwardly. "I need some silence now, but thanks for listening, Jay. You ended up being quite the find back in June."

"What does that mean?" I asked.

"You've been worth it," he said. "I'm glad you've joined Bear and me on this spectacular trip."

My mind raced as I rode my bike home, wondering where

ACADEMY OF UNHOLY BOYS

Bear had disappeared too on that day, clutching a full bottle of Jack Daniel's.

Midweek, I caught up with the All-American, now sober, at practice. Although his high school football career was over, Bear Santos was always on the field—every practice, every game, standing on the sidelines, in street clothes, cheering the players, and clapping away. Obedient and loyal to a fault—that was Bear.

"Did Foster ever tell you about his dad almost killing him?" I asked.

Bear jabbed me hard in the solar plexus with his left fist.

"What the fuck?" I gasped, crouching, out of breath for eight seconds.

Bear's hazel, cat-like eyes were pained. "We support each other until the finale, Jay. That's how all this stuff works. We're a team, remember?"

"Until death, Bear?" I asked. "You're cool with killing yourself?"

"Keep your *goddamned* voice down," Bear said. "You're losing faith rapidly."

"It's not the military, man," I said.

"Don't I know it," Bear replied and walked away.

For all his grace and mastery on a football field, Bear lacked the confidence to lead or think independently in the world. Following his leader's directions was a perfect fit, though. Riding shotgun in Foster's Audi was very natural, so I can only imagine how at home Bear must have felt by the golden-haired young man's side. Dynamic Duo forever.

BEAR SANTOS

10-11-14

In those early days, Foster and I haunted fields, courts, arenas—any place with lines and a ball that kept me out of my own house. During our freshman summer, I talked Foster into coaching a bunch of U10 kids at a basketball camp called Mighty Mites. We'd leave football practice, then grab a foot long at Subway, and head directly to a middle school gym off Boston Post Road, only stopping long enough to change out of our sweaty shirts.

We'd gather the kids around us, kneeling midcourt. The air would be thick, and the place would reek of sweat, the sound of bouncing balls and the squeak of sneakers on the court forcing us to raise our voices. Older teens shot baskets on the other side of the gym—cursing back and forth, practicing their trash talk.

My kids, I felt, were wonderful, so young and impressionable. "Like a big lump of clay waiting for you." Or at least that's how Foster had described them. "Shake these dang Mighty Mites up a little, Bear. Enjoy the anarchy. Say anything that comes to you, mold them, twist them around a bit."

So, I took a deep breath and exhaled and said, "Okay, guys.

ACADEMY OF UNHOLY BOYS

I want you all to bow your heads immediately and pray fervently to the most holy women and men in the wild kingdom, but never, and I mean ever grow up. Sprint away from any signs of puberty, slip out of town when no one is looking. Stand on your head for five minutes each night, and then soar so far away to Peru with a surfboard and some Red Bull and a substantial amount of beef jerky. Your families will understand if you leave baked oatmeal raisin cookies on the windowsills. It's a universal calling card for young boys traveling the world in search of their elemental boyhood."

"That doesn't make sense," one of my little kids, Hank, said. "It's ridiculous."

"I heard we'll get tossed in jail for something like that," another cherubic-faced boy said. "I think that happened to my older brother, in fact."

"How would you both have liked it if that happened when you were our age?" one boy said.

"We did," Foster said. "We made our cookies, stood on our heads. We did all that stuff until the damn cows came home."

"Liar," one bright kid said. "You guys aren't telling the truth, I mean, you both obviously grew up. I thought you guys were going to help us."

"We're all innocent until proven guilty," Foster had added, appearing to get choked up. "That's the American way."

"Bear said we should never mature," the other smart kid said. "Not fair."

I continued to obsess about what Foster's teary eyes meant to me on that day. Was it a fluke? Or was he feeling the same heaviness in the gut, something that pointed to our fear of growing up and the loneliness that came along with it? Or was he just going to miss the kids as much as I did?

Foster's phone that night was flooded with pictures of oatmeal cookies on windowsills, and young kids trying to stand on their heads. We watched on a recording of their faces registering shock, humor, and betrayal. Part of me felt shitty for tricking the kids, but the other part felt an awakening, a hunger —all the power I had over their pliable brains.

Take no prisoners, I told myself.

My negative scheming shook me up, though. Next meet up, I was moved by the kids' belief in me and regretted betraying their trust. On our last day, I wept as I spoke with the Mighty Mites, which confused them—and me. Even Foster looked worried, like he didn't expect all that business. But his eyes watered, too, and neither we nor the kids knew what to make of our open display of grief.

Foster had approached me and for a moment I thought he was going to kiss me in public. He had only done that once.

I was self-medicating big time by freshman summer and all through school, really, either high or drunk, constantly enraged with my dad, and God, however feebly or crudely I imagined him. So, it was hard to think straight, to use any reason. My concussed brain only throbbed. What also thumped steady was a desire for something more. I wanted to share ideas, wishes, and dreams with Foster Gold. I knew it would intrigue him.

But in the meantime, I had elder advisors coming out of the woodwork to preach, to hold forth and tell me what was best for *me.* I was told by famed coaches, by learned and holy brothers from neighboring churches, that if it doesn't make you play better football, basketball, or baseball, it's of little use. It just leads to trouble and grief, just always keep moving, don't bother with all the heavy, philosophical questions *for now.* Faith in the Divine alone will lead you through your individual hells, a friend's preacher told me. Piety is the only medicine needed in battle.

"If you never sin, you never suffer."

The Rev, of course, said nothing. Zilch. He was invisible as ever. His presence, his nothingness was maybe the hardest for me to bear. His ghostly reality shut me down in so many ways. A part of me was disappointed that I hadn't grown thicker skin by then. The Reverend still could wound me so brutally.

Did he ever grasp that? I wondered. *Does any part of him wish we were closer?*

BASIL SOUS

10-11-18

It was Thursday, October 11, 2018, and Peg and I were staying at a new house in Gently—a lovely white clapboard structure with rose shutters, a library, and a spectacular view of Long Island Sound. We thought it a perfect place to hunker down with books as my academic year got rolling. We had recently moved from the blue house on the marsh off Route 146, and the social agency in Gently connected us with this wonderful spot.

It wasn't often our circumstances improved with each move, so we carried our cardboard boxes of clothes and towels across the sunny slate entry as if we were being rewarded for exemplary behavior. One night, I was knee-deep in a math book when my cell rang.

"Hey, who's this?" I asked, knowing exactly who it was. Jay Souther had finally built up the courage to ask for my number at the Green. I'd scrawled the digits on his forearm outside the café.

"It's Jay," came a deep voice. "I'm looking for the girl they call Basil."

ACADEMY OF UNHOLY BOYS

"You found her," I said. I tossed the math book aside and wandered downstairs as he attempted to get it together on the other end. I sat on a comfy wicker chair with chubby pillows and a comforter and studied the Long Island Sound through two large windows on the first floor that rattled in the wind.

"The first thing I wanted to tell this Basil character is that she's so hot," he said.

"Now you're talking," I said.

"I was going to tell you more, but maybe I shouldn't now," he said.

"Tell me," I laughed. "Don't be a silly tease." I pulled at a thread in my shredded jeans, carefully avoiding the painful scab I'd gotten during a cement-eating kick-flip attempt near the center of town.

"Your pastel ribbons and colorful locks make you shimmer like some female version of James Dean," he said.

"Whoa," I said, stifling a laugh. "Maybe just pretend we're regular teens before pontificating away like that."

Jay went on, unfazed. "The one and only Jimmy Dean is so contained... I have no idea how he does it. He holds back, you know? But then, boom, he lays everything out on the table, howling."

"Like those two buddies of yours at St. A's," I said. "You all howl like hyenas."

"I love chatting with you, Basil. But I object to being called a hyena, you saw what they did to Mufasa."

"Well," I said, laughing. "Why do you like being with them so much?"

"Truth is, they give me free drugs, though I'm not really a druggie in the traditional sense," he said. "One thing about the edibles is they allow me to relax, to de-stress, understand?"

"I'm not a fan," I said. I was quiet for a moment, giving him a chance to explain. I could hear him exhale on the other side of the cloud.

"Granted, if I was being totally honest, Basil," Jay said. "I'd point out that periodically the gummies are laced with some nasty shit, and then I don't feel confident or relaxed, only paranoid and terrified about what I'm doing with my body, flying past our little world at a thousand miles per hour."

"That doesn't sound sane," I said. "You need to stop it now."

"Well, like I said," Jay went on. "I like what I'm doing now with you more."

"Yeah?"

"I mean, you got the best name ever," Jay said. "Basil Sous... it rolls off the tongue like a fresh and minty Mentos."

I laughed. "You sound like an old hat at this romance jazz, Jay."

"I got a long way to go, Basil," Jay said. "Never kissed a girl in my entire life. Maybe someone can change that luck for me?"

"Maybe so," I said. "Does that weigh on you? The fact that you've never laid your lips on anyone, save for your family?"

"Yes, it does weigh on me," he said. "That's why we need to get together soon. Just a simple kiss, though. That's all I'm speaking of."

"Nothing else?"

"Not right away," Jay said. "But then my lawyer will call your lawyer and work out all the fascinating sexual details later."

"You're such a goof," I said.

"So, I've heard."

That was the gist of our first call. I didn't quite know why— Jay was awkward and goofy as hell—but I was grinning when I hung up.

ACADEMY OF UNHOLY BOYS

* * *

I see the name Avery Rutherford Sous in my diary a lot, and sometimes when I'm blue I write his name ten times in a row, like I'm about to write a letter to my one and only brother.

Avery had the same roommate freshman and sophomore year at Cornell, a young man named Levon Gilbert, who played the flute so sweetly for me in his room I almost wept. It was early October and foliage season, and the perfect time for Cornell's Family Weekend in Ithaca, so Avery's girlfriend, Mallory, picked me up in Gently and drove me all the way back to campus. So, I hung out with the two roomies for a few days. Levon's mom was from Beijing and his dad was an African American artist and they both resided in Brooklyn, New York. His mom was apparently a professor for a time, his father a multi-media artist.

Levon showed off his dad's work in the main space of the dormitory. Mr. Gilbert was also a carpenter, sculptor, and painter who had revamped the album art of "Goodbye Yellow Brick Road" with Levon in place of Elton John. The painting took up a whole wall with its lovely greens, yellows, and pinks.

"This is wonderful, Levon," I told him.

"I can't get over how sweet it is to have my father's art here with me every day when I wake up," he said. "It's a memorial, a tribute."

And so, I learned that day Levon had terminal bone cancer and didn't have much time left.

"That's gotta be difficult, Avery," I said later at a café, when it was just my brother and me.

"Levon's always a class act, though," he said. "It's just I know he won't be around too much longer, so that kind of wrecks me, destroys me, actually."

DAVID FITZPATRICK

I swirled my cup, so the marshmallows spun in my hot chocolate, thinking of the gorgeous mural made by an adoring father. "Do you ever think about Mom or Dad?" I asked.

"I try hard not to," Avery told me. "They abandoned us, Basil. Cut us loose like we were nothing but the lint on their cheap, ugly clothes. Dusted us off and disappeared into the jungle, left you on your fifth birthday, for Christ's sake. They're such irresponsible maggots in my mind."

"Yeah," I said.

"How about you, though?" he asked. "Do you still miss them?"

"Only like today, at a family weekend where the focus is strictly on parents," I said. "I see responsible dads throwing a football or loving moms playing tennis, or bike riding with their kids, telling them how proud of them they are. Someone to rely on down the road, to visit on holidays."

"Yes," he said.

"Someone to raise them properly."

"I'm sorry it's been so rough," Avery said.

"Yeah, me too," I said.

"I remain proud of you, though," Avery said. "You're *resilient*, Basil Sous. You keep bouncing back from adversity. I think the world of you, remember that okay?"

He hugged me then, kissed my forehead, and the next day his girlfriend drove me back to the Connecticut shoreline and I never saw my brother alive again. Three days later, he died from a fall off a fraternity balcony while binge drinking. At his funeral, Levon played the flute to one of Avery's favorite tunes, "Ripple" by *Grateful Dead*.

"He was a truly sweet soul," Levon told me. "My best friend. I already miss him an impossible amount."

"Yeah, me too, Levon," I said. "Thanks very much."

ACADEMY OF UNHOLY BOYS

"He loved you tremendously," Mallory told me, embracing me as she wept. "He was always talking about you, day and night."

I nodded and hugged her back.

"Thanks," I said. "Avery talked about you a lot, too."

BEAR SANTOS

10.12.18

It was mid-October, and my dreams were especially magnificent, albeit scary. I took more naps as the year went on, a symptom of concussions. One night, I dreamed of toddlers, the younger brothers and sisters of the Mighty Mites, singing off-key, racing around on an October beach. The kids were in tuxedo T-shirts, orange berets, neon-yellow pull-ups, and too-large penny loafers singing "Happy Birthday" repeatedly as they roasted a pig and giant marshmallows.

Within the blue and purple flames of the fire was an image of Foster calling out, proclaiming his wild and legitimate love. Soon I, too, was a toddler outdoors, falling and stumbling across beach after beach, dressed like the other kids in my pull-ups, berets, and outsized loafers, running for the last house on the right to find that bonfire and save my dear friend.

I eventually found the cottage near the pig roast, but it was all dark, and when I pushed through the door, it was deserted inside. No one was singing birthday tunes, off-key or otherwise. There was no fire left on the beach, no Foster, not a soul, just the smell of charred bacon and soiled pull-ups, and one corner

ACADEMY OF UNHOLY BOYS

where discarded orange berets had been tossed. I rushed to the refrigerator, opened it, and found my dad's head on ice, an apple in his mouth, and his eyes wide open.

I was jolted, but still found myself inside the dream. I rolled over on the bed and rubbed my eyes; I saw I was in my dad's room. I walked to his dresser and opened the top drawer, taking out his hunting knife. Dad also had a pistol, but I never touched that. As I held the hunting knife, a carpenter ant crawled across the lamp, and I crushed him with my thumb, then wiped his black goo on the base of the light.

Right then I thought of Foster. I wished to be rocked in his arms, and be absolved of every silly sin, and I thought, *go back, you fool, don't do this, turn back, Bear*, but instead, I rose, spitting out a strange taste of garlic onto the rug and moved toward the window. I drew back the gauzy curtains, looked down, and remembered myself at four, the hunting knife in my adult hand, trembling out of view.

I saw a mini-Phil Santos in the garden, looking contented. He was blowing bubbles with admirable intensity, huge, expanding creations that flickered iridescently in the setting sun. He glanced up at me.

"Do you need a smile today, my friend?" My younger self asked. "You look very sad."

"Everything's fine, mini-Phil, thanks," I managed, my voice shaky. I backed up and sat on the bed, dropping the knife to the floor. My chest hurt, and I sobbed for five seconds before wiping my eyes and exhaling.

"I'm normal and not that unusual, really," I said. "I'm Felipe, Phil, or Bear, or whatever you wish to say about me, but I love Foster Gold and I don't care what the Reverend and all his collection of tight asses believes."

JAY SOUTHER

10-15-2018

My father had bumps on his arms, chest, and legs. Fat deposits, I believe, "nothing serious," most doctors said; they were like golf balls tucked under the epidermis. I remember having weird urges to rip them out of his skin. He caught me ogling them the summer I turned ten, the same year he broke down. I was convinced one would hatch, becoming a pigeon, or perhaps a dove.

"Just call me Mr. Titleist," my father said. "When doctors remove these beauties, first one goes straight to you, my dear boy."

When he left, I worried that I had sent him scurrying away —that his disappearance was because I had asked him too frequently about the bumps. Perhaps now he was hiding in an apartment in Philly or a sleazy hotel in Toledo, or a dilapidated bar in Littleton, New Hampshire, wearing a dark turtleneck and jeans, fearful people would see his bumps and mock him.

All I had left with my dad were the photos and his ancient brown leather chair. I liked to sit in it at night and unwind before bed. I practiced deep breathing, so I wouldn't be anxious, and I scribbled hundreds of fifteen-word notes: over and over I wrote:

I am so sorry for my jokes about your bumps, Daddy. I love you. – Jay

* * *

Six years ago, I awoke to a hoarse, barking sound coming from the living room. The noise penetrated the walls like my Nana's snoring at her Maine cottage, where it kept me up all night. My initial thought had been, *No worries, it's only Nana.* But then I remembered Nana had died that past December of congestive heart failure. As I sat with my ear against my bedroom door, thoughts raced.

Are wolves, or raccoons chewing through plaster, wood, and brick?

It was right around the time the movie *Twilight* came out, so I also thought, *Are they maybe even vampires?*

There was a bad storm and hail slammed and pounded against our home, cars, and windows. The barking, snoring, grating noise continued inside the house. I knew I needed to be brave and protect mom and dad. I felt I was stronger than wolves and vampires and could scare them all away with my youthful energy.

I rushed into the living room, enraged, set to scream at the intruder, but it wasn't a vampire, wolf, or even Nana's ghost. It was my naked, pale father cowering on his knees, hollering about the hailstorm.

"Why does hail have to be so mean-spirited?" His voice was strained, terror-stricken. "Why is it destroying our house, Jay?"

I tried to be calm so I could figure this situation out for my dad, so he would stand and put his pajamas with the tiny gold golf clubs back on. I wanted him to kiss my cheek, and say,

"You're the absolute king of kings," and then lean forward so I could kiss the balding crown of his head.

"It's just frozen rain, Dad," I said.

"No, no," he yelled, rolling across the living room rug, a maroon-and-white one Mom had recently purchased at Pier One. "Don't you see the hail has already damaged us badly? It's wounded our shelter, cracked the concrete, and splintered our very walls."

Mom emerged from the master bedroom in her red-satin bathrobe, calling 911. She began mixing herself a drink, the phone pressed between her ear and shoulder. All I noticed were Dad's bumps. They appeared to have completed their takeover of his body. Perhaps the awful weather had somehow diminished Dad and obliterated our fracturing family.

I ran to the linen closet and grabbed a fitted yellow bed sheet and wrapped it around my ranting, trembling father so he wouldn't be cold or look so vulnerable, so awkward. I hugged him, but he eventually shook off my embrace. I stood back, gnawing at a thumbnail until it bled, while my dad writhed on the living room floor. An ambulance carrying two severe-looking women came and wheeled him away.

"I can't leave," Dad yelled, terrified as a toddler, clutching onto the yellow sheet as they rushed him down our walk, and neighbors he'd awoken in the stormy night gawking at him like he was an alien. "The hail burns my skin."

"Mom?" I said, tugging on her sleeve for a moment. I wanted some type of comfort or a semblance of warmth. She was already on her third Martini, and she and my Aunt Carol, who had stayed over that night, were now huddled on the blue leather couch, where she was penciling suggestions on a yellow legal pad, ("Hospital? Group home? Shock? Therapy dog?") The two of them would periodically turn and study me, standing by the front door in my pajamas.

"Get away from the door, sweetie, the glass could shatter from that hail," my aunt said, but I assured her everything would be fine once the hail stopped, once the sun rose high the next day. When the weather grew calmer, the nightmare would cease, and perhaps my father would return and make eggs and corn muffins with blueberries for mom and me on Sunday mornings, like he always had.

"Just a few more hours, Aunt Carol," I said. "You'll see."

My mother's *thing,* her main commandment—beyond never referencing her drinking or questioning her habit of buying too much shit on QVC or HSN—was something she set down as soon as Dad left in the ambulance.

"Try hard, if possible, not to discuss him," she said. "Dad's disappeared for now. If I hear from him, I'll tell you, but don't ask—it's too damn hard to examine."

"That's not normal, Ma," I said. "You can't just remove Dad from my life."

She once attempted to clarify. We were watching the 1985 Harrison Ford and Kelly McGillis Amish thriller *Witness,* which she was obsessed with.

"Look, Jay," she said, "it's obviously a painful event for all of us, so for now let's look to the Amish for our emotional cues."

"I don't get it, Momma," I yelled. "Not fair, it's not right what you're doing to me right now."

We argued, but in the end, she remained herself, unrepentantly vague.

"Just watch and learn," Mom said, pointing her fork at the Pennsylvania Dutch men constructing a new farmhouse for newlyweds, or when Amish women were preparing the huge feasts. "Everyone has a role. They do as much as they are

DAVID FITZPATRICK

capable of. Let's learn from them, Jay, and move away from the blame game, which you seem addicted to."

Mom did generously pay for me to see counselors after school, but *they*—the social workers or psychologists—always fooled with their wedding rings, watches, or necklaces too much, sighing and excessively folding and unfolding their legs.

It was maddening, and a sign I felt that there was no certainty left on the globe. I didn't allow myself to believe that somewhere in a room like mine my dad was suffering, doing the hard work so he could return home. I couldn't bear to face the fact that Geoff Henry Souther might *still* be clinging to that damn yellow bed sheet he left our house in, wrestling with some gnawing, flesh-eating despair.

Instead, I imagined he was taking a long, intelligence-boosting break—willfully working on his tennis backhand in Tucson or the Berkshires, doing resistance exercises, enjoying saunas, and yoga or playing golf, or revisiting Shakespeare, Milton, Cheever, Bach, Roth, Dickens, Emily Dickinson, James Baldwin, Joy Williams, Anthony Marra, Robert Frank, Gabriel Garcia Marquez, Toni Morrison, and Frank Lloyd Wright—in order to gird himself up to come back full throttle and blow us all away with his health, stamina, and intellect.

When I spoke with the different counselors, ignored their fidgety habits, and absorbed their theories and oblique guesses, I'd think, *No one is calm or zen in this life, Jay. No one has answers. Get used to it. They don't have one damn clue because your dad went up in flames, or crumpled, so you must find comfort, somehow, in the unknowing.*

All the answers to my unacknowledged queries of Mom were kept locked up in her, impenetrable as a safe on the basement floor. This never ceased to frustrate me, particularly because I knew there was nothing down in our basement other than a furnace and washer and dryer, a purple Hula Hoop,

ACADEMY OF UNHOLY BOYS

deflated basketball, and three cobwebbed ten-speed bikes with flat tires. But that didn't keep me from searching for a key, some sign from her that could trip the hatch, a Narnia-like door, perhaps.

It was an unspoken trade agreement I'd made with Mom: In exchange for leaving me alone with my feeble attempts at studying and my freedom with my flexible curfew and use of illicit substances, I left her alone with her martinis and abstained from my safe-cracking attempts regarding Dad and his psychic illness. Truth is, though, I could feel the taxing weight of my father straining everyone and everything—mom, me, even our cheap roof, mold showing up all over the place. Sagging, drooping, leaking—who knows what? I always saw our abode as a vulnerable structure that could give way at any moment.

* * *

The more my sophomore summer sped into autumn and the chillier temperatures rolled in, I realized just how fragile the world and my own specific life were. Whether it's in a tiny town like Gently, or a huge country like the United States, hell, even the Milky Way Universe and deep space, everything's connected, and we all ache, bitch, and hurt. *Try and be more empathic to your fellow humans and animals going forward,* or at least, that's what my Aunt Carol tells me every day of my life. She's really heavily into horoscopes and astrology and will talk your ear off about all things relating to karma. She made me listen to the "Instant Karma" song by John Lennon three times in a row. "We all shine on, like the moon, the sun..."

I grew embarrassed as Carol danced, twisting, and laughing, although Ma eventually gave in to Carol's demands, and she danced with her, too. I retreated to my room, and I did tap my sneakers for it's a catchy song to groove to, but I felt it wasn't right to dance with all the Greatest Show on Earth issues spinning in my head.

Part of learning about my own fragility was grasping that not everyone at St. Andrew's was caught up in Foster Gold worship. Sure, my mom was a bit suspicious of him, and Mrs. G had her exasperations with her only child, but I'd fully believed everybody else at school either admired him or wanted to be like him, whether it was teen girls at our sister school in North Madison, or middle-aged teachers having a crisis of lost youth. But there was one junior baseball player I knew through Bear named Hank Allan, and I quickly learned how much Hank loathed Bear's pal. I sat by Bear at lunch in the cafe, and this huge guy, maybe six-four, was talking trash about Bear's best buddy. "You shouldn't be doing squat for that cocky asshole," Hank said to Bear. "Especially after Foster nearly killed you with the cheap shot heard around the world last year. So many underclassmen hate Foster Gold for that bogus tackle."

"Oh, he's mellowing out," Bear said.

"The dude believes he's infallible, man," Hank said. "He thinks like he's like the Pope or something, and that's not healthy for anyone."

"No, he's fine," Bear said. "A bit of a romantic, actually."

"Seems like to me that Foster's got a death wish," Hank said. "Sounds stupid, I know, but I wouldn't mind taking him out."

"Cold-blooded murder?" Bear asked.

"Yes, exactly," Hank said.

"That's horrible," Bear said.

"It's his fault, all the many errors he's made over the years," Hank said. "I'm just saying he deserves it."

I tried to get up, whether to get peanut butter cookies or to

ACADEMY OF UNHOLY BOYS

try and process this bizarre conversation I wasn't yet sure, when Hank grabbed my arm like a vice. I was unable to move.

"You don't ever tell on any homicidal juniors, right Souther?" he said.

"No, no, of course not," I said. "I've always kept my mouth sealed tight, although now I'm about to stuff it with peanut butter cookies. Is that okay with you, your excellency?"

"Absolutely," Hank said with an unsure smile. "Enjoy those cookies."

"He's cool, Hank, "Bear said. "No worries."

"Just checking," he said. "From now on, I'll be watching you closely, Jay."

"Wonderful," I said. "Superb."

BEAR SANTOS

10.28.18

My father was chock-full of his own angst, frustration, and rage. For a guy who was supposed to preach about the compassion, love, and kindness of Jesus Christ each Sunday, it was stunning to hear how often he spoke about the depraved souls in his sermons who always seemed to wear colored hair, tattoos, and excessive body piercings. It went on every Sunday, and eventually, I tuned his silly rants out.

Dad never paid me much attention to me; even when I was in the local paper a lot, he passed on by me, never meeting my eyes. Rev never saw me play any sport, never attended one of my games. In many ways, he stayed faithful to his words that he issued so long ago. One day, after I'd put eyedrops in to soothe the redness, he gave a new version of his favorite spiel:

"You, Felipe, are not a significant part of my life and never will be," he said.

"Fine."

"You've picked up a fourth concussion, and the cameras and lights have long since faded. The All-State dinners are

ACADEMY OF UNHOLY BOYS

distant nothings in history. Time for you to contribute to this homestead. Understand?"

"Dad—"

"Who is 'Dad?'" he said. "When have I ever allowed you to call me *Dad?*"

"Sir," I said. "I'm still bringing in good grades."

"You're eighteen now, Felipe," he said. "Not a kid, so please bring home a paycheck. I'm not talking about drug money, either, like your hustling friend."

"That's not true..."

"I've been hearing from parishioners that you spend a lot of time with him."

"That doesn't make Foster a drug—"

"Just go and get a damn job."

"What about the state psych hospital?" I said. "Your friend works over there, right?"

"Your choice, I don't care. Ask them about it," the Reverend said. "See what they say about employment."

Something in my chest was burning. "You've never praised me, ever," I said. "Not once."

"I see enough," he said under his breath.

"Yes, sir," I said, more ready than ever for the Greatest Show.

BASIL SOUS

10-29-18

Dr. Athens' waiting room wasn't fancy—just a quiet, clean nook three floors up in a squeaky elevator ride. The building wasn't far from the library and was about a ten-minute walk to Wave Café. A small printing press hummed along on the first floor of the building, which sounded like a drone as you sat waiting for your therapeutic turn upstairs, and there was also a lawyer's office on the second floor, although they made little to no noise, like everyone must have removed their shoes when they entered the space.

Once the rather rickety elevator dropped you off on the third floor, all you could hear was the whirring of a white noise machine and faint classical music. And in contrast to the intricate yellow wallpaper, huge aquarium, and Salvador Dali prints waiting on the wall inside Dr. Athens's office, the waiting room had one simple IKEA table spilling over with old *New Yorker*, *People* and *Time* magazines. There were three large windows, and one had a thin, rectangular sign reading, ***Thank You for Keeping Your Cell Phones Turned Off.***

ACADEMY OF UNHOLY BOYS

There was one gender-neutral bathroom, a water bubbler in the corner, and on the walls, covers of *Life* magazine issues and a framed photo of *Marcel Marceau,* famous mime and clown extraordinaire. There were four red plastic chairs and a blue Lay-Z-Boy recliner with an old radio playing selections from Chopin, Bach, and Brahms from a windowsill. Patients came in and waited silently, or at least that's how I'd seen others do it. Some breathed quietly, while others fidgeted, or stared into their phones.

Then one day I saw him in the waiting room. The only thing that came out of the real tall guy's mouth that day were mumbles. I had said hello several times, but one day, maybe I was being overly chatty or something, but I said, "Hey, how are you doing today, my friend?"

"Fine, really good," he said, before cupping his left hand over his mouth. His hands were big, long slender fingers and perfectly cared-for nails, which surprised me. I have tremendous respect for well-cared-for hands and nails, to me they're almost as important as a winning smile. I know that may sound absurd, but I do mean it.

I always gnawed mine down to the quick like a fiend, or at least those on my right hand, so I had extra admiration for those around my age who had kept their own nails far from their nibbling teeth. Aunt Peg was frequently getting on my case about not taking proper care of my cuticles.

But the tall, skinny guy seemed laser-focused on his iPhone. "Do you like her?" he asked me suddenly, as he played a scene from the film, *La La Land.*

"Who is it again?" I said, and he blushed.

"Emma Stone," he said. "She won the Oscar in 2017 for *La La Land.*"

"Best Actress, right?" I asked, and he smiled.

"Indeed, great movie, very freeing to watch," he said, which was more words than I ever thought I'd hear from him. "Emma and Ryan Gosling star together and they have a wonderful chemistry, an impressive back and forth. You can only smile about it — it's a magical thing. Check it out sometime for fun, will you?"

"Sure," I said. "I promise to... I'm Basil. Basil Sous by the way."

"Tucker Reis," he said, nodding, and when I offered my right hand to shake, he hesitated a few seconds before gripping mine. "Or Tuck, if you prefer a more informal style."

"How long have you been seeing Dr. Athens, Tuck?" I asked.

"Two or three years now," he said before our therapist opened the door and said, "Tuck, you're the next lucky contestant."

"Yes," Tuck said, nodding a goodbye to me, and walked inside Dr. Athens' office.

"Basil," Dr. Athens said. "I'll be seeing you before too long."

"I'll be here," I said. "Not going anywhere, Doc."

JAY SOUTHER

10-31-18

"My slap-happy father died recently, he had a massive stroke, and they're celebrating his life today at the church, so I thought, 'Screw him royally and let's dish out some old-fashioned destruction for our loyal and royal audience.'"

It was Halloween and Foster Gold sent Bear and me a text requesting we meet him at the barn. My warning bells went off. Mrs. G had always made it crystal clear that the red barn was like Fort Knox. But Foster was done with limits.

So, while Foster's mom, our principal, Brother Tomas, and some of the insurance execs in the region packed into the pews at St. Andrew's, paying condolences and farewells to Foster's child-beating dad, who had died of a massive stroke. Soon after, Foster, Bear, and I were picking the lock to his dad's gold bullion.

"How come it's not at a temple?" I asked. "The funeral, I mean?"

"Pop is a lapsed Christian," Foster said. "Mom's Jewish, it's on her side."

"Ah, I get it," I said.

141

The barn was where Foster's deceased father's antique cars, model planes, and trains were housed. It was spotless and pristine. Models hung neatly on the walls or were set up on perfectly kept display tables. Most were miniatures. Some were stashed in carpet-lined drawers—a precise spot for each. The temperature was not too dry or cool, and the windows small, so that any glare was reduced.

"Things are far too clean and shiny in here, boys," Foster said.

The largest, most expensive display was a Model T—a half-scaled-back replica his mother had told us was worth many thousands of dollars. The whole collection was something Foster and his mom had won in the divorce proceedings, and Mrs. G had wanted him to put toward paying for college. The Model T was about the size of a Toyota Prius.

"No can do, Pop," Foster Gold said, mumbling curses and insults as he squatted down to open a Cost-Co-size bottle of Pepto-Bismol that he had carried to the barn in a grocery bag. He dipped his finger in the pink liquid, wrote in the most careful script on the driver's door:

Visualize. Organize. Execute.

Then he asked Bear and me to put on sunglasses and retreat to a corner. As Foster Gold slipped on his Vuarnets, I tried to offer some perspective.

"Foster," I said, "I don't get why we can't save it and you get more money—."

"One should never interrupt a good plan, Jay," he said, and proceeded to pour the remaining bottle of Pepto-Bismol over the models. He continued this precise procedure with the rest of the bottles, which he pulled out one-by-one from the shopping bag.

There were tiny Christmas villages with a chubby little Santa, numerous train engines, boxcars, and lots of miniature

ACADEMY OF UNHOLY BOYS

folks skiing or enjoying the winter scape or taking a dip in a tiny hot tub on the other side of the slopes.

There were Studebakers, Cadillacs, Continentals, Mercedes, classic Jags, along with fighter jets, 747s, a Hess Truck, even the cruise ship, *QE2*. All of it now slathered in pink anti-diarrheal liquid.

"There's no need to destroy everything, Foster," I said.

"Bear," Foster said, "re-start our recording, please. There's a definite problem with our newest recruit. More of an annoyance, really."

"Perhaps a malfunction in his motherboard?" Bear asked.

"Oh come on, not you t—"

"Come destroy the models, *Skunker*," Foster said, clapping his hands twice.

I swallowed, my face flushing. "Why don't you both stop acting like cloying assholes?" My words seemed to echo off the miniature steepled roofs. I rarely stood up to either of them, but I was tired of their incessant death-droning and doomsday musings.

"What did you just say, Skunker?" Foster asked.

"Why the constant obsession with suicide and self-annihilation?" I asked, my pulse pounding in my ears. "Why not something real, something positive? It's cowardly to say life sucks and just give up on it and mope our damn year away, right? I mean, where the hell is the challenge in any of that?"

"Hey Skunker, here, Skunker," Foster said in a singsong fashion. "Skunker…"

"Don't call me that," I said, beginning to shake. "It's bullshit. You sound like a fucking freshman."

"Skunker," Foster said. "Destroy this antique collection or your name on grounds of school, at football practice, at home, online will forever be Skunker."

"Bear?" I said, turning to him for some sanity, but he only smirked.

"Why is Skunker not grasping basic commands, Foster?"

Are these shits serious? I thought. *Is this petty crap actually going down?*

I made a dash for it, trying to sprint out of the barn, but Foster tackled me hard on the beige-carpeted floor, and we smashed into Lionel trains and railcars, knocking them over and onto us.

"What the hell?" I cried out.

"Everyone pays the same dues around here," Foster said, and when I stood, he elbowed my stomach hard, and I lost my breath, before he shoved me into a table of shiny and small but expensive muscle cars. I felt the little pieces shatter against me, which drew much blood on my arm.

I rose slowly, only to see Foster crouching close, his orange jock and lavender socks fluorescent in the museum-quality lighting. He looked ready for a kill.

"Jesus Christ," I said, breathing hard, my belly sore. "What the hell, man?"

"No worries, bro," Foster said right near my face, trying to bite or kiss me, I wasn't sure.

"I'm done, you pathetic shit."

"Just listen," Foster said, slapping my chest a moment, then stepping back.

"Get the hell away," I said. "Stop touching me."

"No, no, no," Foster said, then he began barking. Bear joined him a few seconds later, and the two of them barked fifteen times in unison, not silly-funny-jokey *arf, arf,* but like two rabid German Shepherds.

"Let me leave," I said.

"Slow down," Foster said, almost in a whisper. "Slow it down, be calm, easy."

ACADEMY OF UNHOLY BOYS

"Enough," I said, holding my hands up. "This is so screwed up, so very whacked."

"Everything will be okay, Jay," Foster said.

"No, it won't be okay," I said. "*None of it is okay. I'm outta here.*"

"Easy..."

"Let me pass," I said, needing to get by them to reach the only door.

"Not yet," Foster said, holding both hands up.

"Your pathetic, melodramatic suicide plans," I said, my body trembling, "are nothing more than a yellow flag. Nothing's legitimate or true about your death surprise, and to me, it's nothing more than a pompous, deceitful joke. You can stop this nonsense, Foster, both of you can, you're both so terrified of *hope.*"

The three of us were silent, signaling calm, but I could still feel my heart pounding.

"We're finished with violence, I promise," Foster said. "Sorry about all that."

"Yeah, right," I said.

"No, I mean it, no more violence ever again," he said. "And I'd be willing to speak with you at any point about how our Thanksgiving fundraisers will have great and powerful meaning."

"Oh, horseshit, Foster," I said. "It's a permanent solution to a temporary problem."

"Did you read that off an inspirational calendar written by some New Age fool? That's a stock Freudian quack response," Foster said. "We made a blood brother promise—we need to stick to it. It's our core integrity, beliefs, our souls at play here."

"Why throw me around like you did?" I asked, hands on my knees.

"Easy now," Bear said, approaching me to pat my back.

DAVID FITZPATRICK

"No, no, *don't touch me*," I said. "You're both savages, cut from the same cloth."

"We love you, though," Foster said. "We just needed to know we can trust you."

"Bullshit," I said. "That's just—" *what you know I want to hear.*

"Granted, it's a warped initiation rite," Foster said. "We had to check if you were up to the task."

"Life is going to be smooth sailing from here on in," Bear said.

"Smooth sailing until our idiotic Thanksgiving self-annihilation bash," I said.

It was silent for at least twenty seconds after I said that, so I stared at the ground.

"Okay," Foster said. "We're both overstepping, said things we regret here today."

"I should probably just go," I said. "It's easier, simpler for everyone if I quit right now, just zip right out the door."

"No, no," Foster said, his voice like something you'd use on a frightened child. He had downshifted into a more soothing, calming groove. His face seemed to strain less at that point, as if he were meditating. "You can't go now, Jay." The tone was still soft, nearly melodic. "We need you, man. You *complete* our circle here—Bear and I would cease to function without you." He smiled. "You ground us, so please don't leave, okay?" This last sentence was said with gentle pleading, and a whisper of triumph, because some part of him knew he had me.

"You indirectly destroyed the antiques—you did what was asked, so no more Skunker. I'll never use that title again; I swear to God."

My head was rushing, whirling. I thought, *what kind of cult am I trapped in here?*

"Sit with us, okay?" Foster said, his hand on my shoulder

146

ACADEMY OF UNHOLY BOYS

gently leading me to a chair in the back, away from one door. He sat me down, placing his own expensive pair of Vuarnet sunglasses on me. "After Bear takes swings at the models, we'll order pizza and get Monster out for some fun."

So, I remained sitting, still trembling, and Bear took swings with a bat on the antiques, and Foster, true to his word, went and got Monster in the house and brought it back to the barn. The three of us got quite high, I was given the edibles, of course, and we drank Canadian Club and some cheap Scotch, pretending that we were worldly sophisticates, that everything was civil, grand, and above board.

* * *

It was about 3 p.m., and we were still in the barn, listening to Yo Yo Ma playing Bach, and I was trying to get comfortable. The weed had eased me, and I enjoyed the music. I even laughed a few times despite myself, but then I recalled what went down forty-five minutes earlier, with my scraped calf only stinging faintly now, and arm still oozing blood, and my belly sore as hell.

A pepperoni pizza was promptly delivered by Al Basque. As he entered the barn and looked at the destruction around him, he rolled his eyes and shook his head.

"You guys are too bizarre for words," he said, before offering me a slice of pie. I took off Foster's pricey sunglasses.

The man's eyes gave nothing away as they slid over my injuries and surely stoned-out-of-my-gourd expression. "Hi, Jay," he said. "Everything fine?"

"I guess, Al," I said. "Pretty weird, to be honest."

Al smiled slightly, nodding, as if he knew exactly what I meant. I wondered if Al Basque took his own copies of Foster's constant filming and uploaded it with color commentary on a private cruelty-themed subreddit. *It's all getting so goddamned warped,* I thought. Al took the camera then and started recording Foster like it was just another ordinary afternoon with the gang.

Foster finished his share of the pizza, stood up inside his dead dad's barn, and obliterated the Model T and everything else with an aluminum bat, destroying the remaining toys, Pepto-Bismol flying every which way.

"Foster, *stop it!*" his mother shouted, rushing into the barn, her black cashmere wraps billowing behind her. "Shut the damn music off."

"Yes, Mrs. G," Bear said, turning it off pronto. Mrs. G looked at Foster as if she didn't recognize him, his naked torso coated in pink paste, gripping the bat with both hands like a sword.

"What the hell is wrong with you?" she screamed, taking in the mess and decimated treasures. "You've destroyed all these collectibles, and Al, why didn't you put a stop to this?"

Al shrugged and kept recording.

"Back off, Ma," Foster said, catching his breath, wiping his brow.

"Shut up and put some clothes on, Foster," she said. "You're becoming an embarrassment to me, to all your friends."

"Ma," he said, "don't be so—"

"Grow the *fuck* up," Mrs. G said, throwing her hands in the air. "And Al, put the damn camera down for once, and come inside with me. Time to shut the twenty-four-hour Foster's Life Story down forever. I'm sick of it, I can't take it."

* * *

Later that night, our trio met inside the town's old quarry, and Foster handed Bear some multi-colored pills, and me some

ACADEMY OF UNHOLY BOYS

edibles. "Brothers," he said. "Put these on your tongue, and dissolve away into the lovely, libidinous land of luscious lollipops. We are, of course, three weeks away from Thanksgiving, from the Greatest Show on Earth. I also wanted you to absorb and feel it in your marrow that Halloween is the time when the veil between the living and the dead is the thinnest, opaque in so many ways. We're so close to it now, men, you can almost taste the smoke and ashes on our skin."

Foster started a fire pit, and the three of us danced around it, tripping, drinking beer, and smoking pipes. We stripped down to our boxers, Foster to his jock, of course (I forget which color), and did the obligatory bloodletting, slicing our palms. Not very deep.

We collected the blood, added water, and heated it up. It wasn't sanitary, or wise, but we painted our faces and chests with the words *Visualize, Organize, Execute.* Then we downed too much tequila.

"We're tighter than ever," Foster howled. "Undoubtedly revved to do the deed."

"Proclaim it," Bear shouted. "Speak truth, fearless leader."

I felt out of my head at the fire pit—the smoke, heat, and drippy, trippy colors on my body, doing tumbles and whirls in my eyes. My mystic bones catapulted straight through the moon and sun, and ricocheted around the cosmos, leaving bits of myself at each new planet and star. But at the same time, I was obsessed, thinking, *do these guys understand I'm not going to die with them?*Foster asked for some sacrifice from me, a deep secret, something to prove my trust and faith in the brotherhood, *to the cause.* I wanted to tell the tragic story of my father's fall into near oblivion, but I wasn't ready to part with it, didn't yet want to set that horrific fact loose in the world.

Witnessing my father completely disintegrate was *still* too precious to reveal, even high. I had already told Foster part of

149

the loss, but I wasn't ready to talk about the full story yet. So, as I lay on my belly close to the fire, feeling the grass imprinting on my skin, an older, more sinister secret rose.

It was something that had occurred when I was four and it still tormented me. I was in our first home, and a thirteen-year-old girl named Sally and her fifteen-year-old boyfriend, PJ, were babysitting me. PJ showed up five minutes after my parents had left for dinner and a movie. The teens decided to play Truth or Dare, and PJ said he'd give me a special drink if I sprinted around the house naked three times. Being four, I thought, *Sure, why not?*

As I streaked around the house, a station wagon drove slowly past. I lay down in the cool, thick grass on the front lawn. I can still feel the dampness below my belly, and the sound of tittering laughter erupting from PJ and Sally in the doorway. After thirty seconds, the car drove on, its headlights slipping across other parts of the neighborhood.

When they let me back in, PJ and Sally were drinking my dad's vodka, and they let me try a bitter sip—but I couldn't take any of it.

"This kid's game for anything," PJ said, "so let's up the ante on him."

The radio played ancient oldies stuff, like Sam Cooke's, "Chain Gang," and they put their drinks down and twisted around. PJ instructed me—still bare-assed—to move closer, and then he picked me up around the waist with one arm and pulled up Sally's orange T-shirt with his other hand, pushed aside her bra, and bared her right breast.

"It's not right," Sally said.

"If you're not mature enough for this simple act of fun and mischief, Sally," he said. "Perhaps I should ask your pal, Jen, to the dance. You know, the girl with those big *honking...*"

"Fine," Sally said, downing vodka. "I'll do it."

ACADEMY OF UNHOLY BOYS

"See," PJ said. "It'll be fun. Go ahead and kiss it, Jay. Seems like old times with your Momma, I bet, huh?"

"Right," Sally said, nervously laughing.

"This is so cool," PJ said, as I leaned in and kissed her breast, and played with the nipple. I heard the breathing of PJ —whispery, disturbed. I was transfixed, liquid, ashamed, and terrified, as he kept pushing me into Sally.

I'm going to be sick, I thought. *I don't like how PJ laughs— he pants like a dog. He makes me feel sick and terrible.*

"Jay works the teat like a pro, huh?" he said. "You'll remember this day forever."

"Still don't think it's a great idea," Sally said, looking away.

And then out of PJ came this high-pitched, cackling laughter, and it terrified me. The sound freaked me out more than anything else. I was placed down on the floor, and, per PJ's directions, Sally undressed, eventually standing nude in the kitchen. She spun and danced around to Marvin Gaye's "Mercy, Mercy Me," shaking her behind, throwing her arms high in the air, wiggling her hands and fingers. She watched me watching her and I blushed, looking away, but then returning my eyes back to her bare body, her legs, and that little tuft of hair, and her breasts.

When there was a noise from outside, Sally dressed quickly and came toward me, and I flinched, gripping her hand, and began sobbing. She helped me get into my Superman pajamas, consoled me, and took me to my room.

"It's okay, Jay. It's all over now," Sally said. "We're all done, I'm so sorry this happened to you. Never again will this occur, I promise, I swear to God on that."

As Sally tucked me in later, she sat down on my bed and kissed my forehead:

"This is our secret forever," she said. "Never again."

I can still feel every ounce of awkwardness and anxious

discomfort from that night but also the wicked thrill of seeing something and touching something I wasn't supposed to.

When I fell asleep, I had a nightmare about a gargantuan spider spinning its sticky web, its pincers nibbling on my family. I screamed but couldn't get out of the vision. The spider moved toward me, floating across my bedroom with his prickly, far-reaching legs. I saw my parents wrapped dead in silky cocoons, and I looked for an escape.

Suddenly, a door opened, and naked Sally stood there, slouchy, watching me, holding on tight to her vodka, moving provocatively, gesturing for me to come closer. I tried to reach her, but the only thing I heard was the heavy breath of PJ, hovering unseen, and his incessant cackling.

I awoke hollering and had wet the bed for the first time in my life, but not the last. I sprinted to the master bedroom, finding my parents sleeping soundly. I rushed toward them, crying and stammering about the spider.

"Okay, we're here now," Mom said, half asleep. "No spiders. A nightmare, a bad dream, no one's going to grab you, hon."

"They did, Mom," I said. "They already got me."

"Easy," she said. "Get changed out of the wet clothes and sleep in here on the spare cot. Everything's going to be fine, I promise."

Two months later, my folks went to another movie and hired a babysitter the same age as Sally. At night I laid my head on her and listened to her gurgling belly and giggled. We watched part of the box set of *Gilligan's Island* together, and when she shifted my head onto the couch, I raised my left hand and tried to caress one of her breasts.

"*Stop,*" she said, snatching my hand. "You can't do that, or I'll tell your mom."

ACADEMY OF UNHOLY BOYS

After I shared the story with my senior buddies, Bear balked.

"I don't believe that ever happened, Jay."

"Why would I make that up, Bear?"

"I can't see it going down," Bear said. "Babysitter would never do it—females aren't like us. Girls aren't designed the way guys are, they only go so far."

"I believe you, Jay," Foster said. "Humanity can get ugly, male and female, there's no doubt about that."

I looked over at our leader.

"People can be so damn manipulative," he went on. "They can be wooed into doing almost anything with the right... *pressure*."

I watched him study me.

"Does it still haunt you, Jay?"

"Once in a while," I said, flushing.

"Do you still have nightmares?"

"Not really, but sometimes, I guess," I said, fidgeting under his gaze.

"Does Sally leave you all bloody? Chopping off your tally whacker for fun?" he asked, snapping his teeth twice.

"Screw you, asshole," I said, and he laughed and tousled my hair.

"Life's hard, it's a chore, it's a bitch, boys, we all know plenty of stories like that," Foster said. "It's why the three of us are getting the hell out of Dodge on Thanksgiving morning."

What I didn't say to Foster or Bear that night is that each time I see a four-year-old boy I think of it happening all over again to me, and how peculiar that was. When I sank into bed that night, I felt as if I'd been violated somehow, and so I cried, sobbed, really.

I didn't understand why it hurt so much. Or why Foster was so damn lost. Had he always been like that? He said

153

suicide was the only sane response to a human life. Who in the hell believes that kind of bullshit?

I realized he was pathological—and could carry us all over the falls.

Mom heard me crying, of course, and knocked on my door.

"Mom, I'm good."

"Let your mother in, Jay, right this second."

When I unlocked my door, she came in and sat on the bed, massaging my shoulders for a few minutes. "Teenage life isn't always pretty, is it son?" she said.

TUCK

10-31-18

It was Halloween, and by then I'd learned Dr. A doesn't shy from life's messy moments—he embraces whatever challenges face me and exudes vitality and warmth. One day I asked him, "Can we discuss an odd dream of mine?"

"That's a peculiar way to start our session, Tuck."

"I suppose," I said. "If anything, it's more like a short story."

"You don't usually share those," he said. "Why tell me this one?"

"Mine usually don't hang around in my memory bank that long, but this one did," I said. "Remember, it's a story."

"Fire away."

"Of course, I couldn't sleep, so I stayed up until 4 a.m. and jotted it all down. Even had my own father read it, can you believe that?"

"No, but that's wonderful, what'd he say?"

"He loved it, plus he's ecstatic that Dr. Benzo is no longer in our lives," I said. "That guy was a major pain in the ass."

"Cool," Dr. A said. "Amen to that."

"What do you think?" I asked.

DAVID FITZPATRICK

"Listen, I don't give a whole lot to what goes in your head, in the subconscious."

"Right."

"I know that makes me a bit unusual, but I like it when you're awake and conscious."

"I suppose."

"Tell me your story, Tuck," he said. "You're getting to have a knack for these types of things."

"I was a year older than most kids in high school, so I was gangly, towering over the others. In the spring of freshman year, Dad drove me to my first religious retreat in Mystic on the Connecticut Southeastern shore."

"'I'm proud of where you're taking your life with all its ups and downs,' my dad had told me that afternoon. 'You don't quit; I admire that.' I wasn't sure why he said that, but it made me feel older, more grown up, and a little scared. It was my first retreat in high school, and after a day of groups, God-talk, and food, a wiry Greek kid from class, Tony, convinced me to slip out after dinner with a young, flirty girl he wanted to fool around with named Abby."

"Was she pretty?" Dr. A asked.

"Yes, I, too, lusted for Abby McKenna, she had lovely tan, smooth skin, tiny wrists and forearms that were hairless, and her thighs and calves were muscular, ropey, and I wanted to smother them in kisses."

"Let's hear it for healthy teens!" Dr. A said.

"The ten-acre island we were on was also a home to retired priests, and had two chapels, a small, tiny rock one built into the edge of sea, and the larger, more modern and spacious one with stained glass up on land, containing an enormous copper Jesus with toned abs hanging from the ceiling."

"Every deity needs good abs," Dr. A said.

"Yes," I said. "And, as we ran over, escaping the chaperones, I leered at Abby's frame shifting and bouncing in front of me. It was misty but warm, so she was dressed perfectly for the affair, and I loved her outfit. She had a bulky bra beneath a T-shirt, and white shorts with peach panties that hugged her ass so profoundly. I first came upon my butt obsessions while visiting Disney with a grandfather.

"It was almost proto-sexual," I continued. "I looked up that word for you."

"That impresses me," Dr. A said.

"It was like an early warmth, a groove in my belly, as I watched the parade of folks in warm weather attire in Orlando. Suddenly, everything I focused on were behinds—butts, heinies, tushies, asses, and cheeks. It was old ladies, young girls, busty divorcees bouncing around, statuesque movie star-type of women, and chubby K-mart ladies. Some looked exactly like the models they had each Sunday in the newspaper fliers back home, posing just so in their underwear and bras."

"What were you searching for?" Dr. A asked.

"Something hidden, and mysterious inside them drew me —*what exactly lurks there? I* asked myself. *"What's behind the seams of each person?* It wasn't necessarily the fabric—it was the perspiration, the physicality of it, a slippery sheen that appeals to me, which I would describe as succulent. What pulsed beneath the skin? Deep down, way below where secrets fester, where they lay dormant, ready for desire to sprout and erupt into possibility?"

"When Tony, Abby, and I entered the big chapel, the lights were still on, and she shouted, "Let's fuck this world up, boys," and her voice echoed, and I felt fearful, nervous as hell."

"Why the nerves?"

"That we would get caught or insult Jesus, or that he might zap us with a yoke of lifelong suffering. I was acutely aware that Abby had a villainous, mysterious charm, a type of bionic

DAVID FITZPATRICK

superpower over me, and a freedom that I would never feel, never possess, and for the moment, I loathed her and wanted to spank her, punish her for it."

"What did you find within Abby?"

"I couldn't stop studying the female creature—how she moved, breathed, laughed, coughed, sang, cursed, and danced. And when she stretched her hands up toward the giant copper Christ hanging above her, I thought perhaps a new God was emerging. I studied her thin back exposed, and goose bumps up and down her arms and shoulders, and like a geyser, I ejaculated."

Dr. A rubbed his palms, and said, "This is great that you're telling me all this, no shame. I love that about you, Tuck."

"I was fourteen, and I felt intense shame at the time, but also a misplaced and wonderful, glowing kind of reverence. I figured it was a holy orgasm, the closest I'd get to sharing myself with Jesus. It was the mind of a distorted, naive teen, but it was also faith, I felt, and for a few days after, I thought Abby was a type of spirit, an elfin that could lift me to a higher plain of existence. But she went home a day later in a red Dodge van with a broken rear bumper, and I never saw her again in my life."

"That's wonderful," he said.

"That evening, while I'm pulling my royal and gold rugby shirt down to cover the stain, she took a joint out of her back pocket, shocking us both, and said, 'Who wants the first hit?' Soon I felt holes rip open in the sky, and fantasy and magic entered our realm, or at least, mine.

"As Tony and Abby giggled and made out in the corner pew, I sat in front near the altar, and studied a thin, solitary lit candle in a nook beside the Third Station of the Cross. My vision grew fuzzy after a while, and I noticed layered colors dance before me, along with many types of people: athletes, strangers, and the town's drug store owner, and each of them

ACADEMY OF UNHOLY BOYS

levitated before my eyes, and was crying, and sobbing, begging for my time."

"And what did they wish?"

"They wanted me to absolve them," I said. "I never got that, and so, I tried to explain that I was bad, unholy even, that they shouldn't worry about what I thought, I was just a damn kid, but they only grimaced, and pleaded, 'yes, but we come before you, nevertheless.'"

"They presented bizarre gifts to me; honey, bread, meats, bras, watermelon, ice cream, hockey sticks, bars of gold, records, and even dark chocolate. The first gentleman, who owned the pharmacy, confessed how he killed a broken-winged raven and a bunny with a hammer as a young boy, pummeling them into the earth, bones cracking, blood spurting. Next, an athlete wept about his grandma hollering as mental hospital aides in bleached-clean white uniforms dragged her off the porch, and shocked her brain with induced electric seizures, wrecking her, stealing her intricate history from her like a Hoover vacuum stuck on the skull."

"Jesus, what an image," Dr. A said.

"Most tragic was a sweet boy from a distant city stolen off the streets, thrown in a van, and kept underground in a basement for thirteen years. When the evil one that used him in every way possible had a stroke and died, the boy had morphed into a twenty-six-year-old handsome man. People celebrated, gave him drinks at the bar, women were all over him, and he even threw out a first pitch with the all-star baseball catcher at the Stadium.

"There was a tragic crash eight months later, and the famous catcher died, and next day they found that twenty-seven-year-old sweet man in his autographed Yankee T-shirt, hanging from a pipe.

"Oh, that's awful."

DAVID FITZPATRICK

"That being said, it wasn't strictly horrid material—there was mirth, and joy, as well. Photos of a baby's first steps, and shots of that child receiving her diploma from a women's college in the south twenty years later, next a marriage proposal, and the birth of her own child. Whole positive life tales and visions flowed before me."

"Sounds amazing, Tucker," Dr. A said.

"It was," I said. "Each of these people, with ghosts in their mind like flickering cinematic classics and how they zoomed flew around me that night on that island. They wished to be forgiven, mourned, celebrated, scolded, and built up again, redeemed. I felt both overwhelmed and curious about the vision—it was the first time they moved in sync like that, speeding through my mind's eye."

"Go on," he said. "Did you want to touch Abby in the same way or were they on their own wavelength?"

"Kind of both, believe it or not," I said. "She was lovely to look at, obviously, or I wouldn't have had that earlier reaction."

"Of course," Dr. A said.

"Tony and Abby continued their lovefest in the pews, kissing, and petting, and me, Tuck Reis, I looked straight up, way above the trio of us, and caught a glimpse of a fluttering, flamboyant bird on a skylight. It was a sizable pigeon, bleached white, with sky-blue and maize below the eyes and an almost sweet, odd maroon hue at its throat."

"Its large shadow reflected down to the floor where we were, and it reminded me of a favorite photo I took many years earlier as a child. It was of a boy fishing off a pier in Newport, Rhode Island, with seagulls eating breadcrumbs out of his hand, their wings etched like perfect check marks in the bruised sky. And just like that, I was positive God was above me in the chapel."

"Interesting," he said.

ACADEMY OF UNHOLY BOYS

"After witnessing this bird, and the faces flew past with their tragedies and triumphs, I felt a spot, a fold open up above my collar bone, and just below my Adam's apple, and the people with their many desires, sins, and neurotic tales twirled into figure eights before disappearing into my throat where they've been kept safe ever since."

"Okay, go on, which adult came around and ruined the surprise?"

"Lee, a counselor came hustling around the bushes as I left the chapel."

"'Mr. Reis, you've been missing for over an hour,' he said. 'I didn't expect this behavior from someone responsible like you.'"

"What'd they do to you?" Dr. A. asked.

"No snacks for me that night," I said. "But that was cool, I was so moved by that bird, I'll tell you."

"What do you think about all of it today?" he asked. "And why tell me now?"

"I don't know... it was like half-memoir, half-novel: a hybrid effort. I was high from the weed, but still, it made me adjust and have more room in my life for belief. And so, I became a lot less cynical."

"Would you say it was a hallucination?" Dr. A. asked.

"Probably, but it's not like I ran off and became a brother or monk or joined the seminary. I just didn't chase every doubt down a collection of rabbit holes, and in a weird way it kept me from walking too far away."

"Right."

"I mean, I guess have more faith in a God somewhere up there, observing," I said. "Does that sound asinine?"

"Far from it," he said. "Makes total sense."

NOVEMBER 2018

JAY SOUTHER

NOVEMBER 3, 2018

NINETEEN DAYS TO GO

"Theater and drama and fire are essential in this rebellious, driven, and copulating world of ours," Foster announced. It was Saturday, November 3, and the Greatest Show on Earth was lurking two and a half weeks away. In the basement, Foster had donned an oversized red T-shirt that read, "Ski Powder Ridge... or Else!" He stood before Bear and me on his tattered couch, T-shirt, purple jock, jade socks, and navy flip-flops completing his bizarre ensemble. Al Basque circled around me, recording it for posterity, chuckling occasionally.

"Tell us all about it," said Bear.

"Sometimes you have to put yourself out there to achieve the greater good," Foster said.

"How so?" I asked.

"Before our Greatest Show," Foster explained, "we needed to prove to authorities we had the mettle to get things done. So, I fired a warning shot across their bow."

"Indeed," Bear said.

"We had a fantastically fried flesh-fest the other night," Foster said. "We rented out some space with a lady filmmaker

NINETEEN DAYS TO GO

of some renown in the Hartford area. We needed to make some loud and ugly noise. Frankly, we wanted to make the world more curious."

"What went on?" I asked.

"A savvy director rounded up some theater friends and their allies," Foster said. "*Most* of legal age, and they agreed to... what's the word I'm searching for, Al?"

"Was it a collaboration?" Al asked.

Foster laughed, offering a thumbs up. "We collaborated." He was in a jolly mood. He squatted, hunkering over Monster for a bit. For a change of pace, he had passed the teal bong around only once. Bear and I were working on light beers.

Foster exhaled a thick rope of smoke, and paced, his muscular frame in motion.

"I needed a disguise, a façade, so my name was... Al, what was it again?"

"Chewbacca," he said. "Just Chewbacca."

"I bought a Chewy mask at Walmart," Bear said. "And there was a special cameo by a legendary murderer."

"No, no, don't tell him everything, Bear," Foster said. "Just enjoy it, Jay."

"Right."

"Read the poem and return with your honest responses," Foster said. "We'll be posting everything on TikTok, YouTube, Instagram, Facebook, etc., and sending the link to newspapers, blogs, websites, magazines, and TV stations."

"It's cool," Al said.

"Yes," Foster said. "Although, we did miss your presence, Jay."

"You mentioned fire," I replied. "Why select that particular word?"

"It's a lovely noun, adjective, and verb to me," he said. "So amazingly potent and severe yet lovely, one emotional and dynamite force."

"Right."

"We're going to singe, fry, blister, immolate one thing after the next," he said. "Start with very small acts, a photo of a cigarette, then a little bigger, maybe a fire pit in someone's backyard."

"Burn, baby, burn," Bear said, "disco inferno..."

"Thank you, Felipe, for that wonderful rendition," Foster said. He was pacing again. "As time passes, the intensity of our flames will increase. We'll work up to a Port-o-Potty and keep the momentum going. As we get closer to Thanksgiving, there's a secret. Would you like to know a sweet, juicy one?"

"Go for it," I said.

"I'll work alone on this project," he said. "I'll set a goal post on fire at a football field far from us, maybe in a neighboring state, possibly as far off as Delaware."

"Why, though?" Bear asked.

"Try *why not?* It's a lot more fun."

"It all sounds very cool," Bear says.

Foster handed me a piece of notebook paper covered with his surprisingly neat handwriting. At home an hour later, I sat on my father's leather chair in my room and read Foster's poem;

That Damn Tree
By Chewy

Varying gusts whip the naked
Stalk outside my window. It
Strips and blooms ten autumns.
The scene exhausts—

NINETEEN DAYS TO GO

A weathered flag,
The bare lot,
The stark gymnasium
With gargantuan windows.

Up here, I hear drunken
Undergrads cursing at midnight
Occasional traffic accidents,

A rare taxi exploding
in last summer's blaze.
In the city's main artery
Sirens whine.
It's a decent view, especially when
A coat of silencing white falls mid- winter.
If you catch the traffic
After a concert, the merging,
Growling,
and charging

Leaves a yearning
Imprinted within.
One some hungry, ragged boy

Will try to

Name staring out this
Same window
Next fall.

Mom was knocking. "You in there tonight, Jay?"

"What's up?" I rose to unlock the door.

"No partying, huh?" She stepped into my room with her drink.

"Mellow evening," I said. "Want to read Foster's poem?"

"Not really," she said, before examining it. As mom sat on my bed, she sipped her martini and made sounds of appreciation and intermittent grimaces. She stared at me.

"Foster's pen name is Chewbacca?"

"What'd you think?"

She pursed her lips. "Mediocre but harmless work, I guess," she said. "He's no Robert Frost."

"No," I said.

"Foster's clever and handsome," she said. "But ever since he gave you that fancy tote bag of books in the summer, I've sensed something wasn't right."

"Too quick?"

"Something like that," she said. "Cunning *and* chivalrous— not a typical combination."

"I thought that's what every girl wants," I said. "He's like the perfect package."

"He frightens me, Jay," Mom said. "I just think you should be more careful with him, show some caution."

"He's harmless, Ma." I hoped she wouldn't notice the fear on my face or hear how it lodged in my throat. "He only thinks he's king of the world."

"See, that doesn't sound so harmless."

NINETEEN DAYS TO GO

"Huh," I said, before she hugged me, and went off to mix herself another martini before preparing supper.

* * *

Later that night, I slid the thumb drive into my laptop. When I pressed play on the mp4 file, a British-accented female Siri asked, "Who exactly is Chewbacca? Who, whom, whomever, whichever, wherever are you racing with your artistic visions today, my dear lad?"

The black-lit video took place in a sunken wide parlor room, draped with white bed sheets along the perimeter so that you couldn't see out the windows.

"Some frat house," I recalled Bear saying.

A disco ball dangled and spun from the ceiling and an extended mix of "Funky Town" by Lipps, Incorporated blasted along with thumping house music. Foster Gold in a Chewbacca mask, only recognizable by his muscular body and a glow-in-the-dark purple sock taped over his penis. I doubted anyone but I and Bear could recognize him in such a form. He did handstands before an audience of ten young women and ten young men, each wearing only scarlet Fedoras, oversize white sunglasses, high-top Chuck Taylor's, and scarlet scarves covering their naked bodies. They hooted and whistled, applauding the performance.

What the fuck was I watching? Some come-ons from a deluded cult leader? Or maybe a charismatic narcissist burning off his manic energy? The ten young men and ten young women glowed in the dark, body paint turning their skin into horrific alien-like mutations under the purple-blue light. Some cheered with pom-poms, others with confetti, kazoos, and noisemakers, while still others chanted, "Chewy! Chewy!"

The lights swirled through the mist pouring in from fog

machines. The whole thing seemed like a low-budget eighties music video, with enough schlocky touches to make you afraid of glancing away.

As Chewy stood in the mist, he pointed toward two old-fashioned color TV sets in a corner. One showed a fundamentalist snake-handling preacher praising Jesus Christ. The preacher's voice irritated my skull like a hangover—excruciating and relentless. The preacher insisted God would always be there, no matter how many venomous snakes bit him.

The other TV featured a wild orgy. The two screens battled it out, a defiant-preacher with serpents praised the heavens versus moaning, silicone-enhanced porn-stars. A bright red S had been drawn on Chewbacca's chest, which was now smudged with sweat, and Foster squatted for a moment, then leaped into the air, the purple sock somehow remaining as he bounced around, which looked both ridiculous and oddly erotic.

"I'm a capital-S slothful sinner," came Chewbacca's voice. "And I'd like to introduce my fabulous femme fatale, Michael Myers."

A young lady in a white hockey mask rushed center stage, twirling onto the floor with a huge chef's knife in her hand. She was head-to-toe covered in neon body paint, complete with black pasties on her nipples and black bikini bottom. Her white hockey mask glowed as gas-fire blue. The overall effect made her appear as if she were a photo negative as she matched Chewy leap for leap as they moved around the stage.

She jabbed, stabbed, and thrust at him with the large knife, but Chewbacca managed each time to twist away at the last second. This Michael Myers from the vintage 1978 movie *Halloween* had obvious dance training, and her coiling body was the perfect foil for her battle against Chewy. They whirled and the crowd whistled and applauded. Ms. Myers' body paint left glowing blotches on Chewbacca's skin whenever they met one another. Her body had dark streaks where paint had rubbed off or melted.

She eventually dropped the knife, and the two shook, shimmied, and tried a version of the tango, followed by the hustle, until they attempted every damn wedding dance in the book. The crowd applauded and tossed Mardi Gras beads, jewelry, Gingko leaves, butt plugs, and penny candy. The couple strolled down the aisle as the music changed to an organ-heavy wedding march. Up next was vigorous calisthenics with three hundred jumping jacks to Olivia Newton John's ancient, goofy anthem, "Let's Get Physical." Chewbacca and Myers did pushups, sit-ups, some yoga planks, before ending it all with a downward dog. They had gone strong and hard, dancing, spinning, faux-stabbing, and twirling for quite some time. They had leered at each other, but other than the occasional incidental contact while dancing, their bodies had remained separate.

"I feel," Chewbacca's voiceover pronounced, "the need for some physical release."

So Chewy and Meyers lay supine beside each other on a mattress, continuing to ogle one another, but without touching. I paused the video, bracing myself wondering how they'd pulled all this shit off and whether they had rehearsed.

I hit the space bar on my laptop. Chewbacca crawled across the floor to the color tv's in the corner of the room, and leaned forward, kissing the preacher on the screen, and did the same to the people having the loud orgy on the other set. Myers timidly approached Chewy and whispered in his ear.

Chewbacca nodded at her, before picking up a sledgehammer beside the mattress, and, in a sudden rage, proceeded to destroy both TV sets, which crescendo-ed to Pavoratti singing "La Boheme." Screens shattered and burst, glass raining down on the floor like hail on a winter pond. The porn stars were the first to be destroyed, followed by the preacher, rattlesnakes, and believers.

The crowd cheered and the opera music ceased. Celebratory champagne was uncorked and poured over the heads of Chewbacca and Myers, still in their masks.

Up next, Carly Simon's take on "As Time Goes By" played: *"You must remember this, a kiss is still a kiss, a sigh is just a sigh. The fundamental things apply as time goes by..."*

Chewy and Meyers danced formally, as if they were awkward fifth graders. When the dance ended, an older man, a judge in a black gown on stilts with an enormous yellow wig and hot-pink face came to center stage and blew a penny whistle. Myers turned and kissed Chewy on the cheek, her unyielding face pressing grotesquely into Foster's pliable but hairy rubber mask, and the lights went out.

When the spotlight returned, Chewbacca was in a purple bathrobe, halfway secured, his feet trailing some blood from shattered TV sets. He held hands with Myers.

"I want people out in the world to understand I know exactly what they're about," he said. "And what they scheme, and fake in public while doing other crap behind closed doors. What the world has witnessed here today is nothing short of beauty and style with a capital BS—time for cultured snobs to face our toned, wonderful, and impassioned brilliance. I also wanted to give a shout out to the killer herself, Ms. Myers, my favorite anonymous college girl-boy in one delightful package. I love you both."

Myers turned and waved, before she quickly disappeared into the crowd.

"See you soon, my dearest lonely souls of the Connecticut shoreline," Chewy said. "Keep an eye out for the Greatest Show on Earth coming to rock you to your very core."

NINETEEN DAYS TO GO

The screen faded to black and then I didn't know what to do, so I took a cold shower, impressed, and flabbergasted.

* * *

I locked my door and planned to get myself off. My tripping mind envisioned Foster in a steamy shower when, instead of a naked high school homecoming queen with impossibly buoyant breasts and a heart-shaped ass, a surprise guest showed up.

A naked Basil Sous sauntered over to Foster. I felt wildly conflicted, but incredibly turned on. Basil serviced him, before she pushed him down onto the floor, and slid her body onto Foster's shaft, and gradually, slowly, they had sex together, Basil's lovely breasts bouncing every which way, her back arched.

I couldn't ignore my excitement as I saw this vision take place, but I tried with all my might, goddammit, not to grab it. I didn't want to give in to the wild itchy need—it felt wrong, both of my fantasies co-mingling together like that. Something my ailing dad would truly be disappointed in me for having done. So, I stood and tried to do ten pushups. I stopped after four. I did three sit-ups. While doing this, I was as quiet as possible. Mom's hearing usually didn't miss a thing.

A minute later, though, I was on the bed, thinking of Foster and Basil Sous getting down, madly stroking away. Amid it was the dilemma rattling my psyche: *How fucked up am I?*

Eighteen Days to Go
Bear Santos
11.04.18

I feel like I had my mom's cassette tapes in my possession for several years, but I think I started appreciating them, becoming aware of their importance, in early November of senior year. I felt a spinning, whirling pit in my belly each day that grew bigger the closer we crept to Thanksgiving. The only proof I had of my mother's existence besides photographs is her voice on one black cassette tape labeled "Carly Laughing." The opposite side reads "Carly for President and Her Numerous Isssssues," spelled with five S's. On them, Mom, known as Carlita or Carly, was fourteen and playing games with her sister, Rose. Apparently, Rose had labeled the recordings.

"Generally, Rose, what's your political stance on monarch butterflies?" or, "How many Twinkies do you think Jesus Christo would have devoured in one sitting if they were around when he was alive?" or, "If I'm president, could I automatically declare Puerto Rico a state, no questions asked?"

Silly, I know, but when I hear the tape, it keeps me smiling and feeling buoyant. My mother was funny, clever, relatable, and undoubtedly alive—the tape had a legit spark of truth, you know?

The cassette featured her kicking back and being true, showing her real self. She was born in America, so her accent was only slight, but the emotion in her voice, even if it was just a laugh, or a sarcastic retort, seemed to move the sands around in my chest, like the eddies of outgoing tides. Somebody could easily claim the voice on the tape might be Rosie Perez, Viola Davis, or Michelle Obama's voice asking about colorful butterflies or the consistency of Twinkie cream in heaven.

What I mean is how does one really know what's fact and what's not? The Reverend preaches that one had to have faith about such things. So, I guess I felt that way about the cassette tape—I just *knew* it was her. That said, Carly couldn't carry a tune to save her life, but she giggled so freely, like a class clown.

Her older sister, Rose, visited my father and me nine years ago and told me Carly also enjoyed oversized black, cable-knit Irish sweaters, Fig Newtons, Dr. Seuss books, Stephen King and Danielle Steele novels, macadamia nuts, black and white photographs, Honeycomb cereal, and the mosaic of colors at sunset.

Carly has been gone eighteen years, my whole life. She became a legal adult on her wedding day. I realized this meant she was my age when she brought me into the world, only four short years after she made the cassettes. Funny, because whenever I've listened to the recording, which was frequently before the Greatest Show, it felt like she was in the room with me, straddling the divide between the living and dead. Life, death, Mom, Bear, Carly, Felipe, laughter, tears, sometimes the tape reduced me to tears, while other times it charged me up, filling me with optimism.

Carly died from an overdose of painkillers and anti-anxiety medications—or at least that's according to Rose. The Rev, though, always disputed that. He loathes illness, whether that's physical or mental. Various cancers, varicose veins, influenza, heart problems, arthritis, diabetes, pancreatitis, warts, and obesity. He especially hates "melancholia," which was what shrinks once called clinical depression.

My father didn't mind me holding on to my mother's cassette, which I kept in my bottom drawer and pulled out periodically, listening to it on an ancient Boom Box. After her first overdose, the Reverend sent my mom away to live with her people. I like to pretend I remember her soft breath on my nose, maybe the colors of a bright yellow dress, or the chenille fabric of it against my cheek, or her wide pupils and blue irises, but Dad insists that is not possible.

"I don't care," I told him stubbornly. "I know her in a yellow dress with all her toes painted rainbow colors, humming off-key to 'Celebrate' by Kool and The Gang." My father also hates the word "addict;" the Reverend believed self-help groups were without any worth and refused to recognize them. He fought against the face of addiction, even in his congregation, or his dead wife.

"Those folks lack vertebrae," he ranted once. "It was weakness, pure and simple, lack of faith and determination, broken souls. Who has room for the broken?"

I responded with, "Aren't we all broken sir? Wasn't Jesus a bit fractured, human, and damaged? Isn't that what makes his tale more relatable to the masses?"

He slapped me so hard it tore my bottom lip open, and said, "Don't ever talk about the Lord that way, or I'll send you to live with your San Antonio relatives."

I was on the floor as he rattled on.

"You start that sensitive, humanism gibberish and you can join the mainstream Christian powder puffs," he continued. "That's pure homosexual crap."

"Maybe San Anton has something not available around here," I said through my fingers, which were wet with my own blood, "like love and support."

"You're nothing but a betrayer," he hissed. "A Judas figure in my eyes."

So, I clamored to my feet and left him in his lonely storefront church and walked home to do 333 pushups in my room, trying to concentrate on tangible results. Sit-ups, pushups, and then more stretching. Some breathing exercises, maybe, even try a few yoga positions, in and out, breathe slowly, fully. Just stay in the physical and not let my father destroy my mind with his caustic, ugly thoughts. Our toxic conversations really haven't got any better since that time, but I try not to let it ruin my day.

JAY SOUTHER

MONDAY, NOVEMBER 5, 2018
SEVENTEEN DAYS TO SHOWTIME

I saw Foster at practice the following day on a damp November afternoon, and we walked out to the field together. Nearly every deciduous tree surrounding the school appeared naked and stripped, thanks to a blustery dawn rainstorm.

"That Chewy recording you made was nasty and wicked," I acknowledged, my cleats feeling heavy in the mud.

"I wanted to keep it tame," Foster said. "Almost every actor was an adult—I wanted for us to dress like sluts but offer only a brief kiss."

We crossed over the track and onto the soaked field.

"Where'd you find Myers?" I asked. "She was smoking, and sledgehammering the TVs was pretty wild action."

"She was a UCONN first year, believe it or not," he smiled, "and so damn fierce. She appreciated my natural affinity for destruction."

"It was a tasteful yet risqué performance," I said.

We watched a W. B. Mason truck back up across the street: *Beep. Beep. Beep.*

"Were you jealous of Myers last night, Jay?"

"Huh?" I said, blushing.

"It's okay to desire me," he said, grinning. "Nothing to be ashamed of."

"You're projecting, I think," I said, hoping to distract him with some psychobabble I'd picked up in my long hours of Dad therapy.

Foster knocked my arm. "Handle it as you see fit, man."

I watched him study me, both of us waiting.

What the hell does he want me to say now? I wondered.

Thankfully, he moved on. Bored of waiting, maybe. "What'd you think of my poem?"

"Did it represent your life?" I asked. "Autobiographical, maybe?"

"I don't know," he said. "Everyone struggles. I just got my crap out of the way early."

He seemed to be leading me, encouraging questions. "What kind of crap? Therapy or something?" I shrugged. "That's no big deal. Not like a psychiatric hospital or anything."

"Must you know every itty-bitty detail of my early life, Jay?"

"Doing a cover story on you for *Esquire*," I said. "A tell-all."

He spat on the field and wiped his chin. "I took the Yale University tour once with my mom around New Haven," he said. "Many years ago, now."

I stayed quiet, waiting for more.

"We walked by a group home on Broadway, in a questionable area of New Haven," he said. "Place used to be a funeral home—I was convinced I'd lived there in another life."

He was gesturing, smiling.

"I wanted to take a thousand photos of the building," he said. "I'm positive I'd spent time there. Mom got furious at me for taking so many pictures. *'This has nothing to do with the Yale tour,'* she yelled. *Nothing whatsoever. You're missing all*

SEVENTEEN DAYS TO SHOWTIME

the important facts about Yale education, son. Why mess your life up like this?"

"I didn't know you were into reincarnation," I said.

"Neither did I," Foster said. "Until I saw myself breaking bread with the hurting souls, or what's the politically correct term for the psychically ailing nowadays?"

"Mental illness has morphed into MI, I think," I answered, trying to be helpful.

"Maybe mad denizens of the delirious depths?" he continued like I hadn't spoken. "Or are they just called those with lived experience now?"

I shrugged, and he went on.

"Regardless, I nearly fell in with some truly disturbed, chronic souls. Not in New Haven, but with younger kids, a long while back."

"Where?"

"Guess."

"West Coast?"

"No."

"Midwest?"

"Yep."

"Kansas?"

He shook his head. "Close. Missouri," he said, "outside Columbia—a real buggy place."

"Can I be frank with you?"

"Please do," Foster said, gently guiding us away from the field, where other players stretched and tossed footballs to the dugout built on the practice field. There was scattered trash on the ground around it, Milky Way wrappers, Diet Coke cans, and Foster gathered it all slowly, methodically, and disposed of it in a dumpster.

"Do you believe you're so different now compared to when

you were depressed?" I asked. "Years pass, and you're still as suicidal and destructive as ever."

His face flushed.

"What if you got serious therapy, Foster?" I asked. "Your family has the cash."

"You're naïve, Jay," he said. *"Acutely so."*

"Life doesn't have to end right now, man," I said. "It really doesn't—you'd be a kick-ass actor in Hollywood, I think. The Chewbacca thing was terrific. Emmy material."

"The three of us will die on November twenty-second, 2018," he said. "Don't you see the inherent beauty in all of it?"

I stopped and investigated Foster's face, handsome as ever, eyes dancing with their different colors. His pupils were tiny black beads, his lips forming a slight grin.

"Beauty of *what?*"

"Mr. Death dances on *my* terms," he said. *"I* make the choice, *I* set the mood, *I* tighten the noose. I'm the master of the whole goddamned proceeding."

"You could do all those things and still live, though," I pleaded.

"Enough," he yelled, then elbowed my left cheek, knocking me to the ground.

"You're an asshole, Foster," I said from my knees, holding my face. "That was a cheap shot from a real bastard."

"I didn't mean to hit you so hard," he said, trying to pull me to my feet.

"Get away from me, man," I said, staying down for several seconds. Players and coaches were looking over at us, and Foster was obviously cognizant of that.

"Come on, Jay," he said, "stand up with me now. It's only a bruise, I promise. I'll put some ice on it myself..."

I shook my head. "You can be such an arrogant tool and foolish shithead."

SEVENTEEN DAYS TO SHOWTIME

He rubbed my back. "I'm truly sorry about the wild elbow, okay?"

"Can't just hit people whenever you feel like it, Foster."

"A little rough love, that's all it was," he said, tone trying for playful, fingers massaging into my shoulder now. "Seeing if you have a taste for that type of thing."

"Whatever."

"Don't be blind to the hell that exists around us all out here, man," he said, frustrated now that I wasn't playing along. "Nothing's waiting there for you either, Jay, nothing but the ugly, unfathomable abyss."

He slammed both of my shoulders ten times fast. It reminded me of when we'd first met. Then, it had been thrilling, the way his fists sent vibrations through my football pads. There was something deeply unnerving about it now, his palms stinging my skin.

"Zilch! Zero! Nada!" he shouted, spittle flying everywhere. Then he stalked off towards the other players, leaving me stunned, partly dizzy.

* * *

After Foster exploded that day on the practice field, I kept seeing all those anonymous notes from T in my mind, from the whistleblower, whomever he or she was. By the time I'd arrived home after practice, the story of a Chewbacca-masked teenager with a glow-in-the-dark-purple-socked cock being chased by a sexy co-ed in a Mike Myers mask swinging a chef's knife was everywhere—on local and national channels like CNN, CBS, ABC, PBS, and MSNBC. FOX was running commentaries on the decline of western civilization as they played frequent clips of scantily clad Chewy and Meyers dancing and shaking around. Pundits from around the conservative universe weighed in on the recording.

Even the BBC, Le Monde, and Russian-state TV picked up the story. The Hartford Police were looking into a recent production that Trinity College's theater and film students had produced and were questioning several fraternities where the film was rumored to have been recorded. It was said some actors used in the filming might have been minors.

"FIND.CHEWIE.COM," Foster would say when I spoke to him on the phone later that night.

"What's that?" I asked.

"The name of a new fan-boy site," he said. "Don't you just love show business?"

I joined Mom in the kitchen, washing my hands while she fumbled with the microwave, removing our frozen dinners with the sleeves of her blue bathrobe. I grabbed napkins and silverware and set it up on the blue leather couch. Mom brought the turkey, green beans, cherry pie, and two biscuits to the coffee table.

We stopped eating at the kitchen table some years ago—TV dominating our lives, crowding out conversation, and sucking our brains away. QVC and Home Shopping Network were a constant presence. She had, mercifully, muted the TV tonight. Mom hurried back to the kitchen to grab her Martini.

"Letters coming in twice a week for you, Jay," she said, as she returned to the couch. "I sniff them to see if they're spritzed with perfume or something."

I was acutely aware of those letters, and how they were both alarming and affirming. They floated over my head, not dissimilar to a swarm of hornets, circling, buzzing, waiting to strike. I wondered how the person knew so much about what was going on with our trio. Was he spying, maybe? Was he smarter than

SEVENTEEN DAYS TO SHOWTIME

all three of us, some kind of omniscient teenaged superhero who had my back? And why were the letters always riddled with misspellings? To better hide the author? Who the hell was this soul? Could it be a young woman, even? Or an adult? Was she messing with me somehow? Laughing from a distance as she simultaneously drove me away and toward Foster?

"It's not like that, Ma," I said. "They're anonymous—only signed with a T."

"Could be anyone then," she said. "But whatever you're taking each night is messing with your head badly—I know that much."

"Just booze," I said, "and weed. Mostly edibles, they say it's all harmless."

"You've got to get better at self-care, Jay," she said. "Take a break from those seniors if you can."

"Mom, relax," I said. "Foster can be friendly and warm. Refreshing, you never expect it from someone like him, you know?"

"Foster's a silky con artist, Jay," she said. "You gab about him like you're under a spell, and that concerns me tremendously."

"Oh, what a tragedy that would be."

"Don't be a smart ass," she said. "I don't want you to get involved with something you can't handle, okay?"

"Would that really be the end of the world, Ma?" I asked. "Seriously, would it?"

"Wait a minute," she said, spilling some of her favorite drink on the table. "*What?*"

"I mean, there are worse things in the world, correct?"

"I guess so," she said, her affect blunted, wan. "But you promised me you wouldn't fall for him. We had a deal about all that, correct?"

I rushed to my bedroom, slamming the door, only to come

back a few moments later, holding my forehead as if I'd been shot.

"Nothing to worry about, Ma," I said, feeling dizzy. "Sorry. I think I just need some ice water."

"I don't understand," my mom said, hustling to the kitchen to grab me water and ice, and when she returned, she was teary. "Sit with me on the couch and be rational."

"Affairs of the heart are rarely rational," I mumbled.

Her eyes were bloodshot. I wondered how frequently mine were, too. "So I wasn't that far off with my impression of you?"

"It's—we're... fine. For the most part, it's...nothing I can't handle."

"Who gave you that nasty bruise on your cheek?" she asked and reached out, touching my yellowish-blue contusion, and I recoiled as if her hands were red hot.

"Football is a rough sport, Ma..."

"But you only punt the ball and run off the field, right?" she said.

Her hands trembled, and I stared at the living room rug.

"It was *him.* Foster. Right?" She took a few breaths.

"What about the young lady with the wonderful colors?" she asked, gesticulating. "The public-school girl on the skateboard?"

"Yes, Basil Rutherford Sous. She's great, I'm crazy about her, Ma," I said. "Might even be falling head-over-heels in love with her. My point is you're making me feel weird and wrong for liking a guy. That's old news. It's 2018, if a dude likes other dudes, then whatever, right?"

"But to clarify..."

"I like both, okay?" I replied. "Let it go, Ma."

I felt my gut swirl as Mom dabbed a napkin at the corners of her lips, and I was suddenly outside myself, studying Jay Souther from the ceiling fan, going around and round. *Do I*

SEVENTEEN DAYS TO SHOWTIME

really like guys? I thought. *Have I ever admitted that? Is it true to begin with?*

"I wish I could give everything up," I said, my fingers white-knuckled on the plastic cup. "Drop the hell out, go to an island somewhere and just *veg* out. Go straight to Christmas and forget all about October and November. I just want to skip those rotten months this year. I'm starting to loathe the sport of football."

* * *

Around 3 a.m., my phone went *ping, ping, ping.* More texts. Our fearless leader dictating his goals, no doubt, as he did during English, football practice, or in the middle of the night while I was trying to get some freaking shut-eye. There were only a few weeks to go before the Greatest Show and I grabbed my cellphone off the bedside table, knowing what it would be but feeling I had to make sure. I couldn't fall back to sleep unless I saw it. Yep. There it was.

Visualize.

Organize.

Execute.

"Go back to bed, dear," Mom yelled from the living room. The Home Shopping Network was blaring, but, somehow, she managed to hear every ping. I rolled over and drifted off to sleep.

BASIL SOUS

11.06.18

SIXTEEN DAYS TO GO

Sometimes Jay would text me in the middle of the night. We didn't see each other often now that football season was in full swing, and I was working part-time at Wave café, but I liked connecting with him over messages. On one night, a Tuesday, the sixth of November and he called our wee hour texting sessions his sanity check, but he wouldn't tell me why he needed such a thing.

Sometimes I get these night terrors, he admitted at one point.

What are they about? I wrote back.

For the longest time he wouldn't say, but once he wrote, *Seniors' BS can become real at times, and that scares the crap out of me.*

To me, these moments felt somehow more honest, more anonymous even in their intimacy. But then other times, he phoned, and I could tell he was drunk or high, and that pissed me off.

"Hey, there," his deep voice slurred.

SIXTEEN DAYS TO GO

"What do you want?"

He laughed, which was also irritating. "Jus' to talk to you."

"I won't take that bait. It's late, Jay," I said.

"Oh," he said. "Sorry, Dr. Seuss, I was just finishing my green eggs here."

"Wow, you really are a virtuoso of prose and humor."

"Watch it, that kind of teasing hurts," Jay said.

"Is everything a bad joke tonight?" I asked, looking out the window of my bedroom. I could hear the Sound crashing against the dark rocks out there, and the wind was howling. The first-floor windows were having their own type of ghost bash, rattling and squeaking left and right. I was in my pajamas and had been nodding off. Peg had gone to sleep an hour earlier.

"What?" He tried to regain composure. "Is it National Send Flowers to Your Girl Crush Day?"

"Are you high?" I asked. "I don't want to have a ridiculous drug chat."

"I apologize," he said, his tone immediately changing gears. "I'm going to stop, I am. It wrecks me, I get jumpy. I don't know how to act anymore. What I do like... is that I don't have to act with you."

"Sorry, Jay," I said, so fed up. "I don't want to be your best sober friend."

"Don't you still want to be my first kiss?"

"You're sweet," I said. "And charming and kind in your own indirect way..."

"But?" he said in the most hurt voice.

"I don't socialize with druggies."

"I want to tell you about my father," he said suddenly, almost breathlessly.

"I don't want to have this chat when you're wasted, Jay," I said. "I want to hear it from your heart."

188

BASIL SOUS

"He lost it, Basil," he said. "Had a breakdown, I guess, or went bonkers, or whatever the scientific phrase is nowadays..."

"Jay..."

"I don't know where he is now, but still... somehow I want you two to meet."

I listened.

"Look, you're a kind guy," I said. "But you've got to get away from those hyenas."

"Don't I get a couple chances?" he asked. "In the movies, people get multiple chances, right?"

"No, I don't think so," I said. "You've used all your chances up."

"I'm still going to watch you flying around on the Green," he said. "Waiting for your kiss."

"Get a hold of yourself."

"How?" Jay asked, sounding genuine. "How the hell do I do that?"

"Look me up when you're finished with the seniors," I said. "We'll talk then."

* * *

Our family had moved from Missouri to New Jersey and then on to Connecticut rapidly and I was struggling with constant questions about my lack of parents: Just what exactly they were doing so far away from their little girl? What was their plan for me? And why they took off on my fifth birthday to Costa Rica?

Aunt Peg took me out of kindergarten that late morning in Missouri on the day my folks left, and she drove thirteen-year-old Avery and me to an ice cream shop on the other end of town. We had orange and raspberry sherbet on sugar cones with chocolate jimmies.

"First, abandon your five-year-old daughter on her birthday, and leave no note, no gift or cake, nothing," Avery said. "Who the hell does that to their kids?"

"Broken souls," Peg said. "Splintered and wounded people, Avery."

"Still, though," my brother kept saying. "I can't get over their cruelty."

We had McDonald's cheeseburgers that night and warm Dr. Pepper and a waxy number five candle that we only lit for a few minutes, until I blew it out and wished that life would get a lot better for our trio. Peg and Avery tried to sing the happy birthday tune for me, but it was sad, sort of half-assed. I remember we had Cool Whip as an expensive treat that night. I ate too much of it, along with a Hostess cupcake and Doritos, and felt sick to my stomach. Peg and Avery bought a used-looking Paddington Bear for me; I recall that.

Then Avery died when I was in sixth grade—he was twenty at the time and I missed him terribly. My brother had been the only one who resembled a parental figure, although Peg had morphed into her guardian role as the years slid past. Avery schooled me on many life tasks and his absence hit me like a freight train.

I kept telling teachers about my folks leaving the country, but I knew they were only talking points, excuses I used, instead of facing the real anguish of Avery's death. Or so I tried to say to my freshman-year teacher at St. Catherine's in Gently. I was a hardship student, and Mrs. Haley was teaching about the circles of life in terms of birth, growing, maturing, dying, mourning decaying and all of it is part of the circle of families and I got snappy and said sometimes parents break the family circles.

"You may be relatively new to our town, but our students do not disrespect family like that." Ms. Haley answered, and promptly spanked me three times.

"Go to hell," I said.

"Get to the principal's office now and apologize before your God."

I went to the office, my ass stinging, but there was no one there, and I spotted the principal, Sister Annabelle, heading to her yellow Ford SUV. I rushed out of the emergency exit and hustled to the sidewalk and caught up with her just as she got into her vehicle.

I quickly told her the recent events, shouting a little to be heard from outside the car, since she refused to roll down the window. Once I'd finished, I stared at her with all the expectation of Sister Annabelle's timely firing, but my principal waved her hands at me like one does to a pesky fruit fly. "Give me a moment of peace, okay, Basil Sous?"

"I'm sorry, Sister," I said, my face against the driver's side window. "I wasn't insulting Mrs. Haley, and I'm sorry I mentioned not having parents, as well."

Sister Annabelle snorted, shaking her head as her automatic window slid down.

"You keep stumbling around this year, huh, Basil?"

"I don't mean to, but I guess so."

Sister sat for a minute before opening her door: "So you do or don't have parents?"

"Both."

I told her about the dangers of parental chats with anyone in the world. "It's not safe to say I do have parents nor that I don't, but truth is they've abandoned me for the country and people of Costa Rica when I turned five, and they have no real interest in me. They were usually high on drugs when they were around Avery and me before vanishing like ghosts. No apologies, no explanations. Only the smell of weed, a stuffed toilet, and then BAM! They were out the door and never returned."

SIXTEEN DAYS TO GO

I tried to hold back my emotion, but I sobbed, and Sister Annabelle embraced me, and I smelled her sweat and cheap, fruity type of shampoo. Was it maybe Herbal Essence?

"Why did your folks do such an awful thing to a sweet young girl?" she asked.

As I wept, I realized that was the kind of question adults ask when there's no proper answer—they let the words hang out there like someone's laundry on the line.

Sister Annabelle was so concerned that she drove me to our temporary home on the Sound, but not before purchasing two of my favorite things, a candy bar and a Ginger Ale. Sister had called ahead so Peg was waiting for us on the porch and offered Sister some tea, cheese, and crackers. The nun told Peg I had signs of being a depressive, and other concerns.

"Like what?" Peg asked.

"I fear that Basil could turn to self-harm."

"I don't agree," she said. "And I don't see how a modern school, Catholic or otherwise, should be spanking any young woman like Basil."

"Mrs. H definitely over-reacted," Sister said. "But she recently lost her mom."

"We're sorry about that loss," Peg said. "But Basil will attend public school next year."

"I'd recommend some counseling," she said. "Basil's doing a good job at school, but everyone needs help, and our counselors are free, and maybe she could talk about the death of her older brother back in October."

"We've avoided that one—it's too damn raw."

"Grief can shred you," Sister said. "It doesn't help to skip over it, it's always there, and must be dealt with."

So, I saw a female social worker who also taught guitar for a few sessions, but when she pushed me to talk about Avery, she kept handing me Kleenexes, eventually insisting that I hold the bulky blue tissue box in my hand, and I got pissed off and told her I didn't want to discuss Avery or cry on that particular day so I walked out of her office. I waited for Peg to pick me up, and a day later, a FedEx truck dropped off the guitar, so I took it into the cellar and smashed the instrument to splinters with Avery's old Black and Decker hammer.

Peg asked me about the guitar and social worker in a distant way that night, although I knew she felt it wasn't healthy to ignore such open wounds. A day after I destroyed the guitar, Peg installed a pear-shaped Speed bag she'd bought off Craigslist for me to hit in the basement.

She also carted down piles of decaying objects. There were torn shirts, raggedy boots, old shoes, deteriorating football shoulder pads, and cracking rubber balls, and were placed a few yards from the furnace. I punched the Speed bag, which was fastened near the bulkhead door, and wrecked the rest of the objects, embracing the daily exertion. I ripped, kicked, pummeled, and tore with scissors, the hammer, and a trusty baseball bat.

I wrote, "Destroyed," in red pen on yellow legal pad and placed it on the finished pile. The remaining scraps got carried away while I was at school, and shipments of "not yet destroyed" objects showed up twice weekly near the furnace, just as before. I never met the people who delivered the stuff, or took it away, save for Peg.

The rest of that school year, my schedule was straightforward; four times a week I stepped off the bus in the afternoon, had two potato chips and one glass of apple juice, and headed downstairs to the pile. I punched the Speed bag for fifteen minutes with light gloves and destroyed the delivered materials for another sixty.

SIXTEEN DAYS TO GO

I played old and new music. They had a magnificent sound system: Kendrick Lamar, Maggie Rogers, the Beatles, Rolling Stones, Stevie Wonder, Stevie Nicks, Megan the Stallion, Coldplay U2, Tom Petty, The Cure, Counting Crows, Lizzo, Chance the Rapper, Radiohead, Shawn Colvin, Cardi B, Bon Iver, and Beyonce. They surrounded me as sweat, tears, spit, snot, and everything else flew onto the concrete.

The grieving, or "rages," as I refer to them now, continued for March, April, May, and all of June. It was like chaotic precision, one step after the next, four times a week, day after day like measured synchronized outbursts. There was so much anguish, hurt, and swirling turbulence in that dank space, and yet somehow the sweat and visceral kick, shriek, and punch helped me reconstruct a primal, steady backbone.

One week before I finished my first year of high school, I scribbled in red pen on a yellow legal pad, "All Done," and placed it at the top of the cellar stairs. I retreated to the living room and watched *The Simpsons*, and never visited the basement in any significant way again, except to unhook the Speed bag and carry it into the garage. That Saturday, I found new boxing gloves waiting for me there, and I became one fit little girl and a rabid boxing fan for life.

That may sound too vague or negligent on Aunt Peg's part, but she and I never said a lot about Avery's death except to cry together once *real* hard early on—we wept nonstop for about two hours beside each other, sobbing turned into sniffling which became laughing and then back again to weeping. After that, Peg never spoke about my folks' abandonment, or what was occurring in our cellar weekly, although I consider it one of the sweetest, most compassionate acts of love she ever offered me. In her own meandering way, Peg left a trail for me to follow and slowly, awkwardly, I did just that and returned to the world. Never completely healed or eased, but better than I thought I could be.

"I had a pal who helped me in a similar way years ago," Peg said. "I lost two pets within a short amount of time as a tiny girl, and I didn't think I'd ever recover, so she introduced me to boxing and sweet acts of exertion."

Thinking back now, trying to find the precise truth feels futile. I'm just starting to process all this with Dr. Athens, so it'll take a while, I know. I felt the lack of my brother's presence like an expanding cyst in my gut, and for a time I believed if I prayed hard enough, perhaps his spirit would return inside a spunky dog or cat and transform my life.

Is that silly? Or delusional? Or both?

Turns out it was weirdly spot on. A black cat named Trudy sat on the basement stairs and watched my daily efforts over the early spring and summer. All I had for food was unsweetened applesauce and Trudy took to that stuff like it was crack. Afterwards, I let her out and she slipped back into her other life. But she waited for me when I got off the school bus each day, tagged along and came in through a side door.

I fed her in the basement, and she observed me like a wise coach, absorbing everything before rolling onto her back and offering her tummy to me when I finished up. Today I know the eye of ferocious grief, shame, depression, traumas, and brainstorms are hovering elsewhere, obliterating young and not-so-young lives in Calhoun, Gently, Madison, Chattanooga, Wilmington, Chicago, Springfield, Provo, Jackson, and Middletown.

Of course, I wish all of them stability and wellness, wish them an easier time than I had, but who knows how helpful wishes and prayers are? Usually, I stick to the belief that says prayer eases and soothes, like a cooling balm or a warm, crackling fire on a frigid Monday night in February. But there are

SIXTEEN DAYS TO GO

also times when life's nothing but a bewildering struggle, and I wonder just how unattended I really am.

I linger on those difficult days and wonder if there wasn't some force at work, a compassionate goodness keeping an eye on me, Peg, Jay, Tuck, Trudy, Dr. Athens and every other young fool in the Nutmeg State. Helping us to lead halfway decent lives, to defeat the doubts, that aloneness in our chests.

JAY SOUTHER

11.08.18

FOURTEEN DAYS TO GO

Bear and Al retired early, so it was just me and Foster in the basement, drinking beer, downing edibles, listening to Alabama Shakes. It was Thursday, November eighth, and Foster was in a groove, twisting about, barely dressed. I used the bathroom, and as I emerged Foster grabbed my shoulders, shaking them playfully.

"You still buzzing, Jay?"

"You bet," I said, and watched my friend's blue and green eyes dance.

"One cool fact," Foster said, "is that when two pals bond, a communion occurs, a higher type of connection."

He looked exhausted despite his moving and shaking about.

"Ready to be transformed?"

I felt fearful, but Foster grinned—it was all he did that night. "Hmmm...Maybe?" I answered. *Ask him about the elbows, the shoving,* I thought. *Go ahead, Jay, ask him.*

"It'll be festive, and wild, Jay," he said. "Accu-Weather forecast calls for clear blue skies and canary-yellow sunshine for weeks."

FOURTEEN DAYS TO GO

"Why'd you elbow me at your dad's barn and on the practice field?"

"Unbridled rage, I think," he said simply. "You discombobulate me."

I tilted my head.

"I want it gone from us, though," Foster said. "Wiped from our memory banks forever, understand?"

"But why did it happen in the first place, though?"

"Stressful school days," he said. "Like a sensual thunderstorm rolling past."

"Is that supposed to be an apology?"

"Best I can do so late." He patted my face with his palms, as if he were a mob boss sending his favorite hit man to the fishes. He started pushing me to my knees, and I resisted, looking up at him.

"What's this?" I asked, and Foster kissed me instead, his tongue darting in and out of my mouth, a teaser, and his scent was swoon-worthy. I had always thought I'd be disgusted by a man's kiss, but his tongue surprised me, and I kissed him back, shocked at myself for getting hard. His cheeks were surprisingly warm.

"Surprise, surprise," he said. "What on earth do we have here?"

"You assume way too much, I think," I said. "You believe people will do everything you say, just because you're Sharon Foster Gold."

"So?" he said. "Will you do as I say when it's crunch time?"

"Probably... sometimes.... maybe," I said, and he threw me down in the basement—I landed hard on my back and lost my breath. He stood over me, waiting for me to recover, before he slapped my mouth.

"You're a manipulative bastard," I said.

"You got a fire that intrigues me," Foster said.

I gazed up from the floor, stoned and dizzy, and for a second, he appeared like a knight coming to rescue me, only without the horse or armor. Just a bulging melon jock.

"If we continue this way, you'll probably lose a tooth." He helped me stand, and I felt woozy. Foster's pupils were dilated, and his irises bursting with wondrous, swirling greens and blues. I touched my lower lip and found blood on my fingers. I smeared his cheeks and lips with it.

"Not sanitary or safe," he said.

"You look like Heath Ledger now," I said.

He smiled. "And headed to the same place."

The reminder sobered me.

"I don't know what the hell I'm doing here," I said. "Is this normal, Foster?"

"Normal doesn't exist any longer," he said, pushing me down. "You're cool, though."

"Gee, Skipper, thanks," I said, and he laughed before kissing me again. Pulling me close, his warm hands on my back, stealing my breath. It wasn't so much that I kneeled, but that my knees gave way. It all happened like a dream—drugs, booze, hormones mixing and meshing, transcendent music spilling all over the place.

"It's all yours, Jay," he said. "Just say you love me first."

"No, Foster," I said, trembling. "I can't ever, really..."

"I know you don't," he explained. "It's a simple game, just pretend, a charade, of sorts. Go on, not indicative of a damn thing when all is said and done."

"But..."

"Loyalty is repaid in numerous ways, remember?" Foster said.

"I thought all those novels and poems were just kindness on your part?"

"Negative," he said. "Absolutely no."

FOURTEEN DAYS TO GO

"That's a creepy thing to admit to."

"So be it."

I wobbled there, my knees going numb on the basement floor, drugged brain twisting and twirling, Alabama Shakes tunes blaring. My pulse pounded so loud in my head I wasn't sure what was said for a couple minutes. Eventually, I caught the tail end of a few of his sentences:

"Take it for a test drive. Seek and you shall find, my dear..."

What Foster was so proud of strained before me, and became unfettered, wide-awake, and impossible to ignore.

"I've seen you stare," he said. "Say it to me first, though."

"But..."

"*Say it,* or none for you."

"I can't believe it, but I might love you, Foster."

"Music to my ears, Jay," he said, "for I feel the same."

I closed my eyes, stroking, kissing, sucking, and tasting everything, you might think over the next ten minutes—soap, metal, sweat vanilla, salt, patchouli, beer, wintergreen gum. I didn't think I'd ever need or want such a thing.

I tried hard not to think about what it all might mean for my past, present, and future, for my new debts to Foster. I partly loathed it, but there were equal parts of me that adored it.

* * *

"I want to personally drive you home," Foster said, slipping into his sweats, barn coat, and moccasins, and driving his mother's black Audi Quattro through town. My balls and brains were still buzzing so we didn't speak much on the ride, and all I thought was *Holy crap. What have I done? And why did I like it?*

So, does this makes me officially gay or maybe bisexual?

What do I say now? Will Basil be forever ticked off at me? Or will she even care? Am I just an extraordinarily perverted and sentimental fool? Foster was efficient, blunt, and my jaw was sore. *Wow.*

"So, you're definitely in for Thanksgiving's Greatest Show on Earth, right?" Foster asked, business-like as he drove. "No doubts now, correct, Jay?"

"Correct, Foster," I lied. "None whatsoever."

We soon arrived alongside my drive, engine growling.

"Step out when you're good and ready, madame," he said to me.

"So, like, what does this all mean in the grand scheme of things?" I asked.

Foster offered a wry smile. "What do you think it means?"

"I don't know who I am anymore," I said. "Is that okay?"

"Yes," Foster said. "Means you love me, sex is cruel, and Thanksgiving is on."

"Before you leave, though," I said, as I stepped from the car, he lowered the passenger window. "Will any of this happen again?"

"Maybe, but don't be a girl about it," he said. "It'll occur when it occurs."

"You said something to me once," I said. "What feels like a long time ago now."

"Your meter's running, pal," Foster said.

"Do I still have twelve different kinds of laughter?"

Foster beamed, offering his grin.

"You got a whole lot more than that," he said. "But how about quiz time? Which side of the plate do you hit from?"

"Isn't that like yesterday's news?" I asked. "I mean, obviously... *both.*"

"Right, cool," he said, and I watched the Audi peel out. I realized that sedan was another unstoppable weapon in Foster's répertoire; or perhaps I'm just extremely emotive and sentimental. The early November morning was frigid, and the crisp air reminded me with a stomach-sinking sense of dread how close we were to the end of the year. We'd just lost our homecoming game (our record now 5-5); Thanksgiving was a mere fortnight away. Three of us were going to die soon unless I did something. *Would I kill myself for Foster?* I wondered. A hateful part of me wanted to go through with it. Maybe that was why I kept on hedging. Was I just taking the path of least resistance or did a little part of me want to croak? Just wrap the whole show up? A final kiss to the galaxy?

Come on, use your head, Jay, I told myself. *If you can't save them, save yourself! Ask for help and do it fast.* I'd been standing outside my house for about twenty minutes collecting my thoughts when I came to. My bare fingers ached in the cold and my nostril hair had frozen. I felt the need to comment aloud, as if I were the voice-over to my own story. "I don't want to be outside or inside. I want Thanksgiving with Mom *and* Dad, not to be hanging from a frigging goal post on account of a stupid, lame suicide pact, and I don't want to be in love with Foster or whatever," I said quietly, watching my breath vanish into the cold air.

I took a few dramatic inhalations and for no specific reason, I reached down to the frozen ground and slapped the gravel three times with my bare palms before walking to the front door.

TUCK

11.10.18

TWELVE DAYS TO GO

Periodically, I suffer from a profound case of aloneness—I know I'm not unique with any of that stuff. Seems like more of a dreary fact of life everyone must get used to. That said, I find it hard to move through the sludge of life with any ease, as if existence itself is mostly a harsh rip tide, and I'm stuck treading water, or doggy paddling on my good days, not making much headway, faltering, really. The state of being on one's own—enjoying solitude, embracing that solo part of life—I haven't mastered any of that yet.

I texted with my new friend, Basil several times this week; she's a kind skateboarder and lovely girl who waitresses at Wave. She's the first friend I've had in a long while, outside of my special needs peers, I mean. I texted her and she responded right off. She suggested I read the novel *Middlesex* by Jeffrey Eugenides, which won the Pulitzer Prize some years ago. She told me it was an incredible read, and she's right, I loved it.

A novel that made me cry, in fact—I had never had that experience, so at first, I was going to run it all by Dr. A. I'm not exactly sure *why* that happened to me, the emotion, I mean, but

TWELVE DAYS TO GO

it felt wonderful to concentrate on someone else so intensely for a time, it made me forget all about myself. Shared humanity and all that jazz, I guess. I decided to keep that secret emotion tucked away in my own safe, next to my spleen or kidneys or whatever else the hell is way down there. Something deep and low just for me. I don't know, maybe that sounds silly or maudlin, but I don't think so. *Who knows?* Maybe I'm growing up as of late, maturing, even. Scary thought, right?

I also find myself wanting to gaze into Basil's eyes more often—she has the purest, bluest beacons I've ever seen. Dare I say they're sweeter and more poignant than Emma Stone's greenies? Basil's eyes are piercing in a way that even Emma can't compete with. For Emma is larger than life, up on the movie screen, or pocket-sized and intangible in my iPhone, never quite one-to-one. Basil is a real life-size human being, sitting across the table, breathing, laughing, and sneezing.

Moving on, I don't know what to do about the Dynamic Duo, Foster and Bear —it's been two years since I was expelled from their stupid little death club. Once they tried to seduce me into sacrificing my life and joining their morbid trifecta, they piled on the charm. Some free beers and nachos, and a bong hit or five with some help from Monster. False camaraderie. Phoning me frequently like we were so tight, inseparable for months.

As if we had so many wonderful and vivid memories, when really all we had was next to none. Foster was always on camera, showing his best side to the lens and all that bullshit—it was a bit heady and overwhelming. "You're probably the smartest guy in school even though you can't actually speak very well," Foster said.

"You got great hands, too," Bear told me. "You'd make a fine receiver."

"What a trinity we'll become," Foster said. "Imagine the

epic possibilities of all of us bonded together. We'll be a trending topic for eternity; how cool is that?"

Foster spun tales of our trio hanging off the goalposts in the stadium at dawn. He insisted it took bravery, verve, and true grit and asked me if I would join Bear and himself in the ultimate sacrifice on Thanksgiving of 2016? I rejected them and said I wasn't going to try out for the team, either, and soon my face was in a toilet bowl being flushed, and Foster was so high on something that it was scary and raw. Was it speed? Meth? Coke? Opioids? Synthetic drugs, maybe?

"Smiley Reis will perish *tout suite,*" he shouted in the men's bathroom late one evening, and he didn't release me, or let me come up for any air. "Welcome to the ruin and death of Smiley."

Finally, a humane, second-string senior linebacker pulled Foster off me, so I didn't drown. Just gathered myself, dashed out of there and sped home on my trail bike, even leaving my new pair of glasses behind. Why was I stuffed down the toilet by an arrogant sociopath? Because I disliked football, and that kind of disagreement wasn't allowed in Foster's autocratic rulebook. Plus, I'm uncoordinated big time; everyone knows I can't catch a ball or throw one for the life of me, so the two were lying through their teeth.

"You're ruining dreams, Smiley," Foster told me the next morning at school. "Don't you want to live forever like James Dean, Paul Walker, and River Phoenix? If you ever speak of our plans, today, or next year or ever, I'll find you and cut off your left pinky toe."

The Dynamic Duo's act of cowardice was called off a night before Thanksgiving—the two sophomores stepped away from their diabolical plans. Their ideas never quite got going during junior year either, dissolving in a heap. The world rolled on, oblivious as ever.

TWELVE DAYS TO GO

Football rivalries continued and games were played and lost, heroics took place, and trophies were handed out and money exchanged hands, and classes matriculated on, babies were born, and in thirteen or fourteen years, if they're boys they'll be freshmen at St. Andrew's Prep in Gently, Connecticut, just like their dads.

Foster snuck up behind me in the hall last Thursday and said, "There's nothing like the smell of a flushed toilet in the early morning light, right Smiley?"

"Go to hell, Foster," I said without looking back.

"How's your left pinky toe doing?" he asked, and I kept on walking. When I finally turned, Foster was gone, off to another class, kiss up to a coach, or sneak down the back stairs for another pill or more weed. All that was left were his manic giggles, their echo tunneling and grinding into my skull like a stealth syringe sucking out bits of my brain, leaving me aching in my subterranean depths. His left baby toe threat still gives me chills.

So yeah, Foster Gold is the modern definition of an asshole. A dangerous one, at that.

JAY SOUTHER

11.12.18.

Mom was drinking her Martini in her red bathrobe, but the TV was off. It was almost three in the morning, and I could still smell Foster on me. I could taste his acidic breath and feel his clammy hands on my skin.

"A bit late even for you, huh?" she said.

"Sorry, Ma," I said, keeping my face down. "Won't happen again."

"Look at me now, son."

"I'm going straight to bed," I said. "Out of gas, in general."

She rushed over and touched my face: "Oh, my God, your *face*. Is your nose bleeding, too?"

"It's nothing, Ma."

"You saw *him* again, didn't you?"

"I think I'm in love with him, Ma," I said.

"Foster's an abusive master manipulator," she said. "A con man with no heart."

"He's a lot different with me, okay?" I said. "We were rough housing, having fun together, that's all it was, I swear to you."

"I was expecting you to be man of the house," she said, "and this makes you seem less of a man, it really does."

"You drink too many Martinis to tell me what kind of man I should be."

"And you're a lonesome teen with poor impulse control," she said. "Seriously, though, are you okay?"

"I'm going to shower now—to cool off and escape."

"You're high as a kite," she said. "Don't get sinful in that shower, Jay."

"Go to hell, Mom."

"All I'm saying is keep it clean," she said. "I'm trying to run a family here."

"Well, you're doing a shit job so far."

When I came out in my pajamas, I felt terrible for what I had said, so I walked over and kissed Mom's forehead and told her I loved her, which I hadn't done in four months. I smelled the lingering staleness of her breath and her clothes as I moved toward my room.

"I didn't mean to insult you," she said. "But I think you're getting carried away, drugs perhaps, you should... be more cautious, okay?"

"Right," I said, about to go in my bedroom, but I turned around, studying our disheveled, tired living room. Mom looked old sitting on the edge of the blue leather couch, her once luxurious red hair was now patchy and gray.

She'd lost some weight. Her librarian glasses, which once afforded her a wry, intellectual air, gave her a morose, gaunt look. Her cheeks showed new lines making her appear ten years older than her forty-six years. The maroon-and-white rug needed a vacuum, or perhaps more sensibly, the dump. Even the lampshades looked somber and defeated. The only seemingly healthy thing that remained was the flat-screen TV—and

ACADEMY OF UNHOLY BOYS

I had hostile feelings about that device. It had stolen Mom's best years.

All photos of Dad had disappeared, except the one I insisted Mom keep on display, taken when I was two. I walked across the room to the mantle—toward the three of us in happier times, a Christmas in Burlington, Vermont. I held it up to the dim light, Mom giggling, the three of us in a photo booth. I'm wearing a mustard-yellow shirt with a zipper and stare at my dad as if enamored. I'm twisting all the way back, away from Mom, away from the camera, to watch dad. Mom looks like a sleek Jackie O in a black turtleneck, and my dad looks like a young Harrison Ford.

"You okay, son?" she asked.

I looked at her, placing the photo back in its spot.

"Do we ever get any health updates on Dad?"

"Good night," she said, standing up quickly.

"I'd like to keep better track of him."

"No," Mom said. She took off her glasses, draining the remainder of her Martini in one gulp. "Nothing additional, Jay, no calls, letters or texts for Christ's sake, or Publisher's Clearing House balloons, celebratory smiles, or a few million in cash."

"Okay," I said. "Just seeing, Mom, but he's breathing, right? Not dead yet?"

"I get the curiosity, I do," she said. "I remain sorry for your loss."

I strode into my room, only to emerge a second later. "*Sorry for your loss?* Is he still alive?"

"Jesus wept, Jay," she said. "It's an expression... an apt one."

"I'd like to know everything," I said. "I'm nearly seventeen now."

"Dad's absence feels like an ongoing loss," she said. "That was my only point."

"Right," I said. "Okay, you sleep well now."

"You, too."

I looked back at her, raising my hand slightly, like a tentative third grader.

"*What is it?*"

"What would Dad say about me tonight?" I asked. "I mean, where the hell is he living now, Ma?"

"Pick your favorite question and I'll answer it succinctly."

"What would Dad's response be to all my breaking news?"

"He'd be a lot more understanding than I've been," she said. "Wouldn't blink an eye, I bet."

"Why was he like that, Mom?"

"Your father absorbed people's differences exceptionally well," she said. "He was so steady, tolerant, and even-keeled, nothing upset him for the longest time until..."

"Until what?"

"Until *everything did*," she said. "Noise, dust, lack of starch in his shirts, our old cat's breath, dirty fingernails, chatty ravens, and his dress shoes had to not just shine, but *glisten*."

"And the hail?"

"Yes, hailstorms freaked him out something fierce, as you know."

"Right."

"There's a lot more to say," Mom went on. "Aunt Carol insisted I tell you what's been going on with him. I'm sorry I kept quiet on it for so long... but you seemed so out of it all semester, like you weren't even in the same room with me half the time."

"Tell me now, Ma," I said.

"Your dad tried to kill himself five months back," she said. "Overdosed on Klonopin, an anti-anxiety med, but they pumped his stomach in the ER and he survived."

"Jesus *Fucking* Christ," I said. "How do you justify keeping that quiet?"

ACADEMY OF UNHOLY BOYS

"It's only half the story, son," she said.

"Then continue."

"Dad slit his throat with a steak knife four weeks later," she said. "But he survived that attempt, as well, and they stitched him back up and sent him home."

"Where is *home* now?" I asked. "Is he ever coming back to his *old* one?"

"I need to rest, Jay," she said.

"You can't cut me off after giving such dire, catastrophic news, Ma," I said. "What am I supposed to do with suicidal facts about my dad? A man who hasn't been around in six years and then, oh-by-the-way, doesn't want to be alive now, either."

"His social worker said he's growing steadier," Mom said, "more confident, interacting well with others and learning assertiveness training skills rapidly."

"Any clue as to how filled with sappy bullshit that sounds?" I asked, before going into my room and falling onto my bed, sobbing.

Ma came in behind me and rubbed my shoulders. "Take some deep breaths, Jay, don't hold anything back. Let the hurt spill. Let it go now, son."

"Explain to me why life is so harsh, Ma?" I asked. "Tell me that one, please?"

"It just is, Jay," she said. "At least, right now for you it is."

"What happens now?" I asked.

"We just need to help each other and work on a path forward that makes sense," she said, her face, beading with sweat. "Swear to me you're *not* going to commit suicide now, too, okay?"

"*Wait, what?*" I asked, voice breaking. "Where did that come from?"

"I need to hear it from you," she said. "After all this death

DAVID FITZPATRICK

talk from your dad—please swear you won't do the same thing to yourself tonight, okay?"

"I promise, Ma, that's not going to ever happen."

"No, no, here let me rub your back, okay?" she said, coming over to sit on my bed. She found the knots in my shoulder and went to work on them, kneading and working them obeyond me, like the tightness itself was just some bad water bubbles in my veins that were orelieved, gone now, magically evaporated.

I said, "I hope dad will improve."

"All of these events have been so stressful for both of us, right?"

"Yes, yeah," I said. "Definitely."

"I'm sorry you feel so mixed up," she said.

"I want to live, Ma," I said. "That's a definite fact, there's no doubt there."

Another ten minutes on, my mom kissed my forehead, and went on up to bed, closing my door firmly behind her. I returned then to my father in the hailstorm. Although I preferred to think of him at a spa in Lenox, Massachusetts, I couldn't erase the picture of him being wheeled out to the ambulance as he threw feeble punches in the hail over six years ago now.

Dad's work as an architect is revered in America, and abroad. His Seattle and Long Island amphitheaters had won several awards, plus a chair of his is featured in a museum in Zurich, and another one in Brussels. Dad had exuberant moods, some low and dank like the cellar of an old hotel in Maine. But the fact is, he had never been hospitalized. He had never gone that far or tripped into unsteady territory.

Now he's twice tried to destroy himself in the past five months, so I stare at the ceiling, wondering what his days are like now. Is it a well-worn film? Bathrobe-clad patients taking meds morning, noon, and night? Is my dad a bloated soul with a

ACADEMY OF UNHOLY BOYS

runaway beard, scarred arms, chest, and wrists, and several missing fingers? Racing toward nothing but a bleak death, my dad's actions are terrifying. Like another level of hurt, of deep and ugly anguish. "My dad has serious storms knocking around in his mind, as of late," I said. "Watch over him, God or Jesus or Buddha or Allah or Mother Goddess or whomever the hell is in charge nowadays. If you happen to be listening, please send a whole busload of strength his way."

I breathed slowly, quietly, for a solid ten minutes, before saying to myself, "In other breaking news, I appear to be falling for the cruelest boy in Gently, at the same time I'm in love with a wonderful young woman that I have never kissed." *Jesus, why do you do things so ass-backward, Jay?* First, you go full-on with Foster, and then move like an inchworm toward Basil. Did you ever even hold her hand? No—well, once she did scrawl her phone number on me.

After the conflict and confusion dissipated, the realization freed me up somehow. My connection with Foster. I felt a loosening in my chest and a hardening in my groin. I pondered the entire experience in slow motion and gave myself permission to enjoy it. I absorbed the memory of Foster and myself as if it happened again, a reshoot, where there was no fear, only self-acceptance, and kindness.

That said, I was aware of missing Basil, too, needing her beside me, that light of her buoyant personality, and her pliant, nubile body beneath me, or on top of me, or some variation on that. The two of us coupling with a grand and sweaty intensity — I *need* that. Would I ever get to hold and caress her now? To kiss those wonderfully thin lips? Or would she loathe me for messing around with Foster? I mean, would that only convince her of what a fickle and shallow fool I truly am?

BEAR SANTOS

11.11.18

ELEVEN DAYS TO GO

My neighbor Lavinia made high-pitched yodeling sounds when she was having sex. The mating ritual occurred often and kept life on our three-story clapboard condo building buoyant and peppy. When I didn't overhear her in the evening, I spotted her during the day zipping around Gently in her speedy, battery-operated wheelchair with a lime polka dot umbrella protecting her from rain, snow, or sun. She worked at an architecture firm in Madison and was a curvy thirty-five-year-old with lovely, long chestnut hair.

She was kind to me when the Rev and I first moved in and returned some of our mail that had been misplaced. I soon learned she had graduated from a local community college and had been hobbled with atrophy in her feet since she was a girl. One day she told me her name, roughly translated from Greek, meant, "lightning bolt."

Her apartment sat directly across from the elevator and had an eyehole forty inches off the ground. My father and I were a few doors down to the left and I was quite titillated the first nineteen times I heard the sounds. They were a combination of

BEAR SANTOS

calling out, high-pitched squeals, and some sort of spastic vocal cord reaction. At times, it occurred so rapidly that I wasn't sure if I truly heard it in the first place.

In my minor experiences with the fairer sex, I had assumed young ladies prefer the coaxing, the foreplay, *slow it way down* is what sex experts reported on TV, or in a women's magazines. I always assumed anything too fast is hasty. I assumed a lady would prefer being loved with a gentle, solid groove. Like how I treated my trusty baseball glove each season—I oiled that thing for months, just to get it soft enough, perfectly slow, with the baseball tucked deep inside. Slow and easy groove, night after gentle night.

Lavinia, though, wasn't interested in slow and gentle nights. If I were to break the noises down of her sexual encounters it would look something like this: some grunting followed by a slamming door, at first, muffled and increasing volume of groans, repeating yelps which become a yodeling stream of sounds, followed by the phrase, "Take me, Vince!"

Total elapsed time—somewhere around eight minutes. Again, I enjoyed overhearing the intercourse. I was young, and I already knew I leaned toward men, but any glimpse into the sexual world was refreshing and fascinating. My father assumed my lack of lady friends was due to my focus on school and sports. He occasionally fished for info implying that Foster and I were entertaining a string of wanton young women during our late hours together. I saw not correcting him as a form of self-preservation.

The passion fueled a few of my masturbatory fantasies early on. The noises caused quite a bit of tension in our building, though. Several neighbors asked my minister dad to scold Lavinia, but he deferred. "I have my own church to run, people," he responded. "Not interested in becoming the moral

ELEVEN DAYS TO GO

policeman around here. Let the lady live, she appears quite happy."

"Right on," I said.

"It's good to have passion, Felipe," he said. "You must pair up with someone."

* * *

One day, when I returned to the apartment after football practice, Lavinia was being taken out on a stretcher to an ambulance.

"Don't ask," she said to me as they loaded her into the vehicle. Her face was a bruised yellow and purple mess, eyes wet, hair matted.

"What went on?" I asked.

"Will you come see me in the hospital?"

"Yes," I said. "Absolutely."

Some scum beat me up," she said. "See you tomorrow, right?"

"Of course," I said. "I'll be there, Lavinia."

JAY SOUTHER

11.11.18

By now, Dad was closing in on forty-seven. There was something about his nakedness that day he broke down that still shook me. Bare-assed in the yellow bed sheet, my dad looked frail, particularly in contrast to the fierce-looking EMT women who had carried him away. It reminded me of Mary and the disciples taking Jesus down from the cross after he died. It struck me as I lay there, that perhaps my dad would melt away, dissolve, become nothing more than a fondly recalled ghost, forever and ever, Amen.

Coach had selected me to be the starting punter after one senior strained his knee, and the second-stringer was caught cheating on a Trig exam. Basically, he had no other choice on the team. "I need you to punt the ball well, to knock the shit out of it, okay, Souther? Do you understand me loud and clear?"

"Definitely, Coach," I said. "Consider it done."

He bent over, putting his hands on his knees, so we were eye to eye. "Can you really punish the other team?" he said. "Can we send them way back into their own territory? Can you come through in the clutch for us, Jay Souther?"

DAVID FITZPATRICK

"Yes, I believe I can do that, sir," I said.

"Call me Coach, son. Always refer to me as Coach, okay?"

"Yes, of course, Coach," I said. "I can do that, Coach."

"Excellent, Jay," he said. "That's all I'm looking for. Just to find the best in you, understand?"

"Right, Coach."

I hadn't played a single down in any of our previous ten football games, so I was nervous but excited. The first thing that popped into my mind was I needed to share this information with Basil Sous. We'd begun talking and texting again, but I still hadn't kissed her. The idea terrified me, but I felt like it had to happen soon. And after the "unfortunate, sweaty incident with Foster," as my mom put it, I was eager—maybe overly so— to simply kiss Basil. I walked over to the library, and bam, there Basil was. On a break from work. Her ribbons were aflutter as she came flying down a ramp, with her skateboarding friends whistling by, laughing. Basil swooped in and stood in front of me, offering a smirk.

"What's up?" she said. "Haven't seen you around very much."

"I got some decent enough news," I said.

"Out with it," she replied.

"I'm the starting punter at our next home game."

"Cool," she said. "Perhaps I'll come cheer you on in my old St. Andrew's Cardinals sweatshirt."

"I didn't think you were one for school spirit wear."

"It belonged to Avery, my older brother," she said. "On special occasions, the gallant bird does re-emerge."

"Did Avery go on to great fortune and fame?"

"No, he died," she said. "Tumbled off of a frat balcony after a night of binge drinking in Ithaca."

I panicked, blushing. "Oh, shit, I'm so sorry about that, Basil—"

218

ACADEMY OF UNHOLY BOYS

"How could you know that one, Jay?" she said. "No worries, no sweat."

"Can I be frank with you?" I asked.

"I always prefer an honest Jay over Frank," she said.

"Ha," I said. "I have been less than responsible or even honest with you."

"Okay," Basil said. "Shoot."

I fidgeted, looking at my sneakers. "I'm sorry if this hurts you, Basil."

She was silent.

"I fooled around on you," I said, "with a friend, it was something I regret. I'm ashamed of it. I don't know how to properly apologize."

"Ah, well," she said, her blue eyes narrowing and her face flushing. "That's the way of the world now, I guess, right?"

"I messed up. But I'm laying it all out before you. No secrets."

"Do you want an award for that, Jay?" she asked. "It sounds like you think I may owe you something for treating me like shit, and that doesn't make any sense."

"I'm sorry," I said. "Plus, he's a true asshole. I see that now."

"Foster, right?"

I balked for a moment, then nodded.

Basil scowled and said, "I've grown tired of your games, Jay. You're no better than Foster."

I stammered for a little, then finally said: "It's not who I am."

"What does Foster have on you? What precisely keeps you coming back... like an addict, almost. I honestly don't grasp it at all, okay? Is it just the nonstop weed?"

"I don't think it's the drugs, there's like a stupid camaraderie," I said. "A club-like belonging, a pack mentality. It's hard to break out of."

"Same old bullshit that destroyed Avery is going to eviscerate you," she said.

"Sorry, I'll do better," I said.

"Fine, sure," she said. *"Whatever."* And then she split with all her buddies, shooting behind the town hall in graceful single file.

BEAR SANTOS

11-11-18

I had a quasi-addiction to ordering exercise equipment from 1-800 operators growing up. I typically woke before dawn and chatted with them freely, stretching out the conversations at times when I felt quite lonesome. The operators were perky, buoyant, and cheerful to speak with, and they always asked what I desired more than anything.

"That's easy," I told them proudly. "I want to be the greatest tight end the world has ever seen, Puerto Rican or otherwise," I said.

"Excellent," they said. "Well, it's good you're starting so young."

The operators' names were Rosa, Pamela, Sunny, and Andy—or, at least those were the folks I remembered. I knew I could have ordered online, but I preferred the personal experience, that contact. Periodically, if a gruff male voice answered, I would hang up and count to twenty-seven in Spanish—my football, baseball, and basketball uniform number—and try again. Always hoping a lady named Carly Santos would answer.

I would keep the operators on the line asking how the

equipment worked, or what consumers liked or disliked most about the product. It was goofy, I suppose, but I was very young and timid, and I considered them my close friends. I ordered a whole bunch of stuff on my father's credit card until he put an end to it. He cut me off after I bought three of the gadgets from the infomercials in a single night, but he later admitted he was mostly relieved that it wasn't a drug habit. He let me keep the devices, so in a way, I got off without too much punishment.

Most recently, but still several years ago, I ordered something that looked like a giant hand that provided all sorts of core exercises, and also some aerobic dance DVDs from dancer Charlene Johnson; and one time I purchased the Malibu Pilates machine from soap opera star, Susan Lucci.

I was usually faithful and diligent in using the equipment when it first arrived, but years later I had more than a thousand dollars' worth of machines and devices spilling out of my closet doing nothing. My dad said I was overly susceptible to false hope and pathetically gullible.

"It's okay, though," he told me as I showed him the abdomen-strengthening device. "Worse vices do exist in the world."

As I was bringing one unfortunate machine to Goodwill one day, Lavinia saw me in the hall.

"Good for you, Bear," she said, smiling. "One day you have to show me how to work your gadgets, my belly desperately needs some assistance."

"I promise to help," I said. "I shall set you on a healthy trail."

After she was assaulted and carried off first to an emergency room and then to a state mental hospital, my dad suggested that I support her as a friend.

ACADEMY OF UNHOLY BOYS

"She doesn't seem to have a lot of those," the Rev said. "Assist her like a gentleman, aid her, and remember you're representing my church."

"I cannot figure out for the life of me why you care so much. She's not even a parishioner."

My dad smiled and shook his head. "This is almost a grownup conversation."

I was confused as to why he was changing the subject, but said, "Do you see me as an adult, sir?"

"Nah," he said. "Don't be silly. I know you're forever a kid, lost in space with all your various illegal substances rushing and charging through your veins."

"I'm not on that many, sir," I said. "I think your imagination runs wild."

"Lavinia is a good lady at heart, trapped in a cruel universe," he said. "I have no massive conspiracy hovering, I have not the time to be that hateful. Sorry to disappoint you, Felipe."

"Whatever, sir," I said.

BASIL SOUS

11.12.18

NINE...

"There's a lanky, subdued teen I've seen in your waiting room, Doctor." "You know I can't discuss my other clients with you, Basil," he said. "How are you doing in your own life? That's what I'd like to hear a lot more about."

"I'm doing well," I said. "Your fish here seem as cool as ever."
Dr. A looked at me in an amused sort of way as I continued.
"Tell me all about Tucker Reis, Dr. Athens," I asked.
"Basil..."
"We said hello back and forth several times," I went on.
"He told me he's a special needs student at St. Andrew's."
"I can't comment or say much back to you if you continue going like this."

"People called him Smiley years ago with great cruelty," I said. "They did it for eons. He accidentally drank lye water once, and all he could do for years was smile or cry. Vocal cords were shot. Just imagine being silenced like that."

"I can't contribute to this chat," he said. "I can listen to you, though."

BASIL SOUS

"We struck up a conversation..."

"Where?" Dr. asked.

"First in your waiting room," I said. "Later, at the Wave. He comes in to have a soda and brownie now and then, reads some manga."

"Right," Dr. A said.

"Tuck is sharp, but he keeps his left hand up as he tries to converse. Anyway, he ordered a brownie, and I was on my break, so I asked him if I could sit with him."

"And what happened?" Dr. A asked.

"We discussed you," I said. "Agreed you're a great doctor to us patients."

"I prefer the term *clients*," Dr. A said. "But thank you. I'm glad you feel that way."

"I told him about Avery's death that occurred in my life, and he listened intently," I said. "He's hyper-observant, I think. Fiercely intelligent."

"I agree," Dr. A said.

"He said he's working on speaking more often," I said. "Tuck said he had something called selective mutism and PTSD. So, I gave him my number."

"Oh?"

"I said if he ever wanted to talk, or discuss life, I'm here," I said. "If he ever needed a friend or supporter, he could phone me. So, we exchanged numbers and we've been texting back and forth wildly ever since."

"Okay," he said.

"Let me read one to you. 'Basil, you're a kind and unique young lady, wise beyond your years, I think...thanks for sitting with me... I met another Basil in my life as a boy in Italy, but it was an old butcher in Milan with huge, hairy arms but he was malodorous. Thanks for approaching me, Basil—you smell a lot

225

NINE...

better than the Milanese butcher. We should possibly repeat this interaction if possible."

"Good for you," Dr. Athens said.

"I've heard people talk about having a stiff drink to set them right."

"I have as well," he said.

"Tuck was like that for me," I said. "My strong drink. I can feel sorry for myself, drown in self-pity, but Tuck, he helps me be aware of my many blessings. And with how shy he truly is, I know how hard it is for him to reach out."

"Interesting," Dr. A said, fiddling with the heel of one of his shoes.

"I want to stay friends," I said. "I think we can help one another."

"How's that?"

"I'd like to support him as he emerges from his shell," I said. "We can keep one another as buoyant as possible as the year winds on. Selective mutism can be brutal."

"I can't comment," Dr. Athens said, frowning. "But I admire the kindness you're showing him, Basil."

"He played a bit of his favorite leading lady ever, Emma Stone singing in *La La Land*," I said. "I went home and watched the entire film. It's quite good, have you ever seen it?"

"I enjoyed it, too," Dr. A said. "Thought it was sweet. But, next week, Basil, can we talk about everything about you?"

"Deal," I said.

"I'd love to hear more about your huge loss of Avery," he said. "What's it like internally when you think of your parents now? You got to be truthful with yourself, and me, okay?"

"It's just they aren't my favorite topics to discuss," I said.

"Important material, though," he said. "Fundamental talks to continue to have if you want to discover healing down the road."

"Alright. Do you want to hear a quote Tuck shared with me before I go?"

"Sure," he said.

"*One sees clearly only with the heart. Anything essential is invisible to the eyes.*"

"Lovely," Dr. A said. "But I'm coming up empty as far as who penned it."

"Antoine de Saint-Exupery," I said, "author of *The Little Prince*."

"Ah," he said. "A classic."

"I get it, you know," I said. "Where Tuck's coming from; always feeling on the outside. Always being the new, strange kid, the gawky outcast. Observing the local fauna... I was like that too, until a spot opened for me. If it ever really did."

"Yes... I hear you, Basil," Dr. A said. "I look forward to learning more next week."

JAY SOUTHER

11.13.18

Why did I go back to Foster Gold after his insipid games that occurred after the late-night blowjob? It's a fine, probing question, and I don't have a satisfactory answer for my ma, or even myself. Mom mention something about Stockholm Syndrome to me once, and I laughed it off before I hopped on my laptop and read about it. It's where captives develop a quasi-dependence on the kidnappers. And with that phrase lurking in the air, I'll tell you what I did this week. Not that I was kidnapped or anything, but some seduction and manipulation were going on, creepy as ever.

Bear and I were like distraught, impatient disciples hungry for dark manna, chasing Foster around for life guidance like fools, like idiots. Foster met us every Monday, Wednesday, and Friday morning at half court in the school's gym, for something he dubbed, "Crunch Time." Four minutes before the first bell, he passed us the notes: Crib sheets scrawled with three violent terms—like "crush, kill, destroy" or "eviscerate, obliterate, eliminate." He said to use those terms in our conversations during the day and feel the rage roll off our tongues.

What the fuck am I doing here? I thought to myself. *What am I playing at? This is insanity, Jay. Welcome to insanity. Get up onto your feet and get the hell out.* But I couldn't, I didn't. I was trapped in emotive molasses. The three of us discussed our lives and the Crunch Time verbs while I was snuck weed edibles and acted as if I wasn't overwhelmed by the horror of our Thanksgiving plans. For Bear and Foster, everything was copasetic, even sweet; and we never needed to be scared, and the Grim Reaper would only embrace and comfort us like an old pal with Sam Adams and two oatmeal cookies, warmed just so with a single scoop of vanilla bean ice cream on top.

One evening in November, Foster tied blindfolds on Bear and me as we stood with our backs to the mildewed concrete walls in one of the school's decrepit training buildings. I don't know how Foster got us in after hours; maybe they didn't bother to lock the old gym anymore, or maybe it was just Al's connections, but the whole place felt like some bomb shelter. Real apocalyptic and scary as hell. We were told to wear flip-flops. He handed us thin wooden canes to swing around and told us he'd hanged some kind of mystery piñata from the ceiling. It was a dizzying feeling to blindly take aim. I tried to make contact, whirling about, hoping I wouldn't hit Bear or fall on my ass.

"We must leave the fickle and fallible fools behind us soon," Foster shouted. "Let's check out of this chicken-shit universe with determined grimaces, brothers of the sword."

We swung our canes and could hear the mannequin or whatever the hell it was dangling but also crumbling. I had struck the object several times. It reeked horribly. There was a sound of a lot of liquid spilling onto the floor. Foster finally had us remove the blindfolds, and Bear and I both stood agape at a large rubber pig body stuffed with tomatoes and tomato paste. The black marks on the wall were now dotted with red spatter that had gotten everywhere. I dry heaved, much to the delight and laughter of Foster and Bear.

"You're getting carried away with all this frat-boy bullshit, man," I said. "It can't go on. All these false ideals reek of total crap. I can't take it anymore. You're insane." Then Foster was lunging at me, choking, and knocking me to the floor. My rugby shirt and jeans got soaked in the red goo. If it weren't for Bear dragging Foster off me, I don't know what would have gone down, or how it would have ended. "I'm allowed to state my opinion, for Christ Sake, right?" I shouted from the floor. "What kind of bizarre dictatorship are we living in here?"

"We stand deep into the killing season now, Jay," Foster responded. "You can't doubt me like that. I'm the sanest one here. Study the calendar, we can't afford any more juvenile sarcasm or some quirky quip. *No more of it.* To your point, there will be no more division, only games of trust, and love, there's no going back now, no excuses will be accepted."

"You're both addicted to lying, to embracing false facts," I said, as my eyes watered. I caught my breath, trying to grasp what the hell had been inside the empty rubber sow and what continued to drip from it. My mind flashed back to the last time Foster had knocked me to the floor and towered over me. The promises I had made, the utter devotion my body had offered. "I'm so sorry, okay?" I said, my voice cracking. "I won't say it again, I promise..."

"We only accept love here," Foster said, now subdued. "You see, I do love you, Jay."

"Sure, me, too, man," I said, blushing, as he pulled me up to a standing position.

"What's the deal with you two?" Bear said.

ACADEMY OF UNHOLY BOYS

"We got funky the other night, Mr. Santos," Foster said, "I welcomed the boy wonder into the club, so to speak."

I watched the muscles work in Bear's jaw. "I don't enjoy being taken for granted, so make your fucking amends or you can watch me check out of this whole production on my own."

Foster held me close and whispered, "Everything is fine."

I nodded, and he pulled away.

"Chill out," Foster said to Bear, which caused the former football star to pick up his damp cane from the floor and violently attack the rubber pig body for one solid minute—slam, slam, over and again.

I tried to smile or laugh it off, although I did not get Bear's rage. It was disturbing and downright psychotic.

An hour later, I hadn't even peeled off my tomato paste slimed clothes at home before I received a phone call from Foster.

"Got a minute to chat?" he asked.

My head was thick and throbbing, my skin reeking of tomato-paste. "Didn't we just speak to each other?"

"I'm exhausted, too, Jay," he said. "But I feel one thing needs to be stressed."

"Shoot."

"I want to be clear," he said. "Our obligations and loyalties are forged in steel."

"I'm listening, Foster."

"I know you grasp this somewhere inside your ever-developing brain and body," he said. "But I record every itsy-bitsy piece of my life."

"Yes?"

"If you ever report the Greatest Show to police, a teacher, or Basil Sous," Foster said, "the recording of you blowing me will automatically go viral."

I bent over in my room, my hands slipping on my filthy knees, enraged.

"You idiot," I whispered. "How can it continue? It doesn't make sense to follow through all the way on the Greatest Show now, Foster. Don't you get that yet?"

"I sent you a copy of the dynamic, passionate recording," he said, his voice monotone, cold. "So, you can relive the legitimacy of it for fun."

I fell mute.

"It'll be everywhere, Jay," Foster said. "Every porn site in the world. We're on the same team now, slugger. Let's work together and celebrate our countdown to a historic Thanksgiving event. No more wandering away from the trail, okay?"

"Foster," I said. "Please, there's no need to continue like this. You, Bear, and I can be free of this ridiculous burden. What's so scary to you about the word *hope*? You can have a lot better life; you could do more acting roles, maybe, become a bush pilot, I don't know...be anything you wish, you can do it all. Why go on like this?"

"Life is an intricate riddle, my friend," Foster said. "Or is it more like a dirty limerick?"

"You have no idea what you're doing now, do you?" I asked. "You're driving with your eyes closed down the middle of the road—you'll only crash and kill others."

"Maybe that's how I want it to go," he said. "It all rests on your good behavior and dedication to an important promise, forged in steel."

"I can't believe you," I said.

"Sleep well, Jay," Foster said. "And make tomorrow a great day."

BEAR

11.14.18

EIGHT DAYS...

My dad seemed almost pleased when I started working part-time at a state mental hospital five towns away. It was officially a five-story white-brick institution for those who had little to no insurance. Getting to the hospital was simple enough for me; I took a city bus from outside the gourmet market in Gently and it dropped me off a block away from the mental hospital.

My position was called, "Peer Support Force." I earned twelve bucks an hour while I worked, which wasn't huge money but still a decent wage. Basically, it was me trading in my All-American jock title to make a little income, and the Reverend was pals with a psychiatric APRN employed there, so it was easy-peasy getting the job.

The key is to find the right balance, our boss told us. *Assist those clients who are hurting, but don't unload your personal woes on them. Always remember who the helper is in the equation.* There were brochures in the main lobby about depression or schizophrenia, anxiety disorders, schizoaffective disorder, bipolar disorder, bulimia, and other eating disorders. We

EIGHT DAYS...

assisted these people as they waited to be seen by their social worker or a new doctor.

My duties were to keep the client company and offer a shoulder if they needed it. I played cards and fetched glasses of water. It was a mental health facility, so, of course, there were some long-gone individuals, but most people were hurting, clinically depressed, and lonesome. I only worked three times a week for three hours a shift. It was nothing money-wise, but still, it felt good to lend a hand, and to take home a paycheck, however miniscule. Plus, it kept my father off my back.

Of course, I was in fact nothing but a liar while I was at the facility. I was the antithesis of destroying the world and myself with Foster's Greatest Show agenda. A part of me kept whispering, "You are the biggest, two-faced hypocrite in town, Bear."

But when I focused on Lavinia, I felt ease. Her face looked brighter and less bruised when I saw her that afternoon. She had a lovely silver necklace—a mini wheelchair with wings—and wore a navy dress and hospital booties.

"Hey, neighbor," she said. "I may be only half-machine here, but whining about my life isn't going to change that, right?"

"We don't have to talk at all if you don't want," I said. "We could only play cards, or do anything at all..."

"What should I call you—card shark?"

"Bear or Felipe is fine with me," I said.

"Yes, Bear Santos, apartment B4," she said. "The phenomenal athlete."

I smiled.

"Everyone in our building saw me escorted out into the ambulance the other night," she said. "You missed a real circus —I don't think I have a lot of friends left in that place."

"That's not true," I said, and she smiled.

234

BEAR

"Why come to visit me, Bear?" she asked. "You just trying to get in my pants?"

"No, no, nothing like that," I said. "You're just... kind and sweet, and I enjoy your company."

I had found Lavinia to be an inspiration. I thought, *if she can go on through all her trials and tribulations and continue, why the hell can't I do the same?*

"We're all splintered in one way or another, Bear," she said. "What got you, if I may ask?"

"Too many concussions, booze, and drugs," I said. "Easily influenced by a bossy guy that doesn't love me."

"Don't they test your pee in high school sports all the time?"

"I've learned there're ways around almost everything," I said. "I got brutal anxiety, as well. So, what about you, though?"

"I try to find good men," she said, "but I stumble in that noble pursuit."

I watched her gesture like she was conducting an orchestra.

"I see my reflection in store windows on the Gently Green and I get nauseous," she said. "I don't make enough money, I'm too often alone. I met a guy who wanted to watch me burn myself the other night. That's all. No kiss, or touch, or even sex, he just wanted to observe a wheelchair-bound lady burning herself. W-T-F, right?"

"What an asshole," I said. "And then he hit you?"

Lavinia nodded and swept her hair out of her eyes, deep brown pools filling up.

"I want a new soul, or body," she said. "I mean, it's November, do you think it's too late to be adopted by Angelina Jolie? What do you think my chances are?"

"You never know," I said.

"Finding a new guy makes me feel hopeful. Fools me every damn time."

235

EIGHT DAYS...

"I'm very sorry about all that," I said.

"I want to hear you say we'll be good friends back at home," Lavinia said.

"Oh, of course," I said. "You can count on that one."

"Say it out loud to me, though, Bear."

I looked at her and said, "We'll be good friends back home, Lavinia."

"Yes," she said. "Thanks for that."

"Monopoly, anyone?" I asked the room with a smile, and three or four folks joined us.

BASIL SOUS

11.14.18

When Avery was young and I was a kid, my folks, sober for once, took us to the St. Louis Arch in Missouri. A beautiful sight, that structure; I got lightheaded from the view—it was like a spacewalk. As we gazed out the windows up there, a grandfatherly type behind us said: "I believe our memories absorb only what our tired psyches can contain, so let this view sink in—we're staring at six hundred and thirty feet of stainless-steel truth, sweat, and love."

* * *

With my folks high almost every day, Avery became my parent and my best friend in the process. He taught me how to floss and brush my teeth, tie my shoes, ride my bike, wash dishes, iron my shirts and dresses, sew, ice skate, make my bed, and cook my own meals. He showed me how to whip up grilled cheese with crispy bacon, attempt to make my own meatballs *with* sauce, and he even braided my hair when it got too long.

Avery also taught me how to properly swing a baseball bat

—sometimes he'd pitch tennis balls to me out in our backyard and get a serious look on his face. "It's all about the follow-through," he'd say. "Good footwork and follow through is all you need to know to be a consistent, big-league slugger, B."

Avery called me B, just B, and it always made me smile. It was like our secret bond, a Morse code between brother and little sister. When my parents were around, I got the sense they truly didn't care about anything outside themselves long before I would realize they'd just up and left. We had wealthy neighbors who were probably thirty-something and had a tremendous amount of money, or so Mom maintained.

"That family can eat out every day and night for the rest of their life," she said. "Do you understand that type of financial freedom, Basil?"

"Yes, I think so," I said like a dutiful daughter.

"No," my mom laughed in a stoned way. "I don't think you can appreciate it until you grasp how much hash that would be."

How do you say that to your own daughter? I always wanted to cross-examine my parents in a courtroom ruled by Jesus, or someone impressive like that. I needed to see my parents reprimanded, dressed down for always being on drugs. It was an empty business, but Aunt Peg had done a good job with me, standing in once my parents split the scene. Losing Avery, of course, was a brutal blow, the worst loss ever.

I remember that Parent's Weekend at Cornell with Avery, when everything seemed ideal and picturesque, like some fuzzy, dreamy impressionist painting. Every older adult playing baseball, tennis, or going for long walks, or enjoys a picnic basket lunch on the soccer field with wine and cheese and whatever else they eat in Ithaca, New York. So many smiles and much laughter. I'm sure there was tragedy or despair or dysfunction happening all over the place on that specific week-

ACADEMY OF UNHOLY BOYS

end, it's just I didn't see it. It was also the last time I saw Avery alive.

The thing is ever since he passed on, my life has slowly and steadily improved, two steps forward, one step back, and Peg and I are in a better place, too. She's become a kinder and able protector, and empathic lady who loves me for me. I hope that doesn't sound idiotic and naïve on my part, but she's trying to improve our lot and so am I. We had a funny conversation about relationships the other day over turkey burgers and potato salad. I told her I'm enjoying high school, even though I haven't found a substantial soul who wants to run off somewhere magical and fly me around the world in a Lear Jet, munching on lobster and caviar in our own Shangri-La.

"You're sixteen for Christ's sake," Peg said, after sharing some of my musings. "Don't worry. There's a long way to go in your life. Don't rush yourself, don't get negative, you don't need any other person around."

"I get it, I just kind of hate the in-between," I said. "Dr. Athens has helped me, has told me there's nothing wrong in looking out for me. That's called healthy self-care. I'm even learning some poems from, get this, Mr. Jay Souther."

"What's your favorite one so far?" she asked.

"By far, Wendell Berry's 'The Peace of Wild Things.'"

"Fire away," Peg said.

"When despair for the world grows in me,
And I wake in the night at the least sound
In fear of what my life and what my children's lives may be
I go and lie down where the wood drake
Rests in his beauty on the water, and the great heron feeds.
I come into the peace of wild things
Who do not tax their lives with forethought of grief.
I come into the presence of still water.
And I feel above me the day-blind stars

DAVID FITZPATRICK

Waiting with their light. For a time
I rest in the grace of the world and am free."

"I love that one, Basil."

"Me, too," I say. Peg poured a glass of sparkling cider and asked more about Jay.

"Jay Souther and I are very different folks and he does too many drugs and is immature, and is not an even-keeled presence, and he probably never washes his hands properly after using the bathroom, but the way he sent that lovely poem to me, it restored my faith in humanity, do you know what I mean?"

"Does that mean it's back on again with him?" Peg asked.

"No, no chance," I said, "just that on some days he's a great guy and I'd hire him and pay him well, and other days he bores me to tears or exhausts me with his drama, and am so pleased I'm on my own."

"Okay," Peg said simply.

"Now if he himself had read the poem to me, it might be a whole other ballgame," I said. "Is that a goofy statement to say?"

"Crazy lives we all do lead," Peg said.

"Now who said that one?"

"Just me, just Peg, living my humble life in Gently, Connecticut," she said.

"It got me thinking about all I don't know in life, which is a tremendously stupendous amount. Like about the stranger on the bus beside me," I said. "Or the young lady in the bathroom stall to my left with a fever and a migraine, or my old teacher-turned-florist who lost two babies before having healthy triplets, or a retiring fireman who got too much smoke in his lungs to fight fires any longer, so he files papers for a few hours each day at city hall, where he meets his new wife trying to fix a copy machine."

ACADEMY OF UNHOLY BOYS

"Do you know what I love?" Peg said. "I mean, really and truly adore?"

"What?" I asked.

"That my dearest niece has such a wonderful head on her shoulders," she said. "I mean that, you're balanced, kind, and offer a whole hell of a lot to the world."

"Yeah," I said and kissed the top of Peg's head. "Well, my Aunt Peg is the coolest chickadee in our one-horse town."

And on that particular day, we didn't have any more money than usual, and I still had to take out the trash and feed the damn Siamese cats and those giant dogs, and clean up after them, too. But it was okay, Peg and me, do you know what I mean? We were getting through all of it, together.

* * *

That night, Jay called me again and it wasn't long before I was rolling my eyes. Of course, all the toxic masculinity that's going on with Foster and Bear manipulating my friend, Jay, and I know I'm an adjacent slave to this pain cycle, the feeding and abusing of substances, the whole young death dance that the St. Andrew's trio had embraced. It was a huge waste of promise, any way you studied it.

Jay was a good kid, and when he watched me on the Gently Green, or texted me, flirting in his own awkward but genuine way, I felt like being warmed with a heated blanket on a cold night. I never admitted to that, of course, but I wanted to jump his bones. But I held my tongue, waiting for Jay to try to clean up his act.

Was that too selfish on my part? Or not selfish enough? The burden is always on the young women, we must think a few steps head of the boys every damn time. I know no one ever said life was fair, but still...

DAVID FITZPATRICK

"I just want you to come clean," I said. "Because Foster's a slimy kind of guy and at one time you were a good friend of mine, and now you're slipping into these heinous mistakes."

"I'm sorry, okay?" he said.

"Tell me about the appeal of him," I said. "You referred to him as a friend, is that still what you'd say about him today?"

"He doesn't quit, doesn't take no for an answer," Jay replied, his voice sounding tight. "He uses his many gifts, he's very creative and somehow convinces me to do very stupid things."

"Like?"

"Like sleep with him or give him a blowjob after he gets you crossfaded, and with the music so loud you can't even hear your thoughts," Jay said. "He seduces everyone with his free stuff, short stories, and poems, and all his pseudo-intellectual talk. It's like he's a philosophy graduate student hell-bent on destroying you. We drive around for hours, Foster, Bear and I, listening to poems, we recite some verses, all that stuff. And I have to say that books, reading them or listening to them... I don't know, it gives me something to cling on to. Learning about literature—does that sound like a load of pure bullshit?"

"Not entirely," I said. "Of course not. That part is good. But would you say he's charming?

"He can be," Jay said. "But that's with the cover of his drugs and alcohol and gummies. Each time I lecture myself about staying away, and then he whirls and flips and somehow convinces me to join him in the fiery pits."

"I want you to know this," I said. "Three days ago, this oh-so-talented graduate philosophy student phoned me at home late and asked if he could take away my virginity with his God-given endowments."

"Jesus," Jay spat. "He's a fucking monster."

"Yes," I said.

242

ACADEMY OF UNHOLY BOYS

"But how the hell am I supposed to stop that, though?" he asked.

"Good and fair question, but you need to have a little more skin in the game."

"How do I do that?"

"It won't happen again, is that what you'll promise me now?" I asked.

"Okay, yeah."

"Because I like you. But to me, at least, I don't get all that stuff, why you fall for him. This type of bullshit killed Avery and it will certainly kill you. So, wake up. Wake the hell up today."

"Okay, I'll try really hard," Jay said. "I'll get there."

"My Aunt Peg gets wiser by the day, and she told me sometimes it's easier to stand up for someone else than it is to stand up for yourself."

"Right," Jay said.

"I think what you really need to do is to stop being so disillusioned by him."

I watched him just look at me with his even gaze, his eyes so serious under his curls. "Thank you, Basil. Thanks for giving more than a damn."

BEAR SANTOS

11-16-18

SEVEN...

I dreamed I was attending an elite university not far from Montreal. It was an early September morning, and a marching band was rehearsing, "When the Saints Go Marching In," on a vast field. I was at the student center, busy as ever. Students filled up their backpacks at their lockers, gossiping and laughing, when a frightened voice shouted something was going down across campus. First, we heard it was a terrorist attack, next a school shooter; before long, gunfire could be heard coming our way.

Then, I was off to the side near endless rows of student mailboxes, my pants around my ankles and an extraordinarily large butter knife in my hand, which I was using to cut off my excess skin—it bunched up around my arms and belly. The flesh around my ankles was too loose as well, like old athletic socks that had lost their elastic. It struck me as relatively normal behavior in this increasingly frightening world, nothing *that* odd about it, really.

A student ran over to me, asking, "What's the deal with all your blood, man?"

I said I was trimming my body, losing the excess skin.

"That doesn't make sense," the kid said. "You'll only bleed out and die."

The sound of automatic gunfire filled the area, and students began dropping around me left and right, along with a passing custodian and a chubby math teacher. People rushed by, but I stayed right there next to the mailboxes, trimming my flesh.

People wept and phoned loved ones, fearing this could be the end. I wanted to be more supportive and empathic, if not brave and knightly, but all I could think of was getting rid of my love-handles. The shooting and death toll increased for the next several minutes, and I stayed laser-focused on my fat. When I felt the outside world encroaching, I told myself I was stuck inside a brutally realistic video game, nothing more, nothing less.

A bare-chested, barefoot seventeen-year-old, tow-headed white boy appeared alone in the center, toting a bow and a quiver of arrows, and two semiautomatic weapons slung over his left shoulder, his pupils dilated, breath heavy.

"Why aren't you running away from me like all the others?" he asked.

"I would if I had the time, sir," I said. "I promised myself I would slim down."

"What greater purpose does it serve?"

"It makes me more efficient," I said, "aerodynamic, and proactive, sir."

"You're wasting my time with your silly, pathetic buzz-words," he said, nervously looking around.

"Sorry, sir," I said, dropping the large butter knife, which clanged on the tiled floor.

"I'm not a sir or a gentleman, *dammit*," he said. "Only a lousy, cheap boy. Say it."

SEVEN...

"Okay," I said.

"Scream it at me, *or you'll die.*"

"You're a lousy, cheap boy," I yelled.

"Louder," he said, so I shouted the words, my voice quivering, cracking.

"Show me your tongue," he said.

"What?" I said, feeling dizzy, unreal.

"Uncle Leon said that to me once," he explained. "I had no idea what it meant, but I did as he asked, and stuck my tongue out at him."

I opened my mouth and showed him my tongue, and he nodded.

"I saw two headless deer on my tenth birthday near Lake Placid, New York," he said. "A deranged hunter was behind it, police said. They were decomposing near a stream, and there were ravens and maggots feasting away, and my drunk Uncle Leon grabbed me and sat me down on top of them. He took five Polaroids. He said to offer the world my best big-boy smile, like I was only making sandcastles on Coney Island at a Labor Day shindig. I still have the Polaroids in my bottom drawer at home."

"Why does your uncle do that kind of shit?"

"They put him in a state hospital the next day," the boy said. "He's still in there."

"Alcohol and drugs can make people do terrible, bizarre things."

"I don't drink, though," the boy said. "I say no to most drugs, too, but I can't escape the deer. Each night they both await, nudging me awake."

"How did the deer become more important than all these human beings around here?" I asked.

"Deer are a lot quieter, more subdued," he said, and shot me, first with a semiautomatic rifle, and then with two arrows in

BEAR SANTOS

my throat. He ran down the hall giggling, and seconds later an exchange of gunfire followed, and he was gone.

EMTs, first responders, and police soon flooded the area, rescuing, saving, or covering victims with black blankets. There were cameras, reporters, and triage-like conversations and so many cell phones ringing with no one answering. Outside a buzzing police helicopter cut through the sky, searching for accomplices in the woods, or any additional victims.

A woman in an orange turtleneck and khakis with auburn-streaked hair and a white, Red Cross rain jacket approached my black, blanket-covered body, humming a gospel tune. She squatted beside me and caressed my cheeks and forehead with her soft, cool hands.

"Up and at 'em," she said. "Rise and shine, Phil, come with me right now."

I opened my eyes, touching the gaping wounds in my chest and throat, most of it blown away. One arrow was still stuck in my trachea.

"Shouldn't I be dead?" I asked.

"Oh, yes," she said. "Absolutely, and you were for several minutes."

"Why did I come back?"

"I pulled some strings for you," she said.

"Are you an angel, or a Goddess?" I asked. "Or my mom, maybe?"

"No, no," she said, smiling. "Nothing like that—only a big fan of Felipe Santos."

"Why rescue me out of all these innocent folks?" I asked. "I don't get that part."

"Embrace this blessing," she said. "Don't toss it away again."

I woke with a start and shook my head like I was covered in sticky cobwebs. My mouth felt pasty, dry. I gazed down at my

SEVEN...

watch. It was Wednesday at 6 a.m., which meant I was alone in the condo for the next several hours. My father ran a few early morning services.

After I used the bathroom, I ate an energy bar and drank cranberry juice in the kitchen. I wandered down the hall to my father's mostly unadorned pale-blue bedroom. There was a grandfather clock in the far corner stuck at 10:58 p.m. and a large, plain cross on the wall, along with a color photo of Senator John McCain and Governor Sarah Palin when the duo ran for the Republican Presidential Ticket many years ago.

My dad was smiling proudly beside the duo outside of his church, offering a thumbs up. There was also a shot of his wedding day, Ernest and Carly Santos at Niagara Falls on the American side. It was a June day, and my dad had a blue ruffled tuxedo on, blue suede shoes, and Carly was in a lovely white dress and bare feet, so damn young. Up on a bureau was a color photo of my mom in "better days," as the Rev always put it.

She had reddish-streaked hair and wore a sly smile. Even though the lady in my Montreal dream had denied it, I remained convinced it was Carly Santos who raised me from the dead.

"Easy, Lazarus, only a dream," I scolded myself. Then I reached into my father's top drawer, moved aside his hunting knife, and took out his pistol for the first time. It was heavier than I had ever imagined. I felt its heft, fingered the serial numbers, trembling with excitement, and fear. I took my phone off the desk and slipped out of my clothes; not sure exactly why, but I got with it.

I climbed onto my dad's bed bare-assed with the pistol in my hand, and oddly I thought I'd lose control. Was it the portent and danger implied in the weapon? Or just the rage and violence inherent in our wild, squirrely-assed universe as of late? Without an answer, I took many photos of myself pointing the gun at me. I took all kinds of shots—videos and selfies. I must have done it for several minutes, continuing the photoshoot, until I heard an odd whistling sound, and random noises in the kitchen, and Dorothy Ortiz's stunned face appearing in dad's room, before she started hollering and everything moved in super slow-mo. Dot helped the Rev out at church—a middle-aged, no-nonsense lady with two grown boys of her own.

I thought, *how could I have not heard her coming through the front door? Why didn't I hear the deadbolt and lock? Did Dot even call out?*

"Put the gun down, Bear. You're in danger now, and so am I."

"Just letting off a little steam..." I said.

"You're going to listen to me, or I'll phone the authorities immediately. You know your dad, and I do, too, and I know a mistake like this would shut you down for a decade."

"Yes," I said.

"Reverend is a God-fearing man, but he's not an affectionate, nor a very loving presence to his very talented son. I know you've got a legitimate gripe with him, but listen now, get dressed and I'll take the gun. Where does it go? Put it down on the bed and I'll handle it from there."

"Dot, please don't tell him about this, okay?" I commented. "He'll crucify me in a minute. Take it, Dot, I'm very sorry. It was in the top drawer, just beyond the hunting knife."

"It's fine, it's fine, let's throw some cold water on you, brush your teeth and scrub your face well, and let's clean this place up."

"Okay," I said.

"I'm just going to ask you some questions for my own safety, for my own peace of mind. Do you know who the last five Presidents of the United States were?"

SEVEN...

"Biden, Trump, Obama, George W, Clinton. I'm a sane man, Dot," I said.

"Frankly, Bear, I doubt that right now. What you did was childish mixed with a dangerous type of zeal and adult rage. You easily could have killed yourself or me. Now, listen, the Rev has had some bad chest pains during a service, Bear. He needed an EKG at Urgent Care. He's fine, resting."

After we cleaned the bedroom, Dot put the gun away, deep in the back of the top drawer, just beyond the hunting knife. "Don't leave your phone around either, get rid of all those photos," she said. I swore Dorothy Ortiz to secrecy, and she kissed my cheek.

"No worries, Bear," she said. "We all make huge mistakes...the key is just to repent and make proper amends, so it doesn't happen again."

Thirty-five minutes later, I stood beside the Reverend's bed at the Urgent Care, my mind racing. I ended up going to school only a few minutes late, anyway; I just couldn't stand pretending that Reverend and I cared for each other. Plus, if I followed through with the Greatest Show, surely the Reverend would be asking himself, "Why did the apple fall so damn far from my tree? And how did his hope just up and disappear?"

JAY SOUTHER

11.16.18

SIX...

The time between the pig piñata and the football game was a real struggle for me. I avoided Foster during school because of our schedules, but the assistant coaches were giving me a hard time at practice, riding me about my punting skills, or lack thereof.

"Your first string, Souther, no slacking off, okay?" they said. "We can't have a less-than-stellar player. You get that, *right?* Are we on the same page, *guy?*"

"Yes, Coach."

"Push, Jay," he said. "Got to push to win. Punt the pigskin better than you ever have even dreamt of."

"Right, Coach," I said.

"Never stop shooting for your best," they yelled. "You have to dig down deeper than you've ever gone."

"Deeper than ever, Coach," I shouted back.

"Let me hear it one more time," the coaches said.

"I'll go deeper than ever, punt to the best of my abilities, Coach," I shouted.

SIX...

I was too exhausted to head to Foster's after our practices—I had no energy or desire for more drugs or drink. Despite the constant, lurking anxiety about Thanksgiving and the threat of Foster outing me, I caught up on some sleep. After the deprivation of the past months, early nights helped my mind and body heal some. Before I knew it, I hadn't had a drink or any drugs in six days—I know that's not a lot, but for me, it was *something*. I had more clarity in my day-to-day activities, felt more on, more alive.

At the game that Friday, a cold wind whipped through my helmet and my bulky mouthguard tasted like watermelon bubble gum. The stadium was jam-packed for the home game against Morgan, the crowd boisterous and filled with all sorts from the town. I scanned the faces for Basil's, but I didn't spot her angular, bright one.

People stomped their boots, loafers, bucks, sneakers, bluchers, dress shoes and heels on the bleachers, cheering, raising a ruckus. A roaring, rolling energy and heat leapt off them and kept the team, or at least me, warm and primed to play.

Why would Basil bother to come see me? I was thinking. She was healthy, confident, cool, and saw through my pathetic disguises. I had to admit, I'd been fooling myself, believing Bear and Foster's mystique had rubbed off on me by mere proximity.

I didn't even know who I was anymore. Why should Basil give a damn about me? I was no different than the amorphous bacteria I studied under the microscope in Biology lab every Tuesday and Thursday—taking the form of whatever host I encountered.

Instinctively, I also looked for my father. Could he be out there in the audience? Would I even recognize the goddamned guy? Would he have a scruffy, homeless kind of effect by now? A wild David Letterman or Michael Stipe beard? Was he slim or bloated, puffy from all his medications? I imagined him walking onto the field, stopping the game, grabbing the microphone from a zebra and saying, "Jay Souther, I am so deeply sorry for letting you down. Let's go for a walk, son, and have a beer together. Let's start again."

Off to the side of the student section, a tall, skinny guy was staring at me. He was a special needs student and his unruly black mop fell to his shoulders. He wore those darkened lenses, which I disliked, believing people who hid their eyes had nothing but sinister plans. His face—neither pretty nor ugly—was pale, as though the electronic gadgets in his life had sucked all pigment from his skin.

He was usually listening to an actress, volume turned up a bit too loud in the hallways—was it Amy Adams? Or Mary Louise Parker? He was in the same Timberland boots, dark cords, black and blue flannel shirt, and a thin jean jacket that he always wore, fidgeting now and then.

He looked frozen, out of place. What the hell did he want from me? Or was it all wild paranoia on my part? It was just those frigging dark lenses he wore—they freaked me out every damn time. Guy was probably just staring at someone else. *Easy, Jay,* I told myself. *Take it slow, deep breaths, don't obsess over such a silly, mundane—*

"SOUTHER, get your lazy ass out there to punt!" Coach screamed, so I rushed out onto the gridiron. I was buzzing, not from drugs or alcohol, just the hum and whir of being in the game. It felt good.

I took a deep sniff and was flooded by the contrasting scents of vinegar, Johnson's Baby Shampoo, weed, lye, wet cigars, cut grass, and manure surrounding me. Coach had sweat stains on his cheap suit coat, and furious nostril hairs. He gesticulated wildly, his arms slicing through the air like spastic windmills.

I still hadn't spotted Basil.

SIX...

The team gave me a surge of energy. I squinted my eyes and experienced a type of tunnel vision, imagining myself punting the ball in a Zen-like manner, nailing the damn thing seventy-five yards down the field, hearing the roar of the crowd shouting my name, Jay Souther, NFL-level punter, future Hall of Famer.

As reality set in, I realized I stood alone, fifteen yards from my teammates; the ball was snapped to me. The punt itself, my first attempt in a varsity football game, was horrid, pathetic, to be honest. I was even lucky to have the pigskin contact the side of my ankle. Only a glancing blow. It went about two feet over the line of scrimmage, if that.

A few people booed my effort, so I wasn't feeling much confidence from that point on. I felt like I had failed America, failed democracy, too, I know that might be ridiculous and lame but who knows where that thought emerged from? Maybe it's more my abundance of daddy issues. Not to blame everything on Geoff Henry Souther, but I'm pissed at him; I mean, how does he not want to write? Or text something profound and endearing like "Hello, son," or "You know, daily—" or weekly, or even monthly— "I think of you and miss you with all my heart."

What an awful waste of two good male human beings, who truly should be having a beer together or throwing a football around, or going to, I don't know, maybe an art museum. I mean, Dad, I know squat about architecture and you're an architect. Educate, take me around some cities, okay?

Why won't my father write "Jay, I have an awful ache inside me, and it's for you. I'm sorry I hurt you, Jay, maybe we can talk on the phone tonight. I hope I'm making sense, hope my profoundly hollow and spiritual chasms can somehow be filled by you.

Anyway, now it appears I'm an uncoordinated punter trying hard to get through my days, I have no skills with pigskin. During the game, I could hear the crunch of shoulder pads to helmets on the line, cursing of the offense and defense, scattered voices, a whistle, coaches flipping out on the sidelines, a couple of drunken fools ringing cowbells in the stands, the school band playing something up-tempo, and the hometown fans doing the wave together, and one crazed student dressed as the red cardinal, with his bright red feathers and floppy claws and a distinct mango beak. Whenever St. Andrew's scored a touchdown or field goal, the marching band played the fight song and the tireless bird sprinted the length of the field, flapping his wings up and down.

All of it split-second stuff, so much going on and yet at times, everything appeared to progress in slow motion. Adrenaline is better than any drug, or at least, that's what I say now. I didn't kick the football well that day at all—instead, I choked big time. I kept shanking it, so after punting six times, averaging only 1.4 yards per kick, I was unceremoniously yanked off the field by Coach midway in the third quarter.

"Real shitty ass job, Souther!" Coach grabbed me by the facemask, jerking my head all around.

"Easy, Coach. Christ," I said. "You'll break my neck."

"You promised me you'd make a difference," he said. "You fucking blew it, kid. Six goddamned tries—get the hell out of my sight, you truly suck today. That's undeniable."

"Don't worry," Mom said after the game, which she and Aunt Carol had watched from the stands while drinking hot toddies. "You made the Souther name proud, not that the bar is set very high there."

Throughout the entire game, neither Foster nor Bear approached me. No head butts or words of encouragement. It

SIX...

was only after the game ended that Foster approached me to whisper: "Life is over for Jay Souther very soon indeed."

"Piss off," I said.

"Have you chosen your final song, Jay?" he asked. "Something catchy for your funeral? Perhaps something poppy, or a classic dirge to fit the gravitas of the moment?"

"Go to hell," I said. "You're a sociopathic liar. Everything you do, everything you represent, is all about duplicitous deception. Some ugly ploys for death itself are more like it. You offer the world nada, just nothingness."

"Temper, temper," he said in a singsong way. "No one likes a hothead in this social climate."

I spat to the side, not far from Foster. I moped my way down the field and moved toward the locker room with the other players. But someone kept tugging on my uniform. I turned in annoyance, figuring it was Foster, but instead I found Basil in an oversized St. Andrew's sweatshirt.

"Oh! I—I didn't see you in the stands," I managed to say, stumbling over words.

"Got here late," she said. "You sucked raw out there, though."

"I definitely stunk up the joint," I said and both of us laughed, relieved somehow.

"I still don't know how I feel about you," Basil said. Teammates swarmed past us like we were rocks in a stream.

"Fair enough," I said, holding my hands up. "I definitely appreciate you coming to the game, though, that was sweet and kind of you."

"Sure, no sweat," she said, before turning and walking away.

"Kissy face, kissy face with Jay and Basil," Foster said, banging my pads.

"You're such an immature asshole," Basil snapped at him, giving him the finger.

"So long... it's been good to know you," Foster sang. "So long, it's been..."

"Enough!" I shouted at Foster. *"Enough already."*

BEAR SANTOS

11.17.18

FIVE DAYS...

After my wild, bizarre, whacked-out dream that shook me like a seizure, I drifted through my day in a fog. *What does all that mean?* I wondered. *Such storms inside and out, I can hardly figure them. WTF is it all leading me?*

I had a rare day off at the hospital, so I chilled out. It was Saturday and there were only five days to go to the Greatest Show. I was pleasantly surprised to open my door and see Lavinia there. She looked pretty—her brown hair was cut shorter; she still had the hints of a black eye. Her faded jeans had a few strategically placed holes, and she had a long sleeve yellow T-shirt that read *Stop Staring, please!* She looked brighter and smiled easily.

"Hey All-American," she said. "You and your dad make way too much noise around here, and I can only guess what's going on."

"Forgive us our trespasses," I said, before opening the door wider so she could roll on in. "How's your life going?"

"Decent enough," she said. "I'm trying to be nice to me—a radical concept."

I smiled.

"Can you show me something from the olden days for the hell of it?"

"Yes."

"Is the Rev around?" she asked.

"He's at a conference out in Mystic," I said. "Growing mental health problems in his dwindling congregation, apparently."

"Ah," she said. "Well, I'm quite curious about your antique gadgets."

I walked over to my double-closet and slid the door open. "Got a classic one for you, my dear," I said. "This goes way back, they called it, 'The Bean' in its day..."

"What does it do?"

"Everything on earth."

"Can it magically turn me into a break dancer?"

"Not exactly," I said, "but it can clean, scrub, and save your soul."

"*Alleluia,*" she said, slapping her thigh.

"Redemption for three easy payments of thirty-nine fifty," I said.

I dragged the large inflatable hand from the closet across my carpet into the living room. Like a float with handles. I laid it out before the TV, and she giggled.

"Bon voyage," she said and tumbled from the chair down onto her back and landed on the device, smiling all the while. I noticed how weak her ankles were. Her shirt crept up her belly, showing patterns of scars where she had been burned. Her breasts stood out nicely against her T-shirt. She caught me staring and smiled wider.

"So, you're a guy after all?"

"Hardly," I said, blushing.

"What's that mean?"

FIVE DAYS...

"I lean the other way," I said.

"Just my luck," she said. "Will you come show me how to operate this thing, anyway?"

I squatted beside her. She stretched out, holding the handles. "Now simply rock," I said. "Tighten your abs and rock back and forth, feel the pull at your gut."

She struggled with the motion at first, but eventually she got it. I was on the floor beside her, and I watched her determined body from a foot away. Her breath was quiet and measured.

"Good, that's it now," I said.

"Do I sound hungry, Bear?" she asked. "Or was that sound your belly asking for some substantial food?"

"I thought it was me," I said, laughing. "I'm famished, my dear."

"Yeah, I sensed that," she said, voice trembling. "Would you be okay with me offering you a hug?"

"But, of course," I said, and as I held her close, she reached out her hand and stroked my head. I felt so sheltered, protected. It was the most emotionally intimate moment I had had with anyone in years, maybe ever. Just the warmth of her, our connection, our bond.

"Thanks," I said. "It's nice to have you as my friend, did I ever tell you that?"

"No, you didn't, so, thanks," she said.

I heard neighbors' raised voices, toilets flushing, keys rattling in the hall, blaring TVs. I also heard several barking dogs, along with fire and police sirens screeching past our complex. But none of it bugged me. It was all so easy to ignore. We ordered some pizza. I showed her the other exercise equipment and gave her the autographed photo of Malibu Pilates spokeswoman Susan Lucci.

260

"Merci," she said. "And bend down here so I can buss your head."

So, I bent over and she gave me a hug and kissed my forehead.

"You're a grand one, babe," she said. "Plus, you made my day with is signed photo."

"I aim to please," I said.

It was an odd but poignant time—one of my sweetest nights, looking back. Nothing to do with football or any other sport, school, or The Greatest Show. Just me and Lavinia eating thin-crust pizza, hanging out. Holding onto one another so desperately. My special and treasured friend for life, however long or short that would turn out to be.

JAY SOUTHER

11.18.18

FOUR DAYS...

Foster stood in his bare feet in my kitchen, staring into the empty sink, trembling and mumbling. An extra-large maroon T-shirt covered him down to his muscular thighs like a crude minidress. It was Sunday and he had come into my house earlier in a long red overcoat like some flasher with red Crocs on, but he tossed the coat onto Mom's couch, and left his shoes at the door. I was doing my best to extend my sobriety, drinking root beer. I'd been sobered for over a week and it felt good, but Foster was losing it in my kitchen.

My mother was at the Congregational Church four towns away, enrolled in an adult education course called "Yoga, Jazz, and Jesus." My mind was a whirlwind. I felt both trapped inside my head and outside of myself. My thoughts ran an internal monologue that I barely acknowledged. *Ma kept her part of the summer wager – she had found Jesus Christ and now she goes to church weekly and found new friends, too, and you Jay, have you kept your promise to not to fall for Foster? The slickest con man in the county? Earth to Jay? Can we get an answer about love, guilt, and shame, Jay? And would you admit Foster's a slick shapeshifter, Jay? We need a juicy quote, Jay! Would you agree Foster's a dangerous person? What happens next, young man? Jay? What the hell is your next move?*

It was Sunday afternoon, November 18th, and I knew Ma would throw a shit fit if she knew Foster was in her house, and I didn't want him here, either, but I had reacted like a man without a backbone.

Foster had said all sorts of sweet things on the phone, affirming and apologetic like bullies are capable of, and then he showed up on my stoop, slithering and smiling, saying, "I wanted to apologize for acting like a crazed madman as of late."

I behaved like a broken, bruised victim, forgiving and unfailingly kind, so he rushed into the house. His plan for our deaths was four days away. Foster had brought a sapphire ceramic bowl filled with Reese's Pieces, Twix bars, and Milky Ways, and it was still on the counter and stale candy corn lay scattered about, too, and I was nibbling on stray pieces.

"Maybe I should let it go and tumble into the thicket," Foster said. "Definitely want to embrace the act with all my being."

He had his back to me, but I was watching him as closely as if he were a suicide risk. I crept closer, a weary cop trying to rescue a disturbed teenager on a suspension bridge high above the sea. "You got anything on the premises?" He asked, turning his head furtively. "Booze? Does your ma got any meds hanging around? Some Zanax or perhaps a Valium?"

I realized then that he was as sober as I was, or nearly so. "No," I said, "Let's stay here. Let's stay present." This vulnerability, this torn soul is something I'd only caught glimpses of. But in this moment, his shell was fracturing, flaking away and I needed to nurture this burgeoning life.

FOUR DAYS...

He was still then, posture soft and unsure, staring into the sink. "Are you okay?" I asked, feeling like I'd interrupted him doing something rare and private, like praying the rosary. Foster kept shaking his head, but I was missing the gist.

"So simple to stick my left hand down your garbage disposal and remove all my digits," he said. "Haunts me at how easy that can be, just sweep them away with a late-afternoon latte, perhaps."

"Don't lose your fingers, okay?" I replied. "Those are necessary items."

"So easy to do it, though," he said.

"It'd be a sloppy mess, Foster," I said, "and who wants to clean all that up, right?" Finding myself in control for once, I kept my voice calm, kind, even as my words joked. I gently lifted his hands off the sink's edge, tugging one a little to turn him toward me.

Foster's head was slow to turn away from the cyclops' eye at the bottom of the steel sink. He lifted his bowed head and looked at me, really looked at my face, as he had done only once, maybe twice before. He smiled, a genuine sober smile from the kindest, cleanest parts of his darkened, tattered soul. He lifted our joined hands, placing a dry kiss on my knuckles, his eyes wet and glassy. "Thanks for helping me, man," he said. "But can I ask you something? Late in the game, but an important question, nonetheless?"

"Shoot."

"What if the Greatest Show on Earth was never supposed to be anything but a joke?"

"Say that again."

"What if it was only a prank?" he asked, his grip tightening, as if he were afraid I would tear my hands away. "Something I made up freshman year late one night while studying *Bugs Bunny* with Monster. Nothing but a goof."

"Are you messing with me right now?" I asked.

"It's just a question," Foster said. "What if the Greatest Show was never supposed to be acted out? But then came the drugs and booze and games and wild contests, and everyone embraced it as one... two... three... or more years flew by, and now it sits and breathes and it's Godzilla-like. Massive, sweaty, pulsing, and alive. What if—originally—it was just a lark? Meant for nothing but a good laugh?"

"Then call it off right now, Foster," I said. "Call Bear this instant." I scanned him then, looking for the telltale square bulge in his clothes that indicated a phone. But no, no pockets in this get up. I began to turn toward the raincoat in the other room, but he held my hands firmly halting my motion.

"We can't ever tell Bear, Jay," Foster said. "Bear *needs* the Greatest Show; it centers him, gives him an important focus."

"It could kill him," I said. "Isn't that what you mean?"

His eyes in that moment will forever haunt me. All his lost innocence, fear, desperate need to be loved and wanted, to be seen and understood, all of it welled up in his amazing blue and green beacons. I was transfixed.

I couldn't say how long we stood, still holding hands, stunned and a bit paralyzed by our reflective gaze. A diesel engine across the street roared overloud as the nineteen-year-old neighbor gunned his VW to life, causing our little crystal bubble to shatter.

Foster started as if woken from a dream. His eyes darted as his mind raced for an escape, a recovery option. "Just messing with ya, bud," he said, his voice convincing no one. He mumbled some more phrases my brain wasn't prepared to absorb, slipped into his shoes and raincoat, slithering out my door before I even realized he had released our joined hands.

Elapsed time? Eighteen minutes in total, so I grabbed Febreze off the counter and sprayed it around our kitchen, just

FOUR DAYS...

to have something tangible to do, and to get rid of that scent of vanilla, pine, and cutgrass.

"In summation, the Greatest Show is only a prank," I said out loud. "But for Bear Santos' sake, we're moving full steam ahead with the plans. To Foster Gold, that makes total and complete sense."

BEAR SANTOS

11-19-18

THREE DAYS...

"Pop's stroke killed him a while ago now," Foster said. "I think about it frequently, ruminate about my ruined American childhood and how many times I accidentally pissed on my dad's toilet seat growing up. Some by mistake and a few on purpose, but that's another chapter for a different book! Most importantly, what was the response from my patriarch concerning that specific urine infraction?"

St. Andrew's had a big pep rally for the upcoming Thanksgiving game against rival, Madison, and for the hell of it, there was also a keg party afterward at the captain of the cheerleader's house, Kerry Burns. She attended St. Andrew's sister-school in North Madison, St. Mary's. Our trio, Jay, Foster, and I skipped the party and headed into west woods and we seniors drank like fish. There was a dilapidated cabin up near the Bluff, a lookout where it offered shelter but that was about it, no warmth or food. Foster *loathed* that head cheerleader—she nearly had him arrested for sexting her three summers before, and I was there for everything; Kerry was trouble, especially for Foster.

THREE DAYS...

"Let's just stay away from her," I said.

"Amen," Foster said. The three of us wore baseball caps with lights and our bright LED beams bounced around in front of us on the trail like manic fireflies. Jay had only root beer, for he'd be driving home, but Foster and I went full tilt with Jack Daniels, myself clutching it like a pacifier. Foster was sloppy drunk, spewing all sorts of noxious and toxic insults my way. They echoed off the trunks of the trees in the night.

"It might be the booze, but I'm sick of you tonight, Felipe Bear Santos. I'm nauseous from your pheromones."

"What bug flew up your ass, Sharon?" I asked. "You're dishing out non-stop BS chatter. You sound like a bratty girl."

"Take it easy, guys," Jay said. "Go back to your memory about your dad, Foster, that was perfect for a drunken chat about teen-life issues."

"You're suddenly the host of a teenage talk show, now?" I asked, and Jay shrugged and turned away. "Doogie Souther MD, or something?"

"Do any of you guys have a clue about us going forward concerning life and death?" Foster asked. "Any wisdom to offer your captain, oh, captain?"

"All I know is life is a mixture of nature and nurture," Bear said. "That's the extent of my collective wisdom, though, which is embarrassing and deficient."

"I think it's a mixed bag, too," Jay added. "Frequently, life just sucks."

"Gentleladies, on my eleventh birthday, my soused dad destroyed the shiny little kid that he found nestled inside of me."

"Because you pissed on his toilet seat?" I asked.

"More or less," Foster said. "He arrived home from his mammoth insurance company in Hartford, and he beat me badly. Pop started with a leather belt and then started breaking my bones, followed by using a small hammer, and more traditional kicks and punches to the guts."

"A hammer?" Jay said. *"Jesus."*

"Sears brand, Black & Decker. And he wreaked of Smirnoff vodka, too," Foster said. "He always wreaked of Smirnoff—just the name itself gets me nauseous."

"Are you glad he's out of your life forever?" I asked.

"He was sadistic and enraged, Felipe, but he was still my father. What are you doing, trying to analyze me like that? We all know that's not your strong suit. You fall in line and mind your place."

"You know, maybe I'm getting real sick and tired of your attitude, oh fearless leader. You're supposed to have your shit under control, guide us, but you've been completely off the rails —even for you."

"Oh, woe, woe, and woe is you, Felipe," Foster said. "Honestly, I don't think you bring anything approaching wisdom to our table, haven't in many years. Don't try to start now."

"Bite me," I said.

"Every single one of our dads were sub-par," Foster said. "But Philly, you've truly been shat on by the college scouts and your ghostly dad and life in general, nothing but constant thunderstorms, twisters, or lousy, Cat-5 hurricanes, the world seems to hate you, Bear. Face it, you're absolutely jinxed."

"I'd like to smash this Jack against your entitled mouth," I said, walking at Foster. "Send you home crying to your whore mom."

"Now we're insulting moms, too?" Jay said.

Foster stood up unsteadily before I ran at him and threw the bottle just over his head, smashing it against a huge, gnarled oak tree lurking behind him, glass flying everywhere.

"People should respect me," I said. "Is that too much to ask, Foster?"

THREE DAYS...

"Easy, easy," Jay said. "We respect you."

"Don't be a whiner, what's done is done," Foster said. "Concussions will come and go in our lives, but how long are you going to cling to it like a baby blanket, for Christ's sake?"

"Asshole," I said and spat at my best friend and then walked from the woods to find my way to the cheerleader's house and her keg party. I shouted, "I'm leaving you cold, brutal imbeciles far behind."

"Be safe, Bear Santos," Jay called out. "You're a good man."

"Yeah, whatever, pal," I said, before leaving for the other party.

When I got home late, still drunk, I fell asleep. Sometimes as I rest, I imagine my mom ramblings on about life, death, mortality, wild dreams, and all the complications of being a complete and total human. In my dreams, or hallucinations, whatever they are, she converses with me, keeps me up to date, like I imagine she really would if she were alive. I listened closely as she dished out advice, like her spirit understood that I would not be in this world much longer and she had to convince me to stay.

All the morbid chatter made me examine every possibility. My ideas bopped around within me and offered some bloody Shakespearean drama; Titus Andronicus in action, a quote I had to memorize for an English Literature class last year. "Vengeance is in my heart, death in my hand, blood and revenge are hammering in my head."

Or should I hover in the middle somewhere, a limbo, a heavenly space station with snacks, bathrooms, and comfortable pillows? A rest area on the turnpike to betterment was another of mom's spirited discussions.

Each scenario in the survival game ricocheted inside my six-five body. It went something like this... Foster insisted if I stuck it out with him and Jay and died on Thanksgiving, we'd own the world. Three jocks rocking the globe off its axis for ten minutes or so.

Mom asks: what about your own future, Philip Santos? All the dreams and desires to improve your life, why give up so a lonely, dark, megalomaniacal teen named Foster can wrangle you into destroying yourself? What about my son being his true self? Not hiding from anyone? Don't you want to experience the world as the authentic Phil Santos and love whomever you wish?

Yeah, but I'm so damn tired, Ma. My head aches. I either sleep too much or I'm groggy, fuzzy as hell. Any new ideas make me maddeningly dizzy—it seems like I can't absorb anything fresh. Is that how I want to spend the next sixty years? Permanently stuck in high school mode? No skills. No contributions. Nothing to offer the world but my damn physique that can't even do what it's supposed to anymore on account of its bashed-in brain up top.

And honestly, who would miss me? My only friend would be gone, too. Dad wouldn't notice except for the embarrassment I'd cause him.

I'd miss you, my mother's voice whispered. Plus, you have a full and healthy life waiting there just outside the sports realm and beyond the damn athletic fields. And art museums and history ones, and Latino artworks. I know you love that so much when you stop in at that gallery on Gently Green. You're young and who knows what advances the world will make as you grow. No, no way, Felipe, never give up. I refuse to watch you quit the world, understand? Time to grow, to expand yourself into the universe. And just between you and me, I'd like to see you leave the drugs in the rearview.

As this frantic debating went on in my mind, my dad, the right Reverend continued to preach with his fire and brimstone rhetoric every Sunday, passing the hat, offertory collections

THREE DAYS...

getting smaller, or so he reported to me at dinner. An exodus from organized religion—Dad had shown me a copy of *a Time* magazine article three years earlier about the lack of faithful folk.

The article spoke of a brisk walk in the woods, working out, writing, or singing in a choir, each something I could relate to. The only problem with all that, my father claimed, was that it was rarely a church choir, usually just a communal group, or walking group, informal, with no spiritual base. "We need more than a willing group of fit young agnostics," he said. "Where have all the Christian believers disappeared too? That's what I'd like to know? Weddings and baptisms are a rarity, they never happen in our church. It's nothing but funerals for my believers. Bury, bury, bury is all I do now."

The congregation my father preached to had grown older with him and a great deal grumpier. The Rev told me about his growing spiritual alliance with a very conservative group, which blew my mind. Good God, wherever Mom was lurking in the stratosphere, I hoped she was rolling her eyes.

I wish my Ma had been there to keep me balanced through all the lean years. I'd become frightened by everything new. My concussions had snuffed out any glimmer of hope. I felt hampered, my judgment way off. I remember Foster telling me that hanging around with Tuck was the perfect strategy for us —how everyone in school would think we were kind, compassionate, and plain wonderful human beings.

"We're heroes for doing next to nothing, Bear," he said. "We hang out with a bizarre freak like Tucker Smiley Reis, and people worship us. They'll kiss our ass and trust us with everything they got."

What a manipulative creep Foster was—what he did with Tuck Reis was more like an ex-communication, a dismissal. I was complicit in the whole plan, though. I went along with many of Foster's ideas and schemes. I can't pretend I have no responsibility—I'm learning that as I mature. Tuck was a cool person to know, super bright, undoubtedly smarter than Foster, too, which might have played a role in how he was let go by us. Later, I heard Foster took Tuck's head and shoved it into the toilet and gave him a Swirly, nearly drowned him. *Asshole* is the word to describe someone who treats other humans in that manner—I don't care who he is. Even if it's Foster.

It feels awful to see how I've let good people down in my quest to...do what, exactly? End our life, *end my life?* When I first heard our St. Andrew's Principal Brother Tomas discussing the Chewbacca film, a part of me wanted to stand, beat my chest, and shout, "Bear Santos was a key player in all that business. Guess who purchased Chewy's mask at Walmart? Guess who was chilling out in the crowd with his sunglasses, red fedora, and long red scarf? That's right, you wretched idiot, it was me."

But I don't feel that way now—I feel no pride. I don't know what exactly I feel. Shame and fear, I guess. An abundance of fear. Do you hear me now, Carly? I feel like I'm missing a limb, or maybe I'm the limb, missing the rest of me.

JAY SOUTHER

TWO DAYS...

It was Tuesday, November 20, 2018, and as I walked into the Wave Café, one employee with Down Syndrome greeted me with a cheery, "Good afternoon, my friend." I had grown fatigued of the droning employee greeters at Walmart, but this interaction felt different for some reason. Was it more sincere at this place, perhaps? Or was it only that it was a new, fresher face?

Each of the employees with developmental disabilities had a role at the coffee shop, preparing, baking, and serving the coffee, treats, and eats, cleaning up, washing dishes, etc. One young lady in braids named Patty took the orders and collected the money. Another young man, Gerald, his nametag read, carried a tray of oatmeal raisin cookies from the oven to the counter, and cautiously slid them into place on the display shelf.

Basil had told me she felt appreciated there and enjoyed the camaraderie. Before I could order a root beer and pumpkin bread, though, Basil approached me with hot cocoa on the house.

"What's this?" I asked, pointing and Basil leaned in, and as I spooned out the oddly shaped marshmallow, we bumped foreheads. We sat in the corner, near a bubble-like window, an aviary. The spot was jammed with ferns, sunflowers, and succulents, and a little fountain that made sounds of water rushing over tiny stones.

"The free cocoa is because you're an avid, dedicated, but in the end, mediocre athlete," she said, smiling, her lovely, gapped teeth on full display.

"God, that was a nightmare game," I said.

"Chalk it up to experience," she said. "There are bigger challenges in life, right?"

"One can hope," I said. "Foster was a typical asshole."

"He's always been like that, though," she said, shaking her head.

"I never heard you say much about him," I said.

Basil grabbed my hands: "Does Foster like guys, Jay?"

"I'd say so," I said. "Yes."

"What about girls?"

"Not at all, really. He never speaks of girls, unless he's in a real prissy mood, then he sends nonstop lewd messages and pictures of his hard-on to anyone, he does all that shit just to get under other girls' skin. Rarely is he ever interested in that person, sexually speaking."

"Your hands are trembling now, why's that?" she asked.

I shrugged.

"Is there something you wanted to tell me?" Basil asked.

"I've been sobered for over a week," I said. "No more drugs or drink ever again."

"Excellent, keep up the great work," she said. "A good start for you."

"I could share a lot more with you," I said, "but I fear you'd

TWO DAYS...

sprint off. Last time you didn't want to hear a damn thing and skateboarded away so rapidly."

"I was in a shitty-ass mood," Basil said. "Be honest and I won't run away."

"I'm bisexual," I said.

"Right," Basil said, nodding. "I took a wild guess and figured that out after you fooled around with Foster."

"It's more of a blur to me, honestly, everything happened so fast."

Basil put her chin in her hand and said, "Seems like you're trying to rationalize it all way here."

"Weed, music, way too much booze," I said. "I thought I loved him for a few hours, too, which was stupid, because he's long gone, a creep, an idiot, in fact. I frequently get swept away by dreams, music, colors, people, or so my mom says."

She continued studying me, so I shook my head.

"Sorry about all that," I said.

"You piss me off, Jay," she said. "You've disappointed me with your Foster obsessions and the pathetic affair. I'm crushed, if I may use that term."

"A heinous mistake on my part, Basil."

Basil was staring at me quizzically with her lovely blue eyes, so clear and determined. I didn't know what she felt, and I couldn't take her prying stare, so I glanced at the front counter. Near the espresso machine, two employees laughed. I smelled coffee, of course, maple syrup and pumpkin bread, and the sound system played a crappy, uninspired "coffee shop jazz" Spotify playlist.

Basil was waving at me then.

"You still here, Jay?"

"Yeah, sorry," I said. "Zoned out for a few minutes."

"I have something to tell you. Rents are too high here," she said. "So, we can't afford to stay around too much longer."

"You're leaving Gently?"

"Possibly in six months or so, July or August looks like," she said. "Ohio, I think, near Columbus, probably."

"*Crap,*" I said, and watched Basil; I didn't want to lose her. She seemed overly mature, like a time traveler with a decade of extra experience inside her soul. And those narrow, refined lips of hers.

"What are you going to do about your nasty friends, Jay?" she asked. "They're so bizarre it scares me, especially when they're with you."

I nodded. "Strange," I said. "Just stupid boys being cruel..."

"More like sadomasochism in action," Basil said. "Foster texts me too much. What?"

"Sunday, Tuesday, and Friday night—late," she said. "He said Jay Souther 'lacked any decency in his nasty frame.'"

"He's an asshole."

"I don't see why you stick with those idiots."

"We're trapped together somehow, linked," I said. "A warped bond."

"Yeah," Basil said, releasing my hand. "I lost Avery that way—drunken, stupid, bullshit macho games. False brotherhood... so soaked with toxicity that it reeks. Don't let it take you away, too, Jay."

"I promise."

She stood and dusted off her apron. "I have to get back to work."

As I rode my bike home, I was furious, enraged. *Screw the seniors,* I thought. *But Foster's out of his head, Jay. Don't forget the recording—rat bastard has me trapped.*

I turned my phone off and stayed in.

"Why aren't you going out with your pals?" Mom said.

TWO DAYS...

"Sick of them, Ma," I said. "I'm nauseated by who they are."

"Good to hear that, Jay," she said. "Glad you're coming around."

I wondered whether Foster and Bear had ever consummated their extended homoerotic dance and jive. The way we had. It would explain why Bear had reacted so violently the other night when Foster told him we'd been together.

I had my fill of suicidal revolutionaries and I'd grown tired of their petty games. Seeing Foster contemplate slicing his digits off in my own kitchen had done it for me, plus telling me a triple suicide was nothing but a prank he made up freshman year was bracing. The whole thing is an empty, toxic scam. What are my options now? Maybe Basil isn't that into me, and I've been headed down a wrong path.

But what if I pursued Basil more honestly? *Why not care more about your own life, Jay Souther?* I scolded myself. *Give a damn about something, anything.* It was like that ancient rock anthem by *The Clash* clanging around in my skull night and day. *"Should I stay, or should I go?"*

"Nothing like being sixteen to steady my frazzled nerves," I whispered.

As I fell into a deep slumber that evening, I saw myself as a kid, leaping off our porch front steps, imagining myself hang-gliding over snowy cliffs in Switzerland. Then, I was a little older splashing around Wadsworth Falls in Middlefield. The memories sped up, flashing by in glimpses. Playing Whiffle Ball at Shell Beach, giggling on the swings at my elementary school. Then, there were some memories that weren't my own. I watched my nephew marry the girl of his dreams while an elderly man with a four-pronged cane tossed ginkgo leaves on them instead of rice, and then I was an uncomfortable fifteen-

278

year-old, drinking cheap beer at a high school keg party in west woods.

And everything slowed dramatically. I was a substitute teacher, way out of shape and trying to drop twenty-five pounds by sometime in the New Year. The holidays were rapidly approaching, so I was on a kale-and-peanut-butter shake diet, jogging daily and doing fifty pushups and fifty sit-ups at the end of my miles.

I stared at the sunrise, soaking up wondrous, early colors. I saw wispy hints of yellow, tangerine, and raspberry morphing into wild pinks along the eastern horizon. The high school football field had real grass, not fake stuff that wouldn't stain your clothes. I tried to focus one hundred yards away to the opposite end zone. I didn't have my glasses or my cell on me—they were resting on the dash of my Ford—but sometimes when I squinted, I could see decently enough.

As I set my gaze on the far side of the field, a sudden sinking feeling, an ugly ache overwhelmed my core. The worst wasn't the initial and shadowy, unfocused sight of them swaying in the cold gusts, or the raw anguish. You see, it had taken me so long to notice the figures, to acknowledge them. I tried to rationalize the sight away: the big Thanksgiving Game was coming up soon, so the stupid kids had attached something to the goalposts to drive the opponents nuts. Maybe a mannequin or scarecrow of the rival quarterback?

But I knew those figures weren't pillows or dolls or fancy mannequins of any sort. They were bodies—real students. My water bottle slipped from my hands, and I sprinted down the field, shouting and praying, "Jesus, have mercy. Lord, send some kindness and mercy to the kids."

When I was near enough, I could finally see the three boys. One golden-haired, one with a darker complexion, and one a good deal smaller in frame. I was doubling over, dry heaving.

TWO DAYS...

"Help," I shouted. "Someone. Please, lend a hand!"

Their jerseys were vivid red and black, the colors garish, but worse were the starched white football pants, each stained with piss and shit, dripping like leaky faucets.

I fell to my knees, only five feet from them. Their gloriously youthful faces were bloated, pale, and long gone. The frigid air had made each blade of grass feel coarse against my palms. Everything about the field was hostile, from the ground to the looming goalposts, adorned with three nooses and the trifecta of swaying flesh.

BEAR SANTOS

11.20.18

Thanksgiving was only two days away, and I found myself at a community art gallery I visited periodically just off the Gently Green. It was squeezed in between a bakery and an old, cramped bookstore but once you stood inside it didn't feel so tiny because there were two skylights and a wide window. The space was filled with the work of local artists.

Nothing too groundbreaking—just simple examples of cool colors and a few twisting, odd sculptures, one appearing like a giant piece of saltwater taffy. What the hell is a depressed and concussed high school football player doing in a place like that? It's a fine question because I was very tentative when I first stopped by. But then I started to see playing fields—granted, colorful athletic fields, all around me.

There was one talented woman who painted these tiny and colorful erotic triangles. Splashes of orange and yellow, explosions of hues that seemed about ready to spill outside of their frames. At times, she mixed it up and tried swirling spheres. A blue ray of sunshine, a cinnamon moon, an erupting purple and lime comet.

Much of it went way over my head, but I enjoyed stopping in, anyway. I saw baseball diamonds in the reflection of orange and white, or a neon-pink racquetball court. I enjoyed the funky geometric shapes the best—I wished I could carry all of her pieces in my pocket at school and I would pop them like candy. Little visual doses of color assisted me in floating, soaring, and swimming through my afternoons. Like a sober but artistic buzz, something with a real kick. A whole lot better for me than all that illegal crap I inhale with Foster and Jay during the week. One hundred times better, in fact.

"One day you'll have to purchase a few pieces from me, Bear," Eddie the owner said. "Take it home, you could study it like you do here. Sixty bucks. It's a hell of a bargain for all the inspiration it leaves you with."

"One day, Eddie," I said. "I'll be back with cold cash and buy three or four of them."

* * *

When I returned home, I was greeted by a scowling, hissing Lavinia, her eyes wet, mouth enraged, spittle flying.

"You're a slimy, horrific bastard, a true low life," she said. "Not to mention an idiot."

"What the hell has gotten into you?" I asked, immediately defensive and loathing myself for it.

"You lied, and I hate liars, Bear," she said. "I don't know if I can forgive you."

"I literally have no idea what you're even—"

"A young person at the psychiatric hospital, who will go unnamed, said you've stolen several of her prescriptions. She's been unmedicated for days, and now she's back in the hospital because of you."

I tried to take a deep breath, but it became all uneven and

ACADEMY OF UNHOLY BOYS

shaky. "Listen, okay, it's not what you think. I'm not going to say I didn't do it, but...a friend of mine needed those medications so much more. It was a complete emergency situation."

"And this friend was no doubt Foster Gold, right?"

"So, what? When you really get to know him, he's—"

"Just like you, an awful, toxic fraud who gives out nasty drugs to at-risk kids. I'm done with you, kid. Get out of my sight."

"Lavinia." There was heat at the back of my throat, in my eyes.

"You let me down, Bear," she said. "Oh, and you don't have a job anymore, by the way."

"That's not fair to me," I said, tears spilling. "You're gonna throw me out like trash because of one mistake?"

"This isn't one mistake, Bear. It's a lifetime, short as yours has been. You're too messed up to be trusted and I can't let myself be around people like you." She turned her chair away from me, knuckles white over the wheel rims. "There's no excuse for what you've done to me, to this young lady and her life. How you acted so genuinely. You swindled good people, ones who were trying to turn their lives around."

"That's not true," I pleaded. "I was trying to be a good friend to you. I swear."

"Don't you get it? Foster Gold doesn't love you. Man, he's been playing you for a chump for years, stringing you along like some love-struck pup since you were fifth graders."

I don't know when I'd started shaking. "Why say that to me now, though?"

"Smarten up," Lavinia said. "Be real for once. Get your head out of your ass and move on, or you will die in the wasteland of your own making, or in prison."

TUCK

11-20-18

It was Tuesday, November 20 and I was stunned by the early snow we were having—something like seven inches and more on the way. I wore fingerless gloves, and I had shot a lot of black and white photographs around the Gently Green with my SLR this week. As of late, I felt like I was soaring high above the fray, carefree as I rode my trail bike and recorded video with my Go-Pro camera. Spending time with Basil Sous had psyched me up, helped me see the world with more clarity and color, which Dr. Athens said was, "truly a hopeful sign in your life."

"Yes," I said.

"Doesn't mean she loves you in sexual way, though," Dr. Athens added.

"I know, I get that," I said. "It's just a sweet thing, a good event for me. Let me have this real tender moment for a while, okay?"

"Okay, you're right. I'm sorry. My error there."

After I developed the film, I drew ghouls and twisted, bloated faces in neon orange on top of the pics with oversized

ACADEMY OF UNHOLY BOYS

teeth, and scribbled lots of Z words upside down. *Zaire, zeitgeist, Zamboni, zenith, zeppelin, zealot, zero, zebra.*

I shared a brownie and soda with Basil at Wave on Tuesday. I saw her break away from a chat with Jay as he moved quickly out the door. It was the second day in a row Basil, and I hung out together after her shift. I drove her home for the first time in my father's dented green Jeep. Basil lives in a large cottage with rose-colored shutters and weathered shingles and a huge wrap-around porch with expansive windows and skylights, "which leak like a bastard," Basil informed me, so we just sat outside for a while. We chatted in the driveway as the snow became rain, making the loveliest pitter-patter sounds on the roof.

"Real sweet home you got here," I said.

"We're renting it, though—in reality, we have very little cash to our name," she said. "It's hard for Aunt Peg to hold onto the job, I guess. Not exactly sure why that is."

"I'm sorry."

"I'm glad you're alive, though," Basil said. "That helps me abundantly."

"Yeah?"

"I'm happy you're here with me tonight, Tuck," she said. "I forget what's coming tomorrow, or which volcano erupted last year, but you helped me cope well this week, so I'm thankful for that."

"You're welcome, Basil," I said. "Which volcano was it again?"

"A smaller island in Hawaii, I believe," she said. "Many lives wrecked; homes ruined. Recall it?"

"Maybe Kilauea," I said. "Enough lava to fill one hundred thousand backyard pools."

"Yeah, that has to be it," she said. "Just who comes up with such vivid analogies on the fly?"

"A reformed troll out in cyberspace, I guess," I said. "Doing his level best to make up for all his sins, wild treachery, and grave hacking errors."

She smiled. "That's it, I think, a chastened troll starting afresh with good deeds."

Sirens were heard all around us, until a fire engine roared past Basil's driveway, sirens screeching and all lights flashing, followed by four other pickup trucks, volunteer firefighters shooting past, and several Gently Police cruisers.

Basil said, "Why do you keep your left hand up over your mouth when you talk, Tuck?"

"Anxiety and the cruelest of nerves," I said, thinking, *Stop being such a freak*. "It's hard to explain it fully to someone without feeling foolish."

We sat in the dim light of Dad's Jeep. There was no speech, only the music of Bon Iver's "Roslyn." With the steady rain pelting the vehicle, the sound was peaceful, soothing. All I felt at the time was admiration, like I was becoming a big fan of her.

"Nice to enjoy the quiet music and rain, though, no?" she said, and I nodded.

"Yes," I said. "Check out the glove box before you leave tonight Basil."

"Oh, yeah?" she said, opening it, and discovering a manila envelope and inside a black and white photo of Foster Gold dressed up in his home football uniform at St. Andrew's stadium. Scrawled on top of it were upside-down monsters in neon orange and lime, and numerous 'Z' words.

"Ah," she said. "Foster is undoubtedly a zero of a zealot."

"I wasn't sure if you knew him or not," I said.

"Unfortunately, I do," she said. "What's your take on him, Tuck?"

"Possibly a wannabe sociopath?" I asked. "Or just an annoyingly lazy lounge lizard that lacks any self-worth?"

ACADEMY OF UNHOLY BOYS

"Did he ever hurt you?" she asked.

"He tried to once," I said," and Basil slipped out the door, before turning back a few seconds later.

"Damn, I almost forgot all about your wonderful photo, Tuck," she said.

"No problem," I said.

"You're talented, I mean it," she said. "Marketable skills right here."

"Thanks, Basil."

"Just think," she said. "Without Dr. Athens and Salvador Dali, we probably would have never met."

"Here's to psychotherapy, surrealism, and funky, massive aquariums," I called out. She turned, smiled, and offered a thumbs-up. Then the door closed, and she went into her home. I sat and breathed evenly in her driveway for another minute before Basil's outside light eventually flickered on. I heard her dogs barking so I took a deep breath, exhaled, and backed out onto the main street, and drove myself home in the rain.

"That was a damn good day," I said to my reflection in the rearview.

BASIL SOUS

Several hours after Tuck Reis had dropped me off at home, I discovered our friend Benny had died, but Peg wouldn't tell me any of the details.

"People don't just die in this world, Peg," I told her. "Not someone as strong as Benny, a fighter such as Benny. Something fishy is going on with her case, I believe."

Peg shook her head. "I knew you'd think all that sort of business, Basil, but she just flat-out died. Her heart gave out, she was tired, real exhausted."

"From illness or drug overdose?" I asked. "I mean, Benny was an amazing force of life, of light."

Peg shrugged, brushing what little hair I had with a silver-backed brush that once belonged to my mom. Peg used gentle strokes, something that typically relaxed me, but just then I felt ice cold.

"Benny was a class act," Peg said. "No doubt about that one. You could always count on her to be there when she said she would."

"Right," I said.

ACADEMY OF UNHOLY BOYS

"But that's all we know for now," Peg said. "I haven't heard anything new."

"Suicide, maybe?" I asked, and she made a sour face.

"Always a remote possibility," Peg said. "Police said nothing should be ruled out at this point and time. Nothing."

"Where'd they end up finding Benny, though?"

"Not important or relevant to tonight's conversation, Basil."

"Peg?"

"It doesn't mean anything where they found her damn body, Basil," she said.

"Where was she?" I asked. "Come on, Peg, where the hell she end up?"

"A good distance away, I'll have you know. Quite far away from Gently, in fact, over twenty-five miles."

"Please tell me, Peg?"

"A motel bathtub along the Berlin Turnpike," she said. "In the Newington area."

"Christ Almighty," I said. "Another one gone, lost forever."

"I know," Peg said. "But you talk to your friend tonight, okay? I'm going to an AA meeting to discuss more, but you chat with that young man that you like so much, the sophomore. Don't carry all this heavy weight on your own. Call the one who sent you the poem, okay?"

"I will, I promise to phone him," I said.

"You will speak to him, correct?" she asked. "What's his name again?"

"Jay," I said. "I'll phone Jay Souther right now."

She nodded, bending over to kiss my forehead.

"You sure you're good?" Peg asked.

"Yep," I managed, and Peg headed out into the night. It was late, and I never call anyone's cellphone after ten, but Jay picked up. I apologized profusely.

DAVID FITZPATRICK

"No problem, Basil," Jay said. "I always enjoy hearing from you."

"Thanks."

"Is everything okay?" he asked.

"I guess so," I said, thinking, *Don't go into a long, drawn-out chat with him.*

"Tell me what's up," Jay said.

"Something peculiar, I guess. Can I bounce a few things off you?"

"Sure."

"People fade on me, Jay," I said. "Feels like a horrible type of luck."

"Like with your brother, Avery, right?"

"Yes, but that's just the start," I said. "I fear that everyone I know will start dropping over, cancer, heart attack, or a violent death. A friend of my aunt, a strong lady named Benny just overdosed at a motel in Newington, right off Berlin Turnpike."

"Whoa," he said, which made me smile, because it was such a quintessential Jay comment.

"See," I said. "I get afraid that it'll happen to everyone in my life, bit by bit. It hasn't yet, just with my parents, and now Avery and Benny. It's just my anxiety, my worries, and obsessions getting the best of me."

"I hear you, Basil," he said. "I'll be here with you all night long if you need me."

That's deep for Jay, I thought, before correcting myself. *For anyone.*

"One last thing," I said. "I do worry on your behalf though, Jay."

"Why?"

"You got a long life ahead of you," I said. "Beyond the seniors' bullshit games, but somehow they have their meaty hooks in you."

ACADEMY OF UNHOLY BOYS

"Yes," Jay said. "Both of them are idiots."

"You go and say that to me in a sincere, honest way," I said. "But then you still stick with them. Why?"

Jay said, "Truthfully, part of me feels trapped."

"Let's make a vow," I said. "You check in with me, and I'll check with you before we do something stupid, especially if it's dangerous or life threatening. Agreed?"

"Yes," he said. "We'll be like Batman and Alfred."

"Who's Batman in your equation?" I asked, after a second.

"*You're* Batman," Jay said. "But Alfred might be in over his head, so you're going to go help him out, see?"

"Okay, sure," I said and hung up with Jay, but felt better about us. I knew Jay probably wanted to hear more—like maybe I was set to lay my bare body down so he could ravish me, but that wasn't going to happen. *Not tonight, at least.* But he *does* think of me as Batman—which is sort of cool.

JAY SOUTHER

11-21-18

ONE...

I finally took Mom's best advice. She had been impatient with my incessant abusing of self with alcohol and drugs, but I was finally getting nauseous of the seniors and The Greatest Show BS, so I skipped school and football practice one day. Mom had described it as a mental health day, which I thought was cool of her. Plus, she mentioned a greenhouse near the New Haven-Hamden line recently, a charming place called Edgarton Park. She said, "Your father and I both believed it had magical doses of possibility."

Mom rarely used hippy-trippy references in her daily chatter, so I knew I had to check it out, but I felt rotten inside. I would leave Planet Earth soon, or so Bear and Foster told me constantly. I drove into New Haven in Mom's old blue Ford sedan. The snow had already started falling; they were huge fat flakes. I felt numb, like I couldn't ever be touched now.

I stopped first at Atticus Bookstore on Chapel Street and bought a book of poems for my mom called *Bonfire Opera* by Danusha Lameris. It was her favorite new poet. I drove through the city, and past a group of Yale students laughing, slipping, and sliding towards Woolsey Hall for lunch. On that day, I felt I must see growth—flowers and plants. I felt I needed the greenery and the abundance of color. Anything but the incessant winter slush. I spoke to myself a lot during those days of trying to fix my life, not in a completely whacked-out manner, just sort of leaving voice-overs for the scenes my eyes absorbed. I found myself on stately Whitney Avenue and drove through the snow to the park. I kept on repeating a mantra, a theme for the day. I said:

"People, time, and events—they just pass over me."

I walked through the gates of the park and saw several bundled-up kids building a snowman with an older sister, or perhaps a young mom. I had to find that spot, I needed to see life sprouting somewhere. I was so sick of this early winter, and its bracing miseries. I passed a wide basin that worked as a birdbath in warmer weather, and saw it slicked with ice.

There were squirrels, ravens, and pigeons, and a bundled-up figure walking a regal-looking black poodle along the far stonewall. I made my way up a slight hill and spotted the greenhouse. Its windows were fogged up, and when I eventually found a door, I said "hello" twice, but no one answered, so I went past a collection of flowers, some rhododendrons and other plants that I didn't know the name of. There was a symphony sounding on an old FM radio, Mozart, I think.

The radio rested on a wooden, green stepstool with chipped green paint. I found an open door next to it, and a space as small as a closet that was somehow a toilet, and so I went as quickly as possible, feeling like the intruder I was. I looked down at the cleaners surrounding me, Clorox, bleach, Ajax, and Mr. Clean. My thoughts raced: *No one will even miss you, Jay. Your useless flesh by now, guzzle the bleach and say adios.*

"I'm loved by Mom, Aunt Carol, and Dad. And Basil cares

ONE...

for me, too, or at least, I think she does. Stop your pity party, Souther, that shit is not allowed."

I came out of the bathroom, and a squat, balding man with red cheeks glared at me with a water spritzer pointed at my face.

"Whom were you talking to in there?" he asked.

"I mumble to myself a lot," I said. "Gibberish mostly."

"Is that what young people do nowadays?" he asked, lowering the spritzer, which I realized must be for the plants. "Do they just appear out of the cold, and piss in my bathroom whenever they wish?"

"I'm so sorry, sir, I had to go," I said.

"Why not the great outdoors?" he asked, starting to smile. "Why not go out there, a little more yellow snow isn't going to kill anyone, right?"

I shivered a little, not sure what to make of him.

"Speechless?" he asked, clapping his hands up near my face.

"What?"

When he didn't answer he signaled for me to follow him.

"Come with me, son," he said. "Let me show you something, keep following me way down this aisle."

"I got to get going soon, sir—"

He waved a dismissive hand. "You must be frozen in just a down vest and short sleeves—foolish to be out dressed like that on a cold, snowy day."

"Yeah, I guess," I said, and he gestured again for me to follow. "Although, I don't really feel the cold all that much..."

"Just walk right along here," he said. "I want to show you something that I hope might ease you some."

I followed him through two more long sets of doors, and there was so much splendid color surrounding me—I saw orange phlox and brilliant poppies and all sorts of flora, even a little bonsai tree. I also noticed a miniature pool just the right size for some fluttering koi fish doing their thing in white, silver, gold, speckled black, and spotted. It was lovely, really, so many different ones. I could watch koi fish all day.

As I walked one and half greenhouse-length buildings, nature was raging all around us. But I started to perspire and panic, and nearly ran away. A part of me was nearly ready to sprint back to the exit, and to mom's Ford, but the man mumbled something over his shoulder.

"What? I didn't get that, sir."

"Do you like beauty?" he asked. "As a rule, I mean?"

"Yes, I'm a huge fan of beauty," I said. "And you have it everywhere in this damn place."

"Great, wonderful," he said. "It always invigorates me, gets me all juiced up to take on the world in all is blahness, beigeness, and petty mediocrity."

"Yes," I said, and the man squatted down inside the greenhouse for six seconds near a whole row of succulents, and slowly he presented me with a small green cactus, a bright yellow flower blooming on its top right. The air, the bright colors, and the substantial green was everywhere—it was what I needed, what I had wanted to see. I reached out for the cactus, but my face, my head, my eyes, it was like I was treading water in the wonderful hues of growth and life. A botanical garden. There were fronds and buds of kelly green and lime, and pastoral ferns. It was truly sweet.

"Do you like it?" he asked.

"I don't know," I said. "But it's refreshing to be here, I love all the colors."

"I didn't like these kinds of plants, either" he said, gesturing for me to take the alien-looking cactus. "I'm not a big fan of cactus as a rule. Nevada, New Mexico, etcetera, I've got no interest in visiting those states. All those

ONE…

venomous snakes out there waiting for us with our tasty, pasty ankles."

"Right," I said, and then, "Thank you for giving me the cactus, sir. But I don't know much about plants."

"You take it, you'll grow to love it," he said. "I'll give you a little bag to cover it properly outdoors, but it should be fine. It's a hearty son of a bitch. It can handle serious shit in terms of nasty weather."

"Thanks."

He reached up, patting my shoulder. "Your face looks real sore—were you attacked?"

"In a way, yeah," I said, flushed.

He looked concerned. "Who was the lousy bum?"

I hesitated. "An asshole I had a crush on, but he nailed me with an elbow," I said, not sure why I was confessing to this man, but he nodded like he'd guessed it.

"Sounds like a tough punk," he said.

"Real cocky asshole," I said, tilting the little cactus. "Foster is his name."

"Ah, that must be difficult," he said. "I appreciate you telling me the truth."

"Yeah," I said. "No problem."

"Life can be disorienting," he said, "but you seem, unusually lost, like you were going to freeze to death out there in the ice and snow."

"Oh," I said, "I'll make it."

"I watched you wander around outside the greenhouse in the cold snow," he said. "Trying not to be noticed. I wanted to hand you something, I saw your yellow-blue marks, the bruises."

"Yeah," I said, clearing my throat. "I guess it's nothing."

"No, no, don't ever say that," he remarked. "Do you let the

asshole strike you because you're depressed or angry—which one?"

I felt uncomfortable, ugly feelings rumbling inside of me. I said: "Both, I guess."

He nodded. "Life's not always so heinous, okay?" he said. "Light does emerge way down the road, believe me, it truly does. It's lovely, so beautiful when it shows."

"Yes," I said. "I'd like to see that."

"I hope it happens soon for you," he said.

I felt pressure behind my eyes. Was it a migraine? Or perhaps the start of a nervous tic? "That's real kind of you."

"Take good care of that cactus—treat it with respect, the same way you hope to treat yourself on the good days."

"Right, yes."

"You want to come back next week for a visit?" he asked. "I could show you a few things here — working with nature eases the soul, soothes the savage beast, that sort of thinking."

"I'm leaving town," I said, practicing the sound of the truth. "Checking out for good. But at some point, I would like to return here, it has a cool groove."

"Hm. Don't let them screw you over too much, okay?" he said, and squeezed my shoulder, and walked past, and soon we were back at the main door. He shook my hand with both of his again, smiling.

"Thanks. I appreciate this," I said, gesturing a little awkwardly with the cactus in my free hand.

"It's my pleasure. Your father is a good soul, solid and decent and Irish as can be."

"You knew him? You know me?"

"Back in the day, I helped Geoff with stocks and investments. What a talented architect he is. Your mom is great, too. Why'd you say 'knew'?"

ONE...

I hadn't even noticed I'd used the past tense. My eyes went back to the little flower. "I'm afraid Dad's fallen on hard times."

The man nodded. "I heard. He'll land on his feet. You'll see. He'll be back, mark my words on that, okay, Jay?"

"Yes, sir."

"Call me Miller. Miller Fisher," he said. He turned and took in the verdant plant life around us, wiping a drop of sweat from his nose. "I work at Yale University, but I love plants, so I volunteer here. It's a must or I'd go nuts in the ivory towers. That's no lie."

I nodded, studying him.

He watched me watch him. "I got your back, Jay. Call me about anything. I mean it now. My own boy's only a few years older than you. I know how tough things can be, especially in high school, it's brutal sometimes."

"Thanks." I repeated it, a little more emotion leaking through. "Thank you."

"I'm with you," he said, slipping his business card into the pocket of my rust-colored down vest. Then I was suddenly back out into the snow, feeling overreactive, like I would sob at any second. I sped up as the fat flakes came down heavy and wet. I turned back to the door, but Miller Fisher was gone, hidden behind those fogged-up windows. I felt such warmth in my chest, and my gut, that I had to bend over and take several full, deep breaths, hugging the bagged-up cactus close to me.

I've got your back, Jay. I hadn't felt so weepy in years. I stood, exhaled, and walked on, noticing more kids had stopped to help build the snowman. The poodle and his owner were long gone.

Kindness is never bad, I told myself. *It's never bad.* To the left of me, a stooped, older woman with a large persimmon scarf draped around her face was leading an Irish Setter along a trail. I heard voices behind me and turned to watch young lovers dumping snow on each other, rolling around and kissing passionately. They giggled, made out, and boasted of their love's uniqueness. The male was a striking fellow with olive skin and a handsome face. The redheaded girl had extraordinary ice-blue eyes, and a curvy body to match, and she was only half the size of the towering young man.

I turned from them and hustled along, trying to protect my cactus. I put my face up towards the bone-white sky, catching the flakes on my tongue, on my teeth, until it hurt. My cheeks were wet from the snow, my nose, too. The air was sharp, bracing, and I hustled beneath the stone arch of the entrance and was soon on Whitney Avenue. It was as if I felt the cold temperatures, the frigidity, for the first time. I saw my mom's blue Taurus covered in wet snow, waiting like a chariot. I took my hands and pushed them against the windshield, felt the cold sting my fingers, waited for them to turn numb. I repeated the line of the day, but with the blooming cactus now beside me inside the Ford, I didn't feel so distraught. And the line felt less of a morose chant and more a poignant observation.

"People, time, events," I said. "They just pass over me."

BEAR SANTOS

11.21.18

I phoned Jay that evening from The Cove. "Jay, this is Bear and Foster."

"Figured you might be calling me," he said. "Surprised you two are talking with each other after the other night in the woods."

"Our roots go deeper than any petty disagreements," I said. "But why'd you skip school and football practice today?"

"That's not why you phoned me," Jay said. "Can we get to the point?"

"I missed you, pal," Foster said. "I wondered if maybe you were obsessed about the end. Ruminating. Feeling existential in any way?"

"Perhaps so," Jay said.

"Bear and I," Foster started, then stopped, then started again. "You see, to us the Greatest Show on Earth is a like a dream coming to fruition—"

"Bear," Jay said. "Foster told me the Greatest Show was only a prank. A dark scam he thought up as a freshman while

ACADEMY OF UNHOLY BOYS

watching Bugs Bunny and Elmer J. Fudd with Monster, a goof. Never meant to be taken seriously by you, by me, by anyone."

"Hear us out for a few minutes," Foster cut in. "Don't talk nonsense."

"All you got is blackmail," Jay said, "and I'm afraid I'm not biting tonight."

"You should be concerned, though," Foster said. "Maybe you're not biting *now,* but you were certainly sucking *then,* which is recorded for everyone to see."

"I tell myself I'm bigger than your petty, crass maneuverings," Jay said, his voice rising an octave over the phone. "You admitted the Greatest Show was just a lark. A lie you made up while getting high. And now it has blown up, expanded, and Foster Gold is truly scared, Bear. *Real scared.*" Foster looked at me for three seconds, waiting for my reaction. Could this be possibly true? No, no way, of course not.

"Why would he say something like that, Jay?" I asked. "I just don't think Foster would ever joke around like that, I really don't. I've known him for years, and that just doesn't jibe with Foster's typical behavior that I know. Doesn't sound like his humor, either."

"Thanks for saying that, Bear," Foster said. "I can't believe Jay has stooped to this. You're a sad creature, Souther. All I did was ask you several philosophical questions one day, and you go and have a conniption fit like the big pussy that you are."

"You were never going to take part in The Greatest Show, huh, Jay?" I asked, so fed up with the sophomore, tired of him weighing me and Foster down from the get-go. *Why'd we ever involve him in the first place?*

"I felt mixed up," Jay said. "Right from the start, I never knew what to think."

"All you do is overthink, navel gaze, and have *me-time,*" I

301

said. "That's your obvious problem. You're a loser, a selfish goon. It doesn't reflect well on your integrity."

"Kiss my ass, Bear," Jay said, his voice crackling over the speaker. "You're being scammed by your supposed best friend. I mean, do you want to die over a lame and pathetic joke?"

"Gentlemen," Foster said. "Our trio will meet in the visitor's end zone at St. Andrew's on Thanksgiving at sunrise. Six forty-eight a.m. Dress in home uniforms and know that some talented kids may be filming our defiant act for the sake of cinematic history. We'll be revered down the road as magnificent, glorious warriors."

"The world awaits our brazen act," I said.

"You're each so bizarre with your own major mental illnesses at work inside you," Jay said. "Plus, abusing drugs left and right—you're an addicted and feebly-disguised cult. That's how you began in the summer, and that's you now in the early winter, as well."

"You'll be seen blowing me everywhere," Foster said. "Or change your mind and rightly hang in the end zone with me and Bear for good, and your troubles will disappear, Jay. We'll rest for eternity, and no one must see any of your nasty, *dirty deeds*."

"Huh," I said, studying them both closely. "You think you control all the power in the world, but you're just the little lost weasel in the corner named Jay."

"Aren't you so tired of keeping up with the rat race, Jay?" Foster asked.

Jay was silent.

"Life is exhausting, man," Foster said. "School, exams, and following the same path our parents do—alcoholism, heart disease, drug abuse, cancer, obesity, dementia, diabetes, Parkinson's, or clinical depression. Let's escape the hectic pace and sleep in a corner together safe and sound."

ACADEMY OF UNHOLY BOYS

"You'll both miss so many good things in life," Jay said. "Don't destroy your future defending some dark, sardonic joke. It was never meant to be. Don't you want to fall in love with someone new? Or play whiffle ball on a Cape Cod beach with your friends, and the ocean only steps away? Visit the San Diego Zoo, Colorado's Rocky Mountains or even one day see the lights of Paris – there's so much you're going to be missing, for what empty purpose, Bear?"

"You're just being sappy and nauseatingly melodramatic now," Foster said.

"And you're a goddamned liar," Jay said. "Foster wants to quit but he's scared you'll be disappointed in him, Bear. Isn't that true?"

"Stop being an asshole, Jay," I said. "Take it like a man, for once."

"You both give up so much by quitting now," Jay said. "Maybe your life can get a lot better, why is that so damn hard to admit? Why is hope such a scary concept?"

Foster's voice softened and he said, "Remember that night in the hailstorm, Jay?"

Jay was quiet.

"Recall how scared you were with me, trembling, crying out for your broken, lost daddy? And how I successfully chased that fear away? That's what I want for you, Jay. I want to remove your fear permanently, exorcise it. Think about this — if you wake up in your own bed after sunrise on Thanksgiving, you'll have to live with the fact that I'm gone. And you're all that's left behind. Alone and scared of nasty hailstorms, unprotected like some sobbing little orphan boy weeping in a corner."

It was then I remembered Foster telling me this entire story, being as honest as ever. At least, I think I recalled that right, and how Jay was way off. Or was it the other way around? Was Foster scamming me into taking part in the cruelest joke in the world? Killing myself for no reason at all? Would he ever do such a thing?

"I hope you change your mind, guys," Jay said. "For you and your families' sake."

"Before you go, Jay," Foster said. "Please check out the news, apparently hoodlums set fire to a port-o-potty in New Rochelle. Just poured gasoline all over the damn thing and lit it aflame."

"I saw the clip on the news, CNN, I think," I said. "That's the thing about Foster Gold.... he's a man of his word... unlike you, Jay."

Then there was silence for fifty seconds before Jay hung up the phone.

"Son of a bitch," Foster said. "He'll come around—you watch."

"He'll be on that damn football field with us in one way or another," I said. "I'll get him."

"Yes, Bear," Foster said. "He'll pay, there's no doubt."

JAY SOUTHER

11-21-18

A week ago, I wanted to take Basil Sous out and celebrate her, to have a blast, my very own unique and special treat for an amazing sophomore-waiter-skateboarder, and my mom said she'd help pay for it, so she gave me a few hundred bucks. Which we completely didn't have in our budget. *It's fun to pretend sometimes,* she told me. *And tonight, we're all going to do some pretending that my lovely son, Jay is taking his lady friend out for a good meal.*

"It's my treat no matter what you say, Basil," I told her and so we drove way up near Hartford, and I thought she might enjoy some old-fashioned fun. And we'd grab some good food, and if life was really working out, we'd go to a place to throw axes at a bull's eye on the wall. Basil's Aunt Peg knew a manager at the sandwich-and-axe joint, so we got in no problem.

"You don't get more charming than this," Basil said. "But what if we both pay for our own meals?"

"Whatever gets you out with me," I said. "If that's what you wish, we'll go Dutch."

DAVID FITZPATRICK

"Great," Basil said. "I'm sold on throwing axes, too. I'll admit it's a bit current, but we'll do it and have some healthy laughs."

"Cool," I said.

"Can I offer you some sublime advice for the next lady in your life?" Basil said.

"Sure, let's hear it," I said.

"Read Wendell Berry's *The Peace of Wild Things* out loud to her, okay?"

"I thought I already did that with you," I said.

"*Au contraire*, my friend," Basil said. "You sent the poem to me, just an email, a lousy attachment, but sit your pretty lady down, or your handsome young man, whichever you're preferring, and recite it, or even memorize it, that's even better."

We ended up having a sweet time, and we had burgers and fries and these scrumptious malteds. I was sincere, but then I kept asking Basil about if she was truly leaving town over the high cost of living in Gently, which she didn't have a definitive answer to, so she seemed annoyed. Then, Basil took a deep breath, grabbed my hand, and said she thinks I'm a wonderful young man but for now she liked being a solo act, but that she needs all the single friends, females, and males out in this modern world of 2018. I guess I got those wounded, puppy dog eyes when she first told me that, because she gave me a huge hug, but I eventually bounced back, and we ended up laughing.

"Maybe, just maybe," Basil said. "There's some hope for you, Jay Souther. Just promise me you won't ever tell me Foster Gold is like a modern-day Jay Gatsby."

"I swear I'll never do that," I said. "I guarantee it, as a matter of fact."

And so I dropped Basil off at home just before midnight, and I walked her to her front door and kissed her gently, kindly, and I was suddenly impressed with the both of us.

TUCK

11.21.18.

My doorbell rang on Wednesday morning, and when I answered I saw a Dunkin Donuts bag on my front steps. I picked it up and found a glazed donut, orange juice, and a thumb drive. I walked out in my pajama bottoms onto the lawn and looked around. No one out there. Only a familiar jogger, with his black lab on a short leash, shuffling down the hill, so I closed the door and headed upstairs to slip the drive into my laptop.

I saw a nearly naked male in a Chewbacca mask appear onscreen. He wore a purple sock over his penis and stood for a moment inside a spacious garage with a black Audi Quattro and John Deere tractor behind him. He snapped his fingers and the 1983 song, "Crumbling Down," by John Mellencamp played.

Chewbacca-guy spins around three, four, five times, shaking awkwardly, slowly, to the music, before clicking on an electric razor and shaving all his blonde hair off. First his head, then eyebrows, underarms, chest, pubic area, and his legs, arms, and toes.

307

He bent over a cooler, removing a ten-pound bag of ice, frozen solid, set it down on top of the tractor's seat, and turned his face away from the camera, slamming his masked face into it hard, picking up speed as he grunted, eventually knocking the mask off and giving himself what was probably a broken nose and a split lip. When the song eventually ended, the young man bowed to the camera, sans mask, but still obscuring his identity, and said:

"Today's art featured conceptual trailblazer Chewy on the rocks. I've been dried out, pierced, and passed around once too often. All that remains of me is a frail and brittle shell. Please gather your splintered pieces before another goddamned war starts somewhere else and ruins young lives."

I threw out the Dunkin Donuts bag, along with the untouched donut and juice, and I saw a note at the bottom in fancy stationery. It read, *Watch your left pinky toe, Smiley, Love & Threats – Chewy.* I reflexively went to my shredder and put the note through the machine, regretting it immediately. My forehead got beady with sweat, and I felt short of breath, heart pounding rapidly.

"Deep breaths, Tuck," I said to myself. "Dr. A would say take a lot of deep, full breaths. You're bigger than Foster Gold, you know you are... come on... you can rise above this silly, toxic move by an angry and disturbed coward."

I practiced calming breaths for about two minutes, and then said, "Foster needs to be humbled."

I took a shower and texted Basil: "Did you see Foster's recording?"

"Mine came in a Dunkin Donuts bag. Frankly, I shut it off even before his pathetic ideas were shared."

"Yes," I said. "Smart young woman."

"I'm afraid he's worth less and less as days slip by. He

seems to be on a crash course with self-destruction. It's like he can't help himself now, he's doomed to failure. "Yes," I texted. "A loser."

JAY SOUTHER

It was 10:31 a.m. when I got a bathroom pass. Thanksgiving was creeping in, only hours away now. We were to be dismissed for the break soon, yellow school buses probably already on their way over from the bus depot in North Branford. I used to get excited about the holiday—football, leftovers, the chill on my cheeks and fingers whenever I went outside. Now, I felt only dread.

As I trudged down the corridor, I heard footsteps behind me. I slipped into the men's room and took a quick piss. As I was zipping up and making my way over to wash my hands at the sink, the door opened. A tall, skinny teenager stared back at me in the mirror.

He was a special needs student, frequently spotting him around campus solo, or riding his red trail bike on the Gently Green, snapping photos like mad with his old school SLR. He was the guy I thought was gawking at me at the last home football game, but with those dark lenses, it was hard to make any definitive claims. Usually, it was only him, the SLR, and the

310

iPhone around his neck. He moved and twitched the whole time—my mom would've called him a Nervous Nellie.

His iPhone played clips from an Academy Award-winning flick from some years back. It echoed in the bathroom. He had a wealthy father, a loving single dad apparently. Just a lonely, brilliant kid out in the world, doing his best with what he's got. Or so I heard.

"Could you turn down the volume on that one?" I asked.

"It's Emma Stone," he said. "From *La La Land*."

"I like Emma Stone, she's real cool," I said. "But I'm not interested in hearing about any movie she's in right now."

"Tuck," he said in a shaky voice, covering his mouth with his left hand as if he had bad morning breath.

"What?"

"Letters, mailed," he said, stammering. "Sent them... me, I did. I'm Tuck."

"Wait... Say it again, slower..."

He turned the volume down on the iPhone, blushing. "Letters to Jay, you. Mailed, I did, about the assholes. Foster. Bear. Correspondence. I'm the writer. 'T' stands for Tuck."

This guy had so much to say that words formed a bottleneck in his throat. When he cupped his left hand over his mouth, only several words escaped. This guy was nothing like the superhero I had imagined—the one who secretly had my back over all these past months. "Right, okay," I said. I was trying to properly rinse my hands in the sink. I gave up and wiped them, soap and all, on my dark khakis. "You're T, so what now?"

"It's not worth it," he said.

"What?"

His left hand cupped his lips again. "Death. Your planned suicide pact."

DAVID FITZPATRICK

"If you're so certain," I asked, "why not go tell a teacher right now?"

"You're braver than me," he said. "Rough days, nothing. Me, mostly lucky if I make it through. School sucks. Anxiety. Fear. Do it. You do it, please..."

He took a few breaths, his face flushed.

"Be powerful, Jay."

I kept looking at the door, fearing Bear or Foster would barge right in.

"I was in your shoes sophomore year," Tuck said, "but they booted me out."

"Why?"

"I wouldn't try out for the football squad," he said, his face pained and weary. "So, they cut me off, shunned me. Foster gave me a swirly, told me to be silent forever or he'd have to slice off my left pinky toe."

"Jesus," I said. "What happened during junior year?"

"Zilch...their plans dissolved, nothing developed," he said. "They let it slide until this past summer when..."

"The bastards drafted me," I said, connecting the dots. "I was a death substitute, lousy third-string punter... And Foster thought it was *more theatrical* if The Greatest Show happened senior year, claimed it added poetic truth and justice to the *pageantry*."

"Madness," Tuck said. "Empty pricks at play in the house of the Lord."

"Foster said to me the act itself would rock the globe and alter humanity," I said.

We were both silent for a few breaths.

"Save yourself, Jay," Tuck said. "Don't waste time with the shitheads."

"How, though?"

ACADEMY OF UNHOLY BOYS

He took a crumpled note out of his pants. "Text this number anytime."

"Thanks, T, I will," I said, grabbing the note from his shaking hand, stuffed it into my back pocket, then shot out of the bathroom like a pinball into a hall that smelled of dry-erase markers, sweat, and school bus exhaust.

The men's room door swung open behind me, and I heard his actress again on the iPhone. Emma Stone. I was surprised that no teachers ever got after him about it, the volume.

"Jay," Tuck called out, his tremulous voice echoing.

I turned around. Tuck was fidgeting in front of the large trophy case that displayed a century of St. Andrew's athletics hardware. His pale face made him appear as wispy as an apparition. My eyes lost focus, and for a few seconds I saw the trophy case falling, crushing him, fractured bones, glass, and blood everywhere.

"You can do it," he said, bringing me back to reality.

"Yes, right. Thanks..." I said, relieved to be finished with our conversation.

Tuck spun around then, walking away in the opposite direction as I thought: *There goes the loneliest boy in the world.*

BASIL SOUS

11-21-18

Jay Souther showed up on the porch of our current home on a blustery evening at 11 p.m., an hour before Thanksgiving. Our place was in Cliffside, a regal neighborhood in Gently with its large, colorful cottages whispering old money, each set about a half-an acre apart. Ironic that two of the poorest ladies in town live here—Basil and Peg, a step away from being destitute. I mean, sure we're fortunate to be living here, but we operate without a safety net, and sometimes that scares me shitless.

Our place had rose-colored shingles, funky skylights that leak, an impressive library, a wrap-around porch, plus cats who follow me everywhere. There were also two spotted Great Danes, Reg and Clegg, who did nothing but sniff suspiciously at Jay's crotch when he arrived.

We drank tea from Grateful Dead mugs that have Jerry Garcia's smiling face. Grateful Dead bears are everywhere. I showed Jay the bathroom, which has a sweet cottage feel to it, and there's an Irish Blessing in green calligraphy hanging over the sink. A collection of seashells rest on the shelf above the toilet. Sweet-smelling soap and towels with dancing bears gaze

ACADEMY OF UNHOLY BOYS

up at us. I have him listen to the silence of the home, before we return to the main room.

Rumor has it, I told Jay, the owner of this house had a fling with Jerry Garcia in his early days and remains a fan of Bob Weir and company. "She owns these rare photos upstairs as well," I said. So, we find ourselves in the living room, dancing and whirling around. I made faces in front of an antique funhouse mirror. The homeowner told Peg and I that a pear-shaped man on eBay, calling himself Willard the Wombat sold it to her for $2,500. She said the wealthy gentleman in a cranberry-colored Mercedes Benz convertible drove the mirror to Connecticut and signed it with an orange and black magic marker: "With all my love, Willard."

According to the owner, Willard was a quirky antique collector who was filthy rich and found the mirror in an alley behind a Wilmington, North Carolina laundromat-saloon after a nasty hurricane. It stood four feet high and three feet wide. As music blared from the speakers, I watched my own reflection transform into the tallest woman on earth, reaching nine feet, nine inches tall with bright red-haired pigtails.

Soon, I became a skinny astronaut with lots of kittens and cats around me, the cats kept bunting and purring and fascinated by my astronaut outfit and then Reg and Clegg, the Great Danes, were all over me and Jay. Jay and I shook and spun, transforming into all kinds of Greek gods and goddesses, and gorgons. "You be Medusa and I'll be Zeus, God of Thunder," I told Jay. "For a change of pace, okay?"

"Sounds fine to me," Jay said. "I always loved snakes."

"But in your hair, Jay?" I asked and he spun around, laughing.

"Sometimes all I need to do is shake and dance," I said.

"It feels good to move," Jay said. "To work up a sweat."

"Feels so sweet," I said before an unfamiliar phone number

rings on my mobile. I think, *is it another spam call from the DMV in Bangladesh?* I picked it up, and a voice asked, "Is Basil Sous there?"

"Who's this?

"Foster," he said. "Can you put me on speaker, please?"

"No, I'm busy," I said.

"Please," Foster said. "I beg of you."

"Too bad," I said and hung up and Jay and I laughed.

But Jay's phone started ringing and lighting up, so he turned it right off.

"I'm going to snub Foster," Jay said. "That's what that boy needed his whole life, someone to say no, and keep his appetites in check. Maybe ground him for three months and take away his Audi, Monster, and all that weed and other vices."

"Yes, sir. Amen," I said. "Now you're talking."

"I bet he's getting increasingly pissed off," Jay said. "There's no doubt."

"Not your problem anymore," I said. "You can leave him behind forever, right?"

Jay continued to get a whole blitzkrieg of calls and texts from Foster, but then he lost his temper with himself and decided to just ride his bike back home. It's about a two-mile jaunt and as he left, he said, "Would you mind if I stole a kiss?"

"What the hell," Basil said, and we both lean in quickly and bumped our teeth, before settling into a good kiss.

"Thanks so much," Jay said, and I smiled, blushing despite myself.

"My pleasure, Jay," I said. "Be safe out there tonight. I know it's late, but call me if you need me, okay? I'll be here awake for a while with all my furry critters around me."

JAY SOUTHER

MIDNIGHT

I had tried to receive comfort and support from Basil but all the excessive abuse and toxic bullshit from Foster and Bear has thrown my system way off and I slid into a panic mode, jittery as hell. As I rode my bike home, I realized I now have difficulty being around people who are genuine, decent, and kind, which makes me feel like someone kicked me in the sternum. I realized how rare and affirming Basil Sous is. I saw Foster texting about where exactly I lived and I know my life of ridicule, hurt, and manipulation from Foster and Bear is dangerous and could truly destroy me, like, *tonight.*

So, I shout as I bike, Foster's incessant texting driving me insane. As I approach my neighborhood on my bike, I finally answered my phone and told Foster to go to hell and stop putting my father down.

"You don't know squat about my dad, asshole," I said.

"Geoff Henry Souther is living in a dilapidated group home in Seymour, Connecticut and he bums smokes off everyone in town," Foster said. "He's been hospitalized for self-harm four times in this calendrer year, in and out and in again

DAVID FITZPATRICK

he goes. As of late, he slit his throat with a steak knife. He tried to overdose before he got his stomach pumped with charcoal. Scary frigging life he's got."

"How would you know something real specific like that?"

"Got my reliable connections all around the state."

"My dad's living forty-five minutes from me for the last six years?" I asked.

"Don't ask me," he says. *"Ask your mom, man."*

"Everything's out of control, anyway," Foster said. "The world is imploding all around us, the cracks are in every foundation, mass entropy setting in."

"What does all that mean, exactly?" I asked. I realized that I needed support. That I couldn't handle this all on my own. So, I dialed Basil and added her to the call.

"Bear and you got behind my animated pep talks," Foster said, not realizing yet Basil has been added to the line, "and we fed off one another's rage. I started believing in my own rarified BS, saw myself rising above the masses at Yankee Stadium, addressing tens of thousands like a populist politician, or perky pop star with my own traveling dancers, miracles, and laser light shows. Plus, there were too many drugs and my ugly and warped ego galivanting away."

I switch the phone to my other hand because my right arm was getting tired after holding up my body weight on the bike.

Basil cut in to say: "You need to slow down, Foster, you're losing it."

"I'm living my life with true gusto and grit," he said.

"Take some full, deep breaths," Basil said. "Try to slow yourself down."

"Bear and Jay kept winding me up and believing in our morbid cause. Surfing on my Audi in their shoulder pads, helmets, and cleats, telling me to drive faster, *always so much faster*. I flew across Walmart's parking lot, and when I hit my

ACADEMY OF UNHOLY BOYS

brakes, they both tumbled onto the concrete, cursed, and got back up, bruised, bloodied, and only wanted to do it some more. *Only much faster*, of course."

"Those days are long over," I said. "That only happened twice in early September."

"We can't turn back now, though," Foster said.

"Foster," Basil said. "You have another half-century of life on your side, and those could be great, amazing years. Why walk away from it all now?"

"Young, gifted filmmakers are prepping for The Greatest Show as we speak," he said. "People's ears perk up when they hear about the act in New Haven, or even way down in Bridgeport, Darien, or across the border in New Rochelle. Wild rumors spread on the dark web. It's burning like a brush fire. Everyone's jazzed. Lights, camera, action, for the moment, has morphed into something bigger than you or I could have ever imagined."

"You're not connected with reality anymore," Basil said.

"But it's very freeing, nevertheless," Foster said.

"I don't want you to die," Basil added.

"Thanks, Basil," Foster said. "But St. Andrew's students are currently taking bets on who lives and who perishes, and smart money is *not* on me any longer."

"You told me it was a dark and sinister joke," I said. "A lark —something you thought up freshman year while getting high watching *Loony Tunes*."

"Yes," Foster said. "That's true, but it's happening now... it's unstoppable, like the moon and ocean pulling and whirling together like some metaphysical stormfront, like everything's connected. Minds will be blown in the End Zone."

Basil remained silent, listening to Foster breathe on the other line, and I do so as well.

"Where are you right now, Foster?" Basil asked.

DAVID FITZPATRICK

"Naked under a pyramid at a cheap motel," he said, "searching for a third eye."

"Too many drugs again, huh?" Basil said.

"Yes," Foster said. "But I also found a magic closet here."

"Tell me," Basil said.

"That shrink that saved me early on in Missouri, Dr. Hazel Check," Foster said. "She gave me a print by Andrew Wyeth once. And the motel closet here has a sketch of a Black Plague doctor's costume."

"Black Plague?"

"Sometimes called the bubonic plague," he said. "Killed hundreds of millions from Asia, Europe over many centuries. Decimated populations around the globe."

"And how are the two pieces alike?" I asked.

"Both are facades," he said. "European 17th Century doctors wore a birdlike mask stuffed with sweet smelling spices, basil, and lavender, so air-borne diseases wouldn't infect them. Plus, they wore goggles, hats, gloves, boots, coats, cane, a whole wardrobe."

"And the Wyeth?"

"A ten-year-old girl wears a white mask with a long pointy nose covering half her face," he said. "When you study it, you see it's nothing short of exquisite."

"Is that right?"

"*Winter Carnival*'s the title," Foster said. "The small-frame girl wears a white turtleneck, but she's tough. I can see she's real tough."

"Yeah?"

"Are you familiar with the painting, Basil?"

"No," she said. "Aunt Peg loves Wyeth, though, so I'm sure she knows of it."

"The facade fits her," he said. "Suits her, and her single brilliant blue eye."

ACADEMY OF UNHOLY BOYS

"You got a thing for young girls now, Foster?" Basil asked.

"No, no, Basil," Foster said. "Nothing like that. But I have the painting taped to the bathroom mirror in here with me, and she looks like my daughter might."

"I didn't know you had one."

"I kiss my daughter's head," he went on. "It reassures me, and I'm proud of her poise and grace, pleased with how she perseveres in this weak, crapped-out world."

"Right," Basil said.

"I plan to do it more in the future—I keep track. It's a game I play, more fun than poker or cribbage."

"You sound wired, Foster," Basil said, but he didn't respond, and I know she wanted to say more, something pivotal and direct and use words that are empathic, wise, and kind. She wanted to slap sense into the manic, drugged fool spinning out of control on the other end of the phone. Instead, she remained mute, and I feel the quiet space between us all expand, and soon it was too late to say a damn thing. The silence overtook everyone listening, like a rushing white-noise avalanche that obliterates any connection we may have once had.

"Foster?" Basil said at last. "Try to be rational now... we can still extract you from this ugly, dangerous mess."

"*Arrivederci*, Basil and Jay," Foster said in a different tone, colder, more clipped. "Do check your front door, Jay."

JAY SOUTHER

SHOWTIME...

As Foster said, I found twenty-five eight-by-ten black and white photos had been taped all over Mom's door and front window, leering into our simple home. The others were of my mother taking off her pajamas, drinking wine and her martinis.

The photos peered through the thin glass into the living room, the photographer had studied nothing but Alfred Hitchcock's use of shadows and fright. One picture had my mom in the bathroom. Not for public consumption. Mom was sleeping over at Aunt Carol's house, who said she'd take care of all the Thanksgiving festivities tomorrow.

Foster had dropped off the line, but Basil was still there.

"Foster's s such a bastard," I said.

"And how'd they get so close to your mom?" Basil asked.

"Zoom lens, I guess," I said. "Through her bedroom window probably. Real creepy and ugly."

"We must put an end to this stuff, Jay," Basil said. "Destroy them."

I removed the photos, awkwardly carrying them inside to Mom's blue leather couch in the living room. I perused the prints, shaking my head, and went to the fireplace and burned them all.

"The pictures of your mom will soon be online, no doubt," Basil said. "But I think it's a smart idea to burn them, just get that toxic crap away from your home."

"Foster's got me now, Basil," I said, exhaling. "I'm trapped."

"He's out of control," she said, and as I thought more about my nemesis, I felt nauseous and rushed over and threw up in the toilet. I found Tuck's phone number and texted him, hands trembling.

There was a loud noise in my front room with shouts and heavy footsteps. I had left the front door halfway open with all the confusion going on.

"We'll knock the bathroom door down, Jay," a familiar voice said. "Get the hell out now."

I texted, "Real bad news, Tuck. We need your help now..."

Bear Santos busted into my bathroom as I pushed *Send*, slamming me against the cabinet, and my phone tumbled into the trash. Bear held his right index finger over his lips. It was just the two of us in the closed bathroom, and he reeked of citrus and body odor.

"Foster's out of his head," Bear said.

"I don't get why he needs to be higher than any soul ever in the history of drug-abuse," I said. "I never understood that about him."

"I need your help," the All-American said.

"It's a scam, Bear," I said. "How many times do I need to say it to you? A prank, a joke, so, no, I'm not going anywhere with you tonight."

"What choice you got, man?" Bear said, as he opened the bathroom door. "Hank and Scott, take Jay away to the car. Jay, these are two revolutionaries who don't like Foster at all."

"We're fed up with the senior's arrogance," Hank said.

SHOWTIME...

"He's an asshole, and he's been ordering Bear around for too many years, when he wasn't handing out cheap shots and concussions."

"Well, if you're so fed up with Foster, Bear, why do you still need to take me along?" I asked.

"You are a diversion, a brilliant distraction," Bear said. "We'll take it easy on you, though."

"Asshole," I said.

I swore again at Bear, before being dragged into my living room by Scott and Hank in their black tactical gear. "Don't worry, Jay," a voice said. "Here's some chloroform. Sweet dreams to you, kiddo."

A soaked rag pressed over my nose and mouth, and everything went to black.

TUCK

THANKSGIVING, 5:02 A.M.

I woke to my phone vibrating. Outside was pitch black but I didn't recognize the caller. Thanksgiving morning had arrived, and I was flustered, and it didn't look like my father and I had any plans. Probably hit McDonald's or pick up a rotisserie chicken from the market, if they were even open. I hummed Dad's favorite Beatles tune, "Eleanor Rigby."

I looked at the cellphone, not recognizing the number. I declined the call and flipped it to silence. It was then I recognized a text from Jay Souther last night.

"Real bad news, Tuck. We need your help right now..."

What the hell? I wondered. The phone buzzed in my hand, from a different phone, Basil Sous's, actually. Basil's voice was full of panic as she outlined a tale of terror going down in Gently. *This is out of your league, Tuck. Plus, you flip out whenever you're around Foster, don't set yourself up this way.*

The sound of Basil's scared voice gave me a buoyant rush of energy and chivalrous hope. "Something bizarre is happening around here, Tuck," she told me.

"What is it?"

DAVID FITZPATRICK

"Jay's been taken," Basil said. "It's Bear and Foster, I think, they got him at his house."

"Who took Jay?" I asked.

"Bear and two St. Andrew athletes' dressed in tactical gear," she said. "Foster's involved, too."

"Goddammit," I said, and so I resolved to call the Gently police as soon as we hung up.

"If I can get to Wave," she said. "Can you pick me up, Tuck?"

"Definitely," I said. *Just take Dad's Jeep, leave a note, tell him you're at St. Andrew's, and we could use his help.*

Some minutes later, I saw a tiny girl rocket into the parking lot, stumbling as she jumped off her still-moving skateboard and rushed over and climbed into Dad's Jeep with a Louisville Slugger in her hand, her skateboard hurdling into the bushes out in front.

"Looks like you're all set," I said, and Basil nodded.

"This is just in case," she said, slapping the bat. "We can do this together, you and me, Tuck, okay?"

"What's our plan, though?" I asked. "We're not the most intimidating duo, right?"

"Have some faith," Basil said. "This bat is amazing; I've seen it work miracles."

"Okay, I guess," I said. "Here's to miracles then..." *Finally, validation,* I thought. *Greatest Show on Earth is happening at St. Andrew's now, and it involves the trio of Bear, Foster, and Jay, time to wake up. We're coming for you, Jay, hang on, pal.*

BEAR

The end zone, at long last. How many years since we started shaping, whittling, and crafting our grand finale? I stood in my home uniform for the first time in five months, the snug and padded spandex, which was a comfort to me, like those thunder shirts you see on skittish poodles on the Green. My thick helmet filtered out sound and shielded the bright lights, soothing my aching head and ringing ears. I should have put it on days ago when the migraines started ambushing me, pounding away. The only anomaly, the one piece out of place was my father's pistol tucked into my waistband.

But this was not our plan. No glory, no artistry or fancy polish and shine. Just vulgar self-harm and broken necks and ghastly death. I realized I'd been staring at Foster, looking *through* him, really. What the hell is Foster Gold to me now? First crush? Lover? Maestro? Nemesis? Arrogant fool, Coward? Scumbag? *Or was it something even worse?* Now, he's a few feet away, bare-assed except for that ugly lavender duct tape that bound him upside down to the base of the goalpost. It was his idea, after all—the lavender duct tape. At least, that's what

Foster decided to do to the unconscious sophomore, Jay Souther. But Hank, good ol' Hank Allan, whom Foster hadn't expected to see, he decided to treat Foster in that exact way and bound him upside down in lavender.

I felt outside of myself, like I was an impostor. Nothing but a poseur out on the gridiron. "Take it easier on yourself, Felipe," I muttered. "A true man learns to adapt in stressful times."

Foster's affect was reddening as the blood rushed to his head; he had already been punched by both Hank and me several times. It was even more noticeable with his recently-buzzed head. I had loved and foolishly stayed faithful to him for as long as I had known him. Yet earlier today, he'd betrayed everything we were to each other.

"Don't ever tell me how to live again, Foster," I said, punching his face, hard. "You have lost that right. You blew everything to pieces because you had to abuse your synthetic drugs, had to be the coolest, most detached man in town. You blew the whole thing up because you are an extraordinarily selfish prick."

Foster was the most consistent human being in my life ever since elementary school. How many late nights did he and I worship that five-foot teal bong, Monster, in the Cove? Foster was the most self-destructive, impractical planet in my solar system, *right after me,* that is. But I came with my own collapsing black hole, and an anxiety that bewilders and shuts me down. I took a breath and ripped off the duct tape on my old maestro's mouth. "We're the Dynamic Duo, man," Foster blurted. "It's tradition, our sacred quest."

"More like a stupid *pathetic quest,*" I shouted. "Borne of excessive drugs, and undiagnosed mental illness."

Foster shook his head in disgust and spat, which is not so easy to do upside down. Most of the spit landed in his eyes.

ACADEMY OF UNHOLY BOYS

"Where did all this crap begin? I asked. "When did you become the center of the universe, instead..." I cut myself off before I could say *instead of the center of my world.*

"You know all of it."

"Tell me again, though," I said. "I need to hear you justify it."

"William F. Nolan and George Clayton Johnson wrote *Logan's Run* in 1967, the sci-fi novel that rescued me, just as much as a Jay Gatsby or a Wendell Berry ever did. Although I guess you could also say it destroyed me, too. In the novel, all people living on Earth in the 23rd century die at the age of twenty-one. There is also a hyper-disciplined group, *zealots*, led by a charismatic young male and they end their lives at eighteen."

"A type of cult leader," I said.

"More or less," Foster said. "I was like an amalgam of out-of-control evil beings. All that power and control, ala Jim Jones or David Koresh. Just do not ever tell Jay that fact."

"Yes, we wouldn't want to disappoint our dear Jay," I said.

"Don't whine and complain," Foster said. "It doesn't look good on you, Felipe."

Foster's voice was dull, muffled by a sinus stuffed with blood and mucus from his inverted position. "Would you admit to me, to God, that the Greatest Show was nothing but a massive manipulation on your part?" I asked. "A phantasm of your sick brain that you dragged us all into?"

"I don't believe in God," he said. "Belief in the Divine reeks of weakness to me and eats up too many damn hours on Sundays."

"You're a toxic young man," I said. "My God is about faith and a truth, a force that offers comfort and solace in times of joy, or need, or even celebration."

"Spoken like a true preacher's boy," Foster said.

"No, I sound like me, the guy you never bothered to get to know," I said. "Not everything the Reverend said was crap. God's real and tangible, no doubt about that."

Although Foster could be joyful as anyone, at times, a life-affirming young man, it was confusing and exhausting to try and understand him. Up, down, inside out, horny, frozen, enraged, kind, sullen, manic, gentle, competitive, lethargic and/or sickeningly sweet. Foster quoted writers from Salinger to Baldwin to Elizabeth Bishop to Flannery O'Connor to Nietzsche to Plath, Angelou to Cheever, to modern authors like Michael Chabon, Jo Ann Beard, Paul Lisicky, Colson Whitehead, and Anthony Doerr. When he found time for all of his reading, I never learned, but somehow he was constantly listening to his audiobooks. It must be stated that in the end, Foster exhausted me, but he was also an elitist, too, a self-righteous snob at heart.

Foster's gist, his main thrust, was to have himself and two varsity jocks dangle, lifeless, from goalposts on Thanksgiving at dawn from the visitor's end zone in St. Andrew's. I bought into every bit of it. I believed in my soul that God put me on this whirling planet to be Foster's best friend, if not soul mate. That my main purpose in the universe was to valiantly die at the maestro's side; I never carried it all the way through the maze to see myself with St. Pete at the pearly gates. When did I stop believing in all that insipid muck and toxicity inside Sharon Foster Gold's sales pitch? How could I have ever believed in his silly and dangerous lies?

The pre-dawn skies were now filled with news-camera drones and fifty-foot sheets announcing, "The Greatest Show." It's like the saddest finale in the history of the world, understand? For humans to destroy ourselves and slap the term "ancient quest" on it to add some gravitas and heft.

The frigid wind whipped through my ears, making a howl-

ACADEMY OF UNHOLY BOYS

ing, creepy sound, like a soundtrack to some slasher movie. Hank was behind me, pacing, like a tiger to my bear. He muttered incessantly about the importance of vengeance. It was hard for me to stay patient with someone like Hank Allan, and I thought if I had a chance to do it over, I would avoid Foster and Hank from the get-go.

As I stood, my cleats digging into the immaculately maintained turf, I lived up to my longstanding moniker, lashing out like a bear. I punched Foster three more times. "Our plans never got off the ground because Foster wanted to be so clever, ironic, and memorable for the media," I said.

"My memory is fuzzy now about all that," Foster said.

"*No shit*," I said. "You're a convincing ad for not taking drugs."

"Yes," Foster said. "Right."

"And you're the reason I lost Lavinia."

"What happened there?" Foster asked.

"She told the powers at the state psychiatric hospital I was stealing scripts for you, asshole, and now I've lost my job," I said.

"That's where The Greatest Show now steps in to save the day," Foster said. "Let's just go check out together right now like glorious golden warriors."

"Just shut up please," I said, before I turned to find Hank pulling out his semiautomatic handgun and jamming it into Foster's upside-down jugular.

"What the hell?" Foster said. "*Stop him.*"

"I'm tired of you," Hank said simply.

"Felipe!" Foster shouted.

"Your arrogance comes with a steep price," Hank said.

"I don't have a gripe with you, man," Foster said. "This isn't your war, okay?"

"That cheap shot you gave Bear last year added another

concussion to the tally," Hank said. "It told everyone you don't care about a soul." Much spittle with his rancor, then. "Bear Santos was on his way to the big colleges, and maybe even turn professional in the NFL, and we were all going with him. Most of us must work our asses off to grab any scrap the world can offer. All the St. Andrew's athletes were a team. Bear lifted that team and we in turn lifted Bear. When you crushed his dreams, Foster Gold, you destroyed us, too. No more All-American scouts, no chance to be noticed by baseball evaluators spotting me for free rides to smaller colleges, or even half scholarships. It was the absolute end, *adios* for everyone."

And, just like that, I knew Hank Allan only cared what he could get out of me.

Did anyone care about Bear Santos alone?

Hank threw his arm up and fired twice in the air, and I thought he was intent on murdering Foster, and nothing I said could change that. Facing him, I grabbed for the gun, but his reach was longer than mine, and he swung the pistol like the champion batter that he is, striking my helmeted head. I rolled with the blow; I've certainly learned how to do that well this year.

Rolling to a crouch a few feet away, Hank aimed at Foster again. His eyes were clear in the weird halogen lighting, bright and glowing, pupils like pinpricks. With my feet under me, my legs were coiled so I lunged at Hank. More than half my life I'd been spent figuring out how to hit linemen or linebackers, people usually wider and bigger than me, and how to keep them down.

When my helmet collided with Hank's gut, carrying all two hundred and thirty-five pounds of me; I heard a few ribs crack. But some instinct caused Hank's fist to clench and the gun's deafening eruption to occur, so I whirled, leaving Hank gasping

ACADEMY OF UNHOLY BOYS

for breath and sobbing in pain, expecting to see only a hole in Foster's chest.

There was nothing, no more blood than already decorated his face from a burst lip and a broken nose. But there was fresh blood dripping to the ground a few inches behind him.

Jay.

God, how could I have forgotten the unconscious sophomore was still there, tied, helplessly hanging upside-down in bonds of lavender duct tape? And now his blood trickled to the ground from a bullet wound.

TUCK

I slammed the Jeep to a stop, instinctively yanking up the parking brake. At that moment I was expecting the mechanisms to scream, but instead, all sound was drowned out by two thunderous booms in quick succession. Basil and I looked at each other, the word "gunshots" written clearly on her face, and most likely mine. With a shaking hand, I pulled the keys from the ignition, and we bolted from the car racing to the unlocked and open mid-field gates.

Basil and I ran the length of the football field just as the third, lone gunshot was fired in the visitor's end zone with Basil carrying her Louisville Slugger like a baton and myself no more than five feet back. *Keep up now, do not fall behind her,* I told myself.

The home end zone was partially lit, and there were three teens, a boy and two girls, filming the event with expensive-looking cameras and sound equipment. They wore crimson sweats and New York Mets baseball caps backward. I had a pang in my gut seeing everyone, way too many people in one

ACADEMY OF UNHOLY BOYS

place for me, but I only thought, *stay with Basil, Tuck. Five feet back, be her shadow.*

A portable laser projector shined off a huge white sheet strung between the goalposts. The light breeze rippled the stretch fabric creating a nauseating effect if you looked too long at it. It read, **Chewy presents: the Greatest Show on Earth,** stretching along the home goal post, from one upright to the other.

"Kids might die tonight here you, idiots," Basil spat as she darted past.

"You're overreacting," the camera girl said. "It is not a legit thing—it's a gig, a performance art show. Like Chewie's sculpture of life, just fiction, make-believe, our own little Hollywood empire on the Connecticut Shoreline, okay?"

Sirens blared in the distance, cops, fire engines, and ambulances roaring to life. "Does that sound make-believe to you?" I shouted at them.

It took forever and absolutely no time at all to reach the end zone. The tableau there made no more sense as we approached. I could make out a tall, broad figure in a full game-day uniform, his darkly clad form writhing like a great serpent, gasping, and clutching his middle, and two other inexplicable forms glowed in the sharp light. It took Basil no time at all to make an assessment and a plan of action. My only choice was to follow some Neanderthal instinct telling me to keep her safe, while my rational brain knew I was the one in need of protection.

The smallest of the nude forms were clearly Jay, recognizable even in the shadows. His face was hidden, but the near-white light revealed the dark blood as gravity guided it from the gunshot wound in his arm to his shoulder and neck, drip-dripping onto the white lye of the visitor's end zone.

Basil ran to him and I, as her shadow, followed. She began

searching for his bonds looking for a knot or fastening only to realize he was suspended with layer upon layer of lavender duct tape. She patted her body, searching for a lost cellphone, but no, she was looking for something sharp. Suddenly, she reached out and snatched the Jeep keys from my hands and used the largest key like a squirrel-sized machete to hack through the thickly layered tape.

Looking toward the other three people I half-recognized Foster as the other inverted prisoner. I couldn't see past Foster to where the other figure lay on the ground, but the uniformed titan must have been Bear, circling, raging. I don't know if he noticed Basil and I or even cared. It was almost as if there was a one-way mirror between us and them, running up the center line, bisecting the goal post and keeping us hidden as we worked to free Jay. It felt like an eternity cutting and sawing the tape with ineffective tools of car keys and fingernails.

We had Jay almost free without noticing we were freeing Foster, too. I did my best not to have Jay fall on his head or face as Basil slashed the last bands. Jay didn't rouse but he moaned in pain when we pressed my jacket hard on his wound, applying pressure to stop the seeping blood. Foster must have felt the tape loosen because the goalpost trembled when he half-lurched and half-stumbled, landing on his knees facing me.

"Smiley," he said. "So, we meet again."

I couldn't speak. We looked straight at each other for a heartbeat, his face covered in blood, his hair held high in crimson spikes when it had dried and clotted, his eyes were that of a wild thing, bloodshot, with pupils the size of pennies despite the spotlights. He gifted me with a terrifying grin before turning to rise unsteadily. He paused to lift something from the ground.

My blood ran frigid when I realized it was a gun, one I would later learn had been dropped by Bear moments earlier,

ACADEMY OF UNHOLY BOYS

falling from his waistband. Foster stood shakily, unaware that he was naked except for the remnants of lavender duct tape.

Basil pulled my attention back to Jay directing me to offer first aid to our unconscious friend. The sirens were getting louder. Foster began shouting, "I knew I loved that damn Jay Souther kid from day one."

"Why love him more than me, though, Sharon?" Bear asked, producing coherent words for the first time since we had arrived. "Explain that one."

"You are way too clingy and emotional, Felipe," Foster said. "No spark left."

I covered Jay with my sweater, but it nearly fell off. "We'll keep him warm; we'll do our best to keep him safe," I said.

"He's in shock from the gunshot wound," Basil said.

"Let's tie a tourniquet with my sweater for him," I said, so we both wrapped the garment around Jay and applied direct pressure.

The sirens were so close now, the shrieks and wails creating a cacophony of reverberating echoes. The chaos and noise were frightening, harried. Foster's face was all blood and bone from Hank and Bear's recent punches. The sun wouldn't rise until 6:48 a.m., but the stadium grew brighter every second. Pink Floyd's "Wish You Were Here," had already kicked in over the stadium's speakers.

Four Gently Police cruisers pulled up to the visitor's end zone as Foster tried to stand, still wobbly. Basil left Jay with me, grabbing her bat, swinging quickly, bringing the Louisville Slugger against Foster's jaw with a resounding *thwack*.

"Goddamn wench!" Foster shouted, dropping to one knee. Drones dipped closer to the action like pesky fruit flies, their annoying hum guaranteeing replays of the event would be preserved forever on twenty-four-hour TV news.

Foster raised the gun defiantly, still unsteady, swinging it around as if the firearm was too hot to keep still. A Gently cop grabbed Basil and dropped her beside Jay, crouching with his Kevlar-encased body between them and the gunman. Bear and Foster fought for control of the gun for six long seconds with Bear hollering, "Empty, the pistol's nothing but empty."

The third person finally rose from the ground, almost unseen by everyone focused on Foster and Bear and the pistol. Hank stood just as shaky as Foster, his face contorted with pain and rage. He lifted his arm, pointing his hand at Foster. No, not his hand, but a gun, he had a second gun. I tried to tell the officer holding us back about that exact thing, but my throat tightened again, words caught in a bottlenecked traffic jam as they rushed to be let out.

Time jumped to seconds, minutes, hours, even days, but then I'm always back on early Thanksgiving morning on the gridiron on my right side in St. Andrew's visitor's end zone. It was past six and freezing, and my sweater was wrapped around Jay, and my whole body was trembling, and the blades of grass under me were stiff, razor-sharp and I worried that they might somehow slice into my shoulder and arm.

I was behind Basil and a Gently cop's wide, burly shoulder. He had a balding spot and tiny patch of purple skin where a dermatologist had recently burned off some cancerous lesions, or at least, that was my guess. My memory returned to the slow-motion screaming, blood pulsing, and heartbeat rushing in my ears, and Bear putting himself between Foster and Hank, but as far as what centered me that early morning? Undoubtedly, it was the purple bits, little pieces of that heroic cop's scalp.

The images are like individual frames of stop-motion film; first, Bear turning on Hank, then barreling into Hank once again with his helmet. The muzzle flashed, and the weapon was so close to Foster, firing point blank into his chest. Was it Bear's fault for ramming Hank twice? Or maybe just the power of Hank's cold, strong fingers? Whatever the combination or the reason, it quickly ended Foster's life.

The smell of gunpowder dominated the air, making me feel nauseous. I heard and felt the thunder of that blast. The truth is, with squealing sirens and Pink Floyd music, guns and flashing lights, it was probably impossible to hear Foster's final words. And yet a part of me insists that I heard Foster cry out, "Why, Pop, why?"

From the drone recordings of that early morning tragedy, I learned Hank had used a Glock semiautomatic handgun. Our small town was on the national news for a time. For me, the fatal shot had landed so rapidly, less than a millisecond, really, as if the two cacophonous blasts from Gently Police that followed it were delayed by an hour. Which was not true at all, of course.

It was just that the impression was coming from me, Tuck Reis, and my fear of loud noises and explosions. All my life I've loathed July Fourth, whether it's Roman candles, bottle rockets, M-80s, or even harmless sparklers. Truth is, I hate them all.

Hank was a wide and tall human being moving so swiftly, with leopard-like quickness. He was shot twice by Gently cops, once in the right shoulder and another bullet on the right shin. After Foster was shot, though, he fell back and was gone.

"No one moves a muscle now people," Gently cops said. "No one even breathes before the EMTs go in."

Hank was hollering in pain crying and cursing and most disturbingly, laughing like a hyena, as he clutched his shattered leg even as the Gently Police kicked away the dropped handgun and trained their weapons on him. Another pair of officers wrestled Bear Santos to the ground, relieving him of the empty pistol. Bear's screams of anguish and grief filled the stadium, "No, Foster, no... Let me say goodbye, okay?"

"You're under arrest, pal," an officer said as they took him to the patrol car.

* * *

Ten minutes on, Hank was still being watched closely as they treated his wounds, so Basil kissed my cheek, embracing me, helping me stand. "You were brave, Tuck. Incredible. I'm going with Jay and the EMTs to Yale-New Haven Hospital, I'll text you updates, okay?"

"I don't want to think about what would have happened without you and that bat, Basil," I said, and she shrugged, and hugged me for a few more seconds.

"You sure you're good, though?" she asked. "Steady inside, and everything?"

"Yes," I said. "I'm good. I'm okay."

So, I watched her load up into the ambulance with a stretcher-bound Jay. Basil caught my eye and offered a thumbs-up from inside, so I did the same.

An hour later, as the sun began to rise, illuminating the true horror of the pre-dawn violence, an angular, white-haired man in a tie, navy sweater—a crisis intervention office—offered me bottled water, an energy bar, and a thermal blanket. He steered me to another ambulance parked in the rear of the lot, where I was checked out by a baby-faced EMT. Several TV news vans had arrived a half hour earlier, and their satellite dishes looked fierce, potent.

My dad arrived in a dark winter jacket and tan leather gloves and a winter ski hat and gave me a bear hug.

"Are you okay, Tuck?" he asked. "Seriously, are you losing it or are you doing decently?"

ACADEMY OF UNHOLY BOYS

"I'm fine, Dad," I said. "A bit exhausted, though."

"Are you ready to be questioned?" an officer asked me brusquely.

"No, no," Mr. Reis said. "My son here, Tucker Reis has dire special needs—"

"Dad," I said holding my palm up. "I got this one, let me give it a shot..."

"Whatever you think," he said.

"Can you tell us a bit about what went on this morning?" the white-haired officer asked. "Like whom was the girl with the Louisville Slugger?"

I felt the silence expand within me and without. I thought of Dr. A. and what we'd been working on three days a week for a couple years. I heard the soothing sounds of his bubbling aquarium with funky, aquatic creatures gliding past and glass hummingbirds all over his office, so pastel and bright, and his Salvador Dali prints offering a touch of the absurd. *Balance,* he'd said, *we all need it. . . Start with good posture and lead with clear, concise language and project your voice now. Try and keep your left hand down from your mouth and only speak when you're good and ready, Tuck.*

"You don't have to do this, you know, pal," my dad said.

"I'm okay. I think I got it, Dad," I said.

"If you can't talk well," the officer started to say, "how do you typically—?"

"Basil Sous," I began slowly. "She's the tiny sophomore from Gently Public High with the Louisville Slugger... S-O-U-S. She's the real hero this morning."

"And you?" the officer asked. "Whom exactly, are you?"

"Tuck... Reis... R-E-I-S, a senior at St. Andrew's," I said. "And Basil's a good friend of mine."

"Are you an athlete here?" he asked.

"No, no," I snorted. "I'm in the special needs program. I

341

take a lot of black and white photographs in my spare time, with my old-fashioned SLR mostly, and draw bizarre faces in neon-orange and write miniature upside-down words everywhere. I sell the pictures on my website and make a decent buck, believe it or not."

"Sounds great," the crisis officer said. "I think your dad should know that you and this Basil Sous saved the day. *That* news is already causing quite a stir online."

"I don't doubt it," Mr. Reis said, eyes wet.

"Did you know Hank Allan, Tuck?" the crisis officer asked. "The young man who fatally shot Foster?"

"I saw him at school," I said. "An athlete, baseball player, but he was out of control tonight. He was frequently out of control when I saw him, hyper as hell..."

"I'll say," the officer said. "Prepare yourself to be fêted by the town of Gently, Tuck. Not every day you prevent two suicides on Thanksgiving morning, right?"

"Word gets around fast, huh? How come there are so many drones, though?"

"Someone posted a teaser for the Greatest Show last night, and it took a while before authorities were able to realize its danger. Now it's like everyone and their cousin has got a drone in the sky. Warped times we do live in, huh, Tuck?"

I nodded and asked, "So what happens now?"

"We will likely need your formal statement soon."

"Thanks," I replied, watching the sun steadily push through the clouds.

"Big football game, intense rivalry, all of it canceled this year," I heard one officer say to another as my father gathered up the snacks and drinks the EMTs had offered us. "What the hell is this world coming to if this is how the young people celebrate their lives? A triple-suicide on a national holiday? How does one explain it?"

ACADEMY OF UNHOLY BOYS

Pink Floyd was abruptly turned off the stadium's speaker system and the silence was deafening, in the brief moments before the noise of the ever-growing crowd started filling it up. Reporters doing interviews, sirens fading, police radio chatter; the worst was the parents arriving on scene, crying moms and dads learning the fate of their young community members.

My dad patted me on the back as we started towards our dented Jeep. "Wonderfully handled, Tuck," my dad said. "Are you hungry?"

JAY SOUTHER

I felt myself raised up onto a stretcher and opened my eyes to the muted colors of the ambulance interior. My nose was scalded by a whiff of clean, sterile ammonia with a lemony hint. An EMT asked questions, rapid-fire, one after the next; Basil answered with impressive calm. I wanted to tell them all to be silent, but nothing worked with my twisted tongue, so I gazed helplessly and, strangely, heard Mom warbling away with a Carole King tune she sang whenever she had more than three Martinis.

"*So far away, doesn't anybody stay in one place anymore...*"

There were glowing colors and a fierce undertow, and an emotive tidal wave tossed me around. An EMT started an IV drip into my hand, and I flinched, exhaled, and discovered a row of trees whipping passed out the oblong rear windows, shadowy, bare oak trees with branches like spiny fingers. My left bicep burned.

"Will he be okay?" Basil asked the EMT.

"A gunshot delivers great trauma to a body," she said. "Your friend's in shock."

ACADEMY OF UNHOLY BOYS

"Yeah, but—?"

"In these situations, I find it best to pray."

I was bouncing in and out of consciousness as I tripped through time, and it felt like there were hallucinogens coursing through my marrow. Basil stretched her smooth right hand out with those nail-bitten fingers. As if in concert with Mom, I heard a slightly off-key, modified version of "Danny, Boy" that my dad sang for me each St. Patrick's Day. "Oh, Jay, my boy, the pipes, the pipes are calling from glen to glen and down the mountainside..."

The ambulance shuddered, too, and flashing lights ricocheted off the glass doors of the ER when we finally arrived in New Haven. I rolled onto a gurney with Basil there but out of reach, and the EMT checked my pulse again. I shuddered, clinging to the ceiling, trapped in amber, as my dad crooned on:

"The summer's gone and all the flowers are dying, tis you, tis you must go, and I must bide. But come back when summers in the meadow, or when valley's hearth are white with snow. For I'll be there in sunshine or in shadows, oh, Jay, my boy, I swear I love you so..."

There was more singing, but I had nothing to offer. I was bereft, drained, and mute. I tried to swim across the hospital room, but there was no pool, ocean, or Long Island Sound in sight, only a narrow space with anxiety-gray curtains and tender helpers offering a thin johnny coat and a scratchy blue blanket. Basil kissed my cheek as I was moved to another bed and whisked away down the hall to an operating room.

"Please don't ever leave me, Basil!" I tried to shout, but nothing emerged from my mouth. She reached out, smiling, and blew me a kiss as I faded away.

JAY SOUTHER

Doctors and nurses removed the offending bullet from my left bicep swiftly on Thanksgiving morning, and after five days I was discharged back home to Gently.

"Everyone in the state is pulling for you now, Jay," Miller Fisher said. I was so touched that he'd come by our home to visit, along with bringing a large cheese and pepperoni pie from Pepe's on Wooster Street in New Haven for my mom, Aunt Carol, and me.

"Thanks, Miller," I said.

"Whenever you're ready," he said. "We—meaning me, the koi fish, and the plants —would love to see you around the greenhouse."

"Sounds good," I said, "Can I do a volunteer gig, maybe?"

"No, it's just me there, so we can afford to pay you. You'll earn a decent wage. Maybe after school two days a week to start?"

"Sounds great."

On my first day at the greenhouse, I set up a bird feeder for Miller. It was a cold day, and I spotted a singular red bird

ACADEMY OF UNHOLY BOYS

prancing on a branch nearby. It was a radiant cardinal and I realized he was the most pure and sacred life force I'd seen in a long while. The proud male bopped around on the branches near the feeder. For three afternoons in a row, the avian creature did his dance—his bright vermillion hues were lovely, and his mango beak looked regal and strong.

On the third day, I saw the bird again. I rested my arms on top of a short trellis. Without hesitation, the red flash left the feeder and flew at me, landing on my left hand, staring me down. My breath halted as he observed me. I could barely feel his weight on the edge of my hand. *What exactly does he see in me?* I thought. *What does he absorb of this teenager from the Connecticut shoreline? Another lost druggie spiraling out of control? Or a decent kid who pines for one more shot?*

The bird pondered me before flying away. It was the most startling sight. There was so much resonant color around that little spitfire and thank God, I was sober and sharp, clear-eyed. I dreamt often of that brilliant bird. As I slept, I felt his scarlet presence fluttering between my cupped palms, and inside my sternum, too, radiating outward from my own pulsing heart. My visions were immediate and alive, and when I awoke, I was buoyant, confident.

Dare I say, renewed?

Tuck Reis showed up two weeks after a church congregation raised $1,700 for me after my hospital stay. Tuck didn't ring the bell or knock on the front door of my mom's home—he just stood on the walk with his untied Timberlands pressed against the lowest step. I don't know how long he waited before I noticed him, but his unruly black curls had become flattened, weighed down by the flurrying snow. He wore no gloves, hat, or scarf, only black corduroys, and a long navy T-shirt. And there was no iPhone in

DAVID FITZPATRICK

his bare hands. He wore the same thin, unlined jean jacket on as he had when I saw him at our home football game a month earlier.

I opened the door, and he took a step back. We stared at one another as his left hand cupped his mouth. "Jay," he said. "Mr. Souther, are you good? Are you fine?"

"I'm good and fine, Tuck," I replied with a smile. "How'd you get here?"

"Trailbike." He gestured behind him and then stared at his boots.

"New boots?"

"Same old ones," he said. "Generally comfortable and supportive."

"Did the snow give you any trouble on the way over?"

"Slick," he said. "Difficult to get a decent grip."

"No Emma Stone along with you tonight, though, huh?"

"Left her at home," he said. "Thought I'd give the good lady a rest, for once. Plus, my battery was shot."

"Yes," I said. "Everyone needs a break, experts say."

Tuck cleared his throat. "I got your text yesterday—you said you wanted me to drop in around this time."

"That's right," I said. "Thanks for coming over. I appreciate it."

"Congrats on surviving Thanksgiving morning, Jay," Tuck said. "I'm glad you lived through all that mess. It was a real wild hell. A terrifying experience."

"*You* and Basil saved my ass big time, Tuck," I said. "No two ways about it, my mom didn't want me watching the drone recordings on the news, but it's been played so many damn times by now, I feel like I lived through it a thousand different ways. Basil and you were legit heroes."

His face flushed. "Mostly Basil when she crushed Foster with her bat."

ACADEMY OF UNHOLY BOYS

"You helped, though, right?" I asked. "Will you agree you helped save my life? You took the call, didn't you? You drove Basil to the stadium? The pair of you untied me from the goalpost, right?"

Tuck laughed. "Okay, yeah. Guess I helped some."

"Would you like a drink now?" I asked. "Or a cookie or something?"

"A cookie and a soda sound perfect."

"Come on, let's have a snack," I said. "My ma's not around, so we have the whole place to ourselves. I'll give you a quick tour."

"If it's okay," he said, "do you mind if you, me, if we... just both hang out here?"

"On the stoop?" I asked. "Aren't you freezing? It's twenty-five degrees."

"Cold is fine, it's okay," he said, rubbing his palms together. "It's not so bad, really."

"That's cool," I said, laughing. "I'll get the snacks and a coat."

"Great," he said. "It's very kind of you."

"I got a surprise for you, Tuck," I called back to him, and left the door ajar.

"Afraid of surprises, me... not sure," he said. "Thanks for thinking of me."

I returned with soda in one hand and a cookie in the other, and offered them to him.

"Lovely," Tuck said. "This is perfect."

I put on my new red winter coat and stepped back inside my house, reached into the front closet, and grabbed Tuck's bulky present. I turned and handed him the large blue gift box. He placed the cola down and laughed.

"What's so funny?"

"A good and sweet day, rare," Tuck said. "Never got many presents, not a typical thing."

"That tradition radically changes starting now."

Tuck finished his cookie. Usually so pale, his face now was beet red, and snowflakes were sticking to his glasses, nose, and shoulders. Flurries were all over him. "I shouldn't take this gift, probably not. Forget, should we just forget all about it?"

"No, no," I said. "The present is absolutely for you."

Tuck opened the blue box and found a blue *Patagonia* parka with a hood.

"Holy, holy, holy shit," he said. "Whoa... is it okay to just take it?"

"Yes," I said. "Try it on, Tuck. See if it fits—it belongs to you now."

He removed his jean jacket, and handed it to me, and excitedly tried on the coat.

"A woman came by and gave me $1,700 in an envelope two weeks ago," I said. "She explained her church had raised it for me. She told me to spend the cash, save it, or pay it forward, and said, *'The people who walked in darkness have seen a great light.'* It's from Isaiah, apparently. Old Testament."

"Sweet," Tuck said. "A whole $1,700 dropping in right from the sky."

"I bought a royal cashmere scarf for Mom, and a Kelly-green coat for Basil," I said. "Cherry-red for me, and a cobalt-blue one for my new friend, Tuck. Gloves and hat are in the pockets, man."

Tuck's lenses were shaded, but silver tears rolled down his cheeks almost immediately—lots of tiny ones, they kept coming so fast.

"It's mine," Tuck said, mostly to himself, I think. "For me, a *friend.*"

"You bet," I said, my voice tight. "Goddamned right."

ACADEMY OF UNHOLY BOYS

Tuck crouched on the ground like a baseball catcher, blue parka enveloping him as he covered his face. He sobbed twice as I patted his shoulder.

"*You* helped rescue me, Tuck," I said. "There's no doubt."

He stayed squatted, shook his head, wiped his eyes, sniffling.

"Thanks much, Jay," he said, as he placed the gloves and hat on.

"Let's see brand new Tucker Reis—just in time for the holiday season."

"*Voila,*" he said, rising to his full height, face still flushed, and the two of us remained outside, eyes wet, laughing, enjoying our new coats, and drinking bubbly, cherry-flavored sodas. I handed him another gift.

"Something else?" Tuck asked, and he quickly unwrapped the package to find a boxed DVD set of Emma Stone's films. "Wow. Wow. I don't have most of these. Just seen some clips."

"She's an obscure new actress," I said. "Ever hear of her, Tuck?"

"Never, a complete and total stranger to me," he said, smiling, before embracing my right side and mumbling, "I got no more words, man." He got on his bike, folded his jean jacket on his lap, rested the boxed set there, and pedaled off into the snowy night.

I waited outside a few minutes longer observing the new snow filling the spaces Tuck's boots, tires, and tears had left behind. I realized I had done a good, even wonderful, thing. Or maybe it was only Tuck—perhaps he was the most wonderful thing. So, I exhaled, wiped my eyes, grabbed the empty soda cans, and stepped back inside our warm home.

BASIL SOUS

Tuck became a familiar, solitary figure loping around the town or riding his trail bike past Wave café, taking photos with his SLR, or using his iPhone to keep himself entertained. A tall, skinny dude with his orange helmet and Go-Pro camera, along with his new blue Patagonia parka that Jay had bought for him. He'd been in a buoyant mood as of late.

When we were featured on the local news around the holiday for being heroic and dismantling two-thirds of the Greatest Show on Earth, we were dubbed "three heroic and puffy people," in a news article. Me, Tuck, and Jay in our down Patagonia coats in front of Gently Town Hall. Several months later, on a Sunday afternoon in March, Tuck and I walked outside on the Green during my lunch break.

"I'm drinking more Merlot, as of late," Tuck said, which was a typical comment from the senior. Tuck offered several non sequitur comments in a single chat. He'd think it and say stuff at the same time, without a lot of editing.

"Do you drink alone, Tuck?"

"I drink while watching Shakespeare being performed on

ACADEMY OF UNHOLY BOYS

stage," he said. "My dad's got numerous productions on our TV from all over the world. Singapore, Canada, Brussels, and Switzerland, wherever drama and theatre exist, there's a production being offered of the Bard's work. I study them with my dad. We get silly drunk, nibbling on grapes, sharp cheddar, and crackers. Some versions are wonderful, others are less so."

"It's so cool that you're getting close with your father, Tuck," I said.

"Wasn't always that way," he said. "Thanks to Dr. A and the enormous aquarium, though..."

"Always give credit to Dr. Athens and his aquatic creatures," I said.

"I got news," Tuck said. "I might attend a school on Cape Cod this summer."

"Lovely," I said. "Will you finally believe in Shakespeare, though?"

"Not on your life," he said, smiling. "No way, José."

"You're a stubborn bastard, Mr. Reis," I said.

"I am indeed that," Tuck said. "Can I ask you to do something? I don't want to intrude."

"Yes, you do, Tuck," I said.

"True," he said with a laugh. "Sorry for your loss with Avery... all that grief, Basil. But I think I can help you out today."

"How so?"

"Just allow yourself some... wild, uncontrollable twisting."

"Sounds dirty, Tuck."

"No, no, but it will give you release," he said. *"I'll come to your emotional rescue."*

I saw his cheeks redden.

"That's from an old Rolling Stones song," I said. "Avery used to blast it in his room."

"I'm only talking about a simple, clean gesture," Tuck said.

"Slight movement of the arms, hands, the legs... every part... of your body working in sync."

"Okay, what do I do?"

"You gather all the angst... and frustration," Tuck said. "Rip it out from every wrinkle, vein, and artery you got, and get unusually active."

"Unusually active?"

"Lose the skateboard, first, Basil," he said. "Put it down."

So, I placed my longboard on the grass. "Done," I said.

"Shift your face toward the sky and do a snazzy Misty Copeland move," he said, "the dazzling, principal dancer for New York City Ballet."

"Is Misty still excelling?"

"Oh, hell yeah, she's always wowing the critics."

Tuck and I had drifted all the way over near the Revolutionary War statue on the Gently Green. It was a cold day, nothing but bone-white sky and three public high school kids playing frisbee in shorts and T-shirts were rushing the season, I felt. I stood next to Tuck and put my hands out, leaned my head way back.

"Like this?" I said, and he laughed.

"Pirouette now like your life depended on it."

"Age before beauty, sir," I said.

"We'll begin together... one, two, three..."

The pair of us spun around ten times or so, and I got dizzy and laughing and giggling but it lifted my spirits, truly, it did. I didn't care that it wasn't mature or an appropriate act to be doing because I learned my finest lesson from a young man named Tuck Reis: there's nothing wrong with being yourself, especially in front of a great friend.

I wrote in my diary that night that Tuck and I had gotten along well from that first tentative chat in Dr. Athens's waiting room, and at Wave Café with our shared cocoa, tea, and brown-

ACADEMY OF UNHOLY BOYS

ies. And outside my house in his dad's Jeep while the rain pelted down on us. Jay and I had drifted apart ever since Thanksgiving and we never said we didn't belong together, but Peg and I were moving in June, so I thought it's better if we nip it in the bud. Tuck and I, however, were tight and we still texted a lot and I knew I'd be close to him forever. At least, that's what I told Dr. Athens the other day.

I also felt proud to have assisted Tuck in making gains with speech and keeping his left hand *mostly* down from his mouth. Tuck still does it sometimes, but I don't want to be too much of a pain in the ass about it. We still text a lot at night, too. He even shows up at my bands' gigs, fidgeting in the back, wearing those dark lenses, but he applauds politely when every song ends, which is more than I can say of others, like Jay Souther.

Jay never applauds, just slouches off to the side, soaking up the scenery, gently flirting with all the girls who pay him more attention ever since the Gently Mayor gave him, me, and Tuck the keys to the city. We all hang out sometimes, but recently I've gotten a lot closer to Tuck than I think I ever could have to Jay. That said, when I spot Tuck gliding around Gently Green aimlessly on his bike, I still sometimes get worried. For whatever else lurks around the next bend in the woods for him. Tuck will turn twenty in August, and I wonder how the rigors of adulthood will claim him. All the pressure and expectation and gaping silences coming his way, waiting to pounce all over him.

And yet, knowing Tuck Reis like I do now, he'll probably be just fine.

EPILOGUE

I saw Basil Sous at R.J. Julia Booksellers in Madison, Connecticut four months later. She had suggested I meet her there—more than a coffee and several cookies were owed after she mostly patiently endured me ramble on about love, lust, fractured hearts, and broken parts of me, myself, and I several times in the last few weeks. Maybe dozens of times. She had a tote under her arms, carrying some books.

"I'm giving you a break on the accuracy of the number, Jay," was the first thing she said to me. "It's closer to thirty-four times but I won't complain too much, since I'm here to say my fond goodbyes."

We had initially sat at the bookstore café, and we laughed when every other person who went by recognized Basil and said, "Excuse me, but don't you work at Wave in Gently?"

"I'm nothing but a figment of your imagination," Basil said. "I only live in café's, I'm unable to function anywhere else. Please send help and money ASAP."

We decided to move all the way to the back of the store because so many people walked up to us to say things like, "Do

ACADEMY OF UNHOLY BOYS

you mind if we take a selfie? You kids are so brave, the way you handled that terrible business that happened over the holidays in Gently."

There was a lull in the conversation, and I couldn't help but ask, "Tell me, Basil, where and when could have I ever stolen your heart?"

"You should always begin with a ninety-year-old poet in the Kentucky woods..."

I watched my friend smile.

"*The Peace of Wild Things* by Wendell Berry," she went on. "If you had simply recited it to me, I would have let you ravish me."

"Seriously?" I asked.

"No, not really," Basil said. "But it's fun to pretend, though."

"Not for me," I said. "Will you miss me at all, Basil?"

"Yes. I mean, who else will stare at me on the Gently Green?"

"Good point," I said.

"Did you hear?" she asked. "Tuck is going to a school on Cape Cod. He is up there now for student orientation."

"I hope they have a good photography studio."

"They do," Basil said. "That's the first thing he told me about."

"What's the bag for?" I asked.

"I bought you five novels with my own hard-earned cash, along with this handy tote. The novels deal with love, hate, rage, loss, joy, sex, drugs, friendship, music, death, and grief. The two of us have experienced it all, Jay. We're also both lucky to be alive."

"Cool, thank you, Basil," I said. "It's very sweet of you."

"Are you still dating the first-year girl at the high school?" she asked.

"No, I'm single now," I said, blushing. "I feel worn out. What went down over the holidays was exhausting. Plus, it was just a matter of inches with all those bullets flying past me, left and right. I think I'd still be in purgatory if I'd perished."

"I'm positive you would've gotten into heaven eventually, though," Basil said. "No problem, there. I'd vouch for you and write a glowing letter of recommendation."

"Yes, and you saved me, rescued me like a knight with that damn Louisville Slugger."

Basil smiled. "There was some grace in that act of aiding you," she said. "Like a queen on a white horse saving my dashing, wounded hero. Something about that appeals to me."

"Like Batman saving Alfred," I said, and she squeezed my hand, grinning.

"You are one of the good guys," she said. "Don't ever forget that fact, Jay."

"Thanks," I said. "Are you excited about moving to Ohio?"

"I'd prefer to stay in Gently, but we simply do not have enough cash. How is the greenhouse?"

"It's cool, my boss is wonderful, part grandfather figure, part friend," I said. "He might be able to give me a better-paying job at Yale University next year, which would be fantastic. Or taking the lead in my very own botanical garden when Miller retires in five years."

"That's wonderful," she said.

"Are you scared? Another new school sounds like a pain," I told Basil.

"My head feels clear, finally," she said. "Having a shrink to bitch to last semester was fantastic. Like a wise friend that eased me for not-so-insane amounts of money. Dr. John Athens was his name, and he offers a sliding scale fee, so it didn't cost a million bucks. I called your mom about it, she said it'll be up to you."

ACADEMY OF UNHOLY BOYS

"He doesn't make you lay on a couch or anything, right?" I asked. "Or get massages or anything cheesy, correct?"

Basil smiled. "No, none of that, just talking and working on your own grief, love, rage," she said. "He helps me, and he can help you. Here's his business card."

"Thanks for supporting me so much," I said. "Even when I was an asshole, you were forever kind to me."

"It was my pleasure," she said. "*Most* of the time."

So, I smiled, and she leaned in and kissed me, just a tender sweet peck on the lips, followed by a hug. And soon Basil Sous slipped out the back door and into the wider world, and the rest of her life.

And me? I took Ma's Ford home and did some reading, and it didn't take long to get hooked on Mary Gaitskill's prose. My head was clear, and life was no longer a burden filled with dread and remorse. Instead, it was decent and almost fun.

Imagine that.

ACKNOWLEDGMENTS

I'd say thanks to Ashley Crantas, the kind and immensely talented Running Wild editor of *Academy of Unholy Boys*, was such a breath of fresh air for me, and was wonderful at steering me through any trouble spots of this novel. Thanks, Lisa Kastner, Evangeline Estropia and everyone at Running Wild and RIZE Press.

Running Wild Press publishes stories that cross genres with great stories and writing. RIZE publishes great genre stories written by people of color and by authors who identify with other marginalized groups. Our team consists of:

Lisa Diane Kastner, Founder and Executive Editor
Cody Sisco, Acquisitions Editor, RIZE
Benjamin White, Acquisition Editor, Running Wild
Peter A. Wright, Acquisition Editor, Running Wild
Resa Alboher, Editor
Angela Andrews, Editor
Sandra Bush, Editor
Ashley Crantas, Editor
Rebecca Dimyan, Editor
Abigail Efird, Editor
Aimee Hardy, Editor
Henry L. Herz, Editor
Cecilia Kennedy, Editor
Barbara Lockwood, Editor
Scott Schultz, Editor

Evangeline Estropia, Product Manager
Kimberly Ligutan, Product Manager
Lara Macaione, Marketing Director
Joelle Mitchell, Licensing and Strategy Lead
Pulp Art Studios, Cover Design
Standout Books, Interior Design
Polgarus Studios, Interior Design

Learn more about us and our stories at www.runningwildpress.com

ABOUT RUNNING WILD PRESS

Loved this story and want more? Follow us at www.runningwildpress.com, www.facebook.com/runningwildpress, on Twitter @lisadkastner @RunWildBooks